# Midni

Chronicles of Heaven's Curse
Book One
Kalverya Johansson

# Table of Contents

For my father.

---

1. http://www.k-johanssonstudios.com

# Prologue

WAR.

It wrought the streets of an ancient Excelian city where death smeared the battlefield.

Silence sung through the bloodstained boulevards.

And bodies laid among the cold ashes.

Distant explosions permeated the air and Natalia Ignatius-Valdis regarded the sight of the aliens from afar—the Xzandians. Haplessly, she observed them as they carried their energetic shields powered by some unknown technology. At this distance, she knew she'd be unable to take them out. As they marched towards her with the intent to kill.

The leader, Prometheus, paused and held up one hand, keeping off his battalion that stretched far behind him. "Hand over Midnight Eclipse," he spoke with an ounce of confidence through his helmet. A technology that kept him secure from the poisonous air that was oxygen.

"And if I refuse?" Natalia questioned, her dark eyes on his.

"Then you'll die," the alien declared. "So, I'll ask again. Hand over Midnight Eclipse."

"To your people. *Never.*"

The aliens discharged their weapons and Natalia avoided the bullets, even if the armour of Midnight Eclipse protected her.

The aliens fired their energy bullets and Natalia leapt into the air, higher than anyone ever thought possible, and with her demon activating, she plunged to the earth below.

The ground shattered beneath her boots, the impact never harming her, and the aliens resumed in firing their weapons, but their heated energetic bullets never affected her as they hit the armour she wore.

The detached stones around Natalia's boots lifted off the ground before she launched herself at the aliens with incredible speed. With her sword in hand, she cut down the aliens.

She was certain there was a moment when she'd die but she never stopped. Cutting down one alien after another, after another. Reinforcements arrived and she paused, gasping for air. Then her gaze drifted to the alien hovering in mid-air on a platform. "Give up Natalia. You'll only cause your premature demise," Xaviaius declared, with a dark smile.

"So, what if I do," Natalia retorted. "I won't hand it over. You'll have to take it by force."

"What about your children? Gothalia and Noel-Len, was it? What about your husband Gaius?" he queried. "You wouldn't want anything to happen to them. Now, would you?"

"Bastard." Natalia muttered. "Touch them, and I'll kill you."

His gaze narrowed. "I'd like to see you try."

A Behemoth, able to manipulate all the Excelian elements, crawled out of the ground and Natalia stepped aside to avoid the shards of ice that the Behemoth threw at her that embedded themselves into the ground at her feet.

Natalia glanced up at the Behemoth.

She was tired but she had to keep going. Fighting was all she knew. Fighting for herself, fighting for her children, fighting to keep the demon at bay and fighting to stay alive off the battlefield. That was all she knew. And she knew that would never change but now she had Noel-Len and Gothalia because of Gaius. What would she do?

"Fight," she muttered to herself. "I won't give up and won't hand over the Fragments," she declared, loud enough that both Xzandian leaders glared at her. Before launching herself at the Behemoth, which towered over them and spurred ice and fire in every direction killing both Xzandians and Excelians alike.

"See, and this is why women shouldn't be allowed on the battlefield," the Xzandian declared, like it was the most obvious thing in the world. "You're weak, disobedient and undisciplined."

Natalia tasted blood when the Behemoth deflected her attack, with the element of air the gust of wind smashed into the stone rocks behind her shattering them under the impact.

Natalia avoided the lightning bolts the Behemoth released just in time before, she felt the trickle of blood over her face from when she'd hit her head.

"As far as I'm concerned." Natalia replied, "My husband loves my rebellious side."

Then she picked up her sword from where it was embedded in the ground and leapt high and towards the Behemoth.

Air, earth, and lightning attacked her. Natalia used the sword, to slice through the earth. Then used the earth that flew towards her to block the lightning and air attacks before she allowed herself to fall towards the Behemoth. When she was close enough, she embedded her sword in the Behemoth's neck, and it screeched.

She dragged the sword down it's chest and towards its belly, where the sword disconnected, and she fell towards the ground. Then paused, as the air shifted around her and the armour of Midnight Eclipse gave her the ability to hover in the air. The beast swiped at her and Natalia moved out of the way and flew towards her sword.

Once she'd reached it, she yanked out the sword and stabbed it back into the Behemoth. The Behemoth screeched once more. Oil, water, and blood coated her sword and she tore an opening big enough to enter. Then the Behemoth's hand came down to wack its belly and Natalia leapt out of the way in time. The Behemoth struck the sword and forced it further into its belly and out through the other side. The Behemoth dropped to its knees and Natalia moved out of the way. She stood standing in mid-air and watched the Behemoth die.

Then her attention turned to the Xzandian on the platform a few meters above her. "Xaviaius!" Natalia called, the wind that fluttered around her was both cold and loud. "Stand down your arms and I will show mercy." The black armour she wore, gleamed beneath the full moon lighting up the battlefield and her black eyes locked onto the man.

"No, it is *I* who'll make you beg for mercy! Not the other way around. So, don't be so arrogant!" Xaviaius declared, clenching the bar in front of him as he stood on a hovering platform that gave him the perfect view of the battlefield. "I'll have your head Natalia. Count on it."

Natalia held up the sword she procured from the fallen Behemoth and pointed it at Xaviaius. "Come on then. Let's see who'll fall first."

"You will! Women are naturally weaker than men. What could you possibly do?"

"Look around you," Natalia beckoned. "Don't you see the death of your comrades. Most were men, weren't they? Gender has nothing to do with it. I killed them as I'm going to kill you." Natalia threatened.

"Aren't you supposed to arrest me and take me back to your precious Grand Elders?" the alien mocked. "As a war prisoner?"

"That ship sailed long ago," Natalia declared. "You killed too many of my comrades. I can't just let you walk away."

"I see. To the death then," he uttered.

"To the death then," Natalia remarked when the alien stepped from his platform and dropped to the earth below. Creating a massive crater beneath his landing. Rage consumed him and his gaze drifted to where Natalia stood, in the air. The power of Midnight Eclipse at her call. She dropped from the air and towards the earth, the ground shattering beneath her armour.

"Your Midnight Eclipse versus me? Let's see who'll win?" he remarked and prepared to fight. Natalia mimicked and they stared each other down before the battle began. Then they attacked.

The ring of swords clashing in the air, lingered throughout the silent battlefield. In the distance, other Excelians waited on their energetic vehicles and observed the fight. The battle they fought was long won and they knew it was up to Natalia to claim victory. "Come on, you got this," Anaphora muttered as she observed the battle. L'Eiron stood beside her and placed a hand on her shoulder.

"Don't worry. She's a soldier. She'll be fine," he said.

"I know. L'Eiron but she's all alone."

L'Eiron didn't say anything instead, ordered the other soldiers to keep an eye out.

Then an ear-piercing screech sounded in the distance. The Alastorians caught everyone's attention before he shouted, "Hostiles on the east. Squadron A to D defend the main guard." Then he turned to Anaphora. "We can't afford to be sentimental right now."

"I know," she said.

Anaphora pulled out her sword and called war cry. She yelled with all her might and ran forward with L'Eiron and the other soldiers in their energetic vehicles or on foot as they rushed towards the oncoming Alastorians. They needed to defend this side of the battlefield if Natalia had a chance.

Alastorians and Excelians clashed.

Natalia and Xaviaius fought a gruelling battle. She was wearing out and he had enough energy to climb a mountain. As such, Natalia was thrown to the ground and Xaviaius pinned her down pointing his sword at her throat.

"Any last words?" he asked.

Then L'Eiron's voice broke through over the radio. *"Alastorians on the east. We'll hold them off. Hurry up Natalia."*

"Let them through," she told L'Eiron.

Xaviaius regarded Natalia for a moment confused than he heard the Alastorians screech in the distance. He leapt from Natalia when the Alastorians ran towards them.

While the other Xzandian soldiers worked to fight them off, Natalia sat up and rubbed her throat from where his forearm pinned her down.

The armour may have protected her from ballistics, but not once did it save her from being crushed. *"Natalia!"* L'Eiron called over the radio. *"Where are you?"*

An energetic helicopter hovered in the air not too far from her. They were searching for her she knew, and she knew she had to make it out alive.

Climbing to her feet, she ran from the Alastorians and towards the cliffs. The helicopter hovered low and the Alastorians leapt into the air to grab onto the chopper before they were kicked off by L'Eiron and the other Centurions. "I'm here!" she called back fighting off the Alastorians.

L'Eiron recognised her on the ground from where they hovered in the air. She ran towards the cliffs, battered, and injured while the Alastorians chased after her. Then with as much might as she could, she leapt from the cliff.

The energetic chopper without a rotor propeller and mast, instead operated by air users, caught her. Though not without having her fly through the open window. If it weren't for L'Eiron who caught her in time she'd have fallen through. Once the chopper turned up right, he set Natalia beside him. "Let get out of here," he said placing Natalia in the seat beside him then glanced at the Excelian air user.

"But what about the others?" Natalia asked.

*"We're right behind you,"* Anaphora declared on the radio.

Then they returned to the City of New Icarus.

THE NEXT DAY, NATALIA Ignatius piled off the hover craft that dropped her off before retreating into the air and towards the estate only to stop and breathe in the fresh air, one not filled with smoke, blood, and rotting flesh. Instead, she inhaled the air that was filled with a fresh scent of moss, heat, and a light scent of cinder. The cinder she knew was from the lava below that would lap against the solidified earth that kept their city above the lava.

She heard the river in the distance not too far from her home and felt the soft earth beneath her feet and heard it *crunch* as she began to walk once more and towards the doors of her home.

The artificial sun above warmed her skin, and she glanced at the sky above aware of its falseness but similarity of it to the reality of the surface world.

She knew the Grand Elders and the Royal Family worked to make their home like the surface world as much as possible with their natural curves, crevices, trees, gorges, hills and valleys and every other aspect the Humans weren't aware they were blessed with.

Their buildings were different and ancient; with sturdy pillars holding up the rooves of the buildings that almost mimicked the ancient roman buildings but different with a mix of Persian and Egyptian style as the earliest Excelians were from that continent. Natalia placed her hand against the glass panel of the door and declared, "Natalia Ignatius-Valdis." The automated door opened and revealed an empty hallway.

As she entered, she heard the laughter of children and Aiden as he scolded the children. Her pace quickened as she moved to the sound. As they rounded a corner. She saw Noel-Len and Gothalia run from Aiden who pretended to be a monster and she kneeled when they spotted her calling, "Mum!"

Quickly, the children ran into her arms and she enveloped them into a warm embrace. "Hello, my precious babies," she muttered cherishing the embrace and kissed them both on the head.

"You're home," Gothalia declared, squirming in her arms to look up at her mother. "See told you Len," Gothalia remarked. "I said she'd be coming home."

"Whatever," he said, and clung to Natalia.

Then footfalls rounded a corner and Aiden greeted Natalia, "You're home. Welcome back, my lady."

"It's good to be back," Natalia said and climbed to her feet. "How were the little ones?" she asked.

"They were good, until Noel-Len hit her in the head with the ball," Aiden declared. "But she's feeling a lot better now."

"It wasn't me! It was Maximus and Anton!" Noel-Len defended pointing behind Aiden and at the two young boys their age, hiding behind the wall.

"What are you two doing hiding?" Natalia asked them. "Don't I get a welcome home hug as well?" With her brow raised, and a small smile. The other children ran to Natalia and hugged her.

"Sorry Auntie Nat," Maximus, the seven-year-old said. "It was an accident."

"We didn't mean to hurt Gothalia," Anton added, the six-year-old. "It was an um . . ." he began.

"Accident," Aiden piped in.

"Yeah, that's the word!" Anton declared, with a bright toothy smile.

Natalia laughed at the look on Maximus's face as he narrowed his gaze at his brother before walking into the kitchen, "Who's hungry?" she asked.

"Me!" Maximus said.

"Ooh me too!" Anton declared.

"Me too!" Noel-Len and Gothalia declared at the same time before glaring at each other.

"I said it first," Noel-Len glowered at his sister.

"No, you didn't."

"All right, you lot. Time to eat," Natalia said, and pulled out the chairs. Aiden entered the room and declared.

"I made sure they didn't have any dinner as you wanted to cook." Aiden declared, messing up Noel-Len's hair who crossed his arms.

"Thank you, Aiden," Natalia declared, with a small smile at Noel-Len's reaction then turned her attention to Aiden. "I really appreciate that. Have you seen Gaius anywhere?"

"No, I haven't," he said. "But I recall him saying that he went into the city to meet with the Grand Elders. But is it true? You have it?" Aiden asked.

Natalia glanced at the children, a seriousness crossed her features and she turned back to Aiden, "I do but we'll discuss that later."

"I understand." Aiden declared than retreated to the door. "I'll see if I can find Gaius and let him know you're home."

"That'll be great thanks. I would message him myself, but I think it's best to surprise him," she said.

Aiden nodded and said to the kids, "Behave you lot."

"We will!" they replied. Than Aiden vanished from sight and Natalia turned back to the children.

"Okay what do you feel like having?" she asked them.

"BUT LORD MICHALIS!" Gaius Ignatius-Valdis declared, shocked. "You can't possibly think that *that's* appropriate?"

His voice echoed around the Council Chamber and the Cratians regarded Gaius carefully, from where they stood, beneath the balconies of the Grand Elders.

"I do, Lord Ignatius," Grand Elder Michalis said, from where he sat above Gaius. His chestnut eyes lingered over the younger man in contemplation. "The power of Midnight Eclipse should not be in anyone's hands. What makes you think that it's okay for Natalia to wield."

"She found it!" he said. "And she can't remove it without hurting herself."

"I am sure, there are physicians that can remove that weapon. Besides, she may have found it, but it was discovered on *sacred lands*. You and Natalia should know better than step foot on such sacred sites." Grand Elder Michalis uttered; fury laced his voice.

"The only reason *why* I haven't thrown both of you into the prisons below our feet is because you're the General of Dragon Core and she is the accommodator of Midnight Eclipse. You both should tread very carefully from now on."

"Is that a threat?" Gaius questioned.

"It is. Don't think you've been forgiven. That weapon shouldn't be in the hands of man and should be returned to where you've found it. Buried and hidden far from us. No being, Excelian, Human or alien, should be given such god-like abilities it's unfathomable." The Grand Elder regarded Gaius carefully, for a moment, before declaring. "And I've heard news that she bore you children."

"She has," Gaius declared, with a small smile the memory of his children brought him a sense of happiness that only a few could ever comprehend.

"I am happy for you," Grand Elder Michalis proclaimed recognising the doting expression the younger man wore, "But be mindful because of the demon that lurks in her blood. She and your children will not be accepted among our society. As they are danger to us all."

"They're only children."

"And will grow into fine warriors. I am sure."

"What do you intend to do with them?" Gaius asked. His blue eyes narrowing on the Grand Elder.

"Nothing, yet. I plan to turn the other way as I see you and your family choose to live away from us and on the abandoned hill above the magma where the Valdis members claimed their roots centuries ago. None of you have committed any crimes in the past severe or otherwise. As such, I will not harm your family's reputation or take them away from you. However, some may not agree with this decision. As such, you'll be under the protection of the Cratians until we deem you safe."

"Deem us *safe*? Are we endanger of some kind?" Gaius queried, confused.

The Grand Elder never answered and only said, "I trust you'll take good care of those children." Then footfalls entered the room and Gaius was escorted out of the Council Chamber and into the halls of the Cetatea. He stared at the large elegant door and his brows furrowed in thought.

"Why must you be so evasive?" Gaius muttered than travelled the halls of the Cetatea and towards an energetic carriage. He climbed within, and off the vehicle went, and towards his home on the hill. When he climbed out of the vehicle, it hummed gently behind him before the vehicle pulled away and down the stone path. Gaius turned his heel and walked up to the manor. The door opened without him needing to place his hand on the scanner and there stood, Aiden. "Aiden? You're still here?" he asked, eyeing the other man.

"I am but I'm about to leave for the evening," Aiden declared, with a warm smile. Warmer than he'd ever expected.

"I understand," Gaius uttered. "Have a good night." Aiden stepped by Gaius and climbed into his energetic vehicle before disappearing down the road. Gaius entered the house, closing the door behind him he shrugged off his coat stitched with his family's fire crest and placed it on the hook beside his door. "Kids!" he called, into the house.

No response.

He climbed the stairs and toward the children's bedroom. Noel-Len and Gothalia peacefully slept in their shared bedroom and he smiled. They were asleep and no doubt their cousins would be home by now with their parents and in bed as they should be.

Then his attention moved to his bedroom opposite the hall. He entered the room and turned on the fire, which lit up the walls of the room. He was alone and that made him a little sad. He wondered when Natalia would return.

How he missed her but pushed his mind from it aware that it would only bring on unwanted heart ache. He sighed than entered the room and closed the door behind him.

He removed his clothes than moved to the bathtub. He ran the cold water from the faucet then heated it up with his élanocytes. The water bubbled and steamed. He allowed the water to cool before climbing into the tub and relaxing his tired muscles.

Gaius placed his head on the back of the tub and sighed in delight. "Perfect," he muttered, appreciating the warm water after a long day. Than he noticed a figure in the doorway and moved to cover himself only to stare in wonder.

"You think?" Natalia asked, dressed in only her underwear. He recognised her skin covered in scars from countless battles, but it was still smooth to the touch. The colour of her brown skin gleamed beneath the fire like bronze and his arousal rushed through him. "I merely thought the water was too warm."

"That's because you're not an Ignatius. By blood I mean," he said, and relaxed further into the water. He smiled as she removed the silk wrap from her frame and wandered over to him. Lust flashed across his eyes and she moved over to the bathtub and massaged his shoulders.

"There are so many things I could say to that, but I won't," she purred. "I'm simply happy to be back. I missed you."

"I missed you more." Then she leaned over and kissed him. Both, unaware of the figures outside their manor and fallen Cratians in the shadows of the night watching the silent house.

THE NIGHT WAS YOUNG, and Natalia sighed in delight as she laid in bed beside Gaius. The air was cold against their skin but not so cold by the small controlled fire that lined the room.

"Keep this up and we'll have more children," he told her, and Natalia smiled.

"Is that such a bad thing?" she asked, content. "I'm no longer a soldier. I get to live my life in peaceful bliss even if it means with a swollen belly."

"But you are still an accommodator of Midnight Eclipse," Gaius responded. "They could call upon you when they need to, and anything could happen." Natalia sighed and propped herself up on her elbow to eye her husband. Even until this day, she couldn't begin to believe he was all hers and she was all his.

"They most likely will my love," Natalia replied, stroking his jaw. "But I can't ignore the fact that I have a family to take care of." She ran her fingers through his blond hair as he ran his fingers through her black hair. They regarded each other with a lingering gaze and contemplated their lives. Natalia snuggled into him and he held her close. "My family is my number one priority not the Fragments that make up Midnight Eclipse. Not the wars, the famine, the droughts. Not the crimes but you and Noel-Len and Gothalia."

Than they paused, listening to each other's heart beats until they heard a clatter in the distance. "What was that?" Natalia asked, uncertain. The house was normally dead quiet at this time of the night.

"Not sure," he declared, his brows furrowed. "Probably Noel-Len and Gothalia."

"They shouldn't be up," Natalia declared, "It's past their curfew."

Another clatter occurred followed by a loud *thud*. Natalia and Gaius climbed out of bed and dressed before rushing to the children. Noel-Len and Gothalia were still in bed asleep.

They relaxed a little until Gaius regarded his wife for a moment with one single look in his eye, *'someone's in the house'*. Natalia nodded and pulled out a handheld from the cabinet beside the children's room and threw it to Gaius then disappeared into the room with the children.

Cautiously, Gaius stepped down the stairs. Than Lord Michalis's words entered his mind—"some may not agree with this decision"—when he made it to the landing, he pointed the weapon Natalia had given him into the darkness.

Silence greeted him.

His eyes adjusted to the dark than he saw it. A figure in the shadows and he lowered his weapon. "Anaphora?" he questioned, confused. "What are you doing in my house? At this time of night." He turned on the light and he spotted the other people in his house—all of which he knew. Quickly, Anaphora turned off the light.

"We don't have a lot of time," Anaphora declared then rushed past him with L'Eiron behind her than Maximus and Anton's parents. "Come on," she said.

"No not come on," Gaius uttered, annoyed, and bumped into L'Eiron who scowled at him. "What is going on and why are we in the dark?"

"There are soldiers outside," Anaphora declared.

"And they have live rounds," Mia declared, Maximus and Anton's mother. "They killed everyone."

"And I let them know we're in the house," Gaius declared, horrified.

"That you did." Anaphora remarked glaring at him.

"Where are the children: Noel-Len and Gothalia?" Anaphora asked, halfway up the stairs.

"In bed," Gaius declared, exasperated. He wasn't too sure why he was annoyed. If anything, he was scared. Scared that what Lord Michalis had told him was true. His family was in danger and for what purpose? He had no idea. Instead, he regarded his surroundings searching for an answer and knew that his home was home to many other members of the Valdis clan. With Jax, Mia's husband, he exited his home and entered the night, searching for survivors.

It was a risky move, he knew. If there were soldiers, they'd shoot him and Jax with no problem but seeing that there were no laser pointers on him, and their building wasn't heavily surrounded he assumed they were hidden at the edge of the estate waiting in the shrubs. Quickly, he moved across the estate and towards the houses at the base of the hill.

He regarded the darkness around him, and not once did he ignite a fire in his palm even if he wished that he could. As he knew that the fire in his palm would tell the enemy where they were, even if they didn't already know where they were. Both Jax and Gaius crept across the open grass before running to the first house and forcing open the door.

Bodies covered the floor. Gaius regarded his brother-in-law and his wife were on the ground. He ran by them and towards the children's room. Blood smeared the walls and his hand covered his mouth. Jax turned away.

Gaius ran out of the house to the next one, it was the same result. Then the next house, some bodies were strung up as if they were tortured and Gaius grew angrier with each senseless killing, he saw. When they'd checked all the houses Jax declared. "We told you."

"I had to see for it myself," Gaius said. "You should get out of here."

"What are you going to do? You're not going to do something stupid are you?" Jax asked. His fair skin shone beneath the artificial moon as the cool false air greeted them. His dark eyes watched Gaius carefully and Gaius's blue eyes lingered over the garden in the distance.

"Not particularly," Gaius uttered.

"Why is it that I don't like this one bit," Jax prompted.

"I understand you may not like it, but they targeted our family." Gaius said.

"And we must pay them back tenfold."

"That's exactly what I was thinking."

Than the *crunch* of stone not too far from them caught their attention. Gaius and Jax faced the sound and noticed a soldier with a sword on his back and a rifle pointed at Gaius and Jax. "Did you kill them?" he asked the soldier who appeared to not respond until he said:

"Stand down."

"*Never*," Gaius declared.

Another soldier crept out from one house and towards them. Gaius held up his hands as Jax did. "Secure them," one said.

As the soldier moved towards Gaius an explosion struck the soldier in the back from a strand of fire in the air. The soldier screamed in pain and the second soldier fired his rounds quickly, Jax pulled Gaius out of the way and he allowed his élanocytes to consume him and he vanished in a cloud of black smoke and far from the soldiers and closer to the main house—his house. He ran inside with Jax at his feet once they were inside Gaius slammed the door shut and locked it.

Beside the stairs, he spotted Natalia with Gothalia and Noel-Len. Both children appeared to have woken up with their messy hair and sleepy eyes.

Anaphora declared, "We need to get out of here."

"How? We're trapped," Gaius declared. "We'll have to fight our way out."

"You know the law. If we resist than we'll—" Mia began.

"If we don't resist, we'll be dead." Gaius countered.

"Mum, what's going on?" Gothalia asked and her mother glanced down at her.

She kneeled before Gothalia and pulled her into a quick hug. "Nothing you need to worry about."

"They're after the Fragments of Midnight Eclipse." Natalia declared.

"They could be, but I think it's something else." Gaius replied.

"What makes you think that?"

"If they were after the Fragments, they would have attacked us and not the others. They're not just after the Fragments. They're wanting to wipe us out." Gaius replied.

Mia pulled her children close to her and attempted to keep her composure, but Gaius saw it. She was scared and she had every right to be. She had the lowest unstable élanocyte count and was unable to activate her demon.

Her, the soldiers may keep alive, but Gaius wasn't too sure. He couldn't risk placing his trust in something that was only a fifty percent chance but there was something he knew he could do.

Gaius moved to the door once more and told everyone to stay indoors. "What are you going to do?" Natalia asked.

"The only thing I can do. Those soldiers, they're Centurions and as far as I'm concerned answer to me as the General of the Excelian battalions. However, if there orders come from someone else than there's nothing that I can do."

"Do they know it's you they're attacking?" Mia asked.

"They know." Gaius responded.

"How?"

"Honestly, it's a hunch."

"I'm getting the children somewhere safe," Natalia said, guiding the children away from their parents. Maximus and Anton fussed and didn't want to go but their mother Mia told them to and they calmed a little, but confusion wrought their expressions and it broke her heart.

"We'll be together soon," Mia replied kissing both her children on the head. "Go with Aunty Nat and be good." They nodded and the children were on their way out of the house by the back route.

The air filled with a sense of dread and Gaius turned to Mia. "You can leave too."

"No, I'm staying with my husband."

"Mia—" Jax began.

"—No, I'm not losing you," she replied.

"Go with our boys. You'll be safer with Nat."

"No. I'm not losing you," Mia repeated staring Jax down. "I'm not losing you."

"Okay," he said, than they both turned their attention to Gaius. "What are we going to do?" he asked.

"We fight," Gaius said. "If they want to wipe us out. We'll show them *why* the Valdis clan is feared." Everyone in the room carefully regarded Gaius. "And we'll show them what happens when they mess with us."

Anaphora stepped forward, "I'll be happy to fight for my clan and my home."

"Me too," L'Eiron said. "I'm tired of them always giving us a hard time."

"Honestly, so am I," Mia said. "They always find reasons to demonise us."

Gaius placed a hand on her shoulder. "I know it isn't fair but that's why we have each other. We are stronger together than we are divided." Gaius removed his hand and moved to the door. He leaned against it and listened for subtle movement than his eyes drifted to the other members. "We need to cause a distraction and limit their numbers. Here's what we're going to do: Anaphora, you and L'Eiron cause enough noise and distract them enough to draw their attention and out in the open."

"Mia, you and Jax will be with me and work to take them out silently, understand?" he asked Mia, aware she had military training but never enlisted for as long as he, Natalia, Anaphora and L'Eiron.

"I understand." Mia declared, there was a hesitation in her voice but there was a determination in her eyes. Everyone caught it but they never commented. They knew ever since they could remember that for Mia, the sight of blood from others always turned her stomach. Jax held slipped his hand in hers and held it.

"On the count of three," Gaius declared. "We split up and carry out the plan. It doesn't matter how you do it." His eyes on Anaphora and L'Eiron. "Distract those bastards so we can survive. If not us, the children." They nodded. "One. Two. Three!" Quickly, they ran to their positions. L'Eiron and Anaphora ran out the back of the house and towards the side while Gaius found a few rifles he'd brought home from a mission as souvenirs and he was certain there were only a limited amount of bullets than he smiled. "That could work," he muttered to himself and tossed the weapons at Mia and Jax.

"What about you?" Jax asked.

"I don't need it," Gaius declared, "because I'm going to make those bullets have a massive impact."

Mia and Jax shared a look than smiled. "We just may have a chance then," she commented.

"Agreed." said Jax.

# Prelude

IT WAS QUITE THE NOTION to remember these words: "Believe nothing. Regret Nothing. See everything. Fear None".

For it was a law formed by one of the most ancient of societies; a society engineered during the darkest of times painted and orchestrated by blood and discord. How long ago, that seemed.

The Excelian society, long forgotten and if remembered; it contrary is effortlessly discredited or regularly discarded as a fabrication of misinformation and lies. For that ultimate reason alone, humans need not fear their power.

No matter, the absolute goal for their hidden existence. It was the obscurest of times that drove them from the ravages of war; coddled by greed and pride, and into the arms of a world that encouraged peace and prosperity.

This tenure: Excelian. Was often, used as a reminder, rather than a definition. It was a stint contrived from two words by the humans, one of 'excel' and 'alien'.

Not because of they were aliens but rather because of their prospect and nature of alienation. This majestic term gave them the freedom and power to compose their own path. One, many chose to ignore for centuries. As ill notions befell them made by the discriminating humans, they would resolutely become feared.

Their dark past may have occurred centuries ago, but they remembered its history for it was a constant reminder of their current existence; their purpose within the illusion of time and space and who they were and what they were born to be.

# Chapter 1

Fiery lanterns shimmered along the innermost stone walls and steel gateways that enclosed the cathedral plaza off to the east. They kindled the brace poles on either side of the walkway, guiding any lost wanders to the chantry—or further down the west wing, where the vicar conveyed the doctrine for the day. It was that doctrine they lived by and it was that doctrine they died by.

Natural fire sparkled over the masses below, igniting their red and black non-combatant uniforms in a golden summer glow.

Contemplation *lingered* in the depths of the vicar's greying eyes that wandered over the soundless crowd of Excelian Centurions who heeded his words with each breath he bequeathed. He towered over the first row, behind a grandstand on the balcony of the marble stairs, clad in burnt-cerise and silver robes, pressed finely.

In a thunderous yet quavering tenor, coarsened by time, he uttered: "In the past, our people were inflicted with the worst cruelty known to man. When our ancestors, suffered, no one aided them in their time of peril. Instead, they were shunned and shamed for voicing their suffering. Beneath their bruised, bloodied, and blemished skin, they possessed resilience, clarity, and strength of character.

"Despite their squandered hope, something bestowed them with the power to fight their oppressors and encompass liberation.

Those who unjustly suffered torture and death became the first guardians of our people.

"Throughout the millennia, many lost their humanity and evolved as Excelians: beings gifted with their own unique natural skills and power, blessed with blood, which is as sacred as the lands we walk on. All of this must be considered, valued, and respected with every action we take for the rest of our lives.

"Even as our muscles are sturdier than the strongest metal excavated, complementing speed as fast as the winds of a destructive hurricane, our minds are just as quick.

"Our senses are heightened beyond our comprehension, to match our elemental abilities and our wounded hearts. It is our wounded hearts, our progenitors' pain, which drives our connection with the elements and our home and reminds us every day that our carefully cultivated world is a gift to be cherished and not corrupted.

He continued:

"To believe nothing, is to accept and know that the manifestation of manipulation and misdirected truth exists. To regret nothing, is to understand that for every action conducted to save yourself or many will befall criticism and hatred. See everything, with open eyes, open minds, and open hearts, for the truth will be revealed in every decision made—every action taken will always reveal the truth, often hidden by many layers of secrets and deceit.

"Finally, fear none in the lands beyond ours; fear is a tool to control, oppress and suppress. In saying this, may our blood guide us to value our world and our continued survival."

Second Lieutenant of the Princeps Core, Gothalia Ignatius-Valdis, joined everyone in the hall in repeating, "May our blood guide us to value our world and our survival." Then they all rosing to leave the chantry.

They were the Order of the Phoenix, housed within the Cetatea, that was one of the largest fortresses in New Icarus. It oversaw the training and education of future Centurions, as it had for millennia.

The Cetatea overlooked and guarded the Fire Reserve, protecting it from both the extensive, ancient lava-filled chasms and surface dwellers. With high-set walls, the Cetatea had been crafted to deter those who would dare scale it and ensure climbers would not dare reach its peak.

The towers of amaranthine durability were fortified with motion sensors to detect earthquakes, lava spills and any other infiltrations or disturbances that would befall their home, even if many had believed it could not fall to such frivolous things.

The deep crevices of the Earth's crust hid the fortress well, tucking it away and out of sight, from prying eyes and poisonous thoughts that threatened invasion. Powerful wards guarded the city and its people, nurtured by Grand Elders, and guarded by the Foreseers.

Gothalia walked the old stone grounds, evading every person at the corner of her vision. She didn't acknowledge the familiar pieces of the chessboard she passed, nor bother with small talk as she went to meet up with her mentor.

Why provide any chance for their ill words or to incite more gossip? She would often remind herself this, for she knew no one would dare speak to her. They all feared the demon within.

Except for a few, and Anaphora Reagan-Valdis was one of those few. She was a woman of the Valdis clan, by name if not by blood. She never added to Gothalia's discrimination. She didn't care who she pushed aside to keep Gothalia safe, for it was her duty. She understood Gothalia's anathema but never paid it any unnecessary heed.

Anaphora was an intelligent woman, who never hesitated to arm herself with words sharper than her blade.

Even though Gothalia was twenty-three, she was expected, like the rest of the Princeps, to complete one final year under her mentor's guidance.

Then, she would be free to conduct her missions.

Even so, she recognised the mistrust that would befall her, bloom in the mouths of those with paltry understanding of her.

Gothalia lingered in the courtyard.

Her thoughts were riddled with persecute retentions, one that would demand a call for mourning.

She observed the dojang in the distance with despondency, this place she had trained at a few years before. A place she believed she could not return to ever again.

From the day she could never return, she changed in a way she never expected. She became cautious of who she would interact with, aware only very few could be trusted—that is until she had let her guard down and paid the ultimate price.

Across the courtyard, she recognised Anaphora's dark eyes following her, inspecting her. *She can tell*, Gothalia thought unhappily.

For as long as she had known Anaphora, nothing had ever escaped Anaphora's uncanny perceptiveness – regardless of how many times Gothalia had endeavoured to hide in the past.

Discreetly, Gothalia allowed the muscles in her face to relax, but the look on Anaphora's features confirmed it had not made a difference.

The tension in her shoulders was accompanied by a sullen gloom in her dark eyes.

Anaphora waited patiently until Gothalia was close enough before voicing her thoughts, and when she did, her words were detached yet strewn with concern.

"You don't seem happy."

Gothalia eyed her old dojang from over her shoulder before turning away, choosing to not look back.

"I could be better." Gothalia's attention drifted to her mentor, who in turn, studied the young woman, impassively.

"You will be." Anaphora crossed her fingers loosely behind her back.

They walked inside, their black combat boots clicked lightly against the opaque black marble floor, engraved with translucent flowers and ancient symbols whose meaning had long been forgotten. "I have a mission for you—tomorrow."

"To the surface world—why not tonight?" Gothalia pressed, aware her mentor would throw jobs at her left right and centre. Any further questions Gothalia had were halted by the appearance of female Excelians at the end of the hall.

The Excelians were huddled deep in conversation and their focus danced from each other to Gothalia and her mentor and back each other again. Their hushed words were punctuated with muffled giggles. The women gathered at the mouth of a large breezeway that expanded into a lush garden filled with a varied flowers, trees, herbs, as well as one of the many aqueducts found throughout their home, which carried water from a large central lake. The garden housed a main fountain which was shaped to replicate a female Centurion which many had long forgotten even if her legacy survived.

Anaphora continued, responding to Gothalia's question:

"You can't go tonight. I have other matters to tend to, and no, it is not the Northern Reserves this time. There is another matter with the Xzandians that requires our immediate attention. The Northern Earth Reserve seems peaceful for now. No need to interrupt the natural order."

"Not to be uncouth, but what natural order? The previous ruler of the Northern Reserves may have been a wise man. However, his son is power-hungry and takes what he wants, with no regard or respect for the natural order of things," Gothalia exclaimed. "Of all the members in the family to ascend to the throne, why did they have to choose him?"

"It's not our job to understand, only to safeguard. He and his brothers have been warned to be mindful of their actions, but it's his choice should he decide to be selfish, and if he steps out of line . . . we'll know."

Gothalia did not vex Anaphora further with her unwarranted questions. Instead, her gaze dawdled over the women further down the hall, with mild dislike.

The women drew closer to Gothalia and her mentor until their faces became discernible, much to Gothalia's regret.

An unhinged desire to abandon the area arose, and Gothalia stubbornly refused to listen to such ridiculous fear, to submit any further to the anxiety these women could cause.

An exhausted sigh escaped Gothalia's lips when the women met her gaze - a reminder of yet another of the unnecessary irritations she was forced to deal with.

"I think you have a different battle of your own right now," Anaphora hinted, looking with shrewd scrutiny at Persephone Maragos.

As a Lieutenant Colonel, Anaphora had no place intervening in meaningless rivalry. However, as a Triarius, she was regarded highly for her wisdom and tact in such delicate matters.

Anaphora nodded at Persephone and her friends in a silent greeting, which Gothalia did not approve of, then vanished into the shadows of the building, leaving Gothalia alone with the intolerable Excelian women.

Gothalia knew of Persephone's presence without needing to be informed. Her father was here for another business meeting.

Persephone Maragos was the daughter of a wealthy banker from New Icarus, Michelob Maragos. Whatever she wanted, she procured with little difficulty – including all the men Gothalia had ever been interested in. Which was why she no longer bothered.

"Look who decided to crawl out of the mud! Tell me, did you enjoy your bath?" On cue, her group chimed in laughter.

Gothalia wondered if Persephone remembered how that had happened. As usual, Persephone was more concerned with Gothalia's failings, never on their aftermath. If only everyone knew . . . Gothalia pondered, itching to smile at her the thought she wouldn't share.

Instead, she responded,

"Why don't you go and do something worthwhile other than open your legs?" Ignoring Persephone's stunned reaction, Gothalia tried to push by the woman, only to be held up short when Persephone refused to let her pass.

"You think you can speak to me like that? You're nothing but a filthy orphan! No one wants you and I'm certain your parents didn't want you either." Persephone sneered. The other women stepped back, almost burnt by the scorching fury of Gothalia's glare.

Persephone's unsympathetic words met the ears of the male Centurions across the garden, whose curious gazes drifted to the women in the centre.

"You may be a Centurion but you're a lowlife, unworthy of the title. A loner like you doesn't deserve it," she continued. The girls giggled, momentarily forgetting Gothalia's wrath, while Persephone circled her like a vulture preparing to feast. Gothalia didn't waver beneath her scrutiny, holding her head high.

It was the eyes of the men that amused Persephone. Her already dangerous smile grew poisonous.

"Look, we have their attention. No matter, it's not like they're looking at you." She batted her eyelashes at the men, before narrowing her cold calculating gaze on Gothalia.

Gothalia rolled her eyes slowly.

"You're right. They're not looking at me. You're the talk of the town."

"I know." Persephone sung, in a whimsical voice and her friends fell silent. They watched Gothalia with fearful anticipation of her next words.

"Rumour has it, Daddy's losing money because of your family's dirty deeds and illegal affiliations. So, no, those men aren't looking at me, they're watching you. You know, because you descend from a line of criminals, a once-proud family now forever tainted, and not very clever. You sully your reputation and everyone who ever worked with your family. If anyone is unwanted around here, it's you." Gothalia's tone switched from sarcasm to warning: "Now, get out of my way before I have the Peacekeepers arrest you for harassment and defamation."

"You can't do that!" Persephone wailed.

Gothalia's dark gaze tightened and an evil smile curled at her pink lips.

"I can, and I will. Or have you forgotten, Daddy has no power here, princess? You are on my turf now, and technically you are a guest. I'd advise you best behave." With that said, Gothalia left Persephone behind in a bubbling rage. As quickly as Persephone's anger had erupted, it evaporated.

Her gaze narrowed on Gothalia's retreating form. "We'll see, demon."

Persephone stormed away, then paused to glower at the women, who hadn't followed.

"You don't need an invitation. Let's go!" They hastened after her as she crossed the garden, passing the men who had seen the altercation. The men eagerly avoided eye contact with the raging brunette and her friends, before returning to their duties.

From afar, Gothalia saw Persephone vacate the lush gardens, and questioned whether she was too harsh.

"Don't stress about it," a woman said from behind her. Second Lieutenant Princeps Demetria Crystallovis and First Lieutenant Aquilifer Asashin Brutus approached.

Their eyes lingered on Persephone's figure, until she was out of sight.

"I don't understand why you feel empathy towards a person like her. Then again, I'm not female so I wouldn't understand," Asashin remarked.

"I don't think it's a female thing," Demetria responded, displeased by the comment. "Not all women care for each other, remember?"

Asashin eyed Demetria, surprised by her bluntness, though he knew she meant no disrespect by the question. Nor did she push further; she knew he remembered.

He remembered better than anyone, Gothalia recalled but did not mention, for she knew it was not her place. Demetria had hinted at the Earth Reserve and their only princess, and silence followed the insinuation.

"I'm certain, Lieutenant Colonel Reagan-Valdis will expect us to respond should we need to."

"For now, I'm told there's peace in the Earth Reserve and no threats to our home from the surface world. So, there's nothing to really worry about," Gothalia added, not entirely believing her words.

"Right?" Demetria said. "And how long is the peace in New Eorthen supposed to last?"

"As long as it needs to." Asashin interrupted.

His brown eyes peered at Demetria, filled with intellect and acuity. They reflected his strong features, enough so it made Gothalia question how he worked. He was a man that could be difficult to read at times, but there were moments, Gothalia caught a glimmer of his personality—not that she would ever voice this aloud.

Demetria, on the other hand, could be read effortlessly, even when she assumed, she couldn't.

"Then, we have to go and pick up the pieces again?" she probed, dejected. "Why can't some people just not cause trouble."

"Not everyone thinks like we do," Asashin remarked and crossed his arms, peering down at Demetria, amused by the frustration wrinkling her features.

Grudgingly, she responded, "Don't remind me."

How time flies, Gothalia thought, regarding the light blue sky above. She often forgot it was artificial, especially, when she felt the fake heat of the rays on her skin, and the brief cool breeze that filtered through the compound, cooling the warm summer days and bringing with it a lingering, faint smell of dry soil.

"Let's get going," Asashin said. "Otherwise we'll be late."

"For what?" Gothalia asked, confused. She crossed her arms and shifted her hips.

"The tournament. They've announced new competitors." He wandered past her with Demetria following.

"Why is it always violence that people enjoy? What I wouldn't give for a good book," Gothalia muttered despondently beneath her breath, following her friends.

It did not take long for the Centurions of the Dragon Core unit to reach the Colosseo.

As they ventured closer to the amphitheatre, they heard the uproar of the crowd.

Below, and surrounded by onlookers, were men dressed in traditional Excelian armour, their swords drawn and shields steady. With deceased former competitors surrounding them, the two men squared off.

Gothalia was too aware of the deceased competitors. The moderators needed to list every fallen contender and all the injuries sustained. From Gothalia's perspective there were one too many strikes on most of the bodies; she quickly concluded that the competitors were not too skilled.

"That's too many cuts-he shouldn't need that many to take down an opponent. It's a waste of time." Demetria echoed beside Gothalia.

"Look at them. They're going to collapse before they can even deliver the final blow," Asashin declared, jerking his chin at the struggling, sturdy-built men—clearly less than impressed. "Sloppy."

Gothalia did not respond.

A voice from beside the group, emanating from the furthest chair at the back, caught every Centurion's attention:

"Betheous, is struggling. That is a surprise." A middle-aged man stroked his salt-and-pepper beard. His brown eyes watched Betheous with scrutiny, as though he were about to reprimand a child.

"Heard he was drinking it up and whoring last night," another man noted, from beside the older man.

"Serves him right I suppose," the first man declared.

Gothalia, Demetria, and Asashin shared a knowing look before glancing at the timer in the centre of the arena.

Four minutes left until the end of the competition.

If either man did not fall before the timer ceased, the moderators were within their right to call a draw. Considering the time left, Gothalia knew they would not be given another chance to fight each other.

"I say Betheous will fall after two minutes," Gothalia asserted, eyeing his rapid breathing and the hand that held his sword. It trembled from overuse and excessive strain.

"I say, one," Demetria announced. "I bet five silver stones."

"You're on. I say, he'll fall within the next minute and a half," Asashin added. "They don't look like they can last much longer, to be honest."

Gothalia's laughter echoed as the crowd hushed at the intense competition. "Sounds like we have a wager." She watched the men, entertained.

Demetria groaned, aggravated, when Betheous dropped to one knee after just a minute, before staggering to his feet once more. She muttered,

"Why are you so stubborn?"—or—"Why didn't you stay down?" The vigorous fight continued, much to Demetria's palpable frustration.

The bodies that once limited their range of movement faded away. Eventually, Betheous fell, at two minutes and fifty-five seconds until countdown, making the other competitor victorious.

The spectators slowly departed, leaving the older man who had spoken of Betheous in loathing muttering string of curses.

When Demetria and Asashin moved to flee the arena, they were stopped short by Gothalia, who cleared her throat and held out her hand.

"I believe I'm to be rewarded." The sly expression that masked Gothalia's face annoyed Demetria more than it bothered Asashin.

"Don't get smart." Demetria replied, handing over five silver stones, not meeting her gaze.

Gothalia held out her hand to Asashin who hesitated.

"You said at the two-minute mark."

"No, I said after two minutes."

Asashin glanced at Demetria.

"I won't tell anyone if you slap her."

"Oh, believe me. I'm considering it." Demetria folded her arms, disgruntled when Asashin relinquished his silver coins.

Gothalia tucked the coins away in her belt before walking ahead.

"Pleasure doing business with you, both," she called over her shoulder, not looking back before heading to the debriefing room, pleased she'd make it on time.

Demetria and Asashin watched her leave.

"I could always take her out from behind and you snatch the money. Then we run for our lives," Demetria offered.

Asashin's contagious laugh echoed through the halls, catching the attention of nearby Centurions in the middle of their own early morning tasks. He enveloped Demetria in a playful embrace.

"Let's just get to work, okay?" she said.

Releasing her, Asashin sauntered after Gothalia. Demetria huffed and followed, wondering if he knew she was serious.

When Demetria and Asashin arrived at the debriefing room, they discovered it was unexpectedly crowded with other Centurions of different ranks and from different areas across the Cetatea. They noticed Gothalia sat at the front corner seat with empty chairs beside her.

Taking their seats, she uttered,

"Took you guys long enough. What were you doing?"

"Planning on taking you down," Asashin responded. "Demetria's idea."

"Hey!" Demetria growled, glaring at Asashin. "Whose side are you on? I thought you wanted your money back too!"

Gothalia grinned at the statement.

"Demetria," she sang with purposeful mockery, "If you want your money back so badly, you're going to have to win it back."

"I'm considering wiping that smug look off your face first. Anyway, you've always lost in the past, so what makes you think you won't lose?"

"Bring it. But I assure you, unlike the previous time. I won't hold back." Gothalia threatened, holding Demetria's equally dangerous glare. Demetria muttered,

"Yeah, right".

"Do I have to sit between you two?" Asashin questioned sternly. Both Gothalia and Demetria did not comment, before Demetria murmured to Gothalia:

"This isn't over."

"Of course not. It's just getting started."

"Again, do I need to separate you two?" Asashin intervened. His brows narrowed at the presentation in front of them as he folded his arms, and neither woman noticed the rapid tapping of his finger against his elbow.

Demetria and Gothalia fell silent, and, with one final shared glare, they turned their attention to the front. Lieutenant Colonel Anaphora Reagan-Valdis stepped forward with Lieutenant Colonel L'Eiron Augustin-Valdis.

L'Eiron's golden eyes lingered over the gathering of Excelian Centurions, his black-brown hair shimmering beneath the golden torches.

Gothalia was not surprised by their intimidating presence. Instead, she was intrigued by everyone's whispers and astonishment. According to Demetria, it was rare to see two deadly Centurions in the same room at the Cetatea. Gothalia, on the other hand, had seen them together a little too often—not that she minded.

She had become accustomed to their need to chastise her for something she did or did not do. A lot of the time, she was simply confused as to why she was in trouble to begin with, especially when half of the time she had no idea what to do to avoid it.

"Newly found threats have transpired on the surface world." Anaphora proclaimed, sharp as the edges of a new-cut diamond. Her voice silenced any further muttering from the group. "As expected, the chances of Humans stumbling upon our existence increases."

"Extra measures have been put in place to ensure the Alastorian numbers remain limited. Yet, intelligence hints they are spread too thin throughout the world to cause much trouble on their own. In a group, they can take out hundreds. As the upper echelon of the Phoenix Order you are to undergo extensive training or missions to be prepared for this elevated high priority mission, as decreed by the Grand Elders." Around her, Gothalia heard the other Centurions mumble in concern.

"I thought there were safeguards in place to prevent the increase in their numbers to begin with," Demetria muttered to Gothalia.

"I know what you mean. She's being pretty vague about this too," Gothalia whispered back.

Asashin's fingers stopped tapping and tightened around his elbow.

"Shh!" he scolded, glaring at Gothalia who couldn't help but ask,

"What?" She slumped in her seat and crossed her arms and her legs in discontent, unaware, of Demetria smirking at her small victory.

A Centurion woman of the Ranger Squadron heard Asashin disciplining the younger Excelian women.

Both Gothalia and Demetria, returned their attention to the front, without another word, and listening attentively to the rest of the briefing.

Information about the Xzandians did not shock anyone in the room. Then Anaphora informed the group that the Xzandian presence was proportional to the increase in Alastorian sightings–this was when everyone opposite the Triarius collectively inhaled or stared in stunned silence.

It was news that frightened everyone in the room, regardless of how hard they tried to mask their anxiety.

They hadn't expected it; Gothalia knew that the threat of her home being discovered by the world above would only grow, until her people would be thrown into the dark ages they feared most.

# Chapter 2

THE PRISONERS SCREAMED in anger and discontent until they were silenced by passing officers on their last rounds. Thick prison walls secured the criminals, hiding them from the barren bushlands that bloomed with dangerous reptiles, insects, and other fauna.

The office housed above the cells in the far corner, was supervised by two prison officers this evening. Noel-Len Ignatius and Phillip Lee, who were like oil and water.

Noel-Len never predicted that when he embarked on his position within the Watchtower over a year ago, it would be filled with an unsettling culture and dangerous stigma that he could not talk about.

Phillip Lee, on the contrary, freely expressed his honest thoughts, not once biting his tongue. Even now, as he sat beside Noel-Len, he voiced his opinions without much care.

"I can't believe this! This shouldn't be happening!"—he yelled at the television.

Noel-Len listened, however, not as attentively as he once had.

Phillip scowled at the small television in the far corner, forever critical of everyone portrayed on the screen, much to Noel-Len's amusement.

Beneath the white fluorescent lights, Noel-Len's tidy dark hair complemented his fair russet skin, dark, impassive eyes, and straight line of a mouth. His gaze was drawn to the printed ink before him.

His attention briefly flickered to the security camera monitor, exposing the prisoners in their cells and the empty halls, then, to the television once more, taking note of the horrific destruction.

His attention lingered over the carnage of the destroyed buildings and cars, before returning to the local newspaper he held.

The tabloid was frail and grainy in texture, printed in perfect letters that further caught Noel-Len's concentration.

Among the letters and printed pictures, he searched for information that could explain the nascent rumours, until his focus wavered.

"What's that?" Noel-Len, despite his reluctance, felt inclined to ask.

"Why are those people attacking our soldiers?" Phillip cursed beneath his breath. His light brown eyes glistened in detestation.

Everyone else Noel-Len shared a shift with would not bother turning on the television, but this was Philip. A man who felt inclined to watch the six o'clock news regardless of how many times Noel-Len told him not to.

"Because they have a problem with us," Noel-Len flatly replied, not fond of how bitter it tasted in his mouth.

Being an officer of the law in recent years, Noel-Len understood there were both good and bad people amongst humanity. However, his job was to enforce and not criticise. Regardless of where they were from, or what they appeared like, everyone had a choice to do either. A person's actions would always define their character.

'And this is *why* we don't meet outside of work', he wanted to say. Instead, he folded the newspaper loudly.

"Yeah, but what did we do? We fed their poor, healed their sick and allowed their refugees into our country. Some of those so-called Australians we let migrate here are re-joining them with hopes to wipe out the government that sheltered them, and guess where that leaves us?" Phillip growled, running his thick, tanned hand through his oily chestnut hair.

This was a question Noel-Len was far too familiar with and one he never appreciated.

Phillip Lee was a Class Two Auxiliary Officer; as such, it was expected for Noel-Len to show Phillip the proper respect, even if at times, he questioned some of Phillip's actions and assertions.

In these dubious moments, Noel-Len would cease to listen. There were times when Phillip was worthy of attention but now was not one of those times.

While tranquillity invaded the office, Noel-Len was aware of the severe threats that waited for him and his colleague beyond the red door.

The younger man leaned back in his seat. His dark eyes flickered to the pale ceiling above in thought. Stretching his arms behind his head, he folded his fingers beneath and began to contemplate the past and the future.

"That leaves us with traitors and a never-ending war," Noel-Len replied, while his eyes lingered on the ceiling.

Phillip examined the man beside him in disapproving silence.

He was confused by the quietness that assaulted the room. The younger officer peered at the older man, surprised by his critical speculation.

"Are you mocking me?" Philip queried at last.

"No," Noel-Len replied, with a raised brow, before the buzz of the red door evaporated any uncomfortable air between the two men and allowed entrance to a blue-uniformed man.

Both Phillip and Noel-Len regarded the familiar man with surprise and discretely sat up straighter. As usual, Philip switched off the television before their superior officer noticed, but Noel-Len had a strange feeling that the Constable knew, even if he did not mention it.

Before Senior Constable Mark Roberts could speak, the ground quaked beneath everyone's boots.

The fluorescent lights flashed disconcertingly overhead, flickering in response to the shuddering ground, knotting their stomachs and causing further alarm.

Mark unlocked the door connecting the control centre to the rest of the prison workplaces. Scanning the hallway, cautiously, he checked the surroundings.

Voices beckoned over the radio with questions while both Noel-Len and Phillip listened to Mark's inquiry over the channel, confirming the recent quake with the other constables.

"That was strange . . ." Philip muttered apprehensively. Noel-Len eyed Philip for a moment before his attention glided from the high glass window to the cells below.

Vigilantly, the inmates scrutinised the walls of their cells and assessed the flickering lights overhead.

"It's got to be an earthquake or something, right?" Philip prompted.

When Senior Constable Mark Roberts re-entered the room, poignant words slipped coolly from his lips, "We don't have earthquakes in Australia. . ."

The quivering ground intensified, causing the officers to grip the desktop and walls for support.

"Does this mean . . .?" Philip began, distressed, before the Constable hastily fled the room, ordering both men to watch the prisoners.

A little shaken, Noel-Len discovered the monitors showed portions of the prison filled with terrified inmates stationed and confined behind bars. They bawled and shrieked, pleading for release, a sight that terrified both officers.

Moments later, the monitor presented a video of inmates, slaughtered and no longer identifiable in a spray of blood and guts.

Noel-Len smashed the emergency button, and a siren shouted throughout the prison.

Both Phillip and Noel-Len rushed from the room and to the cells below, aware the other officers would at once respond to the unexpected horror.

Human remains scattered the cells of the once alive inmates, and Noel-Len did not attempt to suppress the horror he felt crawling across his skin.

The prisoner's flesh was scattered beyond the cell door in a muddy pool of blood, which reached towards Noel-Len and Phillips' feet where they stood before the cells.

Noel-Len pointed his gun at the only survivor. His clothes were tattered and covered with the flesh of his cellmate.

Voices of the other officers called over the radio. Mutually, Noel-Len and Phillip attentively listened to the distinct orders, aware that their comrades were on their way. Philip confirmed their location before drawing his Glock, aiming the weapon at the man drenched in blood.

Noel-Len tensed when the inmate staggered towards them.

"Don't move!" Philip warned.

"How far away are the others?" Noel-Len asked. Phillip's unsteady hands that caused Noel-Len further alarm. He needed to calm Phillip down.

The adrenaline coursing through Noel-Len's body refused to allow his brain to process that his friend was terrified of the silent inmate.

"Not too far away," Philip said, stepping cautiously towards the prisoner who paused and watched them. "Cover me." Noel-Len held his breath when Philip opened the cell.

The soles of his once-clean shoes were caked in more blood and tissue.

Noel-Len could not make sense of the explosion.

His mind wandered to all different possibilities while his eyes remained alert, analysing spatter on the walls and flickering lights above.

His thoughts paused when Philip panicked.

"I said: stand down!" he shouted, backing out of the cell as the inmate stepped forward. Noel-Len watched the barrel of Phillip's gun tremble as it had before. "I'm warning you!"

When the prisoner did not stop, Philip fired—fashioning a puncture mark into the prisoner's chest. Black blood oozed from the wound, while his exposed hands and head turned grey with a network of black and purple veins running along the surface before the prisoner collapsed.

Phillip declared,

"Let the others know I've neutralised the threat." Noel-Len lowered his gun and turned away to inform the other officers without any further delay. That is, until he heard Philip's gurgling gasps.

Quickly, he turned to face Phillip and saw the man struggling to breathe, struggling to do anything as his body convulsed—prisoner's arm penetrated his chest. His hand, silver and sharper than any knife, transformed back into a normal hand.

Noel-Len's eyes widened in horror.

Effortlessly, the prisoner jerked his arm free and dropped Philip's unresponsive body to the ground.

The prisoner's eyes fell on Noel-Len, who too in in his flaky grey skin and black eyes.

It was at that moment he realized: the prisoner was not human. Especially, when Noel-Len noticed his once-flat Human teeth become serrated, like a wild beast's—ready to devour its prey.

Noel-Len discharged his weapon and two bullet holes punctured the prisoner's bare chest. Blood seeped from both wounds, soaking the prisoner's uniform, but he did not stop.

Noel-Len backed away, as the man persistently stumbled towards him, as if the bullets were never fired.

"What the hell?" he wondered, aloud.

"Stand down!" Mark yelled, entering the room, with more police officers. Even with their pistols, heavy weapons, and armour, the prisoner continued to step forward, ignoring the command of the officers. Shock and terror consumed them all as they saw the black blood stain his attire.

Noel-Len watched Senior Constable Mark Roberts in front of the heavily armed officers, with his weapon armed and ready to fire.

"I said, stand down!" he repeated. Noel-Len heard the fear in his voice but understood the determination in Mark's posture and in his eyes when he ordered: "Fire!" Ammunition emptied into the chest of the prisoner.

Noel-Len felt it was excessive but did not say anything when he watched the inmate stumble away from the group before falling to his knees.

Unaffected, the monster climbed to his feet once more, and Noel-Len did not hesitate to discharge his weapon, leaving a bullet wound between the monster's brows. The man stopped and crumpled to the ground.

Noel-Len was secretly grateful for all those hours he spent practising.

His celebration halted, when his eyes met Phillip's blank ones, studying Philip's dead body. Not noticing Mark when he sprinted over to the fallen officer, he ordered,

"Call an ambulance!" Another officer radioed for aid. However, Noel-Len knew it was too late.

Philip's life seeped from his desolate eyes. It was a few silent moments later before Mark proclaimed, "He's gone."

Noel-Len gaped at Phillip's unmoving frame. He had seen his mother die before and never realised he would react the same way. Noel-Len had known that a person's life was as fragile as the glass lining the windows high above. It was something he knew well.

Mark scanned the officers behind him before observing Noel-Len's stiff posture. The tightness of his jaw and the distress in his stare was obvious to any who would dare look.

Mark climbed to his feet, informing the surrounding officers to secure the area before he wandered to Noel-Len, who gaped at Philip. He hoped that Phillip would get up and say it was just a flesh wound. When he did not, guilt tightened in Noel-Len's stomach.

"Noel-Len," the Constable called, through his troubled thoughts.

His eyes gradually moved to his commanding officer. It was a difficult task on his behalf, though he knew he had to try and keep himself from freezing over. He had to keep himself from ending up the way he did after his mother's death.

"Sir," Noel-Len forced out, struggling to swallow his bile.

"Do you know what happened here?" Mark asked tactfully. When Noel-Len did not find the words, he asked again, "Noel-Len. How did these men die?" It was a battle of determination and shock that shadowed Noel-Len's features. Mark waited for the younger man to find his words.

Noel-Len hesitated.

"I don't know exactly. I remember looking at the monitor. I saw detainees. They were scared." His eyes drifted over the blood on the ground slithering towards the drains, a reminder of the most recent trauma. "Then there was blood everywhere, but this prisoner was unaffected. Phillip entered the cell to restrain him, and the man wouldn't comply. Then, according to protocol, Philip shot him, but that man didn't stay dead." Noel-Len and Mark regarded the body on the ground, "I turned away to pass on the message, and when I looked back, the man's hand had pierced Philip. I shot him. Then. . ."

". . . Then, we showed up." Mark finished; his dark, conflicted gaze drifted over the cameras in the corners of the prison. His jaw was tight, and his lips pressed together. "We need to get this to Major Crimes."

"Do you think they'll know what happened? Will anyone be charged?" Noel-Len inquired.

Mark accepted the emotion Noel-Len refused to show—utter fear—and with that, Mark offered strained a smile.

"Go home. I think you've had enough drama for one night."

With a brief nod, Noel-Len turned his heel and collected his things before heading home, but not without repeatedly replaying the events of that night in his head.

Later that evening, Noel-Len returned to a dark, silent house. The reality of recent events appeared as an illusion, making him unsteady. What surprised him most was how his recently adopted puppy was not there to greet him. "Mike," Noel-Len whispered into the dusk of the oncoming evening.

Flicking on a few lights, Noel-Len searched the house for the dog, only to freeze in his bedroom doorway.

His dog sat patiently and obediently in the shadows of the room, but not for him. The dog sat at a stranger's feet, his tail happily wagging. The woman's slender hand gently and affectionately stroked the canine's head. Her eyes scrutinised the framed photo clasped in her opposite hand.

Noel-Len recognised the photo she held. It was a photo of him when he was eight. His mother held him under the rays of the sun on the day they went for a picnic beside the courthouse—courtesy of his mother's best friend, Julia. He remembered his mother's jet-black hair, black eyes, and brown skin framing him in the photo.

Cautiously, he noted the stranger, taking in her equally black hair that hauntingly fell along her back in smooth waves.

She eyed him shrewdly over her shoulder, now conscious of his presence. Regardless of her calm composure, Noel-Len felt danger swell in the air between them.

He held her unwavering gaze, even if his heavy limbs rooted him in place just like they had in the prison.

The menace in her eyes shadowed her antagonising smile.

"Who are you?" Noel-Len discreetly glanced at the crystals on his bedside table. "Also, get out of my house."

As she turned to fully face him, his body tensed. His feet parted in a wider stance, bracing himself even as she set the cherished photo on his bedside table where he left it, as if it had never been touched.

"Why would you need to ask? You should already know: a stranger. And, I am not going anywhere until I get what I came for. Then again, this world loosely asks 'Who are you' before understanding the dangers. A terrible habit you've been taught. That fear in your eyes tells me everything, child."

Noel-Len regarded the black singlet, jeans, and boots she wore.

"What are you talking about?" he questioned, wondering if he had heard her properly, "Get out!" Her black eyes searched his, as if she were peering through him, unbothered by his raised voice.

*She's enjoying this*, he thought, and his stomach dropped at the curl of her lips.

"You know the people of this world, the Human Race. Odd, you seem to have forgotten about prior years' events. I do not know whether to feel sorry for your kind who work to forget that invasion. Or, if I should be satisfied that you creatures are as incompetent as ever."

"Get out of my house," he demanded but not as forcefully as he had. The fear of her presence constricted his throat. There was a brief flicker of annoyance in her calculating gaze, one engulfed by anger and impatience.

Within an instant, the woman disappeared and reappeared in front of him. She moved faster than he had ever thought possible. *Or had she moved?* He thought.

Within a single bat of his lashes, Noel-Len felt her firm grip around his throat.

The impact of his body cracked the cement wall behind him and winded him, almost paralysing him before his nails clawed at her strong hands, desperate to break the connection.

"You don't need to be so disrespectful."

Noel-Len desperately strained to breathe.

"What . . . are you?"

"That is a question I'm not obliged to answer," she remarked. Lifting her free hand, she curled her fingers into a fist. A long sharp blade glided from above her wrist and stopped centimetres from his eye. It was a weapon he had not seen, fashioned on her bare wrist.

Noel-Len knew that, if she wanted to, she could release that blade quicker than he could make an escape. She was taunting him. She knew he understood his position, as the blade inched closer to him. As it crawled nearer to his exposed left eye, she demanded in a threatening tone,

"Now, tell me where Natalia Ignatius hid it."

"How do you know my mother?" Noel-Len asked through arduous breaths. "And what are you talking about?" Each word strained his lungs. His muscles burned beneath the pressure as she held him. His mind became both fuzzy and distorted, regardless of how hard he fought to stay conscious.

The burden of her hand constricted, then relaxed at his words. Her intention to kill seemed sporadic.

He felt her dithering choice as she regarded him carefully, ignoring Mike's persistent barking at her feet; he was surprised the dog had not attacked her yet.

As the blood rushed to Noel-Len's ears, Mike's yelps hummed in the background. With a raised brow she questioned uncertainly,

"You're her . . . progeny?"

He held her gaze, and she studied him, searching for deceit. She recognised Natalia's features, and released him.

Swiftly, the woman's attention shot to back door at the sound of the Xzandian trackers in the backyard. Their boots trod over the mowed lawn.

Before Noel-Len had a chance to catch his breath, she vanished.

Mike licked his owner's face as he crumpled on the ground, gasping for air. Mike whined when Noel-Len crawled to his feet and gently pushed the dog aside.

"I'm alright, boy," he whispered, through hefty breaths of air, rubbing his throat.

Decisively, he moved to the kitchen and yanked out a knife he had secured beneath the table and inspected his house for the stranger. To his frustration, every room was empty.

It was not until he heard a thump from the backyard and Mike running to the door, growling at the noise that his hope to find her blossomed.

Noel-Len leaned against the backdoor frame, predicting her next move, before opening the door.

To his surprise, the backyard was empty, and the woman—his attacker—was nowhere to be seen.

A knock sounded at the front door, pulling his attention from his backyard, aware his shed was the perfect hiding place.

Discouraged, Noel-Len closed the door and locked it, aware it would not stop her, not even slow her down.

Her odd visit, the man at the prison, Phillip's preventable death, and images of the prisoner stumbling towards Noel-Len lit up a new sense of fear, one he had not felt for years. A fear he had not experienced since the first invasion.

He forced his fear to subside, and his mind to think of other topics, but no matter how hard he tried, it weighed on him.

It was a dangerous feeling, something he could not understand.

*It's the fear of the unknown that frightens me*, he thought as he stared at where the inhuman woman was last seen. Pulling out his phone, he contemplated letting the others know of the assault, only to place his phone back in his pocket. *No one would believe me*, he reminded himself, before moving to the front door where an unexpected guest awaited him.

# Chapter 3

GOLDEN CONFLAGRATIONS sparkled along the silent corridors where Centurion Peacekeepers and their heavy guard waited. Echoing step taken by Anaphora and Gothalia brought to life the silent walkway. It was a rarity for them to be present in such a highly secure area.

Gothalia pulled her dark gaze from the Peacekeepers, feeling the chill of their gaze upon her as they proceeded down the hall.

The corridor echoed with their light breathing and hushed conversation.

"What exactly are you implying?" challenged Gothalia. Anaphora had ventured to the surface world yesterday but had been reticent to share about her venture. Anaphora *only* informed her of the Alastorian presence at the Darwin prisons and the Alastorians lurking at the outer edge of the city's suburbs.

Gothalia hadn't interrogated her further on the topic, but she had wondered if Anaphora had told her everything.

"What I'm implying, Gothalia, is undercover work—you need to head to a club tonight in Darwin's CBD. An Xzandian Scout commander has infiltrated the city and is meeting with an unknown source. You need to lure out the source without being detected."

"And if I am?"

"Fight. They'll kill you if you don't." Anaphora's convincing gaze halted Gothalia's further question and caused her to turn attention from her mentor—contemplating why the Xzandians were clustering around Australia. More importantly, around Darwin, of all places. *If I continue to be observant and be patient, I will find something*, she thought.

"You'll be given additional orders when we arrive at the Council Chambers." Anaphora eyed the grand door less than a meter from her, lined in elegant silver swirls and carved with dancing flames. Within the centre, upon a stagnant silver fire, a shield proudly bore the insignia of the Centurions and Military personnel.

"Aren't we already here?" Gothalia asked, with a raised brow that dared sarcasm. Anaphora displayed a sly smile.

"You were so talkative. I'd wondered if you even noticed."

"Funny."

They waited for the double doors to unlock, beneath the watchful eye of the security cameras, scrutinized by Peacekeepers on the other side.

When they entered, the doors swiftly shut behind them.

The room was a little livelier than the daunting stillness of the hall, equipped with a small bonfire in the centre of the stagnant foyer.

Stairs lined either side of the walls of the spacious room, climbing to the upper level where the Elders sat, surrounded by books in ancient languages, delicate pieces of art, and lost artefacts.

The black marble floors were the same everywhere. Regularly waxed, they smoothly mirrored Gothalia's and Anaphora's forms as they glided across the room.

Gothalia peered at their moving reflection, coloured in a golden glow from the bonfire.

She tore her eyes from the likeness beneath her boots and climbed the marble stairs.

When she entered the open room, she stopped beside her mentor, gazing upon the Grand Elders of their secret society—the Masters and Generals of the Elite Excelian Battalions.

These twelve members passed laws, advised the Royal family of the Fire Reserve of appropriate actions, judged those who committed crimes, and guarded the Land of Fire.

The members of the Grand Council were never voted in, unlike on the surface world. They were the descendants of their bloodlines, but the selection process was strict. Only those worthy of the title as Grand Elders could become Grand Elders.

Each member of the Council sat high on a balcony lining the entire room and carved into the terraces before their seats were the first twelve letters of the Greek alphabet. Beneath it were Hieroglyphics, each representing the elemental techniques their clans were well known for.

At the base of the balcony were their elite guards and those who conducted errands for the Grand Elders, the Cratians. Their powers were rumoured to have no bounds; some who displayed tremendous courage and bravery had their likeness etched into the walls of the hall of honour, a reminder for the many generations that followed to uphold their commandments on the battlefield and anywhere else they may walk.

"I see you and your pupil have returned home unharmed. Well done," proclaimed Lord Michalis Drakeus, the head of the Grand Council.

He was an older adult, with a neatly trimmed red beard peppered with silver. His dark, gentle gaze held wisdom and power as he assessed the women before him. "As for the mission, Lady Reagan?"

Both Anaphora and Gothalia kneeled. Their curled fists steadied their weight as they dropped their heads in respect.

"The mission was a success, Lord Drakeus. As predicted, the enemy is assembling around the Southern Hemisphere. No doubt, to give the rest of the world a false sense of security."

"What about their Scouts?" he questioned, his eyes observing both women with calculating curiosity.

"They've all been eliminated by the upper Centurions. All that remains is the one scheduled to be assassinated tonight. As our informants discovered their appointment is with an unknown contact."

"I've read the report, Lady Reagan. This unknown contact, it's not someone that we've encountered in the past, is it?"

"No, my lord. It's confirmed that this contact may not be Human but rather a fellow Excelian." Gothalia glanced at her mentor, horrified that a member of her race was collaborating with these creatures, aliens who intended nothing more than to wipe everything and everyone off the planet.

Silence blossomed within the council chambers before Michalis Drakeus spoke, eyeing Gothalia.

"I recognise that expression you wear Gothalia. Where does this surprise come from, child?"

"Forgive me, my lord. I just . . . Never expected our enemy to be like us."

"I'm aware you are young, Lady Gothalia. I am also aware of your difficult upbringing, its struggles, and the horrors you have endured. However, I had hoped from all these trials in your short life you'd understand one thing: we may all wear the same name as Excelians, but we are not all allies. There will be multiple times when Humans or Excelians will betray each other or will work to aid each other. Human nature, like Excelian, is often unpredictable."

"Forgive me. I must have lost sight of that."

"It's not unexpected. It happens from time to time. Even your commanding officer had a similar reaction when she found out." He glanced at Lieutenant Colonel Anaphora Reagan before returning his attention to Gothalia. "We've all been created from the same need to survive. Just because our transition from Human to Excelian was necessary at the time to adapt, it doesn't mean everyone created from this or any similar source is going to fight for the idea that no one else should suffer, as we did. And in some parts of the world they still do. Some people will be ringmasters and will not care who they abuse or kill."

"Of course."

"I hereby sanction you, Lieutenant Gothalia Valdis, to return to the surface world anonymously. Find this Excelian man or woman. Determine their intention and their connection to the Xzandians. Then eliminate the source without arousing suspicion from the Law Enforcers. You're dismissed."

Both women climbed to their feet, and, with a final salute, a cupped hand over their heart and slight bow, and exited the room.

Down the stairs, they strode and out the grand doors that reminded any and every person who entered that every action conducted was judged and recorded.

Gothalia turned away to prepare for her mission before Anaphora's words stopped her.

"You'll be expected to carry out this mission alone; two Centurion officers will tail you, should anything go wrong, but they're not to interfere unless you're dead or close to death. Work as if they are not there. Your final test."

Surprised by Anaphora's words. Gothalia composed herself and accepted the computer chip her mentor handed.

"This has all the information you need. Arthur has all your tools, weapons, and transportation prepared. You leave in half an hour for the surface world."

When Gothalia arrived at the Artillery and Combat Zone, the tranquillity of the air calmed her anxiety. Often, whenever she was here, the place would buzz with the activity of other Centurions walking back and forth, carrying car parts, weapons, or gadgets. In the background, she would hear the grinding of metal, the explosion of a tested grenade in the back room. Sometimes she would listen to the pulsing of electric drills as they manufactured or repaired vehicles or gadgets.

It was during those times that a member of her clan was nearby to ensure the fire from the explosion of the grenades wouldn't spread or cause a dangerous explosion that would ruin the entire foundation of the building or the lives of those within proximity.

"There you are!" a cheery voice called, through the clatter of noises, clear as a bell.

Arthur Cicero's brown eyes shone with admiration. He was a man much older than her, but without a doubt, he was the smartest man she knew.

"Surely, you can move faster than that," he taunted, and Gothalia's smile dropped. It had been a while since she has last seen him, and she had almost forgotten his unusual sense of humour.

There were times, Gothalia knew, when his dry humour and sarcastic remarks, would almost get him burnt by members of her clan or buried alive by the quick-tempered Earth users of Regalis blood. He was brilliant, but not smart enough to know when and when not to speak.

Gothalia hastened her pace, frustration reinforcing the folds of her youthful features. *Rude as ever I see*, she thought.

"I've been told you have my gear and transportation ready?" Gothalia inquired, not bothering to comment on his last words.

Once she reached his workstation, she watched him quickly return to a gadget he had fiddled with when she entered the room.

His workstation was covered in various contraptions, both complete and incomplete. The refurbished computer assembled behind Arthur was stacked with a pile of papers off to the side next to a printer, often forgotten and unused.

Whenever Gothalia arrived, she remembered he would be behind a three-dimensional screen with algorithms, shapes, and words. It was something Gothalia could not begin to describe how it worked, but it was still impressive, nonetheless. It worked like any computer just faster.

"I do. Including your outfit."

"Huh?"

Arthur's brown eyes glinted in mirth at her misunderstanding.

"Didn't they tell you; you'll be infiltrating a club to get to your target. So, you need to look the part. You can't show up looking like you want to start a fight." Arthur examined the gadget under the light before his attention returned Gothalia. He was obviously entertained. Her dark eyes glanced to the side, avoiding his beaming smile.

Gothalia did not speak; grateful Arthur held back his laughter.

"Here it is." He held up the dress he expected Gothalia to wear. She walked around the bench and gripped the ends of the dress, noticing the purposely revealing sections. It would show her stomach and back and one shoulder.

"I'm supposed to wear *that*?" Gothalia's eyes cautiously roamed over the dress while her mind crossed out the weapons, she would not be able to take with her into the club. "Where am I supposed to put my weapons? Why this dress?"

"Like I said you have to look the part and there are black heels over there to match."

Internally, Gothalia groaned.

Regardless, of how times she told herself it was to blend in, she could not rid herself of her irritation.

"Well, how am I supposed to get to my target if I'm fighting off weirdos?"

"You'll find a way. Women always do."

At that comment, Gothalia's irritation only intensified.

"You're serious, aren't you?"

Arthur's smile curled dangerously along his lips, and Gothalia fought the urge to throw him across the room, as she knew he did not deserve it.

"Yes, and you will not be unarmed, but you're expected not to draw your weapons on the Humans. You'll be wearing these underneath." He glanced at the short sword, two knives and an earpiece.

"That's all?"

"Yep, but no one said you couldn't use your flames. Just don't burn the entire city down. The usual light beam will transport you, but you will leave here with a standard Centurion bike. I have packed the rest of your weapons on there. Along with your uniform and armour should you need it. And this—" He tossed Gothalia leather jacket. "To cover the big fire emblem on your back when you ride to the arranged hotel room to change."

"Why didn't you just let me use one of the cars?"

"Can't. They are all currently at the disposal of other Centurions, and Anaphora said a black bike. She chose the dress. The weapons and gadgets are prepped and ready to go."

"Do I have to wear make-up too?"

"If you don't mind, it's been set aside." He smiled. Gothalia snatched the dress and jacket from his hand before collecting the make-up and striding to the assigned bike.

Placing all her items on, she mounted the bike and started the vehicle. It roared throughout the lower levels of the garage. Then, she guided it to a large teleportation pad in the centre before glancing at Arthur, who stood behind the controls. "Ready?"

"Ready," Gothalia confirmed.

"Good luck," he said earnestly. Before Gothalia knew it, she arrived at Lust-us, after leaving the hotel room she checked out from, behind. This club was expected to have the Xzandian contact, but she knew by the bouncers lingering at the door and the many people that was not all it was going to have.

Gothalia's black heels touched the ground as the engine ceased, adjusting her balance she climbed off her bike. *The last thing you want to do is show too much*, she thought, disgruntled by the tight dress and its habit of inconveniently rising.

She paused, noticing two figures, one stationed on the roof that provided a perfect few of the car park and the other down the road who would watch her walk into the club. If she had not known they were Centurions, she would have found them very creepy with potentially dangerous motives. *That's unnecessary*, she thought and parted with the bike.

Gothalia knew even after she managed to make her way inside, her comrades' interference would be limited. Too much interference would mean a failed mission, something she and her comrades aimed to ensure never happened.

Examining the items within the bag, she acknowledged their average appearance, the usual items to carry. Perfume, roll-on deodorant, lipstick, lip balm, foundation powder and a wallet with money. She knew the money was the only thing that was real. She had to use it wisely; Anaphora would not take well to the idea of her having a little too much to drink while on a mission.

She felt the weapons discreetly lining her body and trembled a little as apprehension ran through her; she feared she would be caught. Then, feared even more if she was not. "Then they'd have dodgy security," she muttered to herself.

Taking a deep breath, Gothalia joined the end of the line, listening to the drunken jokes of the men before her. Effortlessly, she ignored them when they tried to catch her attention.

She trained her eyes ahead and, on the bouncers, mentally counting the amount present, then observing their builds, and estimating their weight.

The line was slow, but not too slow that she became bored. She showed her ID with a charming smile, and the bouncer allowed her to pay the entrance fee before heading inside.

She heard the buzz of the earpiece hidden beneath her thick hair. She noticed more bouncers lining the club and mentally counted their numbers, taking in their builds before estimating their weight once more and moved to the bathroom, smiling at the drunk men and women around her as if she were having the time of her life.

When she reached a stall, she heard the earpiece ring to life.

"Do you read, Lieutenant?"

"I read," she replied in a whisper.

"Your coordinates are on track. Identify the Contact," Danteus informed her.

"That's easier said than done," she remarked. "What if he or *she* hasn't had anything to drink or worse . . ."

"What's worse than being sober?"

"Ha. Ha. You're so funny."

"I know, right?" Danteus muttered, equally sarcastic. "Stay on mission."

"Sure," Gothalia uttered, then did not speak on the matter any further, aware that Danteus was done with the conversation. The first question that slipped through her mind was where to find the contact, let alone how he appeared. "A picture would have been nice," she grumbled to herself, then fell silent the moment the door opened, revealing more women entering the bathroom. Fixing her makeup and hair, she vacated the bathroom without a glance back.

Music reverberated throughout the club, mingling with a cocktail of various alcohols, sweat, and perfume. Each scent unpleasantly tickled the back of Gothalia's throat like foreign spice.

Cautiously, she moved through the crowd of people, aware of the vibration of each beat, rumbling beneath her heels. Brushing by strangers, who invaded her personal space, she pressed on.

When Gothalia procured her drink, she purposely avoided eye contact with everyone except the bartender whom she ordered from.

With great lines and a thick crowd, it had taken her a long time to acquire a simple drink, not that she minded: it gave her time to think—to plan.

When she caught the eyes of someone else on her, she became conscious of her earpiece. Casually, she brushed her fingers through her hair, ensuring her earpiece was hidden. Even if it were as black as her hair, she was aware that the various coloured neon lights above would reveal its hard edges to anyone close enough to identify it.

Gothalia relaxed her features into an unreadable expression. Even if her mild anxiety peaked within proximity of others, she knew she could not expose her intentions.

"So, how's it going?" Danteus asked in her ear.

"There are fifteen male bouncers. Average height: five to six feet, plus or minus a few centimetres. Weighing approximately: eight-five to one hundred and twenty kilos. All of them, from what I've seen, are right-side dominant."

Her eyes drifted over the bouncer once more; he was looking at her accusingly. She allowed her eyes to slowly drift from his face and to the people in front of her.

Suddenly, a sharp screech pierced her ear, and she bit back a curse. Pressing her hand against the earpiece, she endeavoured to silence the noise and moved away from the bar and the bouncers, feeling their eyes following into her back.

The judgmental gaze of the others was not missed, but she dismissed it as irrelevant. There was nothing she could do about it.

Once the noise ceased, she readjusted her hair before smiling back at the strangers, whom she could tell were too drunk to notice her slight drop in character.

"What happened?" she asked after the earpiece re-connected.

"Interference, you must be close. I have relayed the hostile profiles to the trackers. Don't blow your cover."

Choosing to ignore her Squadron Commander's almost accusatory comment, she scrutinised the remainder of the club: the DJ booth, the bartenders, and their waitstaff. Her eyes were cautious of everyone and anyone in the building.

The club was smaller than she had originally expected, but big enough to fit a crowd of a few hundred. She now comprehended the need for high numbers of security. A crowd of people was often unpredictable.

Standing within the crowd, she was unaware of people pulling away from her, as they closed the space within their cliques, intentionally reminding her she was not welcome.

Her dark eyes dithered over the green neon railings above, lined in emerald lights that laced the steel poles like poisonous ivy. The lights blinded her vision for a second, but not enough to deter her. Then she caught sight of an icy gaze from the upper level, inviting confrontation.

That was enough.

She knew her target had to be on the upper level. Ignoring the crowd around her, she headed up the stairs.

She elbowed one man in the face, who intentionally slipped his hand up the hem of her dress, then disappeared into the crowd, avoiding the bouncers—she didn't want to start an unnecessary brawl.

An image of the target flashed behind her eyes, but she knew it was just her assumption of what the Xzandian contact would look like based on the little information she was given.

At the end of the day, she had no idea what this person would look like, but she knew what to look out for: the person who appeared the least intoxicated.

Gothalia sighed with discouragement when she realised how many people on the upper level were sober. Great, she thought, disheartened, before making her way to the bar.

Later that evening, she waited outside the club.

# Chapter 4

LEANING AGAINST A WALL opposite the club but out of sight, she spotted a woman mingling with people she had met throughout the night, including Noel-Len.

Even, if the evening had turned to morning over half-an-hour ago, it had not persuaded the woman, who dawdled with her friends down the street, to head home straight away. This irritated Gothalia more than she would ever admit.

She was certain the woman had not even touched her drink throughout the night, but it was only an hour before Gothalia realised she was pretending she had. For what purpose? Gothalia needed to know.

*She's not getting a taxi*, Gothalia pondered, scanning the taxi ranks, then the nearby roofs. The trackers were hidden from view, but her eyes sharper than a human and made out their forms easily, hidden within the darkness.

It was the woman's poor acting that provided Gothalia with enough reason to linger behind and observe her impending exchanges a little more closely. *She shouldn't have to pretend to be drunk.*

Gothalia recalled overhearing a conversation in the bathroom by same group, which had sat beyond where the music could touch them earlier that night. However, it was not a conversation, it was more like the woman would speak to them when necessary and they would eagerly respond.

"Found the contact yet?" Danteus asked, sounding bored. Gothalia knew he was only tired and had failed to remove any trace of his weariness from his voice.

"Maybe, not sure yet."

Danteus did not say anything.

The brunette woman travelled from the twenty-four-hour shop, not too far from the bar, then parted with her group before wandering down a street.

Quickly, Gothalia followed the woman. After a few turns here and there, she finally heard the woman's voice and the catcalling of men. Gothalia chased after the woman only to stumble upon the men's bodies lying dead on the ground with their skin blue and cold. Yet no blood coated the grey tarmac alley.

Gothalia whistled into the darkness, before placing her fingers to her earpiece, gently feeling the smooth texture of the device.

"I found her. The Contact."

"Her?" Danteus replied, uncertain.

"Yes. *Her.*" Gothalia rebutted, at his unwarranted surprise. "She left human bodies behind. I have informed the trackers. Tailing her now." She ran after the woman.

Her heels echoed against the concrete ground. She was grateful they were not too high.

"Stay on her," Danteus ordered.

Gothalia dug into her bag and pulled out a silver-black helmet. Tapping the sensor on the side, she pushed her hair back and put on the helmet. A screen slid over her face and provided a live video stream for Danteus.

"I'm trying, as you can see."

"Visuals good," he replied, ignoring her frustration. She rounded another corner then stopped, eyeing the bare and silent street she'd entered.

A few people she recognised from the club stumbled around the corner at the end of the street before disappearing into the shadows. Other than that, the road was empty and stagnant. Thinking quickly, she touched the side of the helmet, and it covered her eyes with a black screen.

"My lady," an artificial male voice replied.

"Kronos. Run thermo-printing analysis now." Within moments, footprints lined the ground before her.

She scrutinised the feet sizes and none matched.

She knew the woman was her height and her weight, so she proclaimed, "Narrow scan to seventy-eight kilograms and one hundred seventy-five centimetres."

The surrounding footprints that did not meet the requested range faded, leaving those within the parameters she was after. She glanced behind her; her lips thinned into a grimace at the trackers bent over the bodies in the alley.

They would assess the bodies, determined to remove the evidence if needed. The worst part about their job was making people disappear, especially when there would be people who would ask where they were.

With difficulty, she pulled her gaze away. She scrutinised the lingering footprints closely as they trailed away from the trackers, beneath her feet, and down the dark street in front of her. She followed the heeled imprints along the ground.

They guided her down a road that ended at the street. Her heels, loud against the concrete ground, irritated her.

Among the shadows of a nearby building, a man slithered out of the shadows, his gaze on her. It was not until she heard his thick tenor that she paused to take him in.

"Well, this is something you don't see every day."

"Kronos deactivate thermo-printing," she muttered, beneath her breath. With a level gaze, she observed the man and knew he'd have seen her protective gear. Furtively, she wished that the darkness had hidden it from his view, where the streetlights could not reach.

"What do you want?" she questioned when he approached, purposely, blocking her path. Her brows furrowed and her right hand gripped her bag tightly.

With his dark eyes on her, he said.

"Oh, nothing much. Just to talk."

Gothalia laughed an empty laugh before silence echoed through the street.

"I doubt men who hide in the shadows want just to talk."

"What, you think I'm going to harm you?" he teased, feigning hurt.

"I don't have time for your pointless games," she replied, irritated, and continued to walk ahead. She tensed when his thick hand wrapped around her wrist. He smiled at her immediate reaction, almost proud he had had such an effect and she scoffed.

Her angered eyes met his dark glare.

"I wouldn't do that if I were you." She felt the threat behind his words; she slipped her hand out of his tight grip with ease and kicked him away.

"Now, you're going to regret that," he snarled and moved to her.

Gothalia dug into her bag and threw the round lip balm container. The already-loose lid slipped, erupting in an explosion of tear gas. Covering her mouth with a cloth, she rushed past the man.

Her eyes stung a little, but she continued after the footprints Kronos had provided.

A metal bar swung at her, and she rolled over her shoulder, avoiding the attack. Her dark eyes fixed on her attacker with spite.

The woman dressed in blue was barely noticeable amongst the shadows until she ran towards Gothalia once more as she climbed to her feet.

A blond-haired woman, with thick curls travelling over her shoulders, clad in a blue mid-thigh evening dress, she glared at Gothalia with an intention to kill.

Gothalia disarmed the woman easily and kicked her away. Readying herself for another assault, Gothalia stopped when Danteus's voice cut through the sound of rushing blood pumping through her ears.

"Police. Get out of there," he warned in her ear. Gothalia ran from the unconscious woman as if a bomb had exploded, vanishing into the shadows of the street.

She gripped the retractable grapple hook she mounted on her wrist. Aiming it at a nearby building, she allowed it to propel her silently off the ground and against the wall. Pressing her feet against the wall. She bounced with the wire as it hauled her up the side of the building until she was level with the top of a neighbouring tree. Lightly, she climbed onto a branch before moving carefully to a nearby roof.

The police slowed when they recognised the unconscious woman on the ground. Their blue and red lights flashed in alarm.

"Well done, you drew attention," Danteus remarked sarcastically before adding, "This is not going to make it easy to find her now. Return to base."

"What? No! I must be close, otherwise why else would she and that man try and stop me? Or do you agree he's just some creep too?"

"The chances of you finding her when her guard is down is zero. What do you intend to do now, knowing that?"

"To find her. If I follow the trail, it'll lead us to her and whoever else she's meeting or wherever she's going. That's a lead is it not?"

She knew if Danteus wanted, he could write up a report about her recklessness and recent encounters while adding they never found the person who threatened their existence, on top of it.

However, she took the chance to press the issue, knowing she would get on his bad side.

"Come on. You can't pull me from this—we're so close."

"Fine but no more than necessary. Understand?"

She knew even though it sounded like a question, it was not: it was an order. She was happy regardless.

"Got it."

"Good. You're lucky I'm here and not you-know-who . . ."

She had a gnawing feeling in her stomach at the thought of Anaphora in her ear. If she had witnessed this, Gothalia would be set back months. Her arduous work, ruined.

She knew Danteus was angry, but she knew he also had faith in her, even over the silence of the radio.

"Guess, I shouldn't let him down," She promised herself then was on the move.

It had not taken long until the footprints she followed led to a house a few streets over. Gothalia paused and observed her surroundings. She had not heard anything from Danteus and figured she was not going to hear anything from him, for a while.

Her shoulder burnt in sudden pain, knocking her to the ground.

In the darkness, she could not make out her attacker. She sought refuge beneath a truck.

"My lady, I wouldn't consider this to be a safe place!" Kronos proclaimed in her earpiece.

"Quiet, I'm trying to concentrate," she growled. "Activate thermo-seeker!"

Gothalia listened for any cars and any loud, sharp sounds that would alert her to danger. Immediately, she rolled out from beneath the truck and onto her knees and with a short dagger in hand. Her eyes scanned the area around her, seeking the heat signature of a living being, alien or otherwise.

Blood slid down her arm to the cold hilt of the short blade. If it were not for Kronos's immediate warning, Gothalia knew she would have felt the full brunt of that strike. *The pain is bearable; just stay alive,* she thought.

Quickly, her feet shuffled to avoid the random attacks while her dagger deflected unavoidable strikes. In the darkness, steel against steel echoed down the quiet street. The flash of metal in the darkness elicited a sharp shriek with each attack.

The enemy was fast, she noticed, clad in a dark leather jumpsuit that hid her core temperature well but not well enough.

Kronos automatically recalibrated, and the woman's form was strongly outlined, which helped Gothalia dodge and block the slashes of her enemy's dagger. With a backflip, she avoided the final attack, but it reinforced her fears—the target was not a human but an Excelian.

"You're quick," a female voice stated, a few feet in front of her.

Gothalia pulled herself up and stood ready to fight, regardless of how parched her throat was or how desperately her lungs cried for air.

"So, you're the Xzandian Contact?" Gothalia asked, seething with malice. "Show your face, traitor."

"You do not scare me, little princess. I wonder how much they've told you." The woman glowering at Gothalia. A deadly smile shadowed her face, hidden from the streetlights and accompanied by a knowing contemplation Gothalia did not like. "Heiress of the Valdis clan, yes? That is, if you were born first. But you were not . . . were you? So, you have no right to act all high and mighty. Rumour has it, you can't even control those flames Daddy gave you out of pity. Not to mention your curse. You really are a pathetic excuse for a Centurion. You don't deserve to be a part of the higher echelons. You don't deserve to be a part of Dragon Core."

Gothalia snapped,

"Enough of your insults!" Her grip tightened around the hilt of her short sword.

"Oh no, I'm just getting started, princess. So, my question remains: how much have they told you about me? Hmmm? That is . . . this was a mission, and you had to assassinate me. Did they ever tell you about your family, or me for that matter? Or rather, what happened to your mother?" Gothalia did not say anything but glared at the mention of her mother. *Is she implying this is all connected?* Gothalia wondered, but only observed the woman carefully.

The woman was pleased by Gothalia's puzzled yet irritated countenance. It gave her a thrill she had not felt in a long time.

"Do you know the reason?" The woman pulled out a weapon from behind her back; one Gothalia was utterly unfamiliar with at first until she peered closely at it.

Shock enveloped her.

"That's an Xzandian rifle," Gothalia uttered, eyeing the sharp silver lines and the light glow of its recharging battery as it hummed in silence.

"Good eye, little princess." she smiled. "Princess . . ." She enunciated deliberately, assessing the sound of the word on her tongue. "No, you're not a princess. You were never pampered nor sheltered but hated and cursed. You are more of a duchess . . . The Duchess of Execration. Has a nice ring to it, don't you think?"

"As if I'd listen to anything you say."

"But you're still here, aren't you?" she questioned, her tone full of mockery. "Anyway, you probably want information before you kill me—yes? How about this to satisfy your curiosity . . . Humans soon will be benefiting greatly from the upcoming war by increasing their military arsenal with something a little more dangerous . . . where the ethics of war will not apply." The purr of her voice caused goose bumps to swiftly run along Gothalia's arms and back. She wanted to shrug her shoulders and rid herself of the feeling but did not.

"Like what?"

The woman smiled at her Gothalia, amused by the question.

"Like, the extermination of the Humans—your people are attempting to remove from this planet. But the Xzandians won't get their hands dirty. That's what Human greed is for."

"What do you mean 'my people'?" Gothalia spat. "You're not like the Xzandians, nor am I. You are an Excelian, or have you forgotten? You imply the Humans have known about the Xzandians for a while." The woman ignored her statement. Gothalia threw her blade forward, and fire extended beyond the blade, stretching over the street towards the woman.

To Gothalia's frustration, she avoided it.

"You think that's going to take me out?" she called through the shadows, the ground where the enemy once stood melted in the shape of her sword. "An attack like that wouldn't work. I'd know, that's how your father tried to take me out protecting your whore of a mother . . ." Her lips curled in anger. "The sight of you disgusts me."

Gothalia avoided her attacks. "You're right, why bother fighting? But last I checked; you still haven't touched me yet. You don't have enough élanocyte power to do so." Gothalia mocked, noticing the woman's attacks were driven by pure anger.

To Gothalia's surprise, the woman laughed.

"Yes and no. Humans seek power. Unlike them and you, I have it and will cleanse this world with it. Starting with your home!" A strong flare of light blinded Gothalia.

She felt the energy force her away like the winds of a vicious hurricane, but her feet remained rooted into the ground, desperately fighting against the current.

Fear gripped her, and she knew by the enemy's confidence, it was going to get worse. She could feel it. It would toss her across the road or obliterate her on the spot.

Suddenly she was forced out of the way. The trackers that trailed her and shared the mission with her stood before her.

She could make out the fire emblems on the trackers' backs and the swirl of the Valdis crest on their shoulders. She was protected by a ward they'd set up. "Maximus! Anton!" she screamed. They had all grown up together in the presence of L'Eiron and Anaphora.

Maximus glanced at Gothalia with a smile, his words haunting: "Not everyone fears and hates you."

But when the energy retreated, and silence befell the street, Maximus and Anton were gone.

The once-sturdy houses ran with thick black cracks that fissured up the side of the buildings and along the ground and shattered glass windows. Screams of the residents echoed through the roads. Gothalia did not care about the street; she only stared at the two piles of white powder at her feet that fluttered away in the evening wind.

"Gothalia!" Danteus called. "What happened?"

"I'm fine. She was stronger than I thought and the others . . ." Gothalia began to sob. She did not care if she was a Centurion—she cared about losing her oldest friends. "It's all my fault."

The journey from the surface world back to her home was nothing but a blur. Upon arrival, Gothalia ascended the stairs robotically, insensitive to emotion now that she had cried her eyes out. She entered her austere chamber and clambered onto her bed, where she sat for the next few hours.

For her, however, it only seemed like minutes. Minutes that were not enough or could ever be enough.

Her feet curled beneath her body as her arms enveloped her knees, protecting her from the external world. Or rather, the memories she continued to relive, whether she opened her eyes or closed them. They were always there.

They were always there.

The memories of her other family member's stagnant bodies on the ground, their faces blank of any expression, then her parents disappearing and her brother . . . Now, her oldest friends. She had not known what to do and the worst part was her head—it felt messy like an unkempt bedroom, too challenging to re-organise.

"How am I going to face them now?" she whispered into the darkness of the room. It was her open windows that allowed the light of the artificial moon to permeate the room. Her damp face glistened beneath the glow of the moon, shadowing her upturned brows above her damp black lashes.

She recalled their words when she was a girl, just after Anton and Maximus's parents were slaughtered and her brother had disappeared. *"Demon or not. We're family, and we'll always protect each other, no matter what."* Unexpectedly, those words returned. Words she had thought she had forgotten.

When she was young, Gothalia had the ill fortune of catching the attention of two Peacekeepers, but these Peacekeepers were not good. They had abused the laws on a regular basis, but no one spoke about it. They would claim to abide by those laws when questioned, but everyone knew they lied. She had seen it firsthand, then run once they noticed her.

Being small, she was quick.

She ran through the Ember Market. As fast as her small legs could take her, she sprinted between crowds, over stalls and under them. Yet, they continued to pursue her, and she climbed one of the older buildings in the corner of the street before opening a window. No one was inside, so she kept low and out of sight, fearful of being caught.

The Peacekeepers ran down the street, and she watched them from where she hid. When they could not find her, they disappeared.

Gothalia climbed out and dropped onto the street—relieved to have lost them. Her relief was her biggest mistake. Without Gothalia hearing them approach, one man grabbed her throat and slammed her against the wall.

"What did you see, you little twerp?" Gothalia did not say anything at first. Instead, she glared at the man even as he threatened her with a knife.

"Monster," she spat, glaring at the man.

"I'm not the one who's cursed," he replied, with a dangerous smile.

The other man glanced over his shoulder, scanning the surroundings, "Stop. Someone will see, and she is of the Valdis clan. The remaining members will haunt us down and murder us if we harm her. It's bad enough you have her pinned by the throat."

At the time, she did not care about his tight grip; she just took in his face, every detail, and every word spoken. It would be another memory burned into her mind, one that could never be forgotten but one that would drive her future.

"Let that demon clan come, I'll take them all on."

When he uttered those words, Maximus picked up a nearby stone brick and threw it at the Peacekeepers. The attack stunned the Peacekeepers. Anton and Maximus attacked them by first taking out their legs before picking up the brick again, Maximus smashed the brick into the face of the Peacekeeper and the other man reached for Maximus while Anton, kicked him in the back of the legs forcing him to his knees. With another kick Anton kicked the man's jaw. The Peacekeeper collided with the ground as Maximus stopped smashing the brick into the face of the Peacekeeper and Gothalia knew it was by chance they had won. After the fighting ceased, Maximus extended his hand to her.

"There you are. Let us go before Lord L'Eiron, and Lady Anaphora find out we've snuck out."

Gothalia recalled the Peacekeepers words: *"I'm not the one who's cursed."*

"But I'm a demon. You should fear me. Not help me." Gothalia replied in a small voice, glancing away from Maximus. She did not want him to notice the tears she had readily shed. It was embarrassing enough she had to be saved. If she were as terrible as they said she was, surely, she would not need his help—but she did, and she was grateful.

Maximus and Anton shared a confused look.

"What are you talking about?" Maximus questioned. "Demon or not. We are family and we will always protect each other no matter what. Now, let's go before we get in trouble and don't get dessert tonight." She recalled their light laughter as they returned home that evening.

Now, within her room, the artificial moon hung silently, tranquilly, against the backdrop of a starry night, lighting her bare floor with black outlines of her window frames and the faint flicker of her curtains that caught the draft of her open window.

Stillness saturated the bare black marble floor, silencing the shadows further and encouraging her tears. Her dishevelled hair and black dress blended with the darkness, but her eyes were bright like the moon; unlike the moon, however, they held an emptiness none would find captivating.

In the silence, a knock thudded against the thick wooden door. Her toes curled and her arms tightened in anticipation.

"Gothalia, please open the door. I know you're in there."

# Chapter 5

"GO AWAY."

Silence strained the air between them.

"I can't do that."

The electronic wooden door permitted entry to Danteus; whose heavy frame was dim against the light of the hallway. His expression was unreadable, but his eyes glinted with a rare concern.

Gothalia's eyes lingered over the door key card in his hand. A dark reminder of the massacre, a day she could remember in parts, but never as one scene. She was aware that if anyone had a high enough élanocyte count, they could remove the entire door from its frame.

"That door was supposed to stay locked. Why do you have *that*?"

Danteus closed the door a little, allowing the fair light to drift over Gothalia's frail form.

"To check on you. Anaphora lent it to me. You were pretty broken up," he said carefully.

This was a mission he had no knowledge of how to approach. A part of him couldn't help but want to say—"you have the worst luck, don't you?"—but, even by his standards, he knew how insensitive that comment would be.

Gothalia scoffed.

"Why wouldn't I be? Should I be okay with people dying?" Her hurt and reproving eyes fell on his and he recognised the fragility of his position.

"No one can ever be okay with people dying but have you forgotten you're a Centurion. A soldier. And so were they. They did their jobs knowing the consequences, it was their duty to their Reserve. Learn to look at things objectively, and maybe . . . it'd be a little easier."

Gothalia exhaled, feeling weaker beneath the weight of his words, tensed her shoulders.

"I haven't forgotten what their duty is, nor have I forgotten mine. I am just wondering how much more pain and suffering is to come before things get better. And when it does, will I no longer see things the same?"

The bed ducked beneath Danteus' weight as he settled himself on the edge.

He had not thought of her at that moment as a soldier but as a friend. He remembered going to class with her and causing trouble with her. It was only by chance he had outranked her.

"No one said living was easy but the freedom to live without suppression and oppression is something we must fight for. Especially, if the Xzandians are planning on enslaving the entire world."

"That's if the Humans live long enough," she darkly added.

"It won't only be Humans who will suffer, as history has it—that's why we're here. We are to do what our ancestors did centuries ago. Even if many will hate and criticise us for it. There will be others who will be awakened in the upcoming war and we must be there to remind them to fight and to not give up. Do you think you can do that? As a Centurion of the Fire Reserve?"

Quietly, she thought over his words, then nodded, surprised by the sudden stiffness of her legs as she stretched them out along the cold dry sheets. Gothalia examined her bare legs, battered with scrapes and bruises. They were a reminder: she was still here and that was enough to keep going.

The weight on the bed shifted once more. She felt the gentle touch of Danteus' forehead against hers. He was close enough that he could smell the salt of each tear.

"Don't ever feel like you're alone. We are here, even L'Eiron and Anaphora. We're not going anywhere."

In the darkness, Gothalia's short sniffles and shallow breathing reverberated throughout the room. Danteus did not move. Without words or thought, he listened, allowing the memories of that evening and everything she had encountered as he had, to resurface. He knew how much harder it was going to become from that moment on.

At last, Danteus parted with a sorrowful look, aware he needed to return to his small, but specialized, company, Dragon Core. Gothalia was grateful that he vacated the room, encouraging him to leave with a false, but convincing smile. Then she, too, abandoned her home, a place that reminded her of both the good and the bad.

The stone streets of New Icarus were not calm but busy with people walking to and from their morning ventures. Earth users used stone boards to skate throughout the streets, while others, with the aid of air users, utilised hovering carriages.

Steadily, Gothalia roamed the streets but did not go to the Cetatea. She knew Argos would want her to debrief.

Instead, she walked the city streets where people prepared for the morning, passing from one suburb to another, before heading to La Volpe Heights. Gothalia paused on the footpath for a second, observing the artificial ocean stretched before her.

It was as real as it could ever be, she realised. Her lips frowned at the thought, then she moved to the small dirt path that led to the cliff-side.

She would often visit this bench when she needed to be alone; it was luckily unoccupied. The air here always smelt genuine, as did the fresh scent of saltwater.

She often wondered, when would the peace change? It was not like she wanted the peaceful times to disappear. It was more that she knew that not everything would last. Or could not last.

Gothalia recognised the call of the rain by the cool oncoming breeze that gently blew past her skin where she sat on the brink of a sharp cliff.

Her observant eyes regarded the gentle sway of the ocean that lay stretched before her, dancing and colliding beneath the wind.

A storm loomed. The dark grey clouds overhead were staunch warnings for her to return home but Gothalia's feet remained rooted in place. In that moment, she did not care, as she observed the peaceful scenery beyond the cliffside.

*A few more moments*, she thought, *and I will work up the courage to face them.*

She knew Danteus had gone in her place to deliver the news of her comrades' deaths to their wives, but she could not get the image of their existence—reduced to dust—from her mind. It could not be erased.

Nor could she remove the guilt and shame from her stomach when her mind sorted through the memory.

Gothalia observed the dark migrating specks which sprinkled the beach below. Kites glided through the air, their wings guided by the ocean breeze, and a small smile pulled at her lips.

The kites' wings flapped, as they aligned themselves to the air's current before circling the beached stingray below them.

Swooping speedily, they easily picked at the remains before soaring back into the air.

It was fake, she knew. Regardless, of how real it appeared.

She eyed the high and sturdy metal railing not too far from her. Deterring anyone who might wish to climb.

The artificial briny air permeated her nose, clearing her mind. In moments like this, she loved the surface world more than she ever realised. Even though her home had managed to create artificial winds, storms, and a sun, it was different from being aboveground. For now, she could only pretend she was.

It was monsoon season in the Northern Territory, the place she had recently abandoned. It would be sticky and hot, but beautiful once the rain showered the city, cooling the warmer days. This was what she loved—being at one with nature—but per usual, it did not last long. When her communicator beeped.

She felt it shudder in her pocket before hearing another, beep. It trembled, once again, against her skin, much to her displeasure. *No*, she thought, *I need more time.*

It was not like she needed to be made aware of what was happening, and it was not like she needed to be a part of whatever it was that was happening. In the end, she knew she would learn about it. It was inevitable.

With her lips pursed in thought, she pulled out the communication device and eyed the screen a little reluctantly.

There, on the screen, was a text from Argos, the Commander of Dragon Core. He was not in the best mood:

"Return to base, immediately." His words were abrupt and cold. She could only imagine the expression on his ageing features.

Reluctantly, she returned to the Cetatea and to the halls of the eastern building where the Dragon Core members lived, trained, and received their missions.

It was a place they cherished. It was something they all had in common.

In the main chamber, Argos Ambrosia's assistant, Christian Antonius, cowered behind his clipboard as Argos threw a pen through the air. Christian was obviously fearful of Argo's undisciplined and yet humiliating verbal abuse.

Argos was angry.

And everyone was scared.

Unfortunately, Gothalia knew it had more to do with her than anyone else. She recognised the scornful looks of the others as she entered the building.

She understood numerous complaints had been filed against Argos. However, she and a few others knew he was not going to be relinquished of his position until the Grand Elders considered he was irrelevant. This thought never sat well with her. At Anaphora's request, she stayed silent on the topic.

Argos's dark eyes assessed Gothalia, patiently waiting for a response to what had happened on her last mission, but those were words were never uttered.

In place of her silence, he continued to reprimand her. Internally, she wondered if he would still be speaking to her disrespectfully if Anaphora was with her. *Doubtful*, she thought, aware of Argos's discontent when the higher-ranking Triarius reprimanded him for his poor management.

Even as he yelled, the guilt still weighed heavily on her, and she vowed at that moment to hunt down the woman who had slaughtered her friends without a second thought. However, for now, she needed to be patient. Her opportunity would arise.

"That's enough Argos." A voice said wearily. Gothalia did not have to look; she knew who that deep rough voice belonged to. It was branded in her memory as much as Anaphora's. "I'm sure Gothalia feels guilty as it is, since she failed."

"I told you what she wanted. What she was planning and what she looked like. There's video evidence, yet you choose to do nothing." Gothalia turned her attention to L'Eiron Augustin-Valdis.

Gothalia noticed Danteus standing beside L'Eiron with a clipboard in hand, she could tell he had returned from his duty to recheck the weapons' stock. Gothalia was monetarily glad it was his turn, a happiness that extinguished when he disapprovingly frowned at her.

Her gaze returned to L'Eiron.

"You told us that extra measures were in place to ensure that the limited numbers of Alastorians stay limited, but you never said anything about trading Excelian information in exchange for Xzandian technology. Or that the Humans would profit from this." Gothalia held L'Eiron's gaze, taking note of the brown smear between the gold in his irises, shadowed beneath his mahogany brown hair that under the golden torches appeared black.

L'Eiron was a tall man, his build equally intimidating and his presence reminding everyone that he was strong and dangerous.

He held Gothalia's gaze, taking in her features, features that reminded him of her mother.

With a reluctant sigh he proclaimed, "I didn't think you'd find out like this or hoped you didn't find out like this. That's why Anaphora made sure you were always with her on missions."

"And not with you, why?" Gothalia questioned, her tone flat and her expression cold. "Your demonic blood is purer than Anaphora's. Why did you only teach me control in the mountains and never on missions?"

"You need to be specific . . . which question do you want me to answer first?" L'Eiron asked, like a patient parent. Danteus shifted his weight uncomfortably beside him.

"The target. Who was she? Better yet – how does she know me?"

"You know I'm still here, right?" Argos commented, attempting to gain the attention of either Gothalia or L'Eiron. "If anyone cares." He was ignored, much to his irritation.

Upstairs, the phone rang, and Gothalia relaxed at the sound. It comforted her in a way she never realised the ring of a phone ever could, even if everything seemed a little . . . strange.

"Whatever," Argos mumbled coarsely, before moving up the fine silver stairs and to his office.

Gothalia's gaze skimmed over her shoulder, drifting to the tentative women concealed around the corner in the distance.

"You can come out now," she said, before returning her attention to L'Eiron.

He crossed his arms, his expression serious.

"So, you're going to listen now?"

Mimicking his stance, she crossed her arms.

"Intelligence suggests that Numitora Faustus-Ignatius is responsible for the relay of information regarding Centurions in the Fire Reserve to the Xzandians in exchange for weapons and technology that will aid the Humans in the upcoming war."

Regardless, of how L'Eiron had worded it, Gothalia knew it was always human nature to manipulate, gossip and lie—and was even so at times with Excelians. This was a habit she hated but refrained from mentioning aloud.

"And?" Gothalia pressed. "You didn't think to tell me that, or the fact that she could wipe out a person or people within seconds? My job was to assassinate, yes, but I had no idea she had that much power. Were you so willing to sacrifice me, Maximums, and Anton?"

L'Eiron eyes darkened.

"It's not that." Conscious of the secret he was forced to keep, L'Eiron worked to control his temper. "It was more like: we assumed it was better if you didn't know. However, we didn't expect she'd master it."

"What are you talking about?" Gothalia asked, genuinely confused. L'Eiron did not speak. Domitia, Melanie, and Christian, the other Excelians who worked in the Cetatea, glanced at each other.

Gothalia recognised the expression they bore. It was the same expression she was familiar with, and, as such she steadily regarded them from where they stood off to the side.

"Are you going to tell me? You guys look like you know something." The malice in Gothalia's eyes caused alarm to simmer within Domitia, Melanie, and Christian. They glanced at L'Eiron with fear.

As he said,

"It doesn't matter right now."

"Whatever. We are going to get nowhere with this. If you will not tell me, I'll find the answer myself." She glared at L'Eiron who sighed, at her stubbornness, not wanting to remind her Argos still needed to speak to her.

"Christian!" Argos shouted from up the stairs and the girls cringed at the subtext woven through that one name. Christian jumped and flew to Argos's office faster than anyone thought possible, even by Excelian standards.

Melanie regarded Gothalia cautiously.

"The only reason why he hasn't fired you is because you're of the Valdis clan, and because of its connection to . . ." She paused contemplating her next words. ". . . Regardless, you're a part of the Echelon. The Xzandian numbers are rising, as are the Alastorians. We cannot afford to lose any more of the upper echelon. Especially, those of the Dragon Core, as we could have a war on Earth soon."

"There *is* going to be a war not could," Gothalia rebutted, not caring how rude she appeared at that moment. Surely, she would be given freedom to express her emotions, even a little.

Red-faced with anger, Domitia Aelius reprimanded Gothalia with her green eyes, daring her to rebel.

"They're close, the Humans I mean. They are close to knowing our existence; it is all over the surface news. Especially, since your fight with Numitora was out in the open!" Gothalia remained silent with worry and her eyes travelled from one girl to the other, in contemplation.

Gothalia twisted with the potential possibilities of how she could have trailed Numitora and how their fight could have played out. However, as she considered it, she knew it would all end the same way.

She did not know what to say to Domitia but knew she had a point: discretion was necessary to avoid any political conflict in the future.

The enemy was gaining the upper hand, and she often reminded herself, it was not her fault, but she knew without a doubt that when conflict dragged out, unnecessary trouble always ensued, even the unnecessary loss of life.

"I guess I'll be a little more careful from now on," she said.

A bubble of laughter escaped L'Eiron's lips.

Domitia and Melanie glared at him. He quickly composed himself, holding back his snicker.

"Sorry." He cleared his throat and avoided anyone's gaze. It was not that he did not believe Gothalia's words; it was more that he spotted the rare seriousness that had crossed her features, sparking a memory from when she was younger.

"What's so funny?" Melanie questioned.

"Were you unable to believe her statement?" Domitia asked, with a single raised brow.

"That's not it," L'Eiron managed, Gothalia could tell he was uncomfortable with this attention.

Still angry with him, Gothalia glared at the man, who was bothered by her irritation but did not allow it to show. He wanted to tell her the real reason for Numitora's anger, but he figured she would need to find out on her own.

Swiftly, she turned on her heel and vacated the Dragon Core's assigned building within the Cetatea, not even bothering to say goodbye.

As she moved through the open garden, she was fuming and preferred everyone kept their distance until she calmed down.

*I need to calm down*, she thought, *my anger must not get the better of me.*

Once calm, she continued, finally entering the eastern wing of the Cetatea, sombrely reflecting on everyone's words. In the middle of her tedious thoughts, Gothalia halted once more. She knew they were hiding something from her.

Beside her, a glass panel stretched along the wall, mirroring her empty gaze as she eyed the garden beyond, cradled beneath the morning sky. Without much thought, she turned her eyes from the gallery and continued further down the corridor, unaware of another pair of feet on approach.

Surprise escaped her lips when she collided with a person she had not noticed. A voice silenced her apology, and she eyed the red-gold eyes staring into hers.

"Are you alright?" The stranger asked, with a bright smile lining his brown skin. She stepped away from the man and out of his grip before apologising once more. "No problem." His golden eyes regarded her critically.

The encounter was brief; with a lingering smile, he moved around her and continued further down the hall. Gothalia's eyes swept over the corridor behind her, staring at the back of the stranger. Wondering where she had recognised him from, she could not at that moment pinpoint it.

Without much hesitation, she strode the silent moiré hall before arriving at the Artillery and Combat Zone. The two double sliding doors she paused before required her to scan her security card. When she did, the doors welcomed her presence, and she entered.

The Laboratory was built with clean marble floors and lined by empty sterile tables; off to the side were untouched wind experiments that often flooded the room.

Arthur, clad in his usual white laboratory coat, marked notes on a clipboard.

"Arthur."

At the sound of her voice, he paused, watching her steadily and with mild curiosity. She smiled at him; then her eyes drifted to the petri dish on the table.

"What brings you here?" His eyes drifted to the wall clock, aware of the early hour of the morning. He internally sighed, he had stayed out all night when he'd promised himself, he would not. He turned his attention to Gothalia; he caught the tiredness in her posture even if her eyes were filled with determination and curiosity.

"I'm hoping you could help me. I'm after information about Numitora. I know it's a bit of a stretch, but why does she hate our people so much?"

"What gave you that idea?" Arthur asked carefully.

"The anger in her eyes when she looked at me before she tried to kill me. It was brief, but it was there. It was . . . pure hatred and nothing more. It reminded me of those times . . ." Gothalia wrapped her arms around herself, not realising her reaction hadn't escaped Arthur.

"Well for starters, did you know that Xzandian scales retract under artificial sunlight?"

"Wait . . . Xzandians have scales?" Gothalia inquired, surprised by the change in topic.

Arthur's brown eyes glinted in delight.

"They do."

"That's new."

"I want to show you something, but first: to help you with your dilemma, have you ever heard of Midnight Eclipse?" He held up a black Xzandian scale, the size of the tip of her finger, with long silver tweezers. Gothalia watched in wonder, as the light triggered a faint rainbow halo. "You've never heard of it?" Arthur asked again.

Gothalia shrugged.

"What is it?" she inquired, her eyes never leaving the unique scale.

"It's a weapon that has enough power to wipe out nations—even Excelians. A couple of weeks ago, there was a signal that had alerted the surrounding Reserves and the Xzandians to its presence. This explains why they're here a second time and why these scales that we know of are so important."

Gothalia raised a brow.

"I'd like to think I'm pretty bright, but Arthur, I'm honestly not following. . ."

"Imagine a powerful weapon that wasn't created by Human or Excelian hands but created by another race. One that may have existed well before the Earth was even formed. That runs off pure energy. Just like these scales. Look at what happens when I add light to it." Arthur handed Gothalia a pair of dark goggles, instructing her to keep them with her. He set the scale in a petri dish with the long tweezers and headed towards the door she had seen on her way here. It was lined in black and yellow tape, a caution to keep everyone out, unless authorised. "This way."

# Chapter 6

WHEN GOTHALIA ENTERED the room, she eyed the steel door accompanying a glass panel that divided the area. From what she saw, the room had a large glass pane that allowed her to investigate the other room which she figured was used for dangerous experiments.

Arthur opened the steel door, closest to her and headed into the other part of the room. He placed the scale on the table and walked out.

"Do you have your goggles?" Gothalia held them up. "Good. I'm going to set up the environment, and I want you to pay close attention to the rainbow."

"Okay," she responded and pulled on the goggles.

Arthur's fingers glided over the touch screen as he played with a few dials on the transparent display that sat on the glass panel.

Then, the room lit up.

As it did, Gothalia could make out the scale under the glowing light. The rainbow grew and grew until it was as big as the room. Then within a moment, she felt a wave pulse through her and set her off balance. Once the light died down, Gothalia pulled off her glasses and asked, "What was that?"

"That's what we're trying to figure out," he informed his eyes on Gothalia. "Most of the research is done with Dr. Legato and her team. I get to assess it now and again and see how much energy it can take or release in response."

"Because of the colour."

"Yes."

"So, we're pretty much looking for something ancient, black, and from a different world?" she asked. Arthur moved through the steel door and over to the experimental area while carrying the black scale in a transparent dish. "Pretty much. Take a closer look," he offered and held up the scale. Gothalia's eyes squinted at the sight as they took in the small, translucent rainbow lines.

"What's that?"

"From what we've gathered, they're capillaries."

"What are capillaries doing on a scale?" she asked. "Wouldn't it make more sense to have it underneath the scale?"

"Normally, that would make more sense, but when it comes to new scales—the capillaries are on the top layer. Later they pull away under the scales to make way for new scales."

"That's pretty cool."

"I know, right? These scales are not from this planet," he added and turned away, placing the scale back down. "Before I forget . . ." He headed back into the Theory Room. "This scale you found on that abandoned alien ship prior to Anaphora's mission, turns out to be a purebred scale."

"Which means?" she asked, before answering herself, "The person who attacked that reconnaissance ship was an Xzandian." Arthur nodded.

"So, then what does an Xzandian have to do with this Midnight Eclipse?"

He held up an object. It was large and curved in the centre.

"What is it?"

"A Fragment of some kind. A puzzle maybe . . . Rumour has it they are spread throughout the world. Sometimes, people have them, and sometimes they don't know what it is—it could be used as nothing but decoration." Gothalia grinned at the statement; she left aware Arthur did not answer her question but thanked Arthur for the demonstration before heading out of the Cetatea. However, he had asked something of her in return for this information, and that was not something she had expected.

NOEL-LEN RECOGNISED the danger. It was peculiar, to say the least. When the crowd pulled away from him, their fearful yet cautious eyes held scepticism.

The woman's her green eyes gleamed devilishly beneath the flashing lights of the club. Noel-Len was aware of how daring they were, and the almost overwhelming power they had over him and every man nearby. He caught the envious glances of the other women who did not keep the attention of the other men.

The men, inched closer with caution, as did he. Then the night ended.

She parted, with nothing more than a few words and a sultry smile. Noel-Len stumbled upon Caprice, who struggled to guide a drunk Michael down the road. He had not recognised his failed attempts at flirting. Caprice did not fail to reprimand him harshly in response to his shortcomings.

Briefly, she noticed Noel-Len and demanded that he take Michael off her hands. When he agreed, Michael saw she did not hesitate to remove herself from his side as if he were contaminated. He pouted at her palpable relief and replied that he was not that heavy.

Irritated by the pointed leer on his face, she replied,

"You're as heavy as an elephant!"

He responded, with the same smile,

"It's all muscle babe."

She replied with a string of curses, annunciating the stupidity of his comment, causing Noel-Len to stifle his laugh, at her abrupt but honest words.

Caprice drove them home. When she dropped Noel-Len off, he secretly wished she had stayed a little longer, but knew she could not, for he had responsibilities that could not be easily relinquished.

Later that morning, Noel-Len was not as mentally exhausted as he thought he would be when the dawning sun peeked over the distant horizon.

"Don't you dare, slow down!" Corporal Ian Kypreos warned from behind the small group of commando soldiers.

Bravely, Noel-Len peered over his shoulder, then instantly regretted the action when he caught Ian's sharp brown eyes assessing his, reflecting an expectation of failure. Panic fluttered along his spine, like nails clawing down a blackboard, and he tore his gaze away.

The group jogged faster and held their pace for the next few hundred meters, pushing through their shallow breathing and aching feet. The packs they carried were light but held enough weight to be both uncomfortable and wearying on their tired bodies.

When the commando squadron relaxed to catch their breath, Noel-Len sat on the dry dirt ground, not caring about the small stones that made his chosen spot uncomfortable. His tender feet and erratic heart made it almost impossible to care.

He welcomed the warm water from his canteen, quenching his thirst.

It had surprised him at first when they had vacated the base, until he recalled that it was planned months in advance that they'd be exercising off the main base and at a smaller camp that was never in the same spot twice.

The rough terrain, filled with sharp shrubs, smooth gum trees, and endless wind removed any hangover he'd previously had. Secretly, he promised himself never to drink again, accepting it was not how he should have dealt with Phillip's premature demise.

He looked intently at the dry soil before him, lost in thought and recollection, unaware of the intense heat rising off the ground, warming his already-perspiring body.

Michael's unnecessary taunting caught his attention.

"How are you doing, Brown?"

Noel-Len's gaze wandered to one of the two women in the group and the entire regiment.

Sweat lined her features, emphasising her flushed face. She was tired just as he was and, to her clear disapproval, Michael took advantage of this. "Can't keep up?"

"Shut your trap, Williams." Tracey barked, her stern blue eyes on his. "I got here before you." Michael shrank in silence, failing to retort.

Noel-Len did not blame him for being slow: Michael said he had thrown up after he had gotten home. With only an hour and a half-sleep, Noel-Len had to knock on his door, forcing him to wake up and prepare for the day.

Laughter reverberated throughout the clearing.

"You're such a snake," Tracey uttered, her lips curled in irritation, and Noel-Len bit back his laugh, aware of everyone else chuckling at their conversation.

"Wait . . ." Michael began, and the group fell silent, hearing the fear in his tone, "Speaking of snakes, you don't think there are any here, do you?" Michael's wide eyes dissected the area around him. Noel-Len knew just like everyone in the group, he was terrified but attempted to play it off as a joke, one that no one believed.

Noel-Len recalled that, when they were younger, wildlife rangers had arrived at their primary school, displaying all the diverse types of animals found in the Northern Territory bush, including, to Michael's discomfort—snakes. It was only a Children's Python, but Michael would not go anywhere near the little reptile, let alone touch it.

"Who knows?" a voice commented with a teasing tone, one that grasped Noel-Len's attentiveness. At the far end of the group waited Corporal Kypreos who eyed the surrounding area cautiously. "Just keep an eye out. The last thing we want is another dead soldier, especially if he's only a private." Michael squirmed beneath their leader's stern and disapproving gaze.

Corporal Ian Kypreos, a mixed indigenous Australian man, was both reserved and strict when he trained teams or led their fitness regime.

Five years ago, soldiers were required to live in certain parts of Australia to be eligible for the commando core. However, given the initial alien invasion that ensnared their country, three years ago, that requirement was no longer necessary.

They were based in the Northern part of Australia where the attack had taken place. After it, the Australian Prime Minister, along with other vital members of Parliament, insisted on travelling to and from the North and to the Australian Capital Territory, with the purpose of strengthening Australia's northern defence.

Noel-Len's break ended and the group returned to camp to complete drills that targeted strength, balance, speed, and stamina, as well as general weapons practice.

Throughout the afternoon, Noel-Len's shoulder grew numb from the sub-machine gun as it recoiled against his shoulder after every round.

Even if weapons training had halted a while ago, he continued to feel the impact of the rifle against his shoulder. He was grateful for the short shower at the makeshift bathroom to clean himself up before they left.

As he ascended the bus, massaging his shoulder, he moved passed the other soldiers on the bus, making his way to the back.

Settling down on his chosen seat, he closed his eyes, relishing in the moment of peace and tranquillity. Before his dark eyes shifted to gaze out the one-way tinted window, scanning the Australian landscape with apathy, his eyes lagged over the colours that glowed under the golden rising sun.

A blue-winged kookaburra landed on a high branch for a moment before flying away. Noel-Len would not have noticed the goanna moving around the base of the gum trees beneath that same tree if he had not been taught to be observant. Regardless of how sharp his eyes were, he never saw any kangaroos or rock-wallabies, much to his disappointment.

"Hey!" Michael greeted, from the seat in front of Noel-Len, which surprised him.

"Sup," Noel-Len replied, unsure as to why his friend was beaming at him as if he had won the lottery. "Did you enjoy that?" he asked, with a raised brow.

Michael shook his head.

"Not really. I mean I understand that the Australian terrain is perfect for stamina and muscle control but come on. I have a hangover still, and the first thing I have to do is exercise? I just want to sleep."

Noel-Len's humour evaporated into irritation as he glared at his friend.

"Maybe you should have thought of that yesterday." Michael did not mention that he was content with the exercise, regardless of how much his head hurt. Noel-Len noticed, but chose not to say anything.

"You can't talk, and besides, I wanted to catch up with Caprice." Noel-Len did not say a word as he studied his friend, with a blank yet cautious expression. "It's been a long time since I've seen her, and it's been even longer since you've seen her. So, I figured it would be good to catch up. Not just that, she said she needed a break from work and her crazy ex, so I figured, why not?" Noel-Len caught the reminiscent expression on his friend's face and the glint in his eyes, but at the sight of this, he was unable to hide his guilt. "What's with the face?"

Noel-Len glanced away.

"I don't know what you're talking about."

Michael watched his old friend for a moment, confused. Slowly, he drew his theories, but before he could question his friend further, a voice stopped him.

"Mind if I sit here?" it asked ceasing any further questions Michael had. Noel-Len acknowledged the woman at the edge of Michael's chair with a brief nod: Leandra Jones. The only other woman in the commando division.

GOTHALIA WAS SO FRUSTRATED with Arthur for not answering her questions that she didn't notice the man in front of her until she walked into him—for a second time that day.

"You again," Gothalia recognised, glancing at his golden eyes.

"And you again," he replied. "Still not paying attention, I see."

Embarrassment flushed upon her cheeks. She cleared her throat.

"That's not . . . um—"

It was his laughter that cut her short and his eyes glimmered dangerously for a moment.

"It's okay," he said. "Just pay a little more attention next time." Gothalia glanced at the hall he had exited and regarded it with suspicion.

"Will do," Gothalia assured him. "You had an audience with the Seers?" He appraised her with a disconcerted expression, which he quickly hid.

"No. I didn't. I just accidentally wandered down the wrong hall. I'm still trying to get used to this place."

"Oh," Gothalia declared. "I see. It is a little overwhelming sometimes, with all the twists and turns."

"You think so?

"Yeah, I do."

"I see," he stated, deep in contemplation as he regarded her for a moment longer. "I'm running late. I better get going."

"Sure, I don't mean to keep you." With that, she stepped aside and allowed him to venture down the hall. Her eyes lingered over his back before drifting to the hall he'd wandered out of. She turned her heel and headed into a room she'd been wanting to find since her talk with Arthur.

Gothalia wandered to the reception desk and regarded a woman she had not seen for a while.

"Gothalia, how are you?" The woman's smile beamed.

"I'm good, Thea. How are you?"

"Excellent, actually. We have new material. Would you like to borrow today?" she asked.

"No, thank you. Not today."

"Well, that's unusual. What are you after?"

"Archives. Can we still access them, or do I need further clearance?"

"No, you should be fine. It depends on what you're after."

"Something from March twenty years ago," Gothalia declared.

"That should be no problem," Thea assured her, but there was hesitation in her voice. "Follow me."

Thea led Gothalia down the library, passing other Centurions or Legionnaires who eyed their books and paperwork with deep concentration. Passing a few large bookcases, Thea guided her to a metal gate and opened it with a key. Entering the archives, she stepped aside, beckoned Gothalia deeper into the room and pointed at one of the far shelves.

"This starts from February to March, exactly twenty years ago." There was a knowing glint in Thea's eyes but Gothalia did not say anything. "If you need anything else please let me know," she said with a kind smile.

"I will, thank you."

Thea vacated the room. Gothalia turned to the archives and frowned. The paper was bound in black binders with white writing. She walked along the bookcase and eyed the black binders. Climbing onto the stepladder, she pulled out her first binder. Dated: March 13, 2000.

"Okay, let's see if you can tell me anything about what happened about that day," she muttered, then climbed down. Moving to the nearest table, she opened the folder and began to read.

After a few hours of reading, Gothalia managed to come across what she needed in the third binder. She read the page titled, "Slaughter of the Valdis Clan" and Gothalia felt her stomach knot.

*March 15, 2000*

*I had, with our team, managed to take out all the members of the Valdis clan, even if our mission was swathed with negative public opinion. We ignored it and continued, as we had to ensure that these monsters would not arise once more.*

*Our mission took place in the shadows of the night, yesterday evening, while most members were asleep. However, upon arrival, we found that the beds were empty, the doors were unlocked, and the buildings were abandoned. Originally, we had thought that they had fled the city, but there were no sightings at the city gates nor any members outside curfew. Instead, it was an ambush led by a member of the Ignatius Clan—Gaius.*

*Their members put up quite a battle; their transformation into these monsters was unprecedented but expected. We had known of their history and of this ability, but we had not ever known that it still was possible, even after so many centuries. So, we fought them, losing most of our own to these mutants. All that remained was one member of my team and me. We battled the rest.*

*"You will not have her," Gaius had told us with a bloodied sword in hand. his eyes held a wave of unexpected anger at me and I had to know why.*

*"Why do you insist on fighting this? You will be spared if you lay down your sword. You do not carry their curse." I said with genuine concern. "Think of the hearts you are breaking by continuing this fight."*

*"I will defend my family even from you."*

*"Then you are a fool and will die with them!" I yelled, angered that he had betrayed our family for a woman we all knew was beneath him.*

*I can recall that battle and that fight as if it were only conducted a few hours ago and know I will remember this battle for many years to come. We eventually won the battle against Gaius, who had taken out the last remnants of my team. We took him to the Grand Elders to await his punishment. But the woman, Natalia, had fled with the children and two other members of the Valdis clan.*

*We will find them. We must.*

*Signed, Numitora Faustus-Ignatius Second Commander of the Upper Echelon, Specialist Division.*

Gothalia's eyes caught on name of the writer: Numitora Faustus-Ignatius. She had descended from the house of Ignatius, yet she hated Gothalia very much and no doubt her brother too. Gothalia stood, faster than expected, the pens on the table jolted by her rapid movement.

"She knew, she was there." Gothalia understood. "She killed them. All of them."

When Gothalia vacated the archives, her head turned at the memories as her heart ached. She could not stop the emptiness she felt. She paused to lean against a wall. Tears streamed along her cheeks then after a moment, she wiped the tears from her face and cleared her eyes. Then she walked ahead as if the tears were never shed.

WITHIN THE HALLS OF the Cetatea roamed a man. His eyes were cold, distant, and calculating as he strode up to the guards. His russet skin glowed beneath the lanterns stationed on either side of the walls, and his golden eyes glowed beneath the light of the nearby fire. The guards regarded the man for a moment confused.

"You have no authorisation to be here," one said. "Leave." Their red armour shone beneath the lanterns and he did not heed their warning. Instead, he pulled out a sword and rushed at the guards.

Quickly, the guards stepped forward with their hands on their swords, then shifted to their rifles. They kneeled and opened fire. The echo of rifles permeated the hall. The man rushed at the guards, with his sword in hand, and avoided the bullets with his swift movements. Once he was close enough, he cut down both guards and kneeled before climbing to his feet. His golden eyes lingered over the guards below before he turned his attention to the door. With a card he had swiped from a Centurion earlier that day, he opened the steel door and he knew was too thick for them to hear the bullets.

Within, he recognised the security lingering throughout the room. When the door opened, no one noticed his presence, their eyes glued to their screens. The man walked up to one guard, who regarded him with indifference.

"About time you returned with my coffee, Xavier," the man said and held out his hand without looking at the man. Without a second thought, the stranger pulled out a pistol and shot the guard.

The echo of the bullet permeated the room and the other security guards reached for their weapons. Quickly, they were slaughtered. Soon only one remained. He crawled along the ground, desperate to get away from the dark-haired man with golden eyes.

"You," the guard said. "What are you doing here? You should be dead."

"I'm very much alive, as you can see," the man uttered, coldly.

"We will hunt you down, Altair. You have our word, my death will not—" Altair's sword tore through the man's chest.

"I'm counting on it," Altair proclaimed, then turned to the security monitor. Pushing a dead Centurion Peacekeeper aside, whose limp body thudded against the marble ground, Altair sat down in the chair and searched the database. "Now, where have you gone this time?" Displayed before him on the screen was an image of Gothalia.

His earpiece buzzed to life.

*"Have you found her?"* the voice asked.

"I have," Altair replied, searching the database further while dismantling security, servers, and other protocols.

*"Will it work?"* the man asked.

"It will. She's an outcast and no one will want to be associated with her after this." Altair smiled and deactivated the security protocol for the Grand Elder's room and the Seers. He brought up a screen of the Grand Elders and Seers.

"*Is it done?*"

"It is."

# Chapter 7

"YOU KNOW WHY I'VE CALLED you here," Argos declared. "I've given you some grieving time, but I need a debrief of what happened along with your report." Gothalia handed him the document and stood before his desk, at ease. Her shoulders were stiff, and her hands relaxed against her lower back, with her legs shoulder-width apart. Her gaze lingered over the back wall as he spoke. "I trust your mission was not a success."

"It was not, Sir," Gothalia responded. Her eyes drifted to his face. There was a sadness and wariness to his expression. Guilt blossomed within her stomach. "I apologise for not ending her when I should have."

"It's not your fault, Lieutenant. She clearly has unprecedented power. Where she has learned it from is another story." After a pause, he asked, "So, is it true? Captain and Commander Valdis fell to her hand?"

"Yes, Sir," Gothalia answered. "Is that all sir?" Argos regarded Gothalia for a moment longer, his eyes glittering with an unspoken truth he did not wish to share. Then he pulled his attention back to the computer before him.

"That is all, Lieutenant. You are free to leave."

She did. Even as her heart and her mind turned with all the possibilities of what could have happened, she travelled to the training room.

In the training room and in her black, red, and silver non-combat uniform, she removed her weapons and her utility belt. She stepped into the dome. After three hours, she was called out of the training room by another Centurion, one she was not familiar with and found out that Anaphora had requested to speak to her. Gothalia returned to the change room and pulled out a device that held a holographic screen. Anaphora let her know she had another mission—a mission that Argos expected her to complete unaided.

It was news that staggered her gradually regained confidence.

"I failed the first mission," she reminded Anaphora, who observed her with an indifferent expression through the live feed. Not once did her expression nor words reveal why she was not providing such sensitive information to her in person. Gothalia guessed she must have a mission of her own. "You want me to complete this mission alone?"

"Yes, even if they had expected you to kill her, I told them beforehand: you were not ready to face Numitora. Since you failed, we have learned more. So technically, your failure is now to our advantage. This next mission should lead us closer to Numitora, but she will be on guard. So, don't expect this to be easy." Gothalia was aware of the package for this mission was different and knew the Xzandians would support their Scouters. However, this time her job was reconnaissance, not interception.

Three hours later, she was back on the surface, and surveying the building below her from a distant rooftop, undetected. She lay on her stomach on the cold rooftop, as she regarded the Xzandian described in her debrief packet. Having arrived only moments ago, he was masquerading as a regular Human, travelling the streets of Moscow without precaution.

He would have been mistaken for any other Russian woman. Dressed in a fashionable black overcoat and deep blue jeans tucked in fine leather boots, he entered the café.

If Gothalia hadn't seen him earlier—a male, she recalled, with broad shoulders and a thick frame that he'd sculpted into a smaller, slenderer version for his Human disguise—she wouldn't have noticed his presence.

If it weren't for Argos's words—"Don't act reckless and don't blow your next missions, or you'll be suspended for the next two weeks without pay!"—she would have taken him out.

On the roof, she observed attentively the duplicity of his adopted character. Blending into society fashionably well, he casually tucked a strand of long black hair behind his ear and discretely turned his face from the other guests.

His isolated table was tucked away from the windows of the café, keeping him well hidden from prying eyes of the unaware citizens outside.

Kronos would not have been able to hack into the surveillance cameras since they were-closed circuited within this café.

This proved the Xzandians were well informed to choose this tea shop, with its reputation for hosting dangerous men and women alike. Gothalia glimpsed the detectives hovering around and within the building but paid them no further mind.

Those who started any problems, she'd already seen, were taken to the alley off to the side and forced into a black car, to never to be seen again as they once were. Her instinct demanded her to respond to this, but she did not, keeping in mind her duty and Argos's potential wrath.

Gothalia perked up when a woman with platinum blond hair, methodically coiffed, entered the same café. She peered briefly at the table where the Xzandian convened, her expression impartial.

Tapping the side of her headpiece, Gothalia listened and ordered Kronos, "Zoom in."

A black screen shrouded half of her face, amplifying the woman's features in fine detail. She was taking images of the woman and the Xzandian when Kronos said,

"My lady. Wouldn't it be wiser for you to request the company of another?"

"No."

"I think it would be," he pressed, once more before allowing the conversation within the café to filter to her ears.

"Lady Emily, I'm pleased you could make it." the Xzandian articulated, with a pleasurable smile. "All that remains is the payment." The blond-haired woman browsed the doors of the café. Discretely, she pulled out a thin white envelope and slid it to the black-haired woman opposite her.

Gothalia observed the interaction, while Kronos stored away the audio and visual. The blond-haired woman thanked the Xzandian and parted, with a silver briefcase in hand. An hour later, after a coffee and a meal, the alien vacated the premises.

Gothalia climbed to her feet and Kronos noted the best route for pursuit, then paused to warn her of a sudden hostile presence. At the same time, she noticed the golden-orange flare at the corner of her eye. She scarcely escaped the flare, and only thanks to Kronos's warning.

She avoided the first assault, but not the second: pain seared her shoulder. The force threw her to the ground, and she climbed to her knees, glaring at the Xzandian towering over her, who held a rifle to her head. The same one that Numitora held.

Gothalia felt the élanocytes in her body rush to heal her injury and the pain faded. Xzandian's rifle barrel glowed red, smoking. With her body numb to the pain, she moved in time to avoid the bullet and engaged in combat. A moment later, the Xzandian was effectively thrown away by an Excelian man that appeared by her side too quickly to expect.

She ran by the stranger and launched herself at the Xzandian, with a flare of explosions. She heard the Centurion demand that she refrain from making further noise.

She avoided the Xzandian's next attack and observed the black-and-silver uniformed Excelian Centurion, working to decipher his features hidden behind a concealed helmet, identical to the one she wore.

NOEL-LEN RECALLED CORPORAL Kypreos's words from a few months ago—"Twenty years ago, there were no women in the Special Forces." But given the past alien attacks, the Australian Defence Force had reluctantly agreed to the idea of increasing their numbers by putting one woman through a rigorous test. When she exceeded expectations, the military passed the plan to allow women into the Special Forces but with only at entry level. Meaning they were heavily screened.

In sum, Noel-Len knew this woman would be able to outrun him if they were under fire, something he felt relieved to know.

"No. Go ahead," Noel-Len said, gesturing to the seat beside him.

"You don't have to ask," Michael taunted, leaning over the back of his seat. "I'm quite certain he would love to be in the presence of a woman."

Noel-Len glared at Michael.

"Why don't you . . . Shut. Up."

Private Jones regarded Noel-Len with a raised brow and a steady gaze.

"Make me," Michael replied with a sinister smile. *He is enjoying how uncomfortable this makes me*, Noel-Len thought and forced a smile to replace of his annoyance, even if would come across as a grimace.

"You two are the same as ever," Jones smirked.

"And that, my friends, is what makes us so . . . *special.*" Michael boasted, and Noel-Len rolled his eyes at his friend's stupidity. Leandra, in turn, shook her head before sitting beside Noel-Len. Moments later, the bus started, and the group was on their way back to the main base.

When Noel-Len's group returned, they descended the bus, expecting to report to their allocated posts. The unit of commando soldiers headed through the busy barracks, their eyes scanning their surroundings—assessing for imminent danger, a habit long-instilled in them since their yearlong training.

The women halted before foreign Marines in a different khaki uniform. Noel-Len skimmed the frozen forms of the women from over his shoulder, noticing Leandra and Tracey's hostile expressions.

Then his attention drifted to Michael, with hopes he would have an explanation.

"What's wrong?" Michael asked, his eyes on the Marines.

"Nothing." Tracey's voice was reserved of emotion, her tone flat and cold, informing them to not press any further. Noel-Len caught the perplexity unfolding on Michael's face when he watched Leandra walk ahead. Mimicking Leandra's actions, Tracey followed, leaving Noel-Len and Michael inspecting their odd behaviour as they walked away.

"What was that all about?" Michael asked, his eyes lingering on the backs of his comrades.

Noel-Len's gaze drifted to the men.

"Not sure but let us keep an eye on them," he murmured, his eyes narrowing on the glint behind their scrutiny, "I don't like that look."

Noel-Len was not certain how to take their distrust to Leandra and Tracey but since it made him uncomfortable, the Marines had better be careful.

"Agreed."

Both Noel-Len and Michael trailed after their female comrades. When the other soldiers returned, both Noel-Len and Michael sensed a different air in the building.

"What's with everyone?" Michael inquired, puzzled.

Soldiers lined up before a woman whom they recognised as Corporal Melissa McGuire. She strode back and forth barking orders, wearing a murderous expression. Unfortunately, though both men were the last to enter the common room, they were the first to receive her wrath.

"You two!" Corporal Melissa McGuire snarled, her eyes falling on Noel-Len and Michael. "You will be outside weeding! Understood?"

"Ma'am!" Noel-Len and Michael responded at once. Satisfied with the orders, the woman turned her attention from them before storming out of the tense atmosphere and crowded room.

Everyone dispersed at once and Noel-Len acknowledged the soldier walking towards him.

"What happened?" he asked, curiosity getting the better of him.

"Someone pissed Corporal McGuire off." Private McFarland responded, his hazel eyes looking over his comrades beneath his short mop of dirty-blond hair. Even if he smiled, they noticed the concern in his eyes.

"How?" Michael asked. "I mean it's not like someone was sexist or something . . . right?" he joked but regretted those words the moment Private McFarland's hostile eyes fell on his.

"I wish I could say that wasn't the case," Dave responded, relinquishing the hostile glare. "But in this case, it was. That's why everyone's cleaning. It's an order and we must obey, but I don't think anyone here cares about the order. It was terrible how they treated her. I'm sure we'd all rather clean than do endless laps around the barracks."

"Totally," Michael agreed, feeling guilty for his negligence. "We just came back from doing that and anymore running, I think I might have to see a Medical Officer. Where do we start?"

Dave told them where to go and what areas to do. With one last look at each other, Noel-Len and Michael deserted the building.

Half an hour later, their fingers were sore from pulling the weeds and Michael beamed in triumph.

"Finished."

"There you two are." Corporal Kypreos declared, stopping behind them. His shadow cast over the kneeling soldiers before him. "I was looking for you two everywhere. Why weren't you at the briefing?"

Noel-Len and Michael stiffened.

"Apologies, Sir."

Corporal Kypreos regarded the basket at their feet and the recently-pulled weeds. "And . . . why are you two . . . weeding?"

"We were ordered to, Sir," they both responded.

"By whom?"

"By Corporal McGuire, Sir."

Ian Kypreos released a frustrated sigh. He glanced at the pale building beside the men and scanned the rest of the garden.

"You're relieved of your duties, soldiers," Ian said. With a salute and "Sir" hanging in the air, the men left the Corporal behind and returned to their respective stations.

Later that day, Noel-Len returned home knackered. Instantly, he fell into a deep slumber, unaware of Caprice's call lighting up his phone. When he finally picked up after the third missed call, he was surprised but eager at her request for an evening out.

The following morning, he woke to an empty bed. His heavy eyes were stiff with sleep and his mind evenly groggy.

Images of blood and Phillip's unmoving body flickered behind his eyes and he sat up fast, forcing the terrible memories to the back of his mind. Swinging his legs over the bed, he eyed his watch on the bedside table, confirming his suspicion that it was exceedingly early.

He heard the toilet flush, then the bathroom door, open and close. Caprice re-entered the room naked, pecked him on the lips, and climbed back into bed.

Noel-Len smiled, amused at her dishevelled hair, before he frowned at the recent nightmare. Pulling on a pair of loose pants, he listened to her deep breathing return when she drifted back to sleep. Silently, he exited the room.

Massaging his tired eyes, a stubborn yawn escaped his lips. Moving to the kitchen, he turned on the light before robotically stirring to make a cup of coffee. As he waited for the kettle to boil, his eyes flicked past the window he had yet to buy curtains for and caught the reflection of the figure standing behind him, leaning comfortably against the counter, studying him with a casual smile. Stunned by the intruder, he wheeled around.

"I see you had a good night." she jested, as if they were old friends.

"You again!" he growled, derisively. He glared at the stranger with vivid hostility, his posture rigid but alert to her movements. "Who are you?"

Slowly, without making it obvious, he drifted toward the set of knives in the kitchen's corner.

"*Who* am I? *What* am I? These questions are always the same, aren't they?" the woman questioned, jaded. She glanced at the silver kitchen knives in the corner. "I wouldn't do that if I were you, child." With cold eyes, she conveyed a deadly warning. Causing to Noel-Len to pause, catching sight of her stirring anger. Her previous strength flickered across his mind and, unintentionally, he peeked at his bedroom door and knew the room within held evidence of her strength.

"I don't want to hurt you too much if I can avoid it," the woman said.

"You should have thought of that before you strangled me." Noel-Len retorted.

The woman held up her hands in surrender and stepped away from the bench, "I thought you were . . . not related to Natalia."

*So, she would have strangled a stranger if he did not give her information*, he thought disapprovingly, but his ears had perked up at his mother's name.

"Again, how do you know my mother?" Noel-Len questioned, fear prickling along his skin in her presence. He still wondered why a stranger had broken, into his home, not to steal anything but just to stare at the photo of him and his mother.

The woman studied Noel-Len, for a moment. There was a darkness in her gaze that matched his, even as her unusually pale skin glowed beneath the fluorescent kitchen light. Assessing Noel-Len with a calculating gaze, she contemplated her next words.

"My name's Anaphora and I'm searching for something; I suppose you could say. To answer your last question; unbelievably, your mother and I have quite a long history."

"In what sense?"

"Friendship. How else?"

He did not respond. Instead, redirected the conversation elsewhere.

"What are you after?"

"Something . . . but before that, I need to find an item. To locate it, I hoped to catch your mother's friend but then I found a clue that led me here. I expected to see the child from that photo, not a fully-grown man but . . . Looking at you, I see the resemblance to both that child in the photo and your mother. Time sure has flown by, hasn't it?"

Noel-Len did not immediately reply. He recalled that many people, especially his father, constantly reminded him of how he took after his mother's dominating features. Not that he complained; between his parents, his mother was the one with the looks. His father was not too bad. He knew he should be grateful that he'd inherited his father's cheekbones and set jaw.

"What was the clue?" Noel-Len inquired, noting Anaphora's avoidance. At the whistle of the kettle, he began making his coffee.

"Before I divulge anything further . . . I need to know: Where is your mother's friend Natasha?"

Once again, Noel-Len did not speak. His haunted eyes drifted over the woman and her eyes assessed his in response.

The woman, by Noel-Len's standards, understood the message. Natasha was far beyond reach and her time here was being wasted.

"I see. Given your relation to her, I may or may not be back." The woman turned to leave.

He caught the confusion flicker across her face.

Her eyes fell on Mike sitting at her feet, his tail happily wagging at her presence. Anaphora patted the dog before leaving.

Noel-Len glared at the dog and muttered "Traitor" when Anaphora was out of earshot. The dog whined in puzzlement and tilted its head at him.

Noel-Len never knew Mike to be friendly with strangers, but, then again, the dog had taken to Caprice.

The dog surveyed his owner with its tongue hanging out of its panting mouth, before turning away.

"What the hell is going on here?" Noel-Len wondered aloud.

His thoughts halted, alarmed by the sudden shaking of the ground, and a loud explosion overhead tearing open the skies.

A loud crack of thunder split in the sky, louder and longer than any natural storm. Moving to the window, he eyed the darkness, hoping to catch an oncoming tropical storm. The sky rumbled again, shaking the kitchen, before Noel-Len briskly marched to the back lawn. In the darkness, he steadily judged the sky, searching for abnormalities.

Within moments, the roaring engines of the F19 Super Hornets soaring through the skies greeted his ears. The jets lined the skies, perfectly in formation, and he wondered, *why are the super hornets in the sky this early? Is there a drill I don't know of?*

A few seconds later, radiant emerald comets plummeted towards the city at rocking speeds and horror enveloped him. Sparking a glitter of detonations in the distance, the jets' payload filled the air with grey-green clouds.

Noel-Len sprinted through the house.

"Caprice! Caprice get up!" He yelled, hearing the outbreak of an aerial war overhead and feeling the ground trembling beneath his feet, desperately struggling to dress in his uniform without falling over.

Fearing the worst, he frantically woke Caprice who jumped in surprise.

"We have to go! Now!" Caprice's groggy ears registered the clatter of sirens ringing in the background and the jets overhead. Without hesitation, but consumed by fear, she climbed out of bed and yanked on her clothes.

Once they were dressed, Noel-Len demanded that Caprice not carry her purse. Only the cards in it, her phone and car keys which took a little longer, but Noel-Len didn't mind too much. Instead, he noticed everyone screamed and evacuating the city. Noel-Len gripped Caprice's hand and guided her out of the house.

"Keys!" he called. She threw the car keys and he caught them as they rounded the car. Danger permeated the air, as warning sirens screamed throughout the once-silent city.

Others shrieked in panic, as the jets above descended on their street, demolishing, and setting alight a nearby house.

Several families piled their children and pets into cars to escape, while others ran to the house caught aflame.

Mike growled at Noel-Len's feet. Opening the car's backdoor, he urged the dog inside. Then he climbed into the driver's seat while Caprice fastened her seatbelt with trembling hands.

Starting the car, he buckled his seatbelt and reversed out of the driveway, racing down the streets. His stomach sank at the sight of humans being taken out by the fallen jets and dropped alien bombs.

A few blocks later, Noel-Len slammed the brakes at the sight of the last person he expected.

"Michael!" Caprice yelled, both surprised and angry at her old friend. He stood shocked in front of the car, equally surprised to see her, as he rushed from the yard of an adjacent house.

"Idiot! Get in!" Noel-Len shouted, watching Michael round the bonnet of the car and climb into the back with Mike. Noel-Len watched men, women and children who did not have cars run down the road and away from their homes that immediately became engulfed in flames by the fighter jets' attack.

"What the hell? Why were you jumping fences!" Noel-Len snarled, whilst aiming to avoid hitting other cars and residents.

"What do you mean, *why*?" Michael growled. "I came looking for you!"

"Shit," Noel-Len grumbled, steering the BMW. His gaze shifted over the road until he recognised a familiar dark figure with black hair running along the side of the road. He wondered how she'd made it across the suburbs so quickly.

Before Noel-Len could pull over, he slammed the brakes once more. The car propelled them forward and Michael almost flew through the windscreen.

"Put your seatbelt on!" Noel-Len yelled, his arm extended, holding his friend in place.

"Sorry, but that wasn't my priority!" Michael yelled back, equally loudly; his raging eyes set on Noel-Len's as he yanked the belt over his shoulder. Both men ignored Mike's persistent barking at the road while they erupted into a pointless argument. Caprice understood why Mike barked. It was a terrifying sight: a large silver pod in the middle of the abandoned road.

Feeling uneasy at both the alien object and her friends for not paying attention, she shifted in her seat and pulled her knees to her chest; she watched the pod with evident fear.

Mike continued to bark at the pod while both men quarrelled.

The pod, Caprice noticed, had an unusually smooth surface emanating a pulsing green hue that brightened and receded in colour as if it were breathing. Within a single breath, the pod shifted into a silver alien with four thick silver legs. Caprice screamed.

Her scream startled both men at first. Then they followed her gaze.

"Crap," both Noel-Len and Michael muttered, staring at the smooth alien that resembled an animal, and was taller than a truck.

It stared at their idle car; the running engine hummed against the stationary street.

The smooth texture of the alien's armour glowed and ebbed in green. All eyes watched the animalistic robot shift into a ready-to-sprint stance.

"Noel-Len . . ." Caprice began, pushing herself against the car seat, as if she could escape.

# Chapter 8

NOEL-LEN'S NAME BARELY made it to his ears, and her fearful eyes never left the robot.

"Drive," Michael warned slowly, his body taut in apprehension.

Within a second, the alien-robot sprinted towards the car and Noel-Len swung the car around and drove as fast as the car could take him. His eyes flicked to the rear-view mirror the approaching robot, as they reversed along the road, avoiding the obstructions it threw at them with its tail, while it gave chase.

Suddenly, the alien was stopped by a powerful force that almost made Noel-Len lose control of the vehicle. It struck the machine hard, halting its assault.

Noel-Len slammed the brakes, disregarding Mike falling off the seat before climbing back up on Michael.

He watched, the black-clad figure of the woman he had seen moments before force the robot into the ground with her fist. She was no longer wearing casual clothes, but a black and silver uniform. A black and silver cloak shifted around her as she moved.

The surrounding windows of the nearby houses shattered as did the car windows, mimicking the ground beneath the alien, which fissured towards the car.

The robot did not stay overpowered. It climbed to its feet. The woman moved as quickly as she did the day, she had strangled him.

"What the . . . hell?" Michael asked, to no one in particular.

Noel-Len scrutinised the battle.

The woman moved with incredible speed, too fast for his eyes to keep up, as she tore concrete from the road and threw it at the alien, stunning its impending assault.

Michael observed the battle in disbelief then uttered,

"I think . . . we're out-classed." With undeniable shock, he watched the woman shred the alien machine to pieces.

Panting, she glanced over at the idle BMW, then removed the last of the machines' silver limbs before tossing the separate pieces of the robot's body into a nearby abandoned park.

The alien struggled beneath her grip as she pulled the alien from within the large metal armour. Within seconds, the alien became limp in her hand as everyone heard the snap of his neck.

Both Caprice and Michael glanced away while Noel-Len regarded the sight in pure horror. He was now aware that the woman who'd entered his home could have easily crushed his throat.

Before long, her eyes settled on him and he returned her gaze. Immediately, she vanished from in front of the alien body into a cloud of black smoke.

"Where did she go?" Caprice calmly questioned. Noel-Len and Michael glanced at her; they'd forgetting momentarily that she was with them.

Moments later, Noel-Len's window echoed with the rap of Anaphora's knuckles. The men regarded the inhuman woman beside the car with trepidation as Noel-Len wound the window down.

Patiently, Anaphora watched the window to descend into the door before declaring,

"There's no further reason to continue down this road."

"Why?" Michael asked, ignoring the glare Noel-Len threw.

Anaphora's dark eyes drifted to Michael who felt a shiver run up his spine.

"There are more of those," she proclaimed, pointing to the mechanical monster on the side of the road. "If you value your lives, then, I suggest you take my advice. If not, well . . . it was nice knowing you."

Noel-Len swallowed as her words sunk in.

"We need to go that way," Noel-Len managed, a few seconds later.

The woman remained silent for a moment then enquired with mild interest,

"Do you now?"

Then Michael added with a firmer tone,

"Yes."

At that, the woman raised a brow. Noel-Len felt her agitation rise and he knew if she wanted to murder Michael for his disrespect, she would. He recognised the antagonism in her eyes and knew Michael held her gaze almost challenging her.

"By all means. Do as you please." With those words, she disappeared, leaving a cloud of smoke behind. Noel-Len shot Michael a warning glare.

"Try not to piss her off," Noel-Len managed, shifting the car into gear, and driving past the monster Anaphora had destroyed. "Or you'll end up like that alien." Noel-Len felt Michael lean away from between the front seats and glanced at the rear-view mirror. He recognised the anger lining Michael's face even if Mike tried to comfort him. No one uttered a word as they travelled through the small city, avoiding potholes and other obstructions.

Their journey to the base did not leave them without having to dodge a few robots, but to Noel-Len's surprise Anaphora had escorted them from a distance. The reason for her intentions escaped him, but he was grateful even as he observed the unease in her before she parted, leaving them to fend for themselves.

Caprice noticed armoured vehicles that carried heavily-equipped soldiers and deadly weapons to and from the barracks, beneath the war-torn skies.

The car halted before the red and white security beam. A security guard clad in the same green-brown khaki uniform that both Noel-Len and Michael wore gruffly spoke.

"I'll be needing an ID from the young woman. The two of you will need to disclose your identification number."

Caprice handed Noel-Len her driver's licence while Michael and Noel-Len exposed their service numbers. Noel-Len handed Caprice's licence to the security guard.

"You're free to enter. Report to your allocated units. The civilian and your . . . canine . . . will need to report to the head office." Noel-Len nodded, surprised he'd allowed Mike to enter, and guided the car through the barracks and to the head office.

Tightly controlled response teams returned to the base with civilians or left with new packs and weapons. Pulling up, Noel-Len watched as some soldiers moved from one part of the base to the other while officers provided the next set of orders.

Caprice, Noel-Len, and Michael climbed out of the car while Noel-Len called for Mike, ordering the young pup to stay outside. The group moved to the reception desk, taking note of the large throng of civilians gathered within, no doubt the family members of the other soldiers.

Noel-Len turned to Caprice.

"You'll need to show the lady behind the counter your ID and inform her that your father is a soldier. Call anyone you need to and tell them where you are."

"What if they don't pick up?" Caprice asked, worry in her eyes.

"Keep trying," Michael assured her, and pulled out his phone. "We need to make sure our loved ones are safe." Caprice nodded, and Michael placed the phone to his ear. Noel-Len heard the hysteric voice on the other line and Michael's attempts to calm down his parents.

Noel-Len knew he would have to call his father too. When Michael walked outside, Noel-Len felt Caprice's hand tremble over his.

"You have to go . . . don't you?" she asked, her voice wavering at the thought.

A loud bang shredded the skies. This one, particularly loud, caused everyone to drop to the ground in fright. Some covered their heads from the loud shock while the soldiers guarding the building observed the trembling walls hesitantly. Noel-Len viewed Caprice's shuddering frame, understanding the fear in her glassy eyes.

"Caprice," Noel-Len gently urged, "Listen, you need to do everything you can to keep yourself safe and alive. Take Mike with you wherever you go. He's trained to listen." At last, the tears fell, and Caprice shook her head, not entirely believing what she was hearing.

She had grown up in another country but called this humid place home—now it was under siege and she feared for her life but feared more for Noel-Len.

"Look at me," he whispered, forcing her attention on him. "Can you do that?" Closing her eyes, she nodded. "Good." Noel-Len placed a soft, lasting kiss on her forehead before climbing to his feet.

She felt the pressure of his grip fade and watched him walk to the door. With one last lingering look at her, he vanished from sight.

In place of all this, a warm, frail hand covered hers. Caprice regarded the woman beside her with a forced smiled; when the woman returned a bright smile, she caught Caprice off guard. With her messy hair and wrinkled flesh, she appeared in that moment as young as she would have ever been, and her smile never wavered. Caprice's eyes glistened at the reassuring smile she bore.

Both women crouched with everyone else who cowered beneath the thundering sounds of explosions overhead, continuously shaking the entire foundation of the building.

Soldiers guarded the civilians; their eyes scanned the walls and ceiling with uncertainty.

Even with her smile, the woman's brown eyes mirrored Caprice's anxiety. The stranger squeezed the younger woman's hand once more, and it was in that moment that Caprice understood her message.

This small insignificant squeeze of her hand might be the last reassuring thing she would ever feel again.

BEFORE GOTHALIA COULD utter a single word, the Xzandian's frame slipped out of the Excelian's grip and away from both, like a snake slithering through water.

The Xzandian slipped from the man, morphing into a passable humanoid form, and struck Gothalia's jaw with her foot. Gothalia stumbled away at the force, wiping her jaw with a smile on her face.

"Nice trick."

Recovering, she battled the Xzandian again, but before she could deliver the final blow, the man called,

"Wait!" He threw a knife, pinning the Xzandian's shoulder to the billboard.

"Why?"

The Excelian's hand suddenly erupted with hot golden electricity. He moved quickly to the Xzandian opposite him, before the Xzandian could yank the knife from his shoulder.

The Excelian man's hand pierced the alien's chest, frying the skin with the loud crackle, and he watched the sharp electricity rip along the rest of its body. When the current died, the alien sagged in defeat, no longer a threat.

"Ah, you wanted to finish him—cute," Gothalia mocked, as he yanked his blood-stained hand from the alien and released his energy, making the blood evaporate.

He glared at her.

"Don't make light of this."

"You sound just like L'Eiron," she muttered, before returning her gaze to him, with fresh curiosity.

His lips pursed into a disapproving thin line. Gothalia's eyes drifted to the rank of Colonel upon his uniform, then to the crest below it that resembled the Dragon Core unit. Consumed by fear, she recognised his status and the potential repercussions of her impudence.

He turned away from her, ignoring the surprise she endeavoured to hide. Swiftly, and with purpose, he strode to the fallen Xzandian and rolled it onto its stomach.

"Isn't that—?" she began.

"—It is none of your concern, Lieutenant. You are dismissed." He quickly replied, then pulled the Fragment from the Xzandian's body, and clipped it to his belt. Without a glance back, he vacated the area.

She returned to the Fire Reserve later that evening, to inform the Commander of the Dragon Core unit of her partial success. Argos was not too thrilled about the Xzandian contacting the Human woman but was relieved to know Gothalia had done her job right that is if she didn't mention the fight.

He informed Gothalia that the trackers would watch the woman who received had the case carefully and that the hunters would pursue the Xzandian who escaped.

Regardless of his reassurances, something had not sat well with Gothalia, and she was not sure what. She was convinced that there was more to their interaction.

So, after curfew, she snuck into the Cetatea and into Arthur's office, searching for answers. He had left her a clue in her room—information on the Fragments—as if he knew she would search for answers to her questions.

She combed through the documentation on the Fragments. It had been everything he had told her, including theories on their clear appearances, enough so it made her grateful she had allowed her curiosity to get the better of her.

In his notes, he theorised that the Xzandians only contacted Humans who'd be willing to give them information on the Fragments in exchange for alien weapons to either sell on the black market or to use for their security.

Despite her shock at this information, she tucked a map of where the Fragments would be into her belt; on it, the City of Darwin was circled in red, then marked with a red cross.

She vacated Arthur's office.

"I'll return the map, but I'm borrowing it for now," she promised herself.

She stalked through the silent Cetatea and to the Artillery and Combat Section, passing by the vehicles to the transportation platform. She climbed the silver crystal steps with determination. She entered the coordinates and a timer on the control panel before stepping onto the platform.

Her eyes lingered over the balcony opposite her, where Arthur's workstation was, peering into the darkness. A shadow shifted.

"Is that a person?" she questioned aloud, but before she could step off the platform, she vanished from the room and reappeared in the streets of Moscow.

"Kronos. Did you get that?" Gothalia inquired, panicked aware her earpiece was still on.

"I did. There was another person—the vital signals confirm it."

"We have to go back."

"I understand, but you can't go anywhere until the light beam picks you up from the position you set, after about two hours."

Gothalia said nothing further on the matter and pulled out the map, refusing to argue with Kronos.

With no way home until her designated time, Gothalia searched the café she had seen that night, then worked from there to where she had met the Xzandian and the Colonel.

Her gloved fingers traced the stone beneath her feet, searching for something her eyes could not make out.

"What are you looking for?" Kronos questioned in her ear.

"Something . . . that I know should've been left behind." Gothalia replied, refusing to elaborate any further, as her mind ran with innumerable possibilities and her recollection of the fight.

She eyed the dried blue blood on the ground.

"Isn't that the blood from the Xzandian?"

"It is," Gothalia affirmed, evoking a memory of when her unexpected comrade stabbed the alien, and her eyes lingered over the smear.

"An unusual, sight."

"That it is," she confirmed, scanning the café before requesting a replay of the footage. Their conversation was repeated in her ears, and the voice of the woman was both aloof and amused. "It's almost like they're not aliens . . ."

"Then that would throw every known scientific theory on its head," Kronos derided. There was sarcasm to his tone that often occurred on such topics. "Well . . . *most*."

Gothalia did not pay his words much mind, as she kneeled once more before the dried blood. Kronos snapped photos of what remained, including the scars from their battle on the roof.

Her eyes drifted to the café once more.

"Play the video . . . before he walked into the café." Kronos did. Her eyes slid beneath her headpiece to the plate covering her features, which displayed an image. She ordered Kronos to pause it. "What do you see?"

"The Xzandian changed his appearance but not the insignia on the briefcase." Kronos retorted. "Which will lead us back to whoever provided that briefcase. And—"

"More information on who we're dealing with."

"That seems too simple." Kronos resolved, almost let down by the uncomplicated answer. "Not that it matters, I've analysed it. Where are you—" he asked her, then paused when she leapt from one rooftop to the other, opposite the street. "—going?"

Gently, Gothalia settled on the roof, gazing at the street below, observing the spot where the Xzandian had been.

"You could be a little more discreet about that next time," Kronos commented.

Her eyes lingered over the street, but there was no one there.

She dropped to the ground. The streetlights revealed her black and silver uniform and her toned body.

Without much hesitation, Gothalia examined the alleyway and shifted to the spot where she had seen the Xzandian last.

Though her mind ran with many possibilities of where he had come from, she knew none of them was valid, especially since the recording had told her more than she needed.

The shield insignia on the case revealed the organisation. The Xzandian's ankles revealed an energetic technique.

There was a dire belief it had nothing to do with the camera angles but the way the earth moulded around his, or her feet.

Both Kronos and Gothalia spent the rest of the evening going over the spot and hacking street cameras until it was time to leave.

When Gothalia returned to the Cetatea on the transportation platform, she scanned the balcony above where she had seen that figure shifting in the darkness.

"My lady that person may still be here," Kronos warned. "Be on your guard."

"I know." And, cautiously, she strode off the platform. She passed the armoured vehicles and average mission vehicles before climbing the stairs that led to the balcony. She felt the danger in the air, but pressed forward, unaware of eyes watching her.

The figure that seen her from the shadows quickly disappeared from the room. Then she noticed the shifting silhouette leaving the room and followed it. Clad in black, the person ran down the halls and around corners.

The Cetatea was quiet tonight. The evening guards were on their shift, patrolling the silent fortress. Gothalia concealed herself among the shadows and out of sight, relentlessly pursuing the target she noticed climb the opposite wall.

Across from the courtyard, behind a pillar, she saw the intruder crawl into a window where the guard was and, before her eyes, the guard fell to the intruders' blade.

"That's an assassin," she understood. "Kronos give me a layout of the room. Including all vitals within twenty meters."

Kronos did as she asked. Gothalia ran to an emergency button and pressed it but to her surprise it didn't work, and the assassin was on the move.

The heat signatures of the guards slowly disappeared. Quickly, Gothalia chased after the man, avoiding the guards whom the assassin spared. If she could not avoid them, she knocked them out with an apology before carefully placing the guards on the ground.

If she did not want to alarm the enemy, she had to pursue him without his knowledge.

"My lady, he's on his way to Dragon Core," Kronos cried. "You need to stop him! Argos hasn't signed out yet!"

She cursed at the news.

"Of all the times to stay back, why tonight?"

She turned down a hall that led into the open courtyard, then to the second balcony that cut across the twisting turns below and to another courtyard, which led to their assigned building.

She spotted the assassin at the far end of the garden. He effortlessly climbed the old architecture, as easily as any Excelian. Gothalia hunted the assassin, her stomach knots as she scaled the building after him and watched him enter a lit room. Moments later, she climbed the loggia and ran past the open balcony doors before gaping at where Argos lay in a pool of blood.

Hours later, Gothalia sat in the interrogation room and regarded the Peacekeeper that stood before her. "So . . . did you do it?" he asked Gothalia, once again. *Stupid question*, she thought, as she ground her teeth.

"Did I do what? You must be a little more specific. What . . . breathe?" She raised her brow defiantly. The Peacekeeper frowned at her retort, then sighed.

"Lieutenant, you understand why we're conducting this investigation, no? Then please refrain from such sarcasm. It makes it rather difficult for me," he said, running his hand through his golden-brown hair. Gothalia climbed to her feet and slammed her hands against the steel table. The sound permeated the stagnant room, lit by torches and chandeliers.

"Someone's been killed. A *General* of all people. And you're telling me to refrain from sarcastic remarks?" Gothalia queried. "Really?"

"Yes, really. And, I expect you to be a little more civilised and co-operate with little difficulty," he responded, uneasily shifting from one foot to another. Straightening his shoulders, he continued. "I'd also ask that you control your anger."

"What you expect me to be happy with the death of a General? *Our General*," Gothalia growled, narrowing her gaze. "Your job is to find who's responsible no? So, do it and bring them to justice. Or is that too hard?"

"Lieutenant!" L'Eiron bellowed, pausing in the doorway. "In my office, now." Gothalia glared at the Peacekeeper, who released her, though not without a word of warning once Gothalia vacated the room. L'Eiron nodded in understanding.

L'Eiron strode down the corridor and towards the end of the hall, where his office sat. Gothalia glared at him once she paused outside the door and crossed her arms. He wasted no time in replying,

"Inside," in a voice so low it caused Gothalia's skin to break out in goose bumps. She entered and sat on the chair in the centre of the room. L'Eiron closed the door, strode behind his desk, and sat upon his chair. His eyes were hard and Gothalia held his gaze unwaveringly. "Care to explain what just happened?"

"You know what happened?" Gothalia responded.

"Yes, we saw the intruder, and yes, we are currently examining General Argos Ambrosia's remains to learn how he died, but that doesn't explain why you snapped at a Peacekeeper. Do you want jail time? Because you're remarkably close." L'Eiron sounded like a stern father.

"No." Gothalia crossed her arms once more, slouching in the chair.

"Then what's going on?"

Gothalia glanced away.

"What do you mean? I'm perfectly fine."

"You know what I mean. It's unusual for you to act like this." L'Eiron pressed, waiting for a response. When none was provided, he continued, "Do you feel guilty for not saving him?"

"Why does that matter!" Gothalia snapped. Her eyes were hard as she gazed upon him.

"Oh, it matters," L'Eiron responded, coolly.

"How's that?"

"Simple: you're overreacting. And I am not saying that you should not feel the loss of our General, but it does not mean you can carry on the way you have. It has to stop." he articulated, smoothly. "And I won't have you behaving in such a manner."

"Oh right, because you're suddenly my dad," Gothalia remarked, again sarcastically. "Here's an idea why doesn't you stop trying to fill those shoes?"

"You may think that I'm filling these shoes but I'm not. I'm just making sure you don't make any mistakes you'll regret. Considering how you're behaving, you're suspended."

"What?" Gothalia burst out, shocked. "You can't do that!"

"Yes, I can, and I have. It's long due and it's about time you see someone," he declared in a gentler tone. His eyes avoided hers; then she understood.

"You mean a shrink?" Gothalia questioned. "No. I refuse."

L'Eiron sighed.

"Gothalia I don't think you realise how much you've been through. It's not healthy. And I am not asking, I am telling you. You're relieved of your duties until further notice."

Quickly, Gothalia stormed out of the office but paused once she saw Domitia in the doorway.

"Hey," Domitia greeted and Gothalia turned from her and marched down the hall. Domitia glanced at L'Eiron who held his head in his hands. A sorrowful look flashed across her features as she entered. "Care to explain what happened?" she asked gently and L'Eiron was surprised by her presence but didn't show it as she shut the door.

# Chapter 9

GOTHALIA STORMED THROUGH the Cetatea and passed the library. Pausing for a second, she realised reading was not what she needed, and continued further down the hall and into the open courtyard. Where she saw Peacekeepers carry bodies out of the surveillance centre.

"Are those . . . ?" she began.

"They are," Danteus announced from beside her, startling her. "Sorry, I didn't mean to frighten you."

"Me? Scared? Never," Gothalia proclaimed, with a humorous glint to her eyes, her anger at L'Eiron momentarily forgotten.

"Right."

"What happened?" she asked the Peacekeeper once he was close enough. Though, when he turned around, she recognised the man from the interrogation room who Gothalia with hostility and she knew she deserved it.

"Now, you want to talk," he remarked and Gothalia's gaze narrowed.

"You don't have to tell me if you don't want to."

"Good, because I'm not going to." With that, he walked away and Danteus regarded Gothalia with a curious expression.

"What was that all about?" he asked.

"Nothing much, just someone who wants to throw me in jail." Gothalia retorted, crossing her arms.

"Why what did you do this time?"

"Nothing, I promise. I just didn't agree with his methods."

"What methods?" Danteus asked.

Gothalia regarded him for a moment. "You don't know, do you?" she asked, her eyes assessing his.

"Know what?"

"Argos. He was assassinated last night."

Danteus was silent for a moment but Gothalia recognised the pain that flickered across his face.

"How are you involved with something like that?"

"I didn't stop the assassin in time," Gothalia responded, feeling weak under those words, and leaned against a wall. Danteus remained silent for a moment. Their eyes lingered over the Peacekeepers in the distance.

"I find it odd, that there was an assassin and now there are dead Peacekeepers." Danteus said.

"What you think it's connected?" Gothalia was troubled. "It couldn't be, could it?"

"I don't know," Danteus responded. "All I know is that two major events occurring within days of each other is unusual, and I'm sure the Peacekeepers are thinking the same thing. I get the feeling that there's going to be a lot more . . . trouble."

"You're serious, aren't you?"

"I am."

"How do you know more will happen?"

"Honestly, it's just a hunch."

Then Cameron Luxendor, a man Gothalia was familiar with, joined them.

"Hey guys," Cameron greeted them. "What happened?" His eyes lingered over the Peacekeepers.

"I'll explain it later, but we have to get going," Danteus declared with a friendly hand on his shoulder.

"Where are you guys going?" Gothalia asked.

"To a meeting. See you later."

"Sure, see you then," Gothalia responded. And like that, they vanished from sight. Gothalia's eyes lingered over the crime scene once more as her mind pondering the different possibilities; not once had she thought they were all connected. Turning her heel, she walked away.

She wasn't on her own for long when she bumped into Arthur. She was surprised to find him—let alone see him so soon—but she had come to recognise the look of fear on his face.

"Are you alright?" she asked him, conscious of the anxiety in his eyes. "You look a little startled."

"I'm fine. Do you remember what I said to you before you parted the laboratory?" Arthur asked. His eyes scanned her face and Gothalia pondered on it for a moment, then nodded. "Good, there is something that I need to ask of you—and only you."

Gothalia regarded him with a level gaze.

"Why only me?"

"Because I fear that there are some of our soldiers are not—*good*."

"Good, what do you mean? They're going to go on a killing spree? Or they've betrayed their country?"

"Not exactly to that extent but quite possibly not too far from such a conclusion."

"Huh?" Gothalia asked, confused. "Wait, so what is it you need to tell me?" He pulled her aside and under the eaves of a walkway, out of sight from the other Centurions and Legionnaires in this part of the Cetatea.

By this time, Gothalia was a little concerned for Arthur but did not voice it. Instead, she listened attentively to what he had to say.

"Do you remember what I told you about Midnight Eclipse?"

"Yes, the weapon that has the power to wipe out thousands," she responded, eyeing him closely.

"It's much more than that," he said. "And when the time comes, I need you to promise me something." He walked away and led her deeper into the silent halls of the castle and towards one a door. He opened it and beckoned her inside. Once inside he closed the door and handed her a map. "You'll use *this* and find the other pieces. The map will lead you to a piece right here in the city. Find it, and when you do, be sure to keep them from the others."

"Arthur?" Gothalia asked, worried. Stepping away, she added, "I can call the nurse if you're not feeling well."

"I don't blame you for thinking I'm ill, but you've seen the power of it for yourself. I am giving this to you because I trust you. Will you trust me enough in return to do as I ask?"

After deep contemplation, Gothalia nodded. Arthur beamed. "Thank you."

"I'll do as you ask, but Arthur, what am I after?" she asked, cautiously.

"The Fragments. You are after the Fragments of Midnight Eclipse. Over a millennia ago, when it first landed on Earth, the pieces were bound together and held power no man had any understanding of. So, civilisations fought over it."

"Wait, I thought they fought over land."

"That's what we tell everyone." Arthur declared.

Then Gothalia understood.

"That explains why there were so many wars."

"Exactly. If something's precious enough, blood will be shed. That is why I give this to you; you hold the power of the Valdis. You'll have the power to protect it."

"But—"

"Please, start your search," Arthur urged. This confused Gothalia even more but did not question it. With the map and

Arthur's first clue she parted the room and wandered out of the Cetatea and down the streets of New Icarus.

Fifteen minutes later—nine hours after Argos's demise, and the peacekeepers' recent investigation and the interrogation of her—Gothalia was confronted in the narrow streets near Solstice Square.

In the Upper North Plerrolt district, five male Centurions taunted Gothalia, while passers-by avoided the group, sensing the danger. They looked at her with fear and uncertainty, when she sprinted into a nearby alley—and ran right into her old friend, Ilenia. L'Eiron would remind her often of her need to remain in control. These men would never understand why she had to show restraint with them, nor the severity of their situation.

Gothalia had not arrived in the district to start a fight. She arrived in search of the clues Arthur had given her, while others scoured the city for clues as to Argos's murder.

This had led her to this alley not a long alley, where she was expected to search for elusive information about Midnight Eclipse, and its connection to the black scale Arthur found.

It was then that Gothalia heard taunts and threats from the lane behind her. She stopped running to face her pursuers; her eyes shifting over the fire-crest on the wall where Ilenia stood, before returning her gaze to the men.

Gothalia felt Ilenia's fear as if it were her own and, without thinking, she stepped protectively between her and the men.

"Do me a favour will you?" she asked, Ilenia.

"What?"

"Prepare yourself. I'm not exactly on good terms with these guys."

Momentarily, Ilenia forgot about the danger and glared at Gothalia.

"What did you do?"

Gothalia shrugged.

"Let's not talk about that for now."

Ilenia crossed her arms; a sour expression streaked her delicate features.

"I could always report this . . . if you don't tell me." Gothalia knew Ilenia would have difficulty finding anyone who would listen.

"Um, we got into a fight, but it was self-defence. They chased me throughout the city, and I had enough."

Ilenia's eyes narrowed on Gothalia before drifting to the approaching men.

"You're not getting away this time," Gothalia heard one say. She stood her ground. Intimidation would not make her falter. Especially, for men with little-to-no respect for their title or what it meant to be a Centurion. Gothalia was sick of their undignified behaviour.

The men closed the distance. Gothalia's irritation flared as she realised, they were out for blood.

"Gothalia . . ." Ilenia whispered, with a trace of distress in her voice.

"Look who it is—Gothalia. How are you?" Gareth Manius questioned. He was the son of Victor Manius, a man who was arrested on charges of terrorism and treason.

Gothalia had the unfortunate duty of being a part of the task force that had hunted Victor Manius, while Anaphora had been the one to arrest him, on behalf of the Peacekeepers. Gareth had wanted to kill Gothalia ever since that day. His hazel eyes, like his father's, regarded her with hatred. And, his lopsided smile bore the scar she gave him the day she hunted his father.

"I was better until I saw your ugly mug. That scar improves it, though." Gothalia responded, with a dangerous smile.

"You think so, huh?" Gareth's hazel eyes darkened with anger.

"You heard me; I don't need to repeat myself. That is . . . unless you want a *repeat* of last year?"

His smile dropped and his frown deepened. His friends recognised the change in his mood and glared at Gothalia spitefully. Earth erupted from the ground beneath them and Gareth smiled in triumph. Gareth manipulated the earth and it wrapped around Ilenia's throat and Gothalia rushed to aid Ilenia only to have it force her back. She glared—she had almost forgotten he was an earth user.

"Let her go!" Gothalia demanded as he threw Ilenia to a man, she had seen walking to the Cetatea earlier that day.

"Make us." he demanded from beside Gareth, with a dagger to Ilenia's throat. Laughter echoed in the alley. Anger flashed across Gothalia's face.

"Gothalia . . ." Ilenia whispered, her fear interweaving each syllable like barbed wire.

A man from beside Gareth attacked with a dagger and Gothalia disarmed him easily. Gripping his unarmed hand, she twisted his wrist hard before forcing him against the wall with little. The man cried out before slipping out of her grip, and she felt the force of his kick against her stomach, reminding her of his Centurion status. She took another few blow from him, but the adrenaline kept her from feeling the pain.

Finally, she gained an opening and struck him hard. He fell forward on his knees. Kicking out an arm, she locked it around his back and in place, pinning his arm to his back with her knee. She curled over him with her hands positioned, ready to snap his neck if she needed.

"Let her go. Or I'll break him." Gothalia threatened. When no one moved, she placed more pressure and listened to his bones creak. "Don't make me repeat myself."

The astounded men regarded Gothalia.

"She's bluffing," one said, wavering a little with uncertainty.

"Let me go!" Ilenia growled and elbowed her assaulter in the sternum. Gothalia acted fast, striking the man below her in the head, and rolled over her shoulder, closing the distance between her and Gareth. She swept at the ankles of the closest man beside Gareth and he collided with the ground, hard. Gareth kicked her, and she avoided the second strike, then flipped to her feet and struck him hard in the nose.

The crunch of bone rebounded around the alleyway when Gothalia's fist connected. Blood splashed against the red and black non-combatant uniform.

The man who had held Ilenia ran at her. She twisted her weight and blocked the oncoming strikes while evading every attack possible, then kicked him in the head, ensuring his face collided with the stone wall. The final men stared at her in shock. They were not Centurions, just ordinary men, so she paused. Her face stung and her jaw felt wet from the blood trailing along the corner of her mouth.

She'd glared at them.

"Now I will only say this once. Leave." Her dark eyes began to glow red and her skin started to burn with black and crimson marks. "Otherwise, I can't promise I'll show mercy." Her fair russet skin crawled with faint black triangles and red diamonds, contrasting the whites of her eyes.

"Filthy Demon!" one shouted fearfully. "They should have killed you the day you were born!"

"I'm not dying today!" the other said and ran away. The other men followed.

"This isn't over," Gareth spat at her. She stared at him with a cold look before he swiftly retreated after the other men.

Ilenia watched Gothalia with sadness then smiled when she had heard her mutter "Cowards" as she calmed her élanocytes.

"You know my lady, I'd be concerned if you couldn't look after yourself," Kronos commented in her earpiece.

"Shut up." Gothalia sharply replied, not in the mood.

"Were you talking to me?" Ilenia demanded, with an incredulous look on her face. Gothalia said nothing and only pointed to her earpiece. Then she turned to Ilenia to help her up, only to pause in surprise at the fuming anger in her eyes. "You said it would be safe! You said and I quote, 'there's nothing to worry about come for a walk'." Ilenia snarled. "I'm not combat-trained."

"What are you talking about? Everyone's taught self-defence," Gothalia replied, confused.

"Against one person, not several!"

"I hadn't expected them to show up."

"Is that why you were judging your surroundings a little more than necessary today?"

Gothalia shrugged, in silent confirmation.

"Do you think we should get him to a doctor?" Ilenia asked, glancing down at the man Gothalia had kicked. He had hit his head hard, and Gothalia was concerned, even if he had attacked her first. "He may have a severe head injury."

*Maybe, he shouldn't dish out what he cannot take*, Gothalia thought, them wondered if she had been too rough.

After Gothalia's enemies vacated the area, Gothalia moved to the stone wall and regarded the fire emblem on the wall. She moved her hand over it; fire enveloped her hand and the wall retracted to reveal a door.

"What on earth?" Ilenia exclaimed from beside Gothalia.

"Wait here," she said.

"Sure."

Gothalia entered the hidden door and walked down a set of staircases into the darkness. Ilenia gasped when the door closed behind Gothalia and shrieked her name. Gothalia ran to the door—but it was too late. She was trapped. Taking a deep breath, she continued walking down the stairs and into the darkness. Then after a few minutes of walking, she heard the echo of laughter and she noticed a ray of light from around the corner. Music permeated the room and Gothalia was surprised to find she was on the other side of a wall.

"There has to be another way to the other side," Gothalia voiced, dust and dirt covering the floorboards beneath her feet. The area she entered appeared as if no one had entered it in years. It was dark, the only light filtering in from the window, and it was dry and empty—a combination Gothalia did not like. "Alright Kronos, what do you think?"

"I think there's no way out, but this corridor has to lead somewhere," he promised and Gothalia continued forward. After a few minutes of walking down the corridor, Gothalia turned around another corner and entered a large, undeveloped area. She regarded the layout: it was a dome-shaped room and in the centre of the room was an object that she knew Human eyes would not be able to make out. Glancing at the unlit torches on the wall, she lit them one by one.

"What's that?" Gothalia asked, eyeing the black disk lined in white markings and letters that she could not remember from any languages on Earth. It was small, no larger than her palm.

"I'm guessing it's the Fragment," Kronos declared.

"Wait, you were listening to our conversation?"

"I was, but only because you left me on."

"Remind me next time to turn you off." Gothalia pulled out the map and regarded the inscriptions and drawings on the side of the map. "Interesting. This sketch looks exactly like this object."

"It's got to be a Fragment," Kronos declared. "Take it and show it to Arthur. He may be able to shed some light on this object."

"Sure." Gothalia lightly remarked. She picked up the Fragment, but as soon as she removed it, something opened. Gothalia edged towards the door carefully. Her faceplate covered her features as she regarded a set of stairs.

"Another door."

"It must lead out of here."

"You think?" Gothalia asked cynically. She did not like that things were popping up unexpectedly, but she knew she had to remind herself that people had once built this with one way in and one way out.

"Yes, I think so," Kronos remarked and Gothalia climbed the stairs. They led to a door, revealing a familiar street. "See, told you." Gothalia found herself in the street not too far from where she had left Ilenia. Turning down another street then down the alley, she saw Ilenia sitting on the ground, playing with her nails. When Gothalia approached, Ilenia sprang to her feet.

"That was fast," she remarked, relieved. "What did you find and where did it lead?"

"One question at a time." Gothalia contemplate not telling Ilenia and just keep her guessing, until she heard the beating of feet entering the alleyway.

Domitia and Melanie, wearing the readily identifiable Centurion non-combatant uniform, approached Gothalia and Ilenia with confusion.

"What are you guys doing here?" Gothalia inquired, with a raised brow and folded arms.

"Arthur . . ." Domitia panted. "He told us to where we might find you."

"I've never run so hard in my life," Melanie added, through ragged breaths. "And, have never been so scared."

"What are you talking about?" Gothalia had a sinking feeling in her stomach. "Where's Arthur?"

And Domitia replied,

"He's gone. They took him. We saw it, and then they came after us. We lost them, though."

"Gone? What do you mean gone? And who is after you?" questioned Gothalia, alarmed.

Melanie must have seen the difficult internal struggle Gothalia had. She stepped forward and placed a gentle hand on her shoulder.

"We should go somewhere safe, without prying eyes." The man on the ground groaned, and it relieved Gothalia to know he would be okay.

She wanted to reply that there was no place where they could go without being overheard. Then she glimpsed the desperation on their faces.

"We can go to mine. It's outside the city and there's a secret entrance."

"Your house has a secret entrance?" Melanie asked, shocked. Gothalia eyed Melanie with a funny look before leading them to one of the many tunnels throughout the Fire Reserve hidden underground.

When the women arrived, they were awed by the well-preserved ancient architecture. Gothalia led them to a common room and was surprised to hear a voice she thought she would not hear for a while.

"Gothalia, where were you?" L'Eiron asked.

"Out," she replied, not caring if he noticed the dried blood at the corner of her lips.

The women greeted L'Eiron and Domitia's face flushed a little. She quickly moved into the common room. Gothalia and L'Eiron stared after her, confused. L'Eiron glanced at Gothalia.

"Well, anyway, just letting you know: Anaphora's on a mission. She'll be away a little longer."

An obdurate silence shifted between them.

"Thanks for letting me know." Gothalia left the foyer. L'Eiron called after her that he'd dropped off extra food. She thanked him once more and closed the common room door.

Once inside, Gothalia leaned against the door, which separated them, listening to the front door open and close. She released a sigh.

"Gothalia, you know L'Eiron didn't mean to . . ." Domitia began and Gothalia held up a hand, silencing her.

"I don't want to hear it. Honestly, I do not think I am in the right headspace to determine why L'Eiron acted the way he did, or in what world he thought not trusting me was appropriate. Regardless, explain to me what happened to Arthur."

"A group that calls themselves 'The Order of the Rukh' has taken him."

"Rukh as in, the bird of prey?" Gothalia asked, genuinely confused. "The one that has the ability to pick up baby elephants and Humans alike?"

"Yes. Apparently, the Rukh were known for two things: one, it causes unimaginable terror and death; the other, it is believed to be a protector of a vast, secret valley that may have been filled with ancient treasure."

"Was it?" Gothalia asked.

Domitia gave Gothalia a questionable look.

"It's a myth."

"But aren't Excelians?" Melanie asked, smiling at Domitia who sat back, crossing her arms with evident disapproval.

"They want a ransom in return for Arthur. That's so messed up. The Grand Elders and the King are discussing it now."

"They must consider him to be of value, so they'll keep him alive until we deliver. How much?" Gothalia prompted, her mind turning at all the recent events. Even to her, everything seemed very coincidental, and she never believed in coincidences.

"It's not money they want," Domitia replied, tentatively. "It's *who* they want. And that *who* is you." Gothalia held her gaze, recognising the fear there.

"Oh no," Ilenia said shakily. "They're after . . . but . . . wouldn't that . . ."

Everyone eyed Gothalia. Distress was noticeable on her features, and her tacit silence confirmed why everyone was afraid. It was a daily struggle to keep her emotions in control, fearful of what would happen to everyone around her if she allowed both the good and bad emotions to arise. If she could barely control her monster, the Order of the Rukh certainly couldn't.

# Chapter 10

"SO, WHAT ARE WE GOING to do?" Melanie asked.

"You're not going to do anything," Gothalia commented. "I am."

"What do you mean?" she questioned. "You're not thinking of going after them, alone are you?"

"Not alone, but after them yes. Arthur is an unbelievably valuable asset. We can't afford to lose him especially now of all times."

"What makes you think now is important?" Ilenia asked.

"Just trust me," Gothalia said. She was certain that the Order of the Rukh would make their lives difficult and she knew she couldn't begin to determine what they wanted with Arthur of all people. Than the more she thought about it, the more she began to question things. Like why was Arthur working on that scale? And why was the General assassinated?

"Even if we do trust you and believe me, we do," Melanie declared. "How can you be sure you'll get him back? And what are we going to do about the ransom?"

"I will. I have my ways." Gothalia declared. After planning the next course of action, they returned to the Cetatea.

High above the Cetatea, in the tallest of towers, men garbed in dark cloaks hid, moulded into the stone walls like statues. Their eyes trailed over the women who strode the silent halls below, unaware of their presence.

Gothalia who felt her skin prickle, but believing she was just being paranoid, she focused her mind on Melanie's next comments about how long the Grand Elders would take in deciding who'd next oversee Dragon Core and who would take Arthur's place.

Melanie had hoped L'Eiron would accept the responsibility as the one to next oversee Dragon Core, but before she could utter her next words, her attention fell on Gothalia, who lingered at the back of the group. Her eyes widened in fear and she screamed Gothalia's name, shocking her into action.

Swiftly, Gothalia evaded an attack by one man but did not move in time to fully dodge the sword he had attempted to run through her heart. Blood dripped down her shoulder, blending with her crimson tunic.

Gothalia's free hand shot to her wound. She cradled it, conscious not to move too much, but equally conscious of her desperate need to survive.

"Alert the others!" She yelled, pulling out the short dagger strapped to her right thigh. She faced the enemy, then frowned at their numbers. "It's one attack after the other today, isn't it?" she muttered.

Gothalia eyes lingered over their lower bodies, fashioned into the earth before their entire bodies stood above ground. Their bodies were moulded out of the hallway walls. *Earth users, why did no one—*

When Domitia hesitated to follow Melanie and Ilenia, Gothalia yelled:

"Go now!" She deflected an attack from one man before attacking another. Domitia ran and Gothalia saw two of the cloaked men chase her. Gothalia slipped around her initial attacker and threw her dagger at the shoulder of one man pursuing Domitia, then blocked an attack from the same man.

Ilenia disappeared around the corner with Melanie, and Domitia ran to the closest emergency button. She screamed in shock when the earth beneath the box shot up like a spear, destroying the alarm system.

A man caught up to Domitia and Gothalia cursed; she couldn't be in two places at once. Blocking attacks with her good arm and her legs, she threw one kick, then another, and finally leapt into a tornado kick, forcing the man to the ground with a strike to his head.

Gothalia sprinted after Domitia, who noticed her approach and kept the enemy in place as he held her against the wall, ready to strike her down with his sword. Even as fear masked her face at the sight of the weapon, she remained steady.

Gothalia leaped on the enemy from behind and wrapped her legs around his throat, throwing him into the ground headfirst.

"Run!" she yelled at Domitia.

Releasing her hold, explosions shot out of her feet. Throwing one man to the ground, she was unaware of the black and crimson triangles scaling up her exposed neck and over her face.

"Gothalia!" Domitia shrieked but Gothalia could not hear her. Her crimson eyes were busy assessing the men.

Abruptly, a cloaked man that Gothalia had not taken notice of threw her into the nearby wall and locked one of her arms in place. With her leg, she forced him away from her enough to twist out of his hold and strike him the head.

Her ears rang and her head ached. She cursed, realising she would not last much longer if she did not end it now. She was at a disadvantage in numbers. As soon as she began to conjure counter-measures, her body numbed.

Gothalia spotted her blood-smeared arm, injured from their initial assault. A needle protruded it. She yanked it from her arm. *When did they . . . ?*

Recognising the danger. Gothalia stumbled away from the men. Fear coursed throughout her injured body.

In the distance, voices screamed her name and she knew from the sound of one voice that Domitia was nearby, but she did not know where, and the world around her was becoming disoriented.

Everything faded and her body heated, emitting smoke like lithe fingers. She dropped to her knees. The men watched her cautiously before one moved to grab her. Then angry fire enveloped her body. Moments later, her once black eyes were stained red, with diamond-shaped pupils like a tiger. The men stared at her in horror.

"Subdue her now!" one shouted in fear, noticing the whites of her eyes become black.

New energy filtered through the thick air, filled with danger and death. Fire exploded in both Gothalia's palms, and the ground beneath her boots split and shattered as she launched herself at her attackers. Her mind had no conscious thought; her body instinctively reacted to every attack.

Her enemies fell one by one, but their screams were white noise in her ears, victims of the crimson flame. Their skin where she touched them slowly seared away, through the tissues and the muscles beneath until nothing was left but bone.

Sparks of red and black flared throughout the hall and fire erupted at her feet. Within the blazing flame, a sterling silver sword shot up and into her right hand, engraved with an ancient language that many had long forgotten.

Gothalia's eyes scanned the area behind her, and she noticed a man. She vanished from sight and into a cloud of black smoke. Then reappeared behind the man and slashed her sword through his chest before slicing off the head of the next man who became lost within the black smoke.

Earth erupted from the ground and with her sword engulfed in crimson flames, she broke through it before slicing the earth user in half. Only two elemental users remained untouched, throwing slabs of the earth at her from a distance. She dodged and sliced through the earth before taking out her final enemies.

Silence filled the halls of the Cetatea and Gothalia could not recognise the sound of distress nor the blood-stained hallway destroyed by her and the Earth users. She did not even recognise the victims at her feet. Turning her back on them, she walked away, her blood-smeared sword aching for its next victim.

BELOW THE WAR-TORN skies, Noel-Len stepped out of the building. A glimmer of fear and curiosity sparked his dark gaze, which drifted over the shifting soldiers below, taking in their clenched jaws, smeared in dirty sweat. Their eyes sang a sad ballad, one of vulnerability and terror, as they carried the injured on stretchers to the medical building. Finally, he caught sight of Mike's tiny build, and heard his abysmal whimpers.

Noel-Len's empathy did not freeze the burn in his heart; it blazed like a deadly bushfire; one he knew he could never extinguish. Nor could he silence the exploding jets above that fertilising the earth below with the blood of both fallen soldiers and civilians alike. A death toll, which would be forever remembered and mourned.

Dropping to one knee, he calmed his distressed pup, but could not cease his trembling. The animal shuddered beneath his touch. Continuing to stroke the dog, Noel-Len called his father.

After a few apprehensive moments, he answered.

"Noel-Len, where are you?" Gaius Ignatius queried, with familiar concern.

However, the calmness in his voice could not silence the frightened screams of his family in the background. Fear weighed the chambers of Noel-Len's heart before pooling into his stomach.

"At the barracks. Are you alright?" he responded, at last.

"Yes. We're on our way out of the city," Gaius uttered, to Noel-Len's relief. His father's final farewell was tender, but easily forgotten at the screams of his step-siblings and step-mother. His father abruptly hung up.

Michael tentatively approached, with a collar and leash. The collar had tape around it, on which was written Mike's name and Noel-Len's number. Noel-Len's gaze drifted to Michael's expressionless face.

The door opened and behind them, Caprice lingered at the entrance. Her curious eyes were held captive by the injured soldiers until Michael stepped before her, concealing her view. He handed Noel-Len the labelled collar.

Noel-Len wrapped the collar around Mike's neck and Michael passed the leash to Caprice.

"Take care of him," he ordered. Without hesitation, she ushered Mike inside. The men lingered beyond the door.

Noel-Len turned to his friend and prompted,

"Let's go." They moved from the building. Moments later, Dave greeted both men, carrying the sombreness of the invasion in his dark frown.

"Michael. Noel-Len." A grim expression scarred his usually clean features with harsh lines. The khaki uniform, he often wore was concealed by tactical armour and gear.

Dave cradled his rifle with a strong grip. His finger rested on the trigger of the weapon—not hesitantly.

"Good, you two are alive. Follow me." As they followed him, Dave delivered an account of when the attack occurred and when the immediate call for response was ordered.

MEN LAUGHED, A DARK laugh that echoed in the lower district streets of New Icarus, and Altair paused before the men—less than amused.

"Care to explain what's so funny?" he asked them, devoid of emotion. His dark eyes held an unspoken ire.

"Lord Altair," one Excelian declared, surprised, he sprang to his feet. "We never expected you to be—"

"Be what?" Altair coldly pressed.

"To be here, my Lord," the first one spoke. "We were told you left for New Eorthen."

"No, not yet," Altair declared with a dark smile. "I can't leave without seeing the show and besides, I came to check in on you two imbeciles." He gazed upon the men before him. "So, how did your confrontation go?"

"Gothalia, that bitch," Gareth declared, infuriated, "beat everyone up. I can't wait until I get my hands on her. I'm going to make her regret making a fool of me and my father."

"You'll get your revenge in time. Your pride isn't what's important right now," Altair declared. "Did you at least draw out her demon? This won't work if you haven't done your part."

"I did, but she has control over her demon. At least we managed to secure Arthur." Gareth stepped aside to gesture at an unconscious Arthur on the ground, gagged and bound. "How do you intend to draw out her demon?"

There was an explosion in the distance from the Cetatea in the distance and Altair smiled, "I already have."

"Serves her right," Gareth declared. Then an earth user pulled himself out of the ground beside Altair, startling both Gareth and his friend.

"I see you've done it," Altair said to the earth user, not once looking at him.

"I have. She has lost control. Many will be killed, and they won't even notice what we've done until it's too late."

"Good," Altair said and turned from the men and to the earth user. "Keep your distance for now. We mustn't draw too much suspicion on ourselves."

"Understood." The earth user said, then vanished into the ground.

Altair's smile grew as he gazed upon the Cetatea in the distance, popping with explosions.

"Perfect. Everything is moving according to plan."

NOEL-LEN, MICHAEL AND the others arrived at an open grass field, surrounded by many buildings, where all Combat and Security personnel attentively heeded the words of the Captain before them, set into disciplined lines. Swiftly, both men joined the back of the line, then Dave parted, searching for arriving soldiers who had survived the journey.

Off to the side, Michael and Noel-Len noticed Corporal Kypreos observe them with a grim expression. He called,

"You heard the man, move out!" His words strained the air like a deadly war cry.

With relevant information, everyone was stationed in response units. Noel-Len and Michael were placed with Dave and Leandra under the supervision of Sergeant Curt McGuire. They donned their Kevlar, rucksacks, and assault packs prior to equipping themselves with their assigned weapons and climbing into a truck.

The open vehicle let everyone see the haunting darkness of the skies above, untouched by the rays of the sun and the open bushlands surrounding them. Their attention drifted to the Sergeant who yelled over the roaring engine and combusting sky about their unit's primary objective. They had not travelled even five hundred metres before another pod dropped from the sky, separating the group of armed vehicles from their formation.

Noel-Len glanced at the Sergeant and the other trucks behind them that could not continue further. Some soldiers remained fortified behind tanks, lining the base, while Noel-Len's unit and a few others continued to press on. Above, he spotted large helicopters move from the base and away from the war.

Dave embraced the silver cross around his neck and whispered a prayer before tucking back beneath his uniform. Firmly, he gripped his gun, his face mirroring the tension in his shoulders. Noel-Len saw his fingers trembling.

Most streets were bare at first, but soon they came upon men and women running towards their vehicles.

Their actions were rapid and their strength immeasurable: they forced several military vehicles from the road and into the bushlands, killing the soldiers instantly. While bullets were fired from on the open vehicles, directed by the lights above their rifles. When the light on his rifle exposed their attackers, Noel-Len froze. He stared at the men and women running towards them, drenched in blood and with a black look in their eyes—one he had seen before.

He was hesitant at first as he fired his weapon. The echo of his discharge rang loudly in his ears.

To his surprise, the rounds only slowed them down.

"Head-shots!" Sergeant McGuire ordered.

The hostile men and women fell quickly to the soldiers' bullets and Noel-Len's stomach twisted in regret as he observed the sight before him.

"Oh no," Leandra gasped from beside Noel-Len. Her hazel eyes travelled methodically over the unmoving bodies on the ground, "We just . . ." she tried.

"No." Noel-Len announced under his breath. His eyes drifted over the fallen civilians as he recalled the actions of the prisoner. "They appear human but they're not." All eyes fell on him, including the Sergeant's.

"You want to explain what you're talking about, Private?" Sergeant McGuire asked but Noel-Len could tell he was thinking the same thing but couldn't say it, so Noel-Len instead remarked:

"It's not anything important sir, just a thought." Holding the Sergeant's gaze, aware of all eyes on him. Pulling his gaze away, his attention fell on the city buildings.

Steadily, the Sergeant examined Noel-Len's face and body language. When Curt found nothing out of character, reluctantly his gaze returned to the landscape, assessing the area for more enemies—even if they were the very citizens he was sworn to protect.

It had been an hour since Noel-Len and his unit were deployed from the barracks. He and his comrades had destroyed several of the animalistic robots by setting strategic traps and luring them in, then taking out the creature that crawled out, without hesitation.

The armoured enemy was able to take bullets from a distance and remain unaffected; however, up close they were as vulnerable as he was. He relayed this vital information to his Sergeant.

"Don't hesitate to exploit their weakness," Curt replied, in response.

The once-peaceful city was forsaken, peppered with destruction, and littered with dead soldiers and civilians alike, collapsed against the abandoned vehicles and tarnished buildings. Noel-Len slipped around a corner, his back planted against a concrete wall.

Adrenaline coursed through his body and sweat coated his flustered features beneath his armoured helmet.

His earpiece buzzed with the voices of his comrades and their locations. He listened to the orders of his Sergeant, crouched in front of him, hidden with his team.

"They've secured another building."

"Orders, Sir?" Dave asked, kneeling with Noel-Len opposite Curt.

"Take it out. Leave no stone unturned and no monster alive. If deemed a mission fail, you know what to do." Both Noel-Len and Dave nodded in understanding.

Once the Sargent moved away, Noel-Len continued with Dave, their steps cautious as they moved along the concrete pavement.

Their grips were tight on their rifles as they rounded a corner and moved to their designated locations.

Moments later, everyone was positioned to await their final order. They remained out of sight from the silver aliens overrunning the abandoned building.

Sargent McGuire commanded his unit to conduct their strategic plan, hoping it would give them a fighting chance. Their plan was to sabotage the relay of information.

Noel-Len waited for the continuous line of expected explosions before conducting his action in the plan.

The ground beneath him was once an alley with smooth pavement—now it was barely recognisable.

Two explosions sounded along the tarmac roads surrounding the shopping centre where the aliens were gathered; Noel-Len waited for the final one before he heard Leandra report her compromised position.

"Move out!" the Sargent ordered.

THE VALDIS CURSE WAS feared because it varied with each descendent amongst the bloodline. Those with the purest bloodline or purest élanocyte levels had the most unpredictable power.

As such, blood coated the empty hall. Gothalia moved throughout the Cetatea flanked by Centurions, who endeavoured to restrain her. Their swords and daggers sliced her skin, and the cuts of her uniform were lingering reminders of their threat to her vulnerable flesh below.

She couldn't feel the pain, even as she bled.

The curse hindered her sense of pain and all worldly sense of compassion. To some, she was a cold calculating beast, innate to kill without regret or remorse. A perfect assassin. To others, she was more of a prisoner.

All that remained in place of the determined and proud soldiers were fallen forms and blank faces—faces that would forever be carved into her mind.

The soldiers that fought Gothalia attacked with malic and hurt, rebellious to her persistence while she travelled throughout the Cetatea.

Not everyone within the Cetatea was aware of the dangers befalling the fortress, even as the alarms blared—it was common to have practice drills. The alarms never even reached the other side of the Cetatea, leaving everyone within defenceless to the oncoming threat.

As Gothalia rounded a corner, the women froze, seeing the blood soaking her Centurion uniform.

The woman ran in fear of her life and Gothalia pursued.

She threw fire at the woman, who moved around objects, through open doors, and downstairs avoiding the flames in time. Gothalia landed at the base of the stairs as the woman twisted around a corner, avoiding more balls of fire. The woman vanished from sight and Gothalia pursued until a voice called from the other side of the hall.

"Gothalia?" Demetria gasped—even with her Valdis perception, Gothalia hadn't noticed her presence. The scientist sprinted behind Demetria, terrified, as Demetria's eyes dawdled over Gothalia's uniform, stained with blood.

Danteus's terse voice called over the radio, permeating the daunting silence with disturbing orders:

*"Lieutenant Valdis has been compromised. All units respond with caution."* Demetria stiffened in response, shivering at Gothalia's exposed fangs and crimson eyes. She observed the marks beneath her collar and around her eyes, and Gothalia's hair, which had turned silver-white. "What in the hell are you?" she whispered, shocked. "You're definitely not Excelian."

Gothalia leapt for Demetria; extending her staff, Demetria threw Gothalia over her, evading her strike, while the scientist scurried out of the way.

Explosions permeated the halls as Gothalia threw fireballs and Demetria attempted to reason with her.

"It's me!" Demetria cried. "Don't make me fight you!" Recalling all the times she had beaten Gothalia in a sparring match, Demetria battled Gothalia, stunned to find that her usual attacks would not work.

The scientist observed the fight with fear, unable to pull her eyes from the battle; while fire thrown from Gothalia and ice thrown from Demetria collided, creating smouldering steam. Demetria called after her,

"Get Doctor Nelson, now!"

The scientist sprinted into a room that would lead her to the Artillery and Combat sector and to the Medical Wards.

When Kale Nelson, another scientist within the Cetatea, rounded the corner, he bumped into a woman he had not seen since their last experiment.

"What's the hurry, Louise?" he asked, noting her fearful expression.

"It's Lieutenant Valdis. The disease—it's taking over."

# Chapter 11

KALE'S EYES WIDENED in horror before he sprinted from the woman and to the security speaker on the wall.

Even as he slid his fingers over the touch screen, his mind returned to images of when the disease had overcome Natalia, all those years ago. They had taken so many precautions to ensure that this would not occur a second time, including examining Gothalia's blood to count the unstable élanocytes. He had wondered if they had done the right thing by not telling her of what really was going on. *Could we have prevented this?* He wondered.

"Where is she?" he asked the woman, frantically as he dialled Arthur's number, who did not pick up.

A crash echoed down the hall and the lights above flickered in response.

Kale and Louise watched the corner, terrified.

"Arthur, this is hardly the time take a break!" Kale yelled into the speaker before muttering, "If she's anything like her mother in this state, we're all dead."

Demetria sprinted from around the corner and into the hall, where Kale and Louise cringed. Seconds later, Gothalia shattered the wall between them launching herself at Demetria.

"Now, you're not holding back!" Demetria growled, furious, before charging at Gothalia with her sword unsheathed. "I will take you down! If it's the last thing I do!" Bloody and bruised, Demetria worked to hold off Gothalia.

"Do something!" Louise yelled at Kale. "She'll kill her!"

Danteus and Asashin rounded the corner, armed, as Gothalia pushed Demetria back. Blocks, kicks, and jabs by her sword were deflected by the armour Gothalia wore. Kale and Louise sprinted from the fight to Danteus and Asashin.

Gothalia tossed Demetria against the wall, avoiding Danteus's earth manipulation that jutted in spikes beneath her boots.

Demetria hit the wall hard and Kale regarded her unconscious form, hoping she did not have internal bleeding.

Gothalia dashed past the group with her sword doused in a crimson flame, slicing through the earth Danteus threw. Surprise engulfed him, as she deflected or avoided most of the attacks.

Finally, he managed to restrain her from behind by wrapping his arms around her then growled in her ear.

"Snap out of it!" In response, she struck him hard in the nose with the back of her head, before spinning around to kick him in the face.

Kale shook Demetria's shoulders and her eyes shot open. She rolled onto her knees and her hands extended ice along the ground.

Gothalia lost balance; then fire consumed her feet, burning through the ice. She glared at Demetria.

Demetria climbed to her feet and yanked out a grapple cord from her utility belt. With a triumphant smile, she threw it so the hook at the end fastened around Gothalia's ankle. Demetria tugged the cord firmly, and Gothalia hit the ground so hard that she passed out.

Demetria turned from Gothalia to Danteus and helped him to his feet.

"Dummy, we're not to supposed hesitate."

Danteus rubbed his bleeding nose.

"I might have forgotten for a moment," he replied, his eyes on Gothalia's unconscious form.

Asashin helped Louise to her feet. Amongst all the action, she had rolled her ankle and struggled to walk properly. Kale kneeled before her, examining her ankle, while Demetria walked over to Gothalia's fallen form, placing her hands on her hips.

"Just when I think maybe we could get along; you go and do this."

"That's a bit harsh, don't you think?" Danteus asked and Demetria glanced away, refusing to reply.

"What happened?" Asashin asked Demetria. "Or the appropriate question: *how* did this happen?"

"Don't know," she replied, her eyes on Gothalia. The odd markings faded from her skin but not without leaving a searing scar on her neck.

WITH HIS RIFLE DRAWN, Noel-Len eyed the area around him, quickly moving to where he knew Leandra was, the echo of her rifle guiding him.

Clearing the area of any hostiles, he proceeded with caution. Rounding a corner, he saw that the alien had cornered Leandra, an array of bullets hitting the metal rear of the dump truck she hid in. Noel-Len pointed his rifle at the back of the alien's head.

Without hesitation, he fired, and the alien fell to the ground.

The sound of a pistol caught Noel-Len's attention—behind him, the second alien crumbled to the ground.

Leandra climbed out of the abandoned truck, with her nine-millimetre pistol pointed behind him.

Seeing that Noel-Len was safe, Leandra groaned.

"I smell like shit," she grumbled, putting her gun away and moving to pick up her discarded rifle.

"You did climb out of a truck filled with everyone's rubbish," Noel-Len agreed. "What did you expect?"

"It was my only option."

Noel-Len observed the thick metal lining of the garbage truck. They waited for a moment in silence, their ears perked for alien footfalls.

When they heard the aliens, Noel-Len glanced at the wall to their right. Leandra hesitated at first, then moved with Noel-Len to hide behind the corner.

They glanced at each other as the shadows drifted down the road.

"Are you sure. They went this way?" an unfamiliar voice inquired; his tone curious.

Leandra relaxed, hearing that the strange voice was Human. When she moved to step out, Noel-Len held her back.

A terrible feeling knotted her stomach, as she stayed braced against the wall for a little longer.

"Of course, they did. Didn't you see one of them head this way? You know our orders."

"Are you sure that they're not Special Forces?" another man asked.

Discreetly, Noel-Len peered around the corner, making out three figures. They all wore the same military uniform as him and Leandra. No voices echoed over their radio; they must have switched off.

"Even if they are. You really think they're a match for us?" one of the men queried.

"Shut up. You'll jinx us. Sergeant Curt McGuire is with them, and from what I heard, he has a few extra medals to his title. But the rest will be easy targets. They're nothing but privates, fresh to battle. The others didn't last long at all. They were too naïve." The man strode by the alien Leandra had taken out, with little interest. His gaze drifted over the wall that Leandra and Noel-Len hid behind, searching for hostiles.

Noel-Len eased away from the wall, waiting. His heart hammered again his chest. Leandra and Noel-Len heard the haunting fall of their approaching combat boots, along with their intense breathing.

"James." a voice whispered. "Let's go. We should keep moving." The man stopped inches from the wall that Noel-Len and Leandra hid behind.

A moment of silence and as he took a few steps closer. Finally, he whispered,

"Whatever you say, Smith."

Another agitated voice added,

"Let's go, Johnson.

The name froze Noel-Len and Leandra on the spot. Leandra felt Noel-Len's tension and anger but remained silent. Noel-Len risked a final glance at the retreating men, confirming his suspicions.

The man was Patrick Johnson. He had dark eyes and a heavy-set jaw—and he was part of his regiment. A man Noel-Len had shared a room with during training.

IN THE THICK SILENCE, the machine beeped, letting anyone within the room know of Gothalia's catatonic state. Cords slithered from the device, like lithe fingers, to her form, which lay peacefully beneath the white sheets.

Off to the side, her Centurion uniform that was once covered in blood had been cleaned and neatly folded. The clothes reminding L'Eiron of the amount of blood spilt within the past twenty-four hours. He stared at his hands, making fists, and releasing them.

"What happened?" he asked, glancing back at Gothalia's unresponsive form.

"We won't know until we look over the footage, but you shouldn't blame yourself," a man said behind him. "It was only a matter of time."

"What are you doing here?" L'Eiron questioned. "It's not like you care for her."

"You're right, I don't care for her. Not the way the Lord of Lightning does. Not that she'll ever need to know—for now. But I am concerned for her in my own way."

"Will you help her?" L'Eiron asked, not turning to face the white-haired man.

"I'll try," he said before disappearing without a sound as he had come. L'Eiron sighed and climbed to his feet.

"You'll be okay," he promised, gripping Gothalia's hand before vacating the room.

Outside of Gothalia's room, voices whispered in hushed tones.

"Care to explain to what happened?" Kale said, and the women glanced at each other, unsure on how to answer.

"Well . . ." Domitia began, cautiously. "Gothalia, she was fine when we were attacked. She was fighting off the intruders as you would expect her to."

"Yes, you've mentioned that." Demetria proclaimed, watching Domitia carefully.

Domitia silently contemplated her next words.

"I don't think I told you about how they injected her with something."

Everyone fell quiet as L'Eiron stepped into the hall.

"Did you say inject?"

"Yes." Domitia declared, holding his gaze. "Then she fell to her knees and exploded in fire."

Danteus leaned against the wall, not too far from L'Eiron, his brows drawn together. He glanced at L'Eiron, who nodded at him. Without a word, Danteus turned and walked to the room where Gothalia laid.

"So, you were attacked?" L'Eiron questioned, deep in thought.

"Yes, how many times do I have to say that?" Domitia queried, growing impatient. "Then there's Arthur. They took him."

"Who's *they*?" L'Eiron asked.

"Not sure; their faces were concealed in black masks," Domitia declared.

"It's true," Melanie added, "I was there."

"What were you two doing there?" L'Eiron asked.

"We were delivering paperwork—you know—the secure kind," Melanie answered.

"You both had to deliver it?" he asked, crossing his arms.

"No, Melanie was, and I just happened to bump into her. We were both heading back to the office at the same time, so we decided to return together."

"Interesting," Asashin declared. "And too coincidental."

"How do you mean?" Demetria questioned, regarding Asashin from where she stood beside him.

"I mean," Asashin began, "First Argos, then Arthur, and now Gothalia attacking her comrades. Something we all know she wouldn't normally do."

"Now that you mention it," Ilenia began, "Gothalia had bumped into Gareth's group as well, and they weren't kind."

"How so?" L'Eiron asked.

"They fought—*literally*," Ilenia enunciated. "Then Gothalia scared them away, but not long after, she . . ."

"She what?"

"Disappeared behind a wall than reappeared down the street."

This caught everyone's attention.

"How did she disappear behind a wall?" Demetria questioned.
Ilenia shrugged.

"I don't know, she just did."

"First thing's first." L'Eiron declared. "We need to find out
what she was injected with, then work from there. And tell no one
of this."

GOTHALIA STOOD ON THE edge of a cliff and perceived the
bodies on the ground before her. Glancing down, she realised it
was not a cliff she stood on—but a pile of bodies. Her jaw dropped
and her eyes widened as she regarded what she held in her hand.
A heart. Her grip loosened, and the heart rolled out of her hand,
plummeting to the earth below. Glancing at the city in the distance,
she observed the destroyed buildings and the carnage on the street.
She had done this.

Then she woke with a start, sweat covering her features. Once
she had calmed down and grounded herself, she groaned. Her head
hammered. Slowly, she climbed into a sitting position and regarded
Danteus sitting at her bedside. *Where am I?* she wondered. She
moved to climb off the bed, only to pause when her hand would
not follow—it was held captive by steel handcuffs. She regarded it,
confused.

"What's happening?"

"You're awake," Danteus announced.

"I am. I think."

He watched her carefully.

"You seem like yourself."

"Yeah just with a massive headache." Gothalia placed her free hand to her head, attempting to calm down her mind.

"Drink some water," he said gesturing to tray beside her that held a paper cup filled with water and some pills.

"What's that?" she asked him.

"Medication."

"What for?"

Danteus did not answer and regarded Gothalia for a moment, uncertain.

"What?" she asked, after some time.

"You really do seem—normal."

She climbed as much as she could out of the bed, despite the handcuff.

"What are you doing?"

"Trying to get a better look."

"Better look at what?" he asked, still sitting beside the bed with his arms crossed.

He met her eyes and had to glance away, overwhelmed by the intensity of the connection and aware of her top revealing her cleavage.

"Gothalia?" he whispered, feeling her move closer. He frowned.

Gothalia smiled.

"That's better. That's the Danteus I'm used to."

"You want me to be grumpy?"

"If it's better than you being depressed, then yeah," she declared with a bright smile. The air shifted, and they held each other's gaze for a moment longer. Neither uttered a word until L'Eiron entered the room.

"Gothalia, you're up," he acknowledged. She straightened.

"I am." Danteus swallowed, glancing away. L'Eiron looked at Danteus, then back at Gothalia, then back at Danteus again.

"Good," he said, slowly. "We need you to clear up a few things."

"What few things?" Gothalia questioned.

There was a heavy silence and Danteus glanced at L'Eiron.

"What's with the strange looks?" she inquired, studying Danteus and L'Eiron.

"You don't remember?" L'Eiron asked. "Do you?"

"Remember what?" Tears began to slide down her face, surprising all three of them. Quickly, Gothalia started to wipe away the tears with her free hand. "Why am I crying?" she whispered, feeling silly. She suddenly spotted blood on her hand and in the surrounding the room—it vanished just as suddenly. "What was that?"

"Gothalia, are you alright?" Danteus asked, climbing to his feet. Tentatively, he stepped towards her as she trembled. Gothalia dropped to her knees and cradled her head. The headache she had woken up with grew to the point where she could not keep her eyes open. L'Eiron dropped before Gothalia and removed the metal handcuffs.

"I need you to focus," he said desperately. "Stay with us." Images flashed behind her eyes of men and women in Centurion uniforms smeared in blood or burnt alive. She could not remove them from her mind and could not halt the sickening feeling as it pooled in her stomach and rose to her throat. There were flashes of splitting Earth and men clad in black silver cloaks and blood—always blood. "I need you to calm down," he declared.

"L'Eiron," Danteus said from beside Gothalia. "What are we going to do?"

"Get her home."

"But what about the Peacekeepers?"

"I'll deal with them—there's enough evidence that this incident wasn't entirely her fault. Whatever you do, make sure she doesn't leave her house." L'Eiron helped Gothalia to her feet and guided her out of the room with Danteus. "Go now, while they're changing guards."

Gothalia leaned against Danteus.

"We'll get you home," he promised. He guided her past a white-haired man who regarded them both with vigilance and despondency. Before long, they had exited the Cetatea to the streets below by the back route. Gothalia did not say a word. Her head felt stuffy and her mind was unable to focus past the images flashing behind her eyes. Danteus held onto her as he guided her down the streets and past strangers, who regarded them suspiciously. Danteus removed his combat cloak and draped it around Gothalia's shoulders before guiding her further up the road and towards her home.

When they finally arrived, he stopped before the door and glanced at Gothalia.

"Where are the keys?" he asked her, then recognised that she did not hear him. She merely cried and trembled. He pulled out his communicator and called L'Eiron.

"They're under the mat," L'Eiron responded.

"Thanks."

Danteus led them inside and locked the door behind them. He was conscious of her behaviour and tried to speak to her as much as he could, even if she did not respond. Guiding her further inside, he set her down on the couch and kneeled before her. Fear coursed through him. There was no recognition in her eyes and her tears did not stop.

"Gothalia," he whispered and wiped the tears from her eyes. "Are you here?" When she did not answer, he sat down beside her and merely held her.

"I'm here," she whispered after some time. Slowly, her eyes drifted to Danteus. "I'm sorry. I'm so sorry, Danteus."

He wrapped his arms around her.

"It's not your fault." Then he glanced at the family photo placed on the table beside the couch. He recognised Gothalia as a child, then Anaphora and L'Eiron when they were younger. Then he recognised her parents and another child. One that looked much like Gothalia. Before he could question her about it, the front door opened.

"We're over here," Danteus called as L'Eiron peered into the house, and Danteus dropped his arm from around Gothalia's shoulders.

"Gothalia," L'Eiron greeted, dropping to one knee before her. "How are you feeling?"

"I'm sorry, L'Eiron," Gothalia declared. She reached out and wrapped her arms around his shoulders. "I didn't mean too. I always tried to control it, but—"

"It's not your fault."

"But it is!" she responded. "I was the one that ran them through. I was the one that killed them. All of them."

"Do you remember what I said before?" he asked her gently. "You've been through too much and it's not healthy. This is a whole new level. And I am scared for you. I'm scared for what they are going to do. So, you're going to have to leave. For your own protection."

"What?"

"Just trust me on this," L'Eiron insisted. "If Amati found you, he'd definitely throw you in jail."

*Amati* . . . Gothalia thought. *Where have I heard that name before?*

Then shock flooded her as she recognised the name: it was the name of the Peacekeeper that had interrogated her.

"You mean *him*? He already doesn't like me, and I've just given him another reason not to." Gothalia's heart hurt as if someone had gripped it and squeezed.

L'Eiron did not say anything. He held her for a moment longer before releasing her and glancing at Danteus.

"Keep an eye on her. I'll call on you when I need you."

Danteus nodded. Climbing to his feet, L'Eiron vacated the premises while Gothalia sat on the couch beside Danteus.

"You can leave if you want." Gothalia told Danteus, feeling guilty for everything.

"I won't leave you," he said and Gothalia held his gaze.

"Why does it matter, if you leave me or not?"

"Because you're my comrade."

"Is that still all I am?" she whispered glancing at her fingers unable to meet his gaze, flooded with memory. "You told me how you felt that day. Or have you suddenly forgotten?"

"I haven't forgotten, nor could I ever forget. But you made your choice," Danteus said. "We're not having this discussion."

Gothalia sprang to her feet.

"And why not?"

"Because you're not well."

Gothalia grew cold.

"So, we'll only speak about it on your terms?"

"No that's not it," he said, then turned to face her. "You told me you didn't know how you felt."

"Yes, I didn't," Gothalia responded. "But I do now."

"What suddenly made you change your mind?" he asked at length.

"Ever since that day," she said, recalling their mission to the Northern Earth Reserve, "when the demon first broke out, I was scared. But we had to protect them. I could not afford to think about myself. But the past few days have made me think. I figured it was best to tell you, but I didn't know when or where, especially considering all that has happened. I'm scared, Danteus, for you, for me, for everyone."

He stepped closer to her. His calloused hand grazed her cheek and cupped her face.

"You can't tell me these things because you're scared," he said. "It's not fair."

"Fine," she said. "Can I freely say I return your feelings, then?"

"No, you cannot, not now."

Gothalia's gaze narrowed.

"And why not?"

"You've just woken up and could have a concussion. You don't know how you're feeling right now, and I won't take advantage of that," he said.

"But I feel fine," she responded. "And I feel something for you. As much as I tried to deny it."

"You're still talking about it, even when I told you not to," he said with a small smile, stepping towards her. She regarded him for a moment, then closed the distance, holding his gaze.

"You told me you loved me. Did you mean it?"

She shuddered when she felt his warm arms envelop her, but she refused to break eye contact, scared he would suddenly change. There was a vulnerableness to his gaze that gave her no doubt about how he felt, but with everything that had happened, was this the right time? No matter. She had to know how he felt—especially if she were going to leave her home. She knew deep down that she may not ever see him again. She worked to remember every detail of his face, the way he smiled, and especially the way he looked at her like no one else mattered.

"I did mean it," he said, after what felt like forever. "And I still do, I always have." With those words, the distance between them closed and they shared an enthusiastic kiss. When they broke apart, he regarded her with a desperate gaze that made her stomach drop. Then he captured her lips once more. Excited, she jumped up and wrapped her legs around him. He carried her to the couch, their kisses growing hot and hungry.

Gothalia groaned beneath him and gasped, feeling his skin against hers. She needed this. There was no denying how much she needed him and wanted him. It was like a miracle—not once did the passion die—not once did Danteus not stroke her gently or hold her close. It was pure love she felt from him—nothing she had ever experienced. It was safe to say, he was all hers.

After, they lay together, snuggled on the couch.

"I just realised what we did," Gothalia declared.

"What do you mean, you just realised?" Danteus queried. There was a caution in his voice that set off alarms in Gothalia.

"That's not what I mean. I mean, we just did that on the couch—in the living room. Imagine Anaphora's and L'Eiron's faces when they find out."

"They're not going to find out," he promised, kissing her neck with a small smile upon his lips. "Unless you tell them."

"Me? Never, I'm too scared to." Danteus laughed.

"Me too. I think I won't walk away alive."

"You won't," she agreed and kissed him.

# Chapter 12

AN HOUR LATER, NOEL-Len Ignatius observed the fallen enemy militias further down the street. He relayed their positions to the rest of his team.

Sweat coated his skin, dripping onto the microphone connected to his earpiece. His squadron leader's orders further informed the team of his and Leandra's position in the war-torn streets. He knew without a doubt that the others would arrive after they removed the aliens from the scouting sites. But he also knew it would take some time before his comrades would show up. He and Leandra struggled to keep the area secure.

Slowly, the aliens pushed towards the Human soldiers. Noel-Len and Leandra's bullets dropped before their feet. They were too far away to cause real damage.

"The world's gone to hell, hasn't it?" Leandra yelled at Noel-Len, shielded behind a concrete wall.

Her hazel eyes skimmed over their surrounding as her grip tightened around the Para Mini.

"It has." he said with the darkness surrounding him. Noel-Len pressed the side of his watch and the screen lit up. It was five-thirty in the morning.

Scanning the sky, he understood something clearly at last above, osculating along the detached skyline, making it easy to identify the shape of a large ship sitting over Darwin. It looked like the green silver pods he'd stumbled upon. Below the alien ship were specks of explosions and black dots zipping across the sky, lighting up in colours of orange, white and green. He had to wonder how much longer the war above would last.

Leandra crouched behind a car, firing at the aliens.

He had not heard the echo of approaching feet to his right due to the roar of his rifle. By chance, Noel-Len caught a glimpse of a figure to his right and pointing his rifle at the attacker. Ready to shoot, Noel-Len heard a voice.

"Stand down!"

Leandra faced the voice with her rifle ready. They both watched as the figure revealed itself. Another soldier approached, clad in Kevlar and a familiar military uniform.

Noel-Len lowered his weapon when he recognised her face, mumbling curses. Leandra regarded the soldier before them: the unit patch, the rank, and the name. Lieutenant Colonel Anaphora Raegan-Valdis watched Noel-Len with a dissecting and unreadable gaze.

Noel-Len considered Anaphora's unexpected presence for a moment longer then scrutinised her uniform. She was an officer. And yet he did not know. Yet the name Valdis was stitched into her uniform.

"Ma'am." Noel-Len greeted, his tone cautious and his eyes mistrusting.

Anaphora observed Noel-Len, with mild amusement at his reaction. She knelt behind a charred car.

"Where is the rest of your team?" Anaphora asked, firing her rounds. Leandra swiftly relayed their most recent encounters, her voice straining at the noise. "So, the recent objectives to take back the remaining alien scouting sites have failed?"

"Yes, ma'am," Leandra responded.

Noel-Len observed Leandra, wondering if she would still be so relaxed around her if she'd seen the darker side of Anaphora that he had.

"We're waiting for further orders from Sergeant McGuire. Ma'am." Leandra's gaze drifted to the sky, observing the largest ship.

"They're closing in," she declared, her eyes on the aliens and her rifle shaking in her grip after each round fired.

The aliens persisted in their onslaught; Noel-Len noticed they never stopped to re-load, a frustrating advantage they had. Resting on the car, Noel-Len supported his rifle and aimed before firing. They were fewer than fifty metres away.

He needed to be closer if he ever wanted to take them out. There was nothing he could shoot that would harm them.

Helplessly, he glanced at Leandra and Anaphora. They were pinned down by incoming fire. Anaphora hoisted her rifle higher.

"Stay here. That's an order."

A jet crashed behind the oncoming aliens, a few meters behind them. The crashing jet landed on another pod, causing an explosion that blew the shell of the pod onto the caved-in building roof.

Anaphora rounded the car as Noel-Len and Leandra drew fire. Anaphora crawled along the ground out of the alien's sight, boldly, working to close the distance between her and the enemy.

"What is she doing?" Leandra growled. Her eyes shifted from Anaphora to the approaching aliens. "She's going to get herself killed."

"I wouldn't worry," Noel-Len said calmly.

"What do you mean?" she cried over the raging alien bullets. The aliens were close enough that a single shot from them at this distance would no doubt kill them both. The weapons the aliens carried were like nothing Noel-Len had ever seen before. They were made from something smoother yet efficient. The bullets were nothing more than hot clumps of light and heat.

The torn cars and unrecognisable bodies made it clear to Noel-Len that those clumps of light would easily pierce him through, and there would be a thing anyone could do save him. He saw a fallen soldier off to the side, with a thick hole through the Kevlar on his torso.

Pulling his mind from the man, he heard a *bang*.

Dirt and debris filtered through the air as the foundations of nearby buildings shuddered; an alien pod had smashed into it.

Then, there was silence.

An alien screeched, in pain and terror.

It was thrown across the street and into the wall of the opposite building. Noel-Len and Leandra could see nothing through the thick cloud.

"Don't shoot!" Noel-Len yelled at Leandra.

At the rear end of their group, an alien froze and fell in pain. The rest of the remaining aliens pulled away from where Noel-Len and Leandra were, their attention on their dying comrade.

Leandra was itching to take them out.

"Not yet," Noel insisted. "They're too far away."

"But . . ."

"Preserve your ammunition."

Another screech sounded closer to where Noel-Len and Leandra crouched.

"No way," she muttered when Anaphora's figure moved through the smoke before them at unimaginable speeds. "Lieutenant Colonel?"

Noel-Len watched as Anaphora used the alien she had recently killed as a shield.

When she was close enough, she flung the body on two other aliens and ducked, before catching the wrist of another alien. Her stance was familiar to Noel-Len, though he didn't know why.

Anaphora shifted one leg behind the alien's leg and hurled him to the ground.

The ground cracked under the force of the motion and Anaphora pulled out her pistol. In close range, she shot the alien in the head. Then she turned her attention to the other alien, the one she had forced into the wall.

She rolled over her shoulder, kneeling before it, she fired her weapon before the alien could aim at her accurately slaughtering it in one shot. She sprinted to the other aliens and took them out hand-to-hand.

Suddenly, Noel-Len realised why he was familiar with her movements.

They were moves taught to commandos or SAS.

When all enemy aliens had fallen, Noel-Len and Leandra stood tall, their gaze never wavering from the super-soldier before them.

"How . . . the . . . hell?" Leandra questioned; her eyes wide as she gawked at their commanding officer.

Within a moment, voices broke through the radio and Noel-Len responded to their Sergeant, who notified them of his imminent approach.

Moments later, as Anaphora returned to retrieve her weapon, Sergeant McGuire and the rest of Noel-Len's unit arrived at the rendezvous point.

"Everyone alright?" McGuire asked. Both Noel-Len and Leandra nodded. McGuire recognised Anaphora's rank and formally introduced himself.

"At ease, soldiers," Anaphora declared, her gaze drifting over what remained of the city. "How many scouting sites have you taken out?"

"Two ma'am," Sergeant McGuire uttered. "The third one was a failure."

"So that means there are eight more," Anaphora said aloud, deep in thought. "Our primary objective is to destroy those scouting sites. The last thing we need is for them to relay our strategies back to the mothership and send in more soldiers." Noel-Len glanced at the largest ship in the sky.

"Ma'am." Curt began, "What intel do you have on what we're up against? That is if you can tell us." Anaphora held Curt's gaze, contemplating his words.

There was only so much she could say. Carefully, she sifted through the appropriate information, determining what could be said and what could not.

"As expected, there's not much I'm permitted to tell you," Anaphora informed the group. "However, what I can tell you is this: these aliens are known as Xzandians. Those aliens you see on the ground there are their foot soldiers, or 'Peon' as we call them, and those pods that you saw are piloted by their officers. They are known as Amorphous. But the rest . . . is classified. I would need permission from the General to give you any further information. As for how to kill them, I assume by now you've figured that out."

Curt nodded. He did not like the idea that his soldiers were fighting a battle almost blindfolded, but he was grateful they were not entirely blind anymore.

Michael had arrived with the Sergeant. When Noel-Len noticed him, he discreetly shook his head at Michael; he knew his friend would demand questions as to why that woman who had taken out the Amorphous was standing before them in their country's uniform. However, he figured he would find out eventually.

Leandra informed both Sergeant and Lieutenant Colonel of what had happened with the suspicious group of soldiers. However, because there was not any evidence, Lieutenant Colonel declared, nothing could be done yet.

Hard evidence, Noel-Len feared, would be hard to come by in a war zone.

At the same time, he could not grasp why another invasion had occurred. Or why the aliens had insisted on destroying their home. Even as Noel-Len listened to Anaphora's next orders, he could not help but wonder—Did they stand a chance? Could they even survive?

He saw Anaphora's strength, but there was only one of her—and, given the scratch on her face, she was not invincible. Regardless, there was a daring look in her eyes. The intensity of it caused him to slide his gaze to the floor.

*She believes we can survive*, he thought. *That is all that matters.*

The group shifted through the fringes of the city, searching for another scouting site, before separating.

Noel-Len's boots snuck over the empty streets. Here, the streets were soiled with fewer carcasses than the central city, but covered in scorched, half-standing buildings. To Noel-Len's left was an abandoned high school.

He observed the empty school with caution. Smoke clouded the air in a fine mist while his surroundings remained silent. As he entered the school grounds, he recalled Anaphora's words before they had split up:

"There are more than just aliens to deal with. Be careful."

Noel-Len had taken down two scouting sites, but he knew that he needed to remove as many aliens as he could. How he would do that was something he could not comprehend. He knew he would run out of ammunition soon, and the thought of battling aliens with a hunting knife was not ideal.

This unfamiliar school screamed danger. Images of the recent firefights and dangerous aliens flickered behind his eyes. He assumed he had seen greater horrors when his mother died. However, that trauma seemed less painful than being attacked by monsters.

Noel-Len could not comprehend Anaphora's warning. The more he thought about it, the more he began to question: what else was there that he would have to deal with? He recalled the strange way the inmate who'd killed Phillip had acted, then the similar behaviour of those civilians. He wondered if they were connected in some way, and if so, what was it that caused their unusual behaviour. From within the open breezeway of the school, a black and white figure raced towards him. Noel-Len fired his rife.

Leaping out of the way, he rolled over his shoulder at the shattering sound of bricks crumbling. On his knees, Noel-Len twisted around and hit the monster in the head with the butt of his gun, shocking the grotesque human. Before the monster could react, Noel-Len pointed his weapon and fired, not stopping until he emptied his round.

The monster's messy black hair was littered with dirt and twigs and hung limp over her thin shoulders. Her casual shirt and jeans were ruined, stained in dried blood.

Stunned but not killed, she remained standing. Noel-Len moved to reload but stopped when she launched herself at him with incredible speed. Her fist struck him in the face and Noel-Len was thrown off balance. His faced ached. The air was knocked out of his longs as he collided with the adjacent wall.

His armour did enough to prevent his bones from shattering under the impact. His helmet protected his head, but his vision faded in and out. Blood flowed in thick wads down his sweat lined neck. He forced his mind to focus on his attacker. She stood fifty metres away and assessed him. He wondered how he was thrown so far away.

Blood pooled at the corner of his aching mouth and over his jaw. He thought it had to be a nightmare. However, the burning twinge in his desperate lungs desperate made it clear: this monster before him was far from any delusion his traumatised mind could conjure.

Her incredible speed stunned him. Swiftly, he pulled out his pistol and fired. She avoided the bullets easily. Her movements were barely visible. When she reached him, fear washed over him, and Noel-Len shielded his face with his hands, hoping it would lessen the final blow.

In place of the blow he expected, an agonising scream pierced his ears. The deranged woman before him had been doused in fire, and now fizzled into a pile of ash. Noel-Len's vision faded, his back slid against the uneven wall, and he crumpled to the ground. The last thing he saw was the fading image of ash at his feet.

When Noel-Len woke, the light of the burning sunset was barely visible over the distant horizon. The warm orange-red glow smeared the sky. He saw the crescent moon hanging beside the familiar Southern Cross. His breath hitched as he groaned, pain shot through his side, and he was certain he had cracked a bone or two.

His mind swirled with a tsunami of images and voices as he climbed to his feet. There was a monster, she had attacked him, then there was fire, but he could not remember how the fire started. He scanned the area around him, his gaze curious as he stared at a pile of ash before his feet.

Awkwardly, he cradled his solar plexus, aware that his hand could not stop the pain of his shallow breathing. He ran his hand over his stomach; everything was untouched. Noel-Len scanned the area around him.

He was alone.

Indiscernible static shouted in his right ear. Frustrated, he yanked out the earpiece to search for the cause of its current abnormalities. The radio itself was undamaged, as was the wire that travelled over his back to his ear. He changed the channels before eventually giving up and placing the earpiece back in his ear. *I'm out of range*, Noel-Len thought, though he did not entirely believe it himself. He located his discarded rifle, the metal cold beneath his stiff fingers. His finger slid over the trigger and when he pulled it, his weapon clicked. Empty.

Battered and beaten, Noel-Len reloaded his rifle and vacated the area, vigilant to the environment around him. He wandered the city, his earpiece buzzing with static, searching. With his rifle at the ready, he slowly passed an empty park; the playground was as empty as the park and scattered with pits of lingering bonfires. The fires reminded him of the day of the Xzandians' first invasion of Earth.

He clearly recalled his mother finding him in the Central Business District of the city, trying to get him to a safe place. Then he remembered her words.

"Stay here. Stay out of sight and stay quiet," Natalia instructed. Her mahogany eyes searched Noel-Len's. There was no sign of fear in them—just the uncertainty of what would play out next.

Gunfire and explosions thundered the air around them. A heavily armed soldier entered the abandoned apartment where Natalia and Noel-Len kneeled.

"Your orders ma'am."

"Hold our current position. When reinforcements come, we'll pursue the target." She watched the soldier walk out before her attention glided back to Noel-Len. With a lingering look, she climbed to her feet, her khaki uniform hidden beneath the Kevlar armour. "Let's go."

With that, Noel-Len was left alone in the apartment. He glanced out the window to the street below and saw silver-armoured aliens shot down by several soldiers.

He had never heard gunfire until that day, nor had he seen fallen soldiers before. Noel-Len recognised his mother's voice, shouting orders. Afraid the monsters were already in the building; he moved from the window and left the apartment. Sprinting down the empty hall, he froze, hearing footsteps climbing the stairs. Noel-Len scanned the hall behind him and ran back into the apartment. He closed the door, but seconds later heard it splinter. He dashed to one of the adjacent rooms. Turning around, he froze when a man opened the door clad in navy blue Kevlar.

"Hello Lenny," the man said, gleam of his teeth shining through the darkness as he leered at the seventeen-year-old boy. "I see you've gotten taller."

Noel-Len stared at the man, unwilling to submit to his fear.

"Who are you?"

"Your worst nightmare, kid."

AN UNUSUAL AND DISTORTED shriek hauled Noel-Len's thoughts back. He scanned his surroundings; certain he was alone. Then he heard an indistinguishable clicking sound, accompanied by frantic footfalls dashing up the road. They were near where he hid in the park behind a tree, waiting for the stranger to reveal themselves. When he recognised her blond hair, pale skin, and fearful sobs, he could not believe his eyes. Then, he heard a shrill voice call,

"She went that way!"

Noel-Len waited. Three soldiers chased the woman down and cornered her at an abandoned police station.

Silently, Noel-Len slipped out from behind the tree and crossed the street, ducking behind a charred car. The woman ran around the corner, and Noel-Len cursed. She was making it difficult for him to stay hidden. At least it was getting darker.

He heard her scream and anger exploded in his chest. Noel-Len rushed over to the men, ignoring the pain at his side, taking two down within a blink of an eye before pulling out a knife and pointing it at the throat of the third man. "Touch her again, and you're a dead man."

Noel-Len recognised the uniform and the soldier before him. Suddenly, Noel-Len and the stranger entered a grudge match of skill. Noel-Len felt handicapped from his recent injuries. When he could not raise his arms high enough to block much of the attacks. Fortunately, Noel-Len was victorious though but not without receiving a few solid blows in return.

"Noel-Len?" Caprice's voice fluttered through the shadows of the oncoming dusk. "It's you . . . isn't it?"

"Caprice, why are you out here?" Noel-Len asked, as he wiped the blood from his lip. Taking her in, he noticed her split lip and the green-black bruises festering over her jaw. "You should be in the barracks. What happened?"

Tears welled in her eyes.

"They killed them." Her voice wavered on each word. "The soldiers at the base. The good ones. They tried to get us out, then these men who looked like soldiers came, but they weren't really soldiers, I think. They killed all the other soldiers and started scanning us with these weird devices. A lot of people were red, but mine was green, so they took me. They killed everyone else, including Mike."

"They did what?" Noel-Len seethed. He then glanced at the ships in the air. He glanced back at her, "Are you sure!"

"I'm sure!" Caprice replied, shocked. She'd never seen him like this.

He recalled the soldiers' conversation that he'd overheard while hidden. His eyes rested on the soldiers at his feet. Swiftly, he searched them. Caprice silently watched him. Noel-Len took the dog-tags from the men at his feet .

"Why are you taking those?" Caprice asked. "How will they be—"

"Identified?" Noel-Len finished. "I was careful to avoid slashing their faces. They will be identifiable. If the Military wants, I'm sure they could hire a forensic anthropologist." *That is, if we're not all wiped off the face of the planet,* he bitterly thought.

"You don't regard your employers very highly."

Noel-Len watched Caprice with indignation, and she felt his anger as he climbed to his feet.

"They've given me enough reason not to. They killed Mike, and they tried to kill you, when their job is to fight for you." He tucked the dog-tags into a side pocket.

"What are you going to do with them?" Caprice asked, her tone softer. Noel-Len could see the shock and fear marring her features. He also saw how much she fought against it.

"Leave them." Noel-Len gripped Caprice's shaky hand and guided her around the corner.

He had not realised it, but he managed to walk from the main city to Palmerston, a smaller town further away. He knew it would be difficult to continue looking for scouting sites with Caprice. He needed her to stay hidden.

"Do you know why that device or whatever you call it . . . turned green?" he asked as they stood before a locked door. He pulled out a tool he'd snuck into his uniform.

He picked the lock.

"I don't know . . . Where did you learn that?" Caprice asked, as he guided her inside and closed the door slowly behind them, carefully peeking between the slit before he completely shut the door.

"My mother," Noel-Len confessed, aware the door would not stay closed if someone were willing enough to investigate the building.

"Your mum? Seriously?"

Ignoring Caprice's question, Noel-Len moved from the door and combed the room. It was a typical office room with a glass panel separating the staff from the incoming criminals. Down the hall, there were more workstations and a small kitchen, plus a unisex toilet.

He waited; when the alarm did not go off, he silently thanked his mother's strange teachings. He spotted a small wooden doorstopper in the corner and wedged it beneath the door.

"Noel-Len?" Caprice began, "What did your mother do?"

"She was a soldier and a detective."

"So, she would know how to break into places and find criminals? Sounds cool," Caprice said admiringly.

"You think my mum was cool?"

"She taught you how to break into a building. Who wouldn't want to know that?" Caprice said. Noel-Len assessed the woman before him with a raised brow. "Not that I'll break into places. I promise."

# Chapter 13

"YOU'RE TOO CALM FOR someone who's been assaulted," Noel-Len remarked, his fingers brushed her blond hair aside eyeing the bruising on her jaw and neck. As she heard the concern in his voice.

"I want to cry . . . but I can't. I think . . . I'm still in shock." Noel-Len saw the slight tremble of her fingers. Swiftly, he found the emergency first aid kit positioned on the wall. Opening the case, he ordered for Caprice to sit. He addressed the bloodied cut on her lip and over her bruise. Breaking the ice pack. He wrapped it in a thin paper towel before handing it to her.

Silently, she accepted it.

Noel-Len studied her a little longer before asking,

"What else happened after they took you?"

Caprice was hesitant and Noel-Len patiently waited for her to continue.

"They threatened to kill me repeatedly."

Hesitantly, Caprice reached out to him, aware of how angry her words had made him.

Noel-Len was unaware that he had climbed to his feet. Her fingers curled in the air after him, empty. Butterflies danced in her stomach. They'd hit her and beat her. She was almost ashamed that she couldn't protect herself.

The thought of it dampened her confidence as memories of his tender touch resurfaced. The way they managed to hit her was not anything like that, and it was a memory she ached to forget. Her entire frame trembled at the memory. She wrapped her arms around herself. The recollection of their beatings and the death of the innocent men and women on the base flooded her mind. It would become a horrible memory she could never relinquish.

Noel-Len called firmly,

"Caprice."

Her name, uttered by his lips, formed a light that shifted her mind from the terrifying memories. He recognised the look in her eyes: It was that same expression he had had when his mother died. The same one when he first saw the death of innocent people. The same one that stared back at him in the mirror, day after day, for the past two years.

Caprice watched Noel-Len. She understood. She knew he knew. A single teardrop grazed her smooth cheek and he closed the distance between them.

Noel-Len's warm fingers traced the skin over her cheek in comfort, and she recoiled as if burnt.

"I will not hurt you," he assured her, hoping his words were enough.

"I know." To her, those words sounded hollow, and Noel-Len's eyes narrowed at her tone.

"You don't believe me." The echo of each syllable filled the space between them.

His hand hung unmoving in the air, centimetres from her face. Noel-Len scrutinised Caprice's pale blue eyes as they slid to his hand then to his face and back again, before he felt the gentle touch of her hand against his. Shakily, she guided it to her face, seared by the memories of her attacker's strikes.

Softly, Noel-Len felt her velvety skin. He sensed warmth radiating off her beneath his touch. It drew him closer, close enough so that he felt her breath against his lips. Images of the night he had given in to his emotions with her played over in his mind, tempting him. Her next words cleared the air between them.

"I believe you. And I trust you. A little . . ."

"A little?"

His brows furrowed. Moving his hand, he brushed his fingers over her loose, messy hair, then cupped her chin.

"Okay. A little more," she mumbled, inching closer to him. He felt her lips graze his. The pressure made him forget about the current dangers of the world around them and the deadly alien invasion at their doors.

Gently, Noel-Len eased out of the tender kiss.

"Caprice," He began. "How did the scanners work?"

She was confused by the sudden question, but she replied,

"They touched my skin with the end of a black device. There was a small screen that lit up green at the opposite end."

Noel-Len stared at the ground between them.

"Why does it matter?" she asked, analysing his reaction.

Noel-Len did not answer. There was something about those scanners that made him rethink every memory of the past few hours and even more so of the invasion day that occurred a few years ago. Caprice's gentle voice broke through his pondering.

"What? What is it?"

Noel-Len straightened.

"Nothing," he declared, climbing to his feet, securing his rifle. The movement reminded him of his aching body and his recent injury. However, he knew he could not rest when he had a mission to complete and when they were not safe. "Stay here until I return."

"Wait," Caprice began. "Where are you going?"

"Out," Noel-Len said pulling the strap of his rifle over his shoulder. Caprice regarded the weapon. Noel-Len turned away from her and to the door, they had recently entered. "I need to do a few things."

Caprice regarded him with worry. She had noticed the flicker of pain across his face as he picked up the rifle. He was injured that much she understood. However, it was his determination that replaced his painful expression. There was a strength to his shoulders that had not been there before. With no other reason to question, she said,

"Okay. Be careful." Noel-Len smiled at her.

"Always," he responded. Pulling out his pistol, he offered it to her.

Caprice took the weapon in hand. Expertly, she removed the magazine, checking the bullets. Turning off the safety, she placed it on the ground beside her. Noel-Len nodded in approval and left before leaving Caprice to secure the door behind him.

He was sure that those men on the base were connected to the men who had pursued him, cornering him and Leandra.

"Where the hell is everyone when you need them?" he grumbled as he stalked through the abandoned streets. He had tried many times to contact his teammates but was always greeted with static. Pain radiated from one side of his body. His lungs desperately fought for air as the pain persisted.

He regretted not telling Caprice to bandage him up. *Stupid pride*, he thought. Attempting to ignore the ache, he scanned his surroundings through his night-vision goggles, and his vision alit on a small pod. He backed towards it. It reminded him of the capsules the robots had appeared in, except, this one was a lot smaller. The capsule was no taller than his waist. On top of the capsule were fibrous fingers sheltering a pulsing cube. Noel-Len regarded the cube and the capsule.

"Did they even tell us how to open it?" Noel-Len muttered as he recalled that day, but it was so long ago he could not recall how the soldiers opened the pods. He was deployed—he was not debriefed in the slightest about how to open it when they came across it. "Great."

He glanced over his shoulder, eyeing the robots at his feet ensuring they were dead. His armour and boots felt heavier.

*I must get that cube and get out,* he thought. *I am not too sure how much longer my body can last.*

He glanced at his left forearm, wrapped in his uniform. Blood soaked his makeshift bandage. The cut itself was large but not deep. He regarded his rifle, aware of his low ammunition. Then turned his attention back to the capsule.

Gunfire echoed. Noel-Len spun around and faced his attacker with his rifle ready. An object fell from the sky. Noel-Len moved towards it, his eyes scanning the surrounding area before he stared at the unusually large, armoured insect. He regarded the exoskeleton armour that enveloped its head and its extra sets of legs, then he heard a voice.

"It's called a Mortius," a male voice declared. Noel-Len swung around and aimed his gun at the man, who walked towards him with his hands held up. "I'm on your side, remember?"

"Who are you?" Noel-Len asked. His eyes scanned the familiar uniform, gear, weapons, as well as the rank patch on his chest and the name on the left side of his chest. Lowering his rifle, he waited for the man to respond.

"People call me Michaels. James Michaels," he said. "I'm with the SAS."

"Really?" Noel-Len asked the soldier, doubt prominent in his voice.

James twisted his body around, showing the patch colours on his arm. Noel-Len recognised the code of arms and the division, he represented. "Believe me now?" he asked.

Noel-Len regarded the man with a pointed gaze. "Aren't you supposed to be in Orange?"

"Everyone who's with the first and second division was deployed here immediately after the initial attack."

Noel-Len glanced back at the pod.

"What do you call that?" Noel-Len asked.

"The Beacon," James said as he moved over to it, pulling out a hunting knife. He sliced the thick, stringy purple fibres. James's goggled eyes landed on Noel-Len before continuing to pry his way to the cube. "Want to watch my ass?" James questioned, smirking at Noel-Len's confused reaction. James nodded down the street, filled with carcasses of both human and non-human alike before he returned his attention to the cube.

"Got it," Noel-Len replied, positioning himself behind James, pointing his rifle down the road. "Where's the rest of your unit?" Noel-Len's eyes looked everywhere except at the unfortunate outlines of human bodies.

"Scattered."

"Why?"

"It's quicker to find the scouting sites by covering more ground. I mean isn't that why you're here—all alone?" James extracted the cube. He held the cube in his gloved hand, pulled out an empty metal box, and placed the cube inside. The box folded around the cube without James's interference as he tucked it away into his pack.

"So that's the thing we're supposed to find and secure?" Noel-Len thought aloud.

"Were you not listening when you were debriefed?" James asked, with a smile on his thin lips. Noel-Len glared at the man, even if the man could not exactly see his scowl.

"Last time I checked, this wasn't exactly planned and no I wasn't." Noel-Len remarked. "It happened when everyone least expected it."

"Is that what you think?"

Noel-Len stared at the man, his expression dark.

"Yes."

James turned from him.

"Well, I'm certain there's a few more left. Looks like we're going to be at this for a while." He marched down the road before calling back to Noel-Len, "Are you coming or not?"

Noel-Len knew he had to complete his mission, but he also knew that he had to return to Caprice as soon as possible. Without another word, Noel-Len followed the SAS soldier, aware that tonight would be a little too long.

Later that evening, both James and Noel-Len crouched behind a wall. Cautiously, James peered around the corner. The silver robots that both he and Noel-Len had constantly run into were presently guarding the last remaining beacon. James consulted the pulsating light of the cube and the beam of light that shot up into the skies.

Moments later, a human girl in a full silver pyjama suit, walked up to the aliens. Noel-Len heard James curse and he regarded the tightness of his jaw.

"What's wrong?" Noel-Len asked.

"There's a girl," James replied. "She's walking up to the aliens."

Noel-Len moved to look but James pushed him back against the brick wall.

"She's going to get herself killed," Noel-Len grunted in pain.

"We can't blow our position if we want that cube," James growled. "How badly are you injured?" His eyes ran over Noel-Len's damaged forearm.

Noel-Len eventually replied,

"I'm not exactly sure. I think I broke my lower ribs because it's sometimes hard to breathe. Not all the time. Painful to move—yes. One of those aliens stabbed their ridiculously huge knife through my left forearm because I stupidly tried to block it. The only good thing is, I haven't been shot yet. So, you tell me how badly I am injured right now because I don't know."

James did not speak, his gaze pinned to the beacon. *It's going to be a long night*, he thought.

Noel-Len jumped in surprise as the girl in the silver pyjamas came around the corner and crouched in front of him with black eyes and a sharp canine smile.

James drew his pistol. The barrel was inches from the girls' head. Before she could attack, he fired.

The sound of that single shot echoed in Noel-Len's mind as he watched the girl fall to the ground. Both, James, and Noel-Len stared at the girl, waiting for her to leap to her feet and follow up with her intent to kill. To their relief she remained on the ground, motionless. Recognising that they would have been heard, James quickly ushered Noel-Len to move; the Xzandians that had been guarding the cube rounded the corner just as both men made it out of sight. The aliens spoke to each other in an unfamiliar language before turning back to their posts.

"We need a distraction," James declared, then glanced at Noel-Len.

"Shit," Noel-Len responded, not liking what he had in mind. Once James laid out the plan, Noel-Len got into position. He took a deep breath, then ran to the other side of the street, catching the

Xzandian's attention. Bullets fired after Noel-Len, who leapt behind a car, cursing as he was struck in the arm.

While Noel-Len was gone, James rose to his feet and moved over to the beacon. Once, Noel-Len ran around the building to make sure he had lost the aliens, he returned to James. James quickly began to remove the cube.

"You sure this is the last beacon?"

"Positive," James said as he held up a screen, revealing a map of Darwin and the surrounding suburbs including Casuarina and Palmerston. There was nothing on the map except for a large yellow dot. "That yellow dot you see is the beacon." James zoomed further out. "As far as I can see, there are no more."

"That's reassuring." A few moment later, Noel-Len asked, "Have you run into others like me?"

"You mean a . . . doe?" James remarked, and Noel-Len rolled his eyes. He was not too sure when he would get used to being referred to that.

"Exactly, gaz."

"I'm not too sure if you're being sarcastic or not," James said, his eyes critical. Neither man uttered a word while the air sparked with ferocious electricity. Finally, James's attention returned to the cube, which, like the others was placed into a metal box.

To Noel-Len's surprise the communication channel connecting him to his comrades skipped to life. Noel-Len's fingers slid over his earpiece, hearing the voices of Leandra and the others. Noel-Len glanced back at James.

"We have the last cube, so what now?" Noel-Len asked.

James pulled out a small gun.

"Now we let the others know." James pointed the small weapon into the air and Noel-Len waited. A yellow flare sprung into the air then James reloaded the small gun and a green flare followed soon after. Noel-Len at once heard the voice of Sergeant McGuire, then Lieutenant Colonel Valdis.

"They're on their way."

Then the Xzandians returned, and Noel-Len and James fired their rifles on them; their bodies fell to the ground.

Not too long after that, Noel-Len's team and James's team arrived at the last de-commissioned scouting site. Introductions were made, and Noel-Len pulled Michael over.

"I can't believe you're still alive!" he said. Michael rolled his eyes.

"Of course, I am! Idiot!"

Sergeant McGuire regarded Noel-Len and Michael and waited for Anaphora to supply the next set of orders.

"Now that the scouting sites have been neutralised and we have the beacons, we're required to return to base to properly secure them," Anaphora said. Pulling out a compass, she marched towards the direction of the barracks.

Sergeant McGuire soon followed, as did Sergeant James Michaels. Noel-Len regarded James's back, conflicted.

"What's wrong?" Leandra asked from beside Noel-Len, eyeing his crossed arms and clear frown.

"Nothing," Noel-Len spoke, watching as the other four members, James's team who followed him. Noel-Len was not too sure about how he was going to return to Caprice so instead, he began, "Lieutenant Colonel, ma'am?" Anaphora stopped and turned to Noel-Len. "There's a civilian. She was on base when it was . . . infiltrated." Noel-Len could feel the calculating gaze of his superior officer as well as those from the soldiers beside him. Everyone remained silent, listening to his next words.

"What do you mean by . . . infiltrated?" Anaphora questioned; her tone inquisitive. The thought of their place of operations and the sensitive information being compromised did not sit too well with her.

"Civilians and soldiers killed, ma'am."

"Can you provide evidence of your claim?" Anaphora asked.

"I can. The civilian is a witness and can testify to it."

"This civilian, what is his name?"

"The civilian is female, ma'am." Noel-Len knew that Michael was beginning to draw his conclusions. By the confused and wary expression his friend's face, Noel-Len knew Michael feared the worst. "Her name's Caprice."

If Anaphora recognised the name, she did not show it.

"I understand, she's a valuable witness. Sergeant McGuire, I will need you, Private Williams, Private Jones, and Private Hugh from Sergeant Michaels' unit to retrieve the civilian. Everyone else will return to the designated area on their devices." Anaphora glanced at her watch and Noel-Len did not need to be told the time to know he had been up all night. The sky in the distance was a little lighter than the west side of the sky. "Your expected ETA, two hours."

"Understood, ma'am." Noel-Len acknowledged with a salute. Sergeant McGuire, Michael, Leandra, and Andrew swiftly saluted. Anaphora returned their salute and dismissed them. Swiftly, the group left. Noel-Len muttered to Michael,

"Fifteen minutes prior to fifteen minutes."

"Sounds about right," he smiled.

BACK AT THE ABANDONED police station, Caprice sat on the ground, her knees pulled to her chest. Her eyes never drifted from the door. She sat like that for hours, waiting for Noel-Len's return. Her rear ached, and her muscles were stiff. She was terrified that Noel-Len would return to find her injured from sitting in the same place for so long, but also afraid that someone might creep in when her back was turned. She'd never thought a war would make her paranoid. But she knew she wasn't the only one.

Suddenly, she heard voices. She glanced around the office, searching for windows, hoping that she could see where the noise was coming from.

A loud bang sounded from behind her. Caprice spun around and faced the sound originating from outside the closed, glass-tinted doors. She crawled to the bench and knelt beside the office chair. Peeking over the counter and through the glass panel, she spotted two figures before the glass and watched as they became larger shadows.

She could overhear their muffled conversation.

"This is where it stops," one said.

There was silence before another voice asked,

"Do you think anyone's inside?"

"Not sure."

"Want to find out?" A moment later, their figures grew. She recognised the shape of their rifles and the outline of their figures. They were soldiers. Caprice started to move to a better hiding spot but froze when she heard the glass doors shatter.

"Hey, what about stealth?"

"What about it?" the other man asked rudely. Caprice's eyes landed on the door that she and Noel-Len had entered. She glanced at the pistol, still on the ground beside her. *I could always shoot them*, she thought. However, Caprice knew that they would be wearing body armour and the thought of her being a perfect shot was far from reality. The last time she shot a gun was over six months ago, at a firing range.

Decisively, Caprice moved to the pistol and crawled to the door, her fingers prying at the wooden door stopper. She removed it and tossed it to the side. Glancing over her shoulder, she saw the soldiers entering the building. Swiftly, she opened the door and snuck out, closing the door behind her quietly enough, that they would not hear it.

As Caprice exited the building, she froze. A familiar man stood before her, clad in a military uniform. Caprice felt her stomach flutter in fear as she gazed upon the man who had originally oversaw her abduction. "There you are. Cannot have someone like you running from me, now can I?" Caprice slowly backed away. She heard the woman beside him, his second-in-command, whisper orders into a Bluetooth device.

"You know misbehaving women ought to be punished," declared a voice. Caprice turned around and behind her were the two soldiers that entered the building. "Told you she was there, Patrick."

Caprice held a fierce glare as she scowled at her hunters, but Patrick simply smiled at her, causing her insides to twist in disgust.

"I'm sorry I didn't believe you, Eric."

"Private Johnson. Private Smith. Find Private James," the female soldier ordered.

"Ma'am." Swiftly, Caprice pointed the barrel of her gun at the man, responsible for the death of everyone at the base. In return, Caprice felt everyone's rifles point at her. She was uncertain why she was doing something so stupid, but she was terrified of this man and the leer on his face. The gun was the only thing that separated him from her, and that was how she wanted it.

"Now, now, Caprice why don't we talk about this?" he asked, his pale lips still smiling. Before Caprice could pull the trigger, someone else did. Unimaginable pain shot through her calf, stunning her entire system, followed by a sudden strike that made her loose grip of the gun.

She fell to the ground, unconscious. The bullet wound on her calf spouted blood as the group closed around her.

"Stupid woman. She doesn't know how valuable she is." The soldier who had shot her glanced at Corporal Melissa McGuire. "Stop her from bleeding, will you?" Melissa knelt beside Caprice and bandaged her wound.

Captain Ethan Wilson inspected the unconscious woman, then grinned. Everything he needed to complete his mission was falling into place. The last thing he needed was Midnight Eclipse. Then he would be ready to negotiate.

# Chapter 14

GOTHALIA AND DANTEUS giggled and kissed and giggled some more. Then his communicator beeped and Gothalia regarded it with a knowing look.

"Duty calls," he declared and Gothalia pouted.

"Do you have to go?" she asked, knowing the answer.

"You know I have to," he stated and pecked her on the lips. "But I'll see you soon."

"Okay. See you soon."

Fifteen minutes later, Gothalia roamed the halls of her home. As she did, she heard a noise echoing down the silent corridors. She knew she should be on edge because she knew this would be the first place they'd look as she walked the halls; she couldn't help but consider that it was for the best they found her. *I deserve whatever happens.*

The clamour grew louder as she meandered the corridors and down the wide marble staircase. Mystified by the noise, she kept her guard up. Stepping down the stairs quietly, she heard the noise echo from the kitchen.

Glancing at an antique weapon beside her, she plucked it from the wall before venturing to the noise. Hesitantly, she moved into the kitchen, ensuring the door swung closed behind her.

Near the commercial fridge was a wooden baseball bat and she wondered when she had put it there. *Unless . . . L'Eiron, a baseball bat? Really?* Ignoring the bat, she twisted the broadsword around in hand. The noise which intensified with each of her steps. *Someone's here*, she thought. Her heart drummed in her chest.

Her silent boots wandered over the white marble floor. A dark figure was illuminated by the lights of the courtyard; she saw it as she leaned against the wall, her sword resting over her shoulder. The external security light in the gardens shone into the house and outlined the kitchen and the figure.

Gothalia's vision sharped, and she made out the coffee machine, pantry, sink and table opposite her. Creeping around the corner, she identified the shape of the person's face and swung. Simultaneously, she felt her sword slice through skin, as an object connected with her jaw. Colliding with the ground, Gothalia's vision blurred. A voice declared,

"I can't believe you're a Centurion let alone an Excelian. Taken out by something like that, you're pathetic."

*That voice*, Gothalia thought.

"*You . . .!*"

"Yes, me. The name's Numitora." Effectively, pinning Gothalia down, she taunted, "So, I'm curious—how did your comrades' family take to their deaths? Did they mourn?" Gothalia recognised the glint of humour in her eyes and anger rushed beneath her skin, before surfacing in an explosion of fire. Throwing Numitora from her, Gothalia flipped onto her feet before charging at the enemy.

"I'll kill you!" Gothalia yelled. The woman, leering, blocked and dodged most Gothalia's stream of fire attacks, kicks, and punches. A flurry of ice and fire permeated the old house, scorching the walls and cracking the black marble floor.

Gothalia was forced through the glass window and onto the roof of a lower building. Rolling over her shoulder, she climbed to her feet and sprinted at the woman, who turned the roof to ice.

Surprised, Gothalia lost balance and the woman threw a kick at Gothalia, effectively throwing her from the roof.

Before Gothalia hit the ground, she threw her hands forward and fire erupted from her palms, slowing her descent.

"That hurt," she mumbled, as she hit the ground and rolled out of the way, barely avoiding the icicles thrown at her from above.

"Why won't you stay down?" Numitora growled, impatient.

"That's not my style," Gothalia replied, Numitora's frustration momentarily allowing her to forget her own internal turmoil.

Numitora's impatience shifted into anger, and she rushed at Gothalia with surprising speed, throwing tornado kicks and punches that Gothalia barely managed to avoid.

The impact of Numitora's punches and kicks made her suspect that Anaphora had been going easy on her in all of her training sessions.

A flare of light surprised Gothalia, to Numitora's delight. She threw a roundhouse at Gothalia's head, forcing her to fall to the hard ground, stunned.

"See, little Valdis, I'm the better fighter," Numitora proclaimed, standing over the other woman.

She whistled and several tall figures moved from the shadows into the light. Black leather armour covered their bodies from head to toe, masking their faces.

Gothalia saw the world through a haze of confusion and disorientation.

"Grab her. She's coming with us."

Gothalia felt hands yank her upright, and she was thrown over the shoulder of one man. Her mind spun and all she wanted to do was sleep, but she knew she should not close her eyes, even as the darkness threatened to pull her under.

They started to move but stopped suddenly.

"She's not going anywhere with you," said a deep voice, within the darkness.

"Well, well, well . . . look who it is . . ." Numitora purred, her voice almost delighted. "Lord Berith Barak of the clan of lightning. The Lord of Lightning. Tell me what business you have with this poor excuse for an Excelian."

He did not reply. His gold-crimson eyes glowed in the darkness, like deadly animal's.

"You cannot take her, Numitora."

"Aren't you at least concerned with why I want her? Or are you just doing Anaphora's bidding?" Numitora questioned. "You're a Colonel of the Dragon Core unit. You don't answer to her to do you? So, who do you answer to?"

He remained quiet.

"Fine. Your silence will be the cause of her death. I will kill her before you can move. Set her down." Gothalia felt the same hands that carried her pull her from where she lay and set her on the ground. Her vision cleared and she glanced up at the man who stood between Numitora and her escape, surprised.

"Lord Barak?" Gothalia mumbled. Not once did he glance at her. His eyes focused solely on Numitora, who quickly created an icy diamond sword that glittered with sharpness.

"So, what will it be? You step aside or I run her through?" Numitora taunted, standing over Gothalia. When Berith did not answer, Numitora gripped her sword and pressed it towards Gothalia's back. Without warning, the Earth shifted like the waves of an ocean.

Numitora and her comrades were thrown off balance and Gothalia crawled to her knees, cradling her tender arm.

Danteus sprinted into the courtyard with Demetria and Asashin following.

"Who the hell are they?" Demetria asked, eyeing the men clad in dark uniforms.

"Who cares!" Danteus retorted, running over to Gothalia as she climbed to her feet. Her head hammered but the world did not shift as it had before. "Careful, you may have a concussion."

"You said that last time. I'm an Excelian, I don't get concussions." Gothalia retorted.

"All Excelians were Human once." Danteus remarked. "Can you walk?"

"I'm fine. Where is she?" Gothalia demanded, with spite and scanned the area for the woman. *I will end her*, she thought breathing heavily between the loose strands of dark hair that framed her face.

A loud noise thundered, and everyone's attention was drawn to Numitora and Berith.

Electricity sparked along Berith's body and to the ground before sliding along the earth and leaping into the air. Gothalia felt her skin tremble at the sudden change in temperature and glanced at Demetria.

"We should get going." Danteus prompted.

"Why? She's my prey. I will be the first to end her. Especially after everything she's done!"

"We get that. You'll get another chance, but let's just say—" Before Danteus could say anything further, Berith called,

"Danteus, get them out of here. It may get messy but keep her safe."

Gothalia glared at Berith.

"I'm not some child that needs protection and Numitora will die by my hand!"

Danteus stepped before her.

"You're coming with us," Danteus said. When Gothalia didn't respond, her gaze still on Barak he growled. "Gothalia! Let's go."

Pulling her away from the fight. Everyone halted, as Numitora's soldiers hindered their escape. "But first, we have to deal with them."

"You think?" Demetria said sarcastically. She froze the first row of soldiers straight away, but the others escaped and ran towards her with rifles and swords.

Gothalia sprinted to the frozen soldiers. Using her fire, she shattered their bodies then fought the unfrozen soldiers while Danteus created mud pools and quicksand.

The soldier's numbers grew and Gothalia wondered where they were coming from. Quickly, she made for an opening and sprinted to the far gate.

"What you are doing?" Danteus yelled, over the sound of the fight.

She ignored Danteus and eyed the open gate, through which the soldiers entered. Effortlessly, she closed old the gate by cutting the rope with her sword.

Then began to fight the last soldiers.

"Next time let us in on your plan," Danteus hissed from beside Demetria, as she froze and cut down several more soldiers with her sword.

"How did you guys get here?" Gothalia demanded, deflecting, and blocking a few attacks.

"The road. Why?" Demetria yelled back as she kicked one solider to the ground. Rolling over her shoulder, she slipped past one enemy and cut his calf. She did not wait for him to drop to the ground, instead stabbing the soldier she had kicked.

"Did you see any more on the way?" Gothalia asked.

"No! Again, why?" Demetria questioned, blocking an attack.

"Because that road leads to the city," Danteus replied in place of Gothalia, annoyed. He cursed beneath his breath.

Gothalia sprinted to the line of soldiers and leapt into action. Kneeing the first soldier in the jaw, she pushed him to the ground as her palms erupted in flames. Her flaming fingers slit his throat as she threw fireballs at her oncoming opponents.

"If they get past the bridge—everyone will be in danger!" Gothalia yelled, loud enough for Berith to hear her, and Numitora's deadly smile shifted to a hardened frown.

Gothalia glanced back at the large gate. They had wanted her to close it. She cursed.

"Danteus you think you can oversee things here?"

"No problem."

"Where are you going?" Demetria asked, avoiding the string of bullets fired by the enemy. "You're going to go after them, aren't you? There's too many, wait for us!"

"I'll be fine. Just remove them from the premises." She called back, not bothering to glance at either of them. Her heart hammered against her chest and sweat dotted her features.

When she reached the top of the wall, she saw that enemy soldiers were advancing down the ragged road that wound up to the small hill at the edge of the city.

Long ago, before New Icarus became a city and before the Fire Reserve became a country—even before it had a Royal family, Grand Elders, and Seers—this place was chosen as a sanctuary by their earliest ancestors.

Gothalia's ancestors had driven out the lava, eradicating the heat from the chamber floor, leaving cold black earth behind. At that time, the ancient Earth users had moulded the city and carved the riverways that forged the early aqueducts.

It was the ancient water users who readily filtered water from the underground reservoirs for those who were not gifted with Regalis blood but were Caligati—this did not mean they were any less than Excelians.

Gothalia knew every elemental user both of Regalis descent and Caligati blood had a purpose. She understood a little bit more now what Anaphora had always tried to instil in her: *"Our job is to safeguard, not to encourage an attack on our home and its people."*

She knew the enemy soldiers were Human.

"Explains why they're easy to take down and why there's so many," she muttered to herself as they moved slowly but cautiously throughout their street.

Their presence would upset the balance her ancestors had worked so hard to keep. She saw their retreating forms and spotted no insignia indicating another Reserve, but their uniform was one colour—black with leather paddings and modern tactical gear. *How did they get inside?* she wondered, as she caught up to the rear of the group.

They noticed her presence immediately. She fought them hard, removing the soldiers from the road with her flames. Still, they pressed forward and to the beginning of the city gates, while others faced her. She cursed; aware they were deliberately slowing her down.

She did not have her gear on, nor any way of contacting L'Eiron and the others, but she knew she could not admit defeat. She had to stop them—this was what she was trained for.

Amongst it all, she had a horrible hunch that she could not stop anyone dying. *But I will limit the body count*, she promised herself.

Terror induced screams pierced the air and her determination lapsed.

Bullets fired from a distance, as Gothalia dropped to the ground and kicked her flames at the closest soldiers. She surprised them, which gave her the opportunity she needed to disarm them. Picking up one of the rifles, she kneeled, aimed, aid fired, taking out several soldiers who had not reacted fast enough.

A soldier concealed himself in the shadows of the shrubs at the base of the road and shot at her. Firing her recently acquired rifle, she moved slowly along the road. A grenade was hurled into the air—with a leap, she twisted in mid-air, kicking the grenade back at the soldier who had thrown it.

She sprinted down the road and leapt over the edge of the cliff and to the ground below, avoiding the bullets they fired at her. She dropped onto an old path that led to the city where the lava didn't touch.

Without another thought, she sprinted up the path and towards the city.

"Looks like studying Human warfare and their weapons has its advantages. I'll never argue with L'Eiron again," she muttered to herself, then slung the rifle over her shoulder.

When Gothalia reached the streets of New Icarus, the capital city of the Fire Reserve, her ears caught the screams of the citizens, who ran in fear of the rifles the intruders held. She followed the pop of the rifles taking out the men who she ran into by chance. After she shot one, she curled over his body and patted down his uniform searching for the radio and earpiece. Putting it in her ear, she heard their orders and their locations.

"The flame is up ahead, two clicks north." the radio said.

Her heart sank and her skin chilled. Gothalia's eyes lingered over the buildings beside her. Then she quickly scaled one. Her muscles burned against the artificial night air as she peered in the direction of where the soldiers clustered within the city.

The worst part was the fresh silence.

Her gaze drifted to a fortress in the distance. It was not the Cetatea. "Oh no," she muttered, and sprinted along the buildings of New Icarus, avoiding the soldiers as much as she could. She cursed under her breath, scolding herself for neglecting her radio.

Finally, she arrived at the Centratus Bastion, the home of the Royal family. Everything appeared peaceful—until her attention was caught by a figure at the corner of her eye, swiftly climbing over buildings a few meters away. A flicker of red in the field of silent darkness pulled her closer to the moving figure.

"He wouldn't . . ." she muttered, then groaned, "but he would." Then recognised the man that jumped over rooves was Prince Leviathan, someone she knew shouldn't be active now of all times. Especially, when the Alastorians and soldiers were after him.

Quickly, she chased after him.

Prince Leviathan, clad in Centurion clothes, fired an arrow, which erupted into a brilliant red explosion. His red hair gleamed beneath the artificial moon, reminding her of an angel of death. He fought the soldiers and Alastorians without fear.

She stared at her enemies curiously, Human soldiers and Alastorians working together . . . The thought would have never crossed her mind.

She dropped from the building and to the streets below. The citizens of New Icarus were momentarily stunned by her behaviour as she sprinted down the road—towards the unsuspecting Alastorians. She yelled at the Excelian men and women.

"Get off the streets!"

"Who are you to tell us what to do?" A nearby man questioned, his wife and child beside him.

Gothalia ignored his comment, seeing the Alastorian behind him ready to kill. Those around the family noticed the danger and screamed in terror, running for shelter. Gothalia pointed her rifle and fired, aiming for the Alastorian's head. The bullet took the monster down. The man and his family ran while Gothalia battled the rest, buying as much time as she could for them to get away.

Her fists burnt in brilliant flames as several Alastorians attacked her from all sides. She launched herself at them, allowing her flames to erupt into explosions at the mere touch of her hand against their rough dry skin.

Her eyes glittered in deathly crimson. Rushing past the houses, she had noticed Prince Leviathan on the furthest house and a soldier aiming a rifle at him. In her ear, she heard one soldier order: "Take him out."

She knocked that soldier down, and her flames engulfed him, but the bullet vacated the barrel. Fear consumed her as once the soldier was taken out and she could no longer see the Prince.

The Alastorians scampered towards her and she battled them, bit by bit edging closer to his Highness. Once there was a break in the Alastorian defence, she took her chances and scaled a building. Her lungs burnt.

"Please don't be dead. Please do not be dead," she muttered repeatedly, running to him after discarding her empty rifle. She picked up his discarded bow and arrows and fired the arrows at the Alastorians, taking them out one by one.

"Prince Leviathan!" she yelled. "Stay down!"

She flipped out of the way as the prince crawled to his feet. She dropped his bow and what was left of his arrows before him, while fire erupted from her fists at the Alastorians. Then arrows took down the Alastorians and Gothalia burnt those who would he missed.

"What are you doing outside of the Palace?" Gothalia growled, fire detonating around them in rapid explosions.

"I was going for an evening stroll," he answered, without a hint of amusement.

"What a great idea," Gothalia replied, sarcastically.

Running to the closest Alastorian, she threw it to the ground before burning it.

"I've been attacked! I could do without the sarcasm!" He rolled over his shoulder and stabbed another Alastorian in the head.

"You started it," she muttered, and she stepped away to the edge of the building with Levi beside her. Levi pulled out and fired a blunt arrow with a bag hanging from it.

"Gothalia!" he cried. Without thought or question, Gothalia tossed fire at the arrow and a large explosion erupted, throwing them from the top of the building and into the open courtyard below.

Levi laughed through winded breaths, after a moment.

"It worked." The arrow had eradicated what was left of the Alastorians.

Gothalia climbed to her elbows and glared at the Prince.

"Gunpowder? really?"

"What? We're alive, aren't we?"

Gothalia's muscles ached. She peered at Levi. He was no better. *They are going to kill us*, she thought, her teeth clenched. Off to the far side of the courtyard, a Human soldier lay flat on his stomach, a sniper rifle in hand.

"If that didn't kill us, he will," Gothalia whispered. Levi glanced at her and she shoved him to the ground.

They never heard the bullet.

Instead they heard only their panting, then Gothalia's ear-piercing scream.

Gothalia's arm burnt in pain as she fell on the ground, rolling onto her back to clutch her injured arm. She forced her mind to relax and listen to Levi's voice as he called out to her fearfully.

Levi spotted the man in the distance, lying in the shadows with his rifle propped in front of him on a stand. Without thinking, the Prince rolled to his knees as fast as he could and fired his arrow.

The soldier fell. Gothalia groaned and pulled herself up, cradling her arm and ignoring the blood seeping through her fingers. She felt pain radiate throughout her body but suppressed a scream.

"Are you okay?" Gothalia asked Levi with a forced smile. Levi smiled down at her; grateful they were both alive.

"I'm okay." Then he noticed the blood pouring over her exposed fingers. "You're hurt."

"I'll be fine," she uttered, mentally, trying to focus on anything else other than the searing pain in her arm. "It's just a flesh wound."

"That's not a flesh wound. It's too much blood." Levi said. He removed his coat and pulled a strap from one of the fallen soldiers before returning to Gothalia. He wound torn the fabric of his coat around her injured arm before securing it tightly with the strap.

Then, he studied her.

Her clammy skin glistened beneath the streetlights and he recognised her rapid panting and unusual pale complexion. "Gothalia are you okay? You don't look too good."

# Chapter 15

"I'M FINE. JUST NEED to rest." After a moment of silence, she asked, "What were you doing outside of the palace walls?" Her dark, accusing eyes rested on him.

"I . . . um . . ." Levi could not find the words and Gothalia's eyes narrowed.

"How many times have you been told not to go anywhere unaccompanied? What would your mother think? I know she'd be horrified to find out something happened to you."

"But it didn't. I'm fine."

"Yes, but you were close. That sniper was not aiming for me. He knew we'd be distracted, and he took his opportunity from the shadows." Gothalia's gaze drifted to the fallen soldier, her gaze staring at the arrow in his chest. "There are others. We need to move."

Gothalia climb to her feet unsteadily, then dropped to her knees, feeling frailer than she had ever felt. She glared at the ground. Her body refused to respond.

"Here," Levi said, threading her uninjured arm around his shoulders and helping her limp down the road. As they travelled, she listened to the earpiece; they were calling for the man Levi had taken out. "Is that them?"

"Yeah, it is." As she listened, she guided Levi in the opposite direction of their forces. They needed to get to the Cetatea, they were under attack. *What of the Foreseers, did they know? What about the Grand Elders?*

"Yes. I don't know how, but they passed the wards. Wards that held against lava, earthquakes, and countless other attacks from other Reserves for centuries . . . Why did they suddenly fall to Humans?" Gothalia spat. Levi did not speak as he guided her.

When they finally reached the walls of the fortress, the guards drew their swords on Gothalia and she sneered at them.

"Listen," she tried. "Humans have breached the Reserve. They tried to kill Prince Leviathan. His highness needs sanctuary!"

Gothalia's stomach stung. Now that the adrenaline had faded, she felt the pain, and her body screamed in agony. She had taken more hits than she realized.

She recognised a voice, Lord Michalis Drakeus, and eyed him as he wandered down the wide stone stairs. Her eyes flickered to the guards; she recognised the Cratians, the Grand Elder's guards.

"Dear child what happened to you?" he asked. Then he glanced at Levi. "Don't just stand there, bring her inside so the physician can see her, and before she gets an infection!" He glanced at the other guards; his gaze hard. "Scan the rest of the city thoroughly to the East and find Numitora. Take the Human Soldiers as prisoners. I want her found and I want her found *now*. She has not left the city walls yet. The Seer has confirmed that."

"Seer?" Gothalia probed. Michalis caught her question but turned away from her, refusing to let her to glimpse the pain and defeat in his countenance as he scurried up the stairs.

Levi followed, helping Gothalia.

"Doesn't he mean *Seers*?" she asked Levi, who remained silent. His eyes mirrored her concern. "They didn't . . ."

"I'm not sure. I heard Rangers speaking to my father in the throne room. They were overly concerned . . . I don't think . . ."

They reached the landing at the top of the flight of stairs. Gothalia ignored the deadly glares thrown at her by the Centurion Peacekeepers. Levi glared at them in response and they faltered at his anger.

She knew she would be dragged away to the prisons to rot with those Humans. Michalis would not allow her actions to go freely without consequence. His sense of justice was what made him a great and respected leader.

"Levi, what did you mean when you said that the Rangers who spoke to your father were concerned?" Gothalia asked when they were out of reach of the hostile peacekeepers and deep in the halls of the Cetatea.

"Concerned probably isn't the appropriate word. Scared. I think whatever they discussed had something to do with the Seers." Levi responded before Gothalia heard Michalis call once more for a physician, this time louder.

Gothalia's reality began to fade in and out, accompanied by a hammering headache.

Her abused body fought to stay awake. Levi's features contorted into concern, as he eyed the pooling blood on the ground at their feet.

Gothalia's thoughts slipped from her mind little by little, and she eyed the Cetatea's marble floors with almost no recognition. She heard a rush of thundering footfalls and saw Levi hover over her but could not hear his alarmed cries. Nor could she feel his grip, tightening around her when she couldn't keep herself upright.

Michalis stood over her too, equally alarmed. Then, darkness washed over her, and in the dark void, she heard a voice cry,

"Gothalia!"

DANTEUS AND DEMETRIA fought the soldiers until there was no threat left; their bodies scattered the courtyard—a reminder of victory. Numitora, the only survivor, barely held her own against Berith's attacks.

"Not so overconfident, now is she?" Demetria remarked cockily, her hands on her hips.

Danteus peered in the direction that Gothalia had set off on.

"Stay here," he ordered, before turning to leave. "I'm going after Gothalia."

"Wait!" Demetria called, reaching her hand out to him. "You can't just leave me." Then he was gone, leaving Demetria staring after where he had left her. "But he did. That jerk. What kind of teammate are you?" she shouted after him before her eyes returned to Berith.

"I won't ask again," Berith declared, with a smooth voice, his golden eyes lingering over Numitora's icy blue ones with indifference. "Stand down, and I will refrain from harming you."

"Never," she seethed forming another ice sword. "Do what you must, but I will not back down."

"Then you leave me no choice," he uttered, his hand erupting in electricity. Without a second thought, he moved faster than she had ever seen him move and struck her down.

"Ouch," Demetria muttered when Numitora hit with the ground. "That's got to leave a mark." Berith straightened and regarded Numitora's unconscious form. Then he placed his hand to his earpiece and said,

"Threat neutralised."

Demetria regarded him and thought, *what's going on here?*

DANTEUS RAN DOWN THE streets of New Icarus with haste.

"Why do I have this weird feeling something's wrong?" he muttered to himself, continuing past the citizens, who regarded him with astonishment. He turned down a few corners, then heard the screech of an Alastorian and the scream of civilians nearby. He sped up his pace and rounded a corner where an Alastorian towered over a family. Danteus knocked the monster aside. Before the Alastorian could rise to its feet, he removed a spear-shaped piece of earth from the ground and threw it at the Alastorian, pinning it to the wall.

The family gasped in surprise, forcing the children to look away. The man uttered,

"Thank you"

He was surprised to the see the Alastorians but supressed his astonishment and nodded, then was on his way once again to the Cetatea. Upon his arrival, the guards regarded him strangely, but he ignored them as he climbed the grand stairs.

Then he saw Levi.

"Your highness," he greeted, with a hand over his heart and a bow.

"Danteus."

"Have you seen, Gothalia?"

"I have."

"And—?"

"It's not good."

Danteus's heart sank.

"What do you mean?" he asked, attempting to hide the fear he felt.

"I mean Gothalia's been taken by the Cratians. She has broken laws. My father told me ages ago but still it's a little hard to believe."

Danteus glanced away, uncertain on how to explain the past happenings to his highness. He wondered if it was best that Levi did not know.

"What?" Levi asked, catching the guilt flashing across Danteus's face. "What do you know that I don't?"

Danteus swallowed.

"There were laws Gothalia broke," he said at last. His words tasted bitter in his mouth. "And because of that, she's expected to be executed."

Levi gasped, his eyes wide with uncertainty and fear.

"What did she do that would warrant such extremes?"

"That doesn't matter right now," Danteus acknowledged, "I need to see her."

"Go ahead and try. Unless you want to be beheaded along with her." Levi commented gesturing to the Cratians not too far from them.

HOURS LATER, GOTHALIA'S eyes opened to the dark room. Her head throbbed in pulsing beats in response to her numb body. She glanced at the bandages on her arms, confused.

A moment later, images of the most recent events came back to her mind. She sat up straight, then groaned, hugging her waist. She felt the texture of a soft bandage swathed around her.

The soft mattress, smooth sheets, and frigid air were welcome to her tired mind, but she could not return to sleep. Not after what had happened.

Sweat doused her flushed skin, reminiscent of the nightmare that had awoken her. It had felt so real. She peered around in the darkness and relaxed. She was safe.

"It was just a dream," she muttered to herself. "The demon won't awaken again; everyone will be fine. I hope . . ."

The darkness surrounding her was accompanied by a hushed stillness. A digital clock flashed repetitively through the obscurity of her room. She did not bother to fix the clock, only regarded it briefly with disinterest.

"Good, you're up. A little fast but . . . you're up," a dark figure in the room said suddenly. "Relax. I'm not here to harm a vulnerable woman." Gothalia wanted to scoff at him, but she knew she was in no condition to fight.

The worst part was his voice sounded familiar—a familiarity she knew was responsible for the rise of her goose bumps.

The man moved closer to Gothalia; his dark eyes boring on her.

"Let's be civil about this."

"What's civil about sneaking into someone's room?"

"It's not your room. It is a medical wing. And while I'm at it . . . what's civil about a society who fears truth?"

"What are you talking about?" Gothalia probed, regarding the man with vehemence.

"You'll find out in due time." He folded his arms behind his back and turned from her to face the window. "I'm not your enemy, young one. I certainly mean you no harm, regardless of how my actions may have been interpreted. However, I'm here to aid you as I did your mother . . ."

"My mother?"

"Yes, the demoness everyone despised." He uttered the words with detachment and peered at his nails beneath the moonlight. It outlined his features clearly and Gothalia knew he did not care if he was identified. "The Heiress of the Valdis clan. The truth behind their slaughter is the reason I'm here, young one."

"You don't look that much older than me."

"And yet, I met your mother when she was about your age. By then, she'd had her heart won over by that Ignatius fellow. Tell me, how is your brother? The one who inherited the power of the Ignatius clan."

Gothalia remained silent, her eyes disdainful at the mention of her brother.

"Oh, not good, huh? Then again it makes sense . . . I suppose . . . somewhat . . ." His eyes returned to her. Her guard did not drop. "Still don't trust me?"

"You were there when the Prince had almost . . . You helped save him. Why?" Gothalia inquired.

"Because I'm not the monster every Excelian makes me out to be."

No falsity flickered across his countenance. Slowly, he walked closer to her.

"Stop right there," Gothalia affirmed, with a tone sharp enough to cut steel. "You may say you mean me 'no harm', but trust has to be earned."

"I see your point." He smiled. "What if I were to offer a piece of information in exchange for your trust?"

"That depends . . ."

He pulled out a device from his pocket and, with a flick of his wrist, it hovered closer to her. He was an air user. She frowned. If he wanted to kill her, he could have done it when she was asleep, and he would not have had to use his hands.

The silver device, no bigger than her hand, was set imperceptibly in her lap.

"What is it?" she asked, feeling the smooth, cold surface against her warm skin.

"A monitor, among other things . . ." he casually stated before turning his gaze out the window and to the city below. "The Elders always had a nice set-up here."

Gothalia browsed the screen. A live audio-visual divulged an image of Human soldiers on the surface world. She recognised the flag they bore on their shoulders. They were Australians and the city they cautiously moved through with armed weapons was derelict and barely liveable.

"What happened?" she asked him.

He turned his head to glance at her. His alabaster skin contrasted the looming shadows, carving his hollow cheeks, and giving him a ghostly appearance. His evocative white eyes resolutely rested on her. "The Xzandians. They are searching for that relic. Not surprising though: your mother made sure it would not be found. Even Anaphora cannot find it. And, when she fails, you know it's difficult."

"Anaphora's searching for Midnight Eclipse?"

"She is."

"For what purpose?"

"To save us all, I suppose. Or rather, to build up anticipation and hatred among the humans before they tear each other apart . . . one by one." His words were cold and detached yet had the ring of truth to them. "I wouldn't know her reason exactly. All I know is that this weapon should never fall into anyone's hands. Humans have been responsible for many things, including the accelerated death of this planet. If the surface becomes uninhabitable where do think they will go? What will they do to replace it? And what would they do to keep it from other countries?"

Gothalia turned away from him.

"Honestly, I really couldn't care."

"You should. Excelians were once Human too. If their numbers die . . . the Xzandians would not be as outnumbered as they are now. Especially, if the Humans suddenly convert to their Excelian nature."

"I don't think the Humans would give up their Human nature so willingly. They love the selfishness that comes with such Humanity." There was no amusement in Gothalia's tone. He contemplated her thoughts, curious yet indifferent. He recognised the hard lines of her scowl on her russet skin, the bruises and cuts around her throat and jaw.

"Are you implying they won't give up their stubbornness to keep their Humanity?" he asked. "A trait both Excelian and Human alike share."

"Excuse me?" Gothalia raised a brow at his words. "Are you implying we're alike?"

He minded her words with a levelled gaze.

"The races are not that different from each other. Even if you, and others like you, prefer to think all Excelians are the 'good guys,' if you will. When that is just an unintentional manifestation of desire. Good and bad rests in everyone, as you know well yourself."

"So, why are you here?"

"To show you what you've been missing and where to find it."

Gothalia's eyes returned to the monitor. The Humans were cornered in a room, and the Alastorians and Excelians flooded the building. The Humans had no idea they were surrounded. Her eyes narrowed on a man, who spoke to another man off to the side, beside a blond-haired civilian.

"Why are you showing me this?"

His eyes glittered in amusement. "Why are you acting as though you don't know? From what I recall, Numitora did a similar thing—had she not?"

Gothalia eyed the man, cautiously.

"I have no idea why you feel the need to be so secretive and evasive about why you're here and what you wish to show me."

He glanced at the screen and back at her.

"If you don't keep watching you'll miss it." Reluctantly, she turned her gaze back to the screen and her heart stopped. In the corner, of the room was a person she never thought she would ever see again. A gasp escaped her lips. "You see it now, don't you? It was not your imagination. Your brother is alive and so is your father."

"Why are they not here?"

"That would have to do with why your family was slaughtered all those many years ago. Even, if L'Eiron and Anaphora are allowed here, they are not blood. They were adopted, as you know and were given the power of the Valdis clan. Your friends gave their lives to protect you. Has it ever occurred to you why they would sacrifice their life for you?"

"They're Centurions. Why else?" She demanded. "Why do I get a feeling you're not going to tell me the reason?"

"Because you will find out on your own, in time. A feat that will benefit your home, its people and more importantly—*you*. These soldiers are here for you; you know that don't you? I suggest you decide what you want to do from here on out. You have attacked your own. Don't pretend to think they'll forgive you." He turned from her and disappeared into the darkest shadows in the room.

She leapt from the bed, enraged, and threw a fireball at the wall, illuminating the room briefly.

"That's not possible," she muttered, staring at the empty space where the man had been.

She heard approaching voices, one of which she recognized as Michalis.

The door opened.

Gothalia regarded Michalis and the heavily-armed Peacekeepers surrounding him.

"How are you feeling?" he asked her, cautiously.

"Fine," she replied, watching him firmly. "What's with the cavalry?"

Michalis contemplated his next words. His brown eyes assessed her before he motioned soldiers behind him to be at-ease. "You've broken the law. There is enough visual evidence and countless witness testimonies that there will be no trial. You are to be taken to the Prisons to await your execution. You are a danger to everyone around you, including those you hoped to protect. I'm afraid, child, the vote is unanimous."

Gothalia's fist curled. She wanted to defend herself, *but then what would I do?* "I understand. It is for the best. Everyone will be safer this way."

"I'm sorry," he whispered. He approached and cuffed her wrists, without difficulty. "You're officially stripped of your rank and title as a Centurion."

"Of course. It's protocol." Closing her eyes, Gothalia thought about everything that happened within the past twenty-four hours and wondered how it had all changed so suddenly. "I blame myself."

Michalis led her out of the room with Peacekeepers surrounding her. She kept her eyes to the ground, allowing them to lead her away. As they walked, Gothalia listened to the sneers of others and the curses—"Serves her right"—"Off with her head" or even, "She didn't believe she'd get away with it, did she?"

Gothalia refused to reveal how much their words shattered her heart, keeping her stoic expression.

When they finally arrived at the cells below the Cetatea, Gothalia observed the other prisoners indifferently, regardless of how some leered. They stopped outside one cell that already held a man.

"This will be your cell," Michalis said sullenly from beside her. "I tried to get you a cell alone, but the prisoner numbers are high and—"

"—It's fine." The Centurion Peacekeepers were not above feeling sympathy for Gothalia as they shared a concerned look. "I'll make do. He looks like he's been in here a while. Malnourished. Is there a reason for that?"

"You know why that is," Michalis replied.

Gothalia frowned and waited as the Peacekeepers opened the cell. The man inside giggled, his grin wide and his mouth foaming with saliva.

"Goodie, I have a new roommate and she's vulnerable." he called, eyeing the bandages on her arm and beneath her thin white shirt.

"Restrain him," Michaelis ordered. Two peacekeepers moved in front of Gothalia and punched some buttons on the wall pad. Gothalia watched as electricity shot through the prisoner's body. *They will have six seconds*, Gothalia thought. Their electronic cards beeped and the bolt behind the door withdrew, revealing the other prisoner in the room.

They pushed her inside and tasered her. She felt the burn and sting run through her entire body. A scream escaped her lips before she fell to the floor, her muscles spasming from the aftershock.

Feet padded out of the cell. The grinding of the cell door closed, followed by the final the sound of the bolt sliding across the door and Michalis's voice:

"Forgive me but you brought this on yourself."

# Chapter 16

GOTHALIA'S MUSCLES ached and the voice beside her laughed.

"Looks like I have you all to myself. How much fun. This room is lined in stainless steel. The perfect conductor of electricity. Not even the strongest Centurion could break it."

He climbed to his feet. Immediately, the ground beneath his bare feet stung and Gothalia smiled.

"You forgot the last part. Metal is a perfect conductor of heat too, as the Greeks learned centuries ago." She felt the fiery energy pour through her body into the floor, and climbed to her own feet, unaffected.

The air in the room became thinner and Gothalia watched amused as her new roommate struggled to breathe.

"Tell me your name," she demanded, with a sinister smile.

"You're . . ." he began, through screams and climbed onto the bunk bed in the corner of the room. ". . . a fire user! A filthy Regalis is what you are!"

"Aww, you think that bed will save you?" Gothalia assessed and placed her hand on the metal bar, watching as it heated it up instantly. The floor and walls blooming into a faint scarlet. The smell of the mattress permeated the air with smoke and the prisoner's laboured breathing.

She felt the élanocytes buzz throughout her body, permeating her cells with a different type of energy, one every Excelian carried and only a few mastered. Her muscles ached to respond with action and her mind contemplated all combat moves, taking in every detail of the room, desperate for an escape.

The mattress was engulfed in fire, emitting more smoke, and the air in the room disappeared with each passing second. She listened to him scream before she asked again,

"Are you going to tell me your name?"

He loudly screamed his name before the fire on the mattress could reach him.

Immediately, the fire and heat disappeared.

The air returned to normal.

"Thank you for cooperating," Gothalia proclaimed lightly before adding a darker voice. "Try anything like that again and I'll make sure to burn to you to a pile of ashes, so no one can ever recognise you. *Understand*?" Her eyes watched him unwaveringly.

He swallowed and nodded.

A bang on the door erupted, followed by a sudden shock, then a thundering voice.

"Keep down it in there!" A peacekeeper called, from the other side, sending electricity through the cell. It threw her to the floor; she groaned and climbed to her feet again.

The man laughed. Gothalia eyed him sceptically, *he is losing it, isn't he?*

"Or maybe I'm just imagining things," Gothalia muttered to herself, still hearing his laughter echo through the silent cell. She felt him staring at her.

She ignored him and reminded herself, *I am not as unstable as him and never will be.*

"You'll let your guard down eventually, and when you do, I will strike. Count on it," he muttered from the corner of the room.

With a single glance, a spark of fire exploded in the air near him.

"You better hope you kill me before you're done. Otherwise, I will make sure you suffer slowly by my hand." An explosion pulsed against his shoulder and he screamed in pain, cradling his shoulder. "I may show mercy and kindness, but don't assume for a single second you're trusted. One step out of line, and I won't hesitate to take you out."

Gothalia knew that the moment she closed her eyes or dropped her guard, he would be there. She contemplated whether mercy was a luxury she could afford. Or must she work to adapt?

Internally, she groaned and settled herself.

Silence filled the room, and Gothalia wasn't certain for how long. To her, it felt like a couple of long minutes, but she hoped it had been longer. There was nothing that could distract her tired mind and tender body, as images replayed repeatedly behind her fluttering lashes. She needed to find a way to get out, but she knew this was her punishment.

There was no other alternative.

Gothalia stared at the blank wall opposite her as her roommate nestled on the burnt mattress. He slept soundlessly, as soundlessly as anyone could in a prison; by the content look on his face, not even an explosion could wake him.

She peered closely at his face, uncertain, if he were genuinely asleep or not. The corner of his lips tugged upward before it settled into a dark grimace.

With a sigh, Gothalia curled her legs beneath her, then allowed her head to relax against the wall. Folding her elbows on her knees, she felt a little more secure. Her eyes shut.

It was a dream she had before, filled with dread and fear.

Even as the dark shadows called to her, she watched in trepidation as her home dissolved beneath her feet, like it had never existed.

The faces of those closest to her—Danteus, Demetria, Asashin, Anaphora, L'Eiron—watched her. They stood at contentedly at ease before they disappeared. Confused, she called out to them, wondering where they had gone. Then, she heard the voice,

"You should. Your people were once Human too. If their numbers die . . . the Xzandians would not be as outnumbered as they are now. Especially, if the Humans suddenly convert to their Excelian nature."

Turning to face him, she saw him standing in the shadows of the room she had been in only a few hours ago. He was clad in a midnight blue business suit, an unusual outfit, and stood watching her.

She looked exhausted, but there was a determination in her eyes.

"Oh, look, you're here. About time. Why do you look so stunned?"

"This is a dream. Why are you talking to me?"

"It's your dream, you tell me. Got anything on your mind?" he inquired stepping closer to her. She glanced away, hoping to hide the conflicting emotions flashing across her face.

"No, I don't," Gothalia rebutted, annoyed that he insisted on questioning her, but she kept her composure. "If it's my dream, you shouldn't be here."

At the edge of her awareness, she realized soldiers took their position outside, clad in black uniforms, their faces concealed and unidentifiable.

MORE PEACEKEEPERS THAN usual wandered the streets of New Icarus and Danteus regarded the sight of them with a blank expression from where he stood behind a wall.

"Do you think this will work?" he asked L'Eiron.

"Not sure," L'Eiron responded.

"Why am I here?" Demetria declared.

"What do you mean? You're a part of the team." Danteus replied, confused.

"I mean, Gothalia attacked me! You may have forgiven her, but I haven't, even if I fought beside her."

"I understand how you feel." Danteus placed a hand on her shoulder. "She attacked me too, but that doesn't mean we can just abandon her. She needs us and so does New Icarus. We cannot afford to be soft and second-guess ourselves. Not now. Especially, when this is what the Order wants." Danteus held her gaze, daring her to question his authority. When she did not pick up her mask, L'Eiron added:

"If she's out of the way, the Order will most likely take advantage of that."

Then Levi entered the clearing with his mask and gear. He tied the bag and threw it over his shoulder, then regarded the group, sensing the tension.

"Is everything still a go?"

"Yes, it is." Danteus handed Demetria her mask. "Please, I won't ask any more of you after this."

Reluctantly, Demetria took her mask and put it on. A few minutes later, Danteus had led them to the prisons of the Cetatea.

Their faces were hidden beneath disguises and black clothes, so they mingled with the night, blended with the shadows of the hall.

They tiptoed past guards, copied security codes and hijacked cameras. Easily moving through the prison, they bypassed all the security systems before finding the cell they needed.

They stared at the steel door. With a nod at each other, they took their positions on either side, with their swords drawn, anticipating the danger within.

Then they unlocked the door.

L'Eiron and Demetria entered to find both prisoners asleep. Danteus knelt before Gothalia, then glanced at the man behind him, awaiting approval.

When he nodded, Danteus placed Gothalia over his shoulder and he ran out. He sealed the door behind the group, and they escaped different route. L'Eiron guided the group through the halls and past the security cameras that re-looped scenes of before they entered the building.

A security guard, with the clan of lightning emblem on his uniform spotted them and rushed at them with lightning in hand. It echoed down the halls and quickly, Levi armed his arrow and fired, an explosion of a sticky substance made with rubber elements covered the guard from head to toe, leaving his face exposed but glued to a wall. "Get back here!" he yelled. Demetria paused and ran back to the man and with her elemental ice ability, she sealed his mouth shut before rushing to catch up with the others.

Danteus ran down the hall, carrying Gothalia who remained unconscious on his shoulder, while L'Eiron silently took out the other men before they had noticed their presence. With everyone armed they made their way towards their designated area, Danteus forced his way through the steel wall after Demetria froze it and shattered it with his earth abilities. Then the earth opened, and everyone ran inside, Danteus handed Levi Gothalia before sealing the wall behind them.

An hour later, the group crawled out of a hole in the ground that surfaced beside an underground reservoir. Gently, Danteus placed Gothalia on the ground and tapped her cheek.

"She's not waking up," Danteus remarked and removed his mask to stare up at L'Eiron. "How much did you give them?"

"Enough. They'd be asleep," L'Eiron replied.

"Are you sure it wasn't too much?" Demetria asked, pulling off her mask and fixing her hair.

"I doubt it, but just to be safe . . ." L'Eiron moved passed Danteus and kneeled before Gothalia, his eyes methodical. He placed a hand on her forehead, and a faint glow permeated the area, lasting less than a second before it faded. Retracing his hand, he removed his mask and waited. He stared down at Gothalia and watched her brows furrow. With a groan, she opened her eyes. "Finally, we were getting worried."

"About what . . . that I was in prison?" Gothalia questioned, confused. Then her eyes narrowed in understanding.

"Maybe . . ."

"I hate you," she responded, not sure why they had broken her out. In her eyes she felt like she deserved to be there even if the others didn't believe her.

"No, you don't. You are grateful—it's okay. You can say it." When L'Eiron ruffled her hair and she slapped his hand away. "No one's going to blame you."

Then she was surprised, by arms around her and a head on her shoulder.

"You're okay," Levi whispered. Confused by his reaction, she did not move. "I was worried. You lost a lot of blood. You are okay, right?"

Gothalia nodded.

"I'm fine."

"Well now that's over and done with, can we get go—?" Danteus grumbled before being cut short by Demetria's elbow in his side.

Gothalia observed Demetria.

"Hey, Demetria. I'm sorry. I never meant to hurt you," Gothalia said sombrely. Demetria glanced at Gothalia, then looked away.

"It's not your fault."

"That's where you're wrong, I—"

Danteus interrupted.

"—No, Gothalia. She means it actually wasn't your fault."

Gothalia regarded her teammates with perplexity. Levi watched her with concern but did not utter a word.

"Huh?"

"Danteus is right," Levi added, "the reason you were turned was because of a psychosis-inducing drug. It's something that hasn't been used since the earliest members of the Valdis clan—there's an antidote that returns you to normal back in New Icarus. It was harvested for years as a form of medicine, taken in small quantities and over a prolonged period. And . . . drugging you was the enemy's perfect distraction while they killed the Seers. Isn't that right, L'Eiron?"

"It is," L'Eiron replied, steadily regarding the young woman, searching for a reaction. "The Valdis clan, centuries ago, harvested it to control the unstable élanocytes within their bodies."

Gothalia's shoulders dropped.

"So, if it wasn't my fault, does that mean it has more to do with the people who kidnapped Arthur and me?"

"Yes and no. We kept looking but made sure no one else was aware of our search, not even the Grand Elders. Everything that has happened in the Reserve and on the surface-world is too . . . efficient to not be a coincidence."

"So, you're implying it has something to do with the Order of the Rukh?" Gothalia pondered, unsure why Danteus was staring at her strangely. Without paying him any further mind, she allowed Levi to pull her to her feet.

"Exactly." Danteus said. "And they want you in exchange for Arthur, if you haven't heard already."

"I've heard." Gothalia contemplated her next course of action, only to freeze as a memory resurfaced. Her attackers were Earth users, but that didn't necessarily mean that they were from the Earth Reserve's capital, but she couldn't shake the feeling that it had something to do with the Fire Reserve's recent interference before the coronation.

She brushed the thought aside as it was only a hunch and she needed more evidence before telling it to anyone.

"So, if it isn't my fault. Why did you break me out, other than to tell me that?"

"Because I asked them to . . ." A familiar voice sounded from off the side of the shadows of the caverns. Gothalia eyed the Grand Elder with surprise and concern. "Grand Elder Michalis . . . why would you?"

"There's not much time to explain, but,"—he handed her a small computer chip— "this will explain everything." He stepped aside, allowing his assistant to hand her a bag. Gothalia glanced back at him questionably, who only provided her with a small smile. "For now, you must be careful."

His eyes held uncertainty, but she accepted the bag from his assistant before her gaze drifted to Michalis. He turned from her with a sad smile, then placed a comforting hand on L'Eiron's shoulder.

"Watch over the young one."

"Of course."

Gothalia heard Demetria mutter,

"Don't stress, old man, she'll be fine." Asashin shot her a warning look, while Levi stifled a chuckle. Without another word, Michalis and his assistant disappeared into the shadows of the underground caverns.

L'Eiron ushered Gothalia in the opposite direction. He directed Gothalia through the caverns, only to pause and silently wait
when Peacekeepers marched back and forth, patrolling the smaller
city and barer areas outside of New Icarus.

Once they were further away, Gothalia glanced to the side
where the tunnel wall opened to reveal the city of New Icarus in
the distance, its massive walls, and sturdy towers. She took one last
longing look.

"I'm not ever going to be welcome home, am I?" she asked,
aloud.

The uncomfortable silence from her comrades answered her
heavy question. She jumped a little when she felt L'Eiron's hand upon her shoulder but saw the genuine concern in his eyes.

"We need to keep moving." Desperation and fierceness cloaked
his eyes, which kept her from arguing further. With a determined
nod, she followed, travelling through the many tunnels that surrounded her home.

The ancient clay maze was a popular tourist attraction for those
travelling from other Reserves. Despite growing up so close by,
she had never seen the maze in person. Gothalia had read about
it when she was younger, and her teacher had mentioned that it
was created eons ago, by nature and Earth users who had accelerated and smoothened the stone that had yet to erode. The endless
mazes were enough to confuse the enemies who had hunted them
so many centuries ago.

L'Eiron guided the unit according to Danteus's advice; as a descendant of the original Earth users, Danteus' untouched knowledge navigated them throughout the dark corridors, lit by the small
security lights on their uniforms. Their footfalls resonated down
the silent caverns, only slowing to stop and slip past more guards.
Finally, they were out of the maze and into the open chasm.

Gothalia recognised the houses surrounding the area, divided by a steep drop into volcanic lava below. They were linked by elegantly designed bridges. The suburban houses carved into the earth on either side, stacked upon each other with lush green vines, and foliage.

Giant silver statues of men and women lined the chasms, their hands stretched out as in offering; out of their palm filtered clean water from the many untouched aqueducts.

No one uttered a word when L'Eiron sprinted towards the closest house.

Gothalia moved to follow, but Demetria informed her they needed to wait. They saw the door open, and a figure ushered L'Eiron inside and closed the door behind them.

Fifteen minutes later, the door opened, and L'Eiron beckoned the group inside.

When Gothalia entered the house, she was surprised by the woman who waited for them in the foyer.

She smiled kindly at Gothalia.

"You must be the little troublemaker," she said.

L'Eiron closed the door behind them.

"She does tend to cause problems," he remarked, dropping his arm around her shoulder. "Don't you, kid?"

"Hey! Cut it out! I'm not a kid!" Gothalia growled, irritated.

L'Eiron laughed, at Gothalia's retort.

"Compared to me, you sure are," he added. Gothalia frowned at the smugness in his tone, not appreciating everyone's collective laughter.

"Ha. Ha. Funny, you can let go now," she grumbled, not fond of the attention. Promptly, L'Eiron rubbed her head and removed his arm; she scowled at him.

Mutely, she watched L'Eiron's strides quicken towards the woman whose house they were in; she wore a warm, pleasant smile at his presence.

He bore a grin that was both gentle and admiring, which amazed everyone in the room.

"Aurelia, how are you?" L'Eiron asked tenderly.

"I'm . . . well, better now, better than you lot anyway." Aurelia eyed Gothalia with a small titter.

"Sorry we're late for dinner."

"No, you're just on time. And yes, I decided to make dinner this time. Next time, you're doing it, *understand*?" She added firmly, with a finger pointed at L'Eiron's chest. He agreed apologetically, only to be rewarded with a flirtatious smile.

Gothalia, Danteus, Demetria and Asashin stared after the couple.

"Did you know he had a girlfriend?" Demetria asked Gothalia.

"No, he never mentioned her. I don't know why."

Before Danteus could say anything, Aurelia's voice echoed down the hall, calling them for dinner.

IN THE EYES OF WAR, no one was safe. In the onslaught of casualties, no one was untouched by the blood-drenched fingers of loss and tragedy. Noel-Len and his group worked to protect what was left of their home, but the City of Darwin had fallen into ruin and served as a reminder to the rest of the world of the war they never saw coming.

The world watched in news coverage in horror. Soldiers worked to protect some reporters, while others were forcibly removed from the war zone and taken off the air.

Amongst it all, governments all around the world clamoured in fear and shock at the sight of the alien and metahuman race only previously found in stories.

On the ground, Noel-Len and his group concealed themselves among the shadows of the ruined buildings, each time Leandra called—"contact".

Beneath the early morning light, Noel-Len and Michael peered from around the trunk of a car and observed the soldiers in the car park. They were distracted, much to Noel-Len's confusion. Noel-Len recognised that the soldiers were outside the building where he left Caprice.

*Please be okay*, he thought before his gaze rested on the figure at the feet of the soldiers in the lot.

"You know if they weren't on our side, they'd be so easy to pick off," Michael muttered.

"Oh really?" a familiar voice sounded from behind them. Swinging around, Noel-Len eyed the stranger. As expected, he was a soldier from the Infantry branch. If the name across his chest hadn't confirmed Noel-Len's fears, James' familiar features and the smugness lining his lips would have. "Last I checked, you're the ones being picked off." His hazel eyes smouldered in victory as he stared Noel-Len down.

Quickly, James pointed his rifle at Michael as he reached for his weapon.

"I wouldn't do that if I were you. Unless you want a chest full of bullets." Michael retreated and placed his hands in the air. James' eyes drifted to Michael. "Come on, you know what to do."

Michael mimicked Noel-Len's surrender while James leered and squatted in front of Noel-Len.

His hands slid over Noel-Len's legs to the large pockets on the side. Tapping each pocket, he heard a familiar clink of metal. Reaching into Noel-Len's pockets, James pulled out the dog-tags.

Noel-Len felt Michael's shock as James dangled the valuable information before his face. "You would have gotten away with that too . . . if I weren't smarter than you," he mocked and pushed Noel-Len's head back.

The radio buzzed between them and James responded.

"Fifty meters south of your position."

Noel-Len heard "Roger" on the other end and knew that he would have back up. A few moments later, two more soldiers arrived.

# Chapter 17

NOEL-LEN RECOGNISED the other Commando soldiers of his team, sitting by and waiting. They were following one of the plans Sergeant McGuire had laid out should they encounter hostiles, even if they were theoretically wearing the same uniform. James before them confirmed their fears.

"There you are, Adrian," a soldier said. Noel-Len eyed the two soldiers who had arrived. They had similar haircuts as Adrian James, but their hair colour was a different shade of brown.

Noel-Len knew he would have to try to remember them, but he also knew that, in a war zone, sometimes the simplest task could be the most difficult. "We have h—" One man glanced at Noel-Len than at Michael. "Who are they?"

"One of those Commandos you saw running around like an idiot, Eric," James growled.

"Oh. *Him*." Eric pointed to Noel-Len as if it were the most obvious thing in the world. Noel-Len ignored Eric and glanced at the surname across his chest—Smith. He was one of the men Noel-Len recognised from the alleyway. Eric Smith. Noel-Len regarded the man beside Eric. His surname was Johnson. He knew this man—Patrick Johnson.

"Remember me, Noel-Len? Or should I say, Private Ignatius," Patrick mocked. "And look who it is . . ." Patrick's attention fell on Michael. "Private Williams. Tell me, did your mommy and daddy make it out of the city alive? Or wait, that's right, you don't have a daddy." Michael glared at Patrick but did not make any moves to attack. Just like Noel-Len's, his eyes rarely drifted to his concealed comrades. "In a way, you and Ignatius here are perfect for each other. Don't you agree?"

"Noel-Len has a father," Michael retorted. "Dickhead." At that, Patrick Johnson punched Michael in the jaw.

"Oh, is that so?" Patrick said calmly, as though he hadn't moved. "I wonder . . . is that where you got your name from? It's such a fucking weird name." His gaze lingered over Noel-Len as he stepped aside to make room for the other member of his group.

"Now, I'm certain the Captain wants to see you." James griped Noel-Len by the front of his uniform. "But whether he wants to see you dead or alive is something . . . I'm unsure about." Noel-Len heard the threat in those words but did not flinch. He knew what he was getting into the moment he applied for the military—fear was an understandable emotion, but one he could not afford.

Without much trouble, Adrian and the others yanked Noel-Len and Michael to their feet. Rifles were pointed at Noel-Len and Michael's backs, forcing the men to stride towards the group in the centre of the car park.

He managed a brief glance at Michael. He understood Noel-Len's thoughts by the tightness of his jaw as their gazes returned to the blonde figure huddled at the feet of the soldiers. The moment they stepped aside; Noel-Len's breath caught as he stared at Caprice on the ground.

"Caprice!" Michael growled, fury lacing his voice as he glared at the dark-haired man opposite him. "What the fuck did you do to her?"

"Nothing," James said easily with a cruel smile on his lips. He held his rifle loosely in his hands before pointing it at her head. "Yet. Get my drift?"

Noel-Len tensed; his heart hammered. His eyes regarded the barrel of the rifle, inches from Caprice's head, and recognised the bloodied bandage wrapped around her left calf. He heard Michael growl *Bastard* as he knew his old friend had come to the same conclusion he did.

Noel-Len searched his brain; he remembered something from seeing him that he could not connect. His gaze slid to the blond-haired, uniformed woman. He recalled her dangerously-marred features, of the Corporal who yelled at him and Michael and ordered them to weed.

"Corporal McGuire?" Noel-Len asked, stunned. "Was it you who shot the civilian?"

"Whether I did or didn't, it doesn't matter," she casually said, moving towards Noel-Len. "I mean . . . it's not like you can prove I shot her. That is, if we take out the bullet." Noel-Len did not respond but silently watched as she pulled a device from out of her pants' pocket.

"But there's a bullet in her leg," Michael growled, his gaze threatening, as Corporal Melissa McGuire wandered towards him with a black device. "That's too much blood for a flesh wound."

"What? Are you a doctor now?" teased Adrian from behind them. "Don't make me laugh."

"Keep him still," Melissa ordered, tapping the butt of the device against Michael's exposed skin, beneath his jaw. "Well look what we have here. It's green. That's a good sign." Her gaze shifted to Noel-Len. "You're next, but I know the outcome; after all, you're an Ignatius." Noel-Len was confused by her words. She placed the butt of the device against Noel-Len's neck. It was cool at first, before he felt it heat up. Moments later, Melissa pulled the device from him and regarded the screen. Her face lit up. "As expected, green. However, I never expected the élanocyte count to be so high. Interesting. Do you know what family your mother descends from?"

Noel-Len glared at Corporal McGuire, who was not bothered by his seething look. He knew it was not an order and refused to tell her. Though, the more Noel-Len thought about it, the more he recalled that his mother never told him of her family's name. Instead, she always referred to herself as an Ignatius.

Melissa waited, and Noel-Len still did not respond.

"Maybe he doesn't know," James suggested. Melissa studied the man behind Michael and nodded.

"Possibly," she said. "But wasn't she the one who raised him for a bit?" Noel-Len scowled at the woman. "Your orders, Captain." A precarious hush fell among the tense group.

"We're taking them with us. I'm certain Chang would want to examine them," said Eric, with a knowing smile. "Move out." The enemy pushed them further away from their comrades. Noel-Len was certain they were not going to see Sergeant McGuire and the others anytime soon. However, Noel-Len also knew he could not give away their position by glancing over his shoulder. He contemplated fighting his way out but realised there was something bizarre going on with the soldiers around him. They often casually uttered unfamiliar terms like *Excelian* and *Alastorian*.

Noel-Len did not understand what they were referring to either, when they mentioned *Midnight Eclipse* or its *Fragments*.

Noel-Len felt Michael's gaze drift over him from time to time, but Noel-Len could not meet it. If anything, he avoided it. Noel-Len knew Michael was frightened. He was aware Michael was unable to look at Caprice's limp form hanging over the Captain's shoulder as they strolled down the empty, blood-stained streets.

It was when Noel-Len and Michael followed the rest of the soldiers into an almost abandoned building, through the shattered glass door that James had happily shot down, that Noel-Len knew they weren't the only ones remaining within this empty city.

Civilians were huddled in a corner of the office room when they entered. Noel-Len's gaze lingered over their wide eyes and quivering forms, petrified of the armed soldiers. When Eric taunted them with the barrel of his gun, by slowly drifting it over their frightened figures, they recoiled against the wall. Noel-Len scowled at his cruelty.

Captain Wilson, the man cradling Caprice over his shoulder, yelled orders, while the terrified, unarmed civilians obeyed, moving to the centre of the room and kneeling. Their hands were placed behind their heads by Corporal McGuire, who restrained them with black Flexi cuffs. The sight of it made him sick, but Noel-Len knew that these civilians were too scared to act, and he could not act on their behalf without putting them in danger. He watched some women silently cry while most of the men in the group looked ready to themselves.

They were terrified and Wilson's team loved it.

One man caught Noel-Len's gaze. His eyes were veiled beneath his short, messy chestnut hair. He remained composed, kneeling a few metres away from Noel-Len, and his attention lingered over Noel-Len longer than expected before sliding over to the enemy wearing his same Army uniform.

Noel-Len averted his gaze as Corporal Melissa McGuire circled both Michael and Noel-Len like a tigress waiting to pounce.

"Throw them into the pile," Captain Wilson ordered.

Noel-Len felt James grip his arm while Eric seized Michael by the shoulders and forced him to his knees. Noel-Len and Michael were restrained with the same Flexi cuffs that held the wrists of the civilians.

The confusion on the civilians' faces was evident, but Constable Mark Robert remained silent and observant. Noel-Len kneeled with Michael at the front of the group.

"You can take her too," Eric said and threw Caprice to the ground, causing Noel-Len, Michael, and the group to react in shock at his careless attitude. "Don't worry. She didn't break." He tapped the tip of his boot on her jaw. "See, she's still in one piece."

"Bastard," Noel-Len spat, his eyes on Ethan.

"Sorry to say, but I have a father and . . . unlike yours . . . he didn't abandon me."

Noel-Len held his tongue. He was not too sure whether he should be angry that it was half the truth or content that it was not the entire truth.

Captain Ethan Wilson's group finally vacated the building, leaving three of the soldiers to guard the door. Both Noel-Len and Michael knew they were the grunts of the group.

"Noel-Len," Michael whispered. "We should bust out of here while they're gone."

"We could," Noel-Len responded his eyes drifting over the layout of the room: a few desks and chairs off to the side, along with a few filing cabinets and closed doors. "But I get the feeling we won't get far. We should sit tight until the others arrive." He knew, with his injuries, he would have to think smarter otherwise he wouldn't be alive much longer.

"You sure?" Michael asked, curious as to why Noel-Len was not acting on this rare opportunity. Then his eyes drifted to Noel-Len's bloodied arm, bandaged in his torn uniform. Michael could see the cogs turning in Noel-Len's head. *Honestly, Noel-Len, you better think of something and fast*, Michael thought, before his gaze fell on Caprice. He could faintly see the rise and fall of her chest.

"Noel-Len," said Mark Roberts. Noel-Len regarded the Constable. "Do you know those men?" He gestured to Eric's back in the doorway.

"Not too well. Kind of only just met them," Noel-Len said.

"Do you know—"

"—Their motive?" Noel-Len finished. "Not really, other than people being green is bad and they're after... something. Not sure what it is yet."

Mark considered Noel-Len's words, uncertain if he was being serious or not.

"Noel-Len, how do you know this guy?" Michael muttered harshly beneath his breath.

Before Mark could say, Noel-Len cut him off.

"That doesn't matter." Noel-Len, Michael and Mark heard bodies fall to the ground. A moment later, Noel-Len saw a figure peek around the corner. Then, Sergeant McGuire stood in the door and scanned the room once more. "Sir!"

"Don't give me that look, Ignatius. It's not like you didn't know we were coming." Sergeant Curt McGuire, Leandra, and Andrew entered the large office room before stationing themselves with their rifles pointed at the door. Sergeant McGuire cut through the Flexi cuffs around Noel-Len and Michael's wrists with his knife. He tossed the blade to Michael. "Remove the handcuffs from the others."

"Sir."

Michael began to slice through the Flexi cuffs of the rest of the group. Leandra tossed Noel-Len his abandoned rifle. Once Michael was done, Andrew handed him his rifle.

Unbeknownst to Sergeant Curt McGuire, Captain Wilson entered the room, and opened fire. Sergeant McGuire ducked away, barely managing to avoid being shot in the chest. To Noel-Len, it happened too quickly—all he saw was Curt turning around, then heard the pop of the rifle.

Noel-Len watched Curt fall to the ground. His upper arm bled, but the bullet instantly killed the woman behind him. Curt gawked at the lifeless woman. Her body revealed the red stain seeping through her pale blue blouse. Uttering a curse, his grip tightened around his rifle and he fired, shooting Captain Wilson in the shoulder.

Noel-Len fired too, but Ethan swiftly retreated behind the wall for cover, shielding himself from the bullets of Sergeant McGuire's team.

Michael spotted Corporal Melissa McGuire, who tossed a steel ball into the room.

"Grenade!" Leandra called. Michael twisted a tornado kick, and the steel ball flew towards the door.

Before it could explode, Michael shielded Caprice's unconscious form, while every civilian ran to the other side of the room and hid below the wooden desks. Noel-Len ran with Andrew, who carried Curt, and hid beneath a desk as well. A second later, the explosion juddered the building, the ground shuddered beneath them, and smoke permeated the room. Michael pulled Caprice into his arms and sprinted further from the door.

Sergeant McGuire uttered his next command. Swiftly, Noel-Len and Andrew followed Curt. They tactfully scanned their surroundings before heading out of the room, while Michael and Leandra remained behind, their eyes vigilant for any sudden movement or the familiar sound of gunfire.

Moments after Noel-Len and the others left, silence greeted Leandra and Michael's ears. A soft groan drifted from Caprice's lips. Michael glanced down at the woman beside him. He saw the crease lines around her eyes as she squeezed them tighter before slowly opening them. She was silent, searching for any recognisable features on the man beside her. It was his voice that made her relax when her vision finally returned.

"Hey, you alright?"

"I'm sore," she complained, glancing around her. Michael remained silent and turned his attention back to the door. "Where are we?" She moved to sit up.

"Stay down," Michael said. Caprice's eyes lingered over Michael's body. She recognised the scorched, torn clothing over Michael's back and arms. She recognised the weapon Michael held over the desk. Fear washed over her as she perceived the dried clotted blood on the side of his head and the bruises and dirt lingering on his cheekbones and jaw. Then her mind drifted to Noel-Len. Before she could ask, Michael said,

"He's alive." His attention was on the door, occasionally drifting to the other doors.

"How did you—?"

"That look in your eyes says it all." Michael chose not to mention how much it angered him that Noel-Len was always at the forefront of her thoughts. If anything, that constant reminder hurt him more than being physically harmed. "He's injured but I'm sure he'll manage." Caprice slowly nodded, and Michael returned his attention to the door once more, ending the conversation.

Noel-Len followed Curt, with Andrew beside him. Outside the room, Curt ordered them to split up. The three men travelled in separate directions. Andrew moved to the right and searched the hall, Noel-Len proceeded to the left, and Curt proceeded outside the building.

Noel-Len remained vigilant, examining every crevice and recess. His mind suddenly stung, pain burned his skull. He squeezed his eyes shut with his fingers pressed against his head in the area where the pain was most excruciating. He gasped. Surprisingly, it ended as quickly as it occurred. Blinking, he scanned his surroundings, before walking on ahead, his index finger on the trigger of his rifle.

Then it happened: his exposed left wrist was slashed with a knife blade, forcing him to relinquish the hold of his weapon. Before he could react, the heel of a boot flew towards him and he shielded his face with his right arm. His rifle swung by the strap around his shoulder.

Noel-Len tripped Eric, who immediately scrambled to his feet. Eric rolled over his shoulder and towards Noel-Len, pulling out his pistol. Noel-Len forced Eric's hand into the air kicking the hot barrel of his gun upward and sending the bullet past Noel-Len's head. Swiftly, Noel-Len kicked in Eric's knees before throwing him over his shoulder. Twisting, his weight around Eric's arm, he acquired the gun. Eric rolled to his feet, then sprinted around the corner. Before Noel-Len could aim, Eric vanished. Hesitantly, Noel-Len moved around the corner, careful of any surprise attacks his enemy could create. When he found no one within the empty halls, he relaxed.

"Shit."

Then he heard it. The sound of a Para Minimi going off. He could tell it was close. Then, orders from his team leader echoed in his earpiece—he required back up.

"Sarge," Noel-Len muttered and followed the sound. When he arrived, he promptly took cover behind the large reception desk. Shattered glass surrounded his feet above the blood-stained beige carpet. His eyes lingered over the two male receptionists dressed in black trousers and white shirt and ties. Dried blood smeared the carpet beneath their frozen bodies.

The echo of bullets flooded the lobby. Noel-Len kneeled and held his rifle above the desk, aiming it in the direction of the bullets and flashing blue lights.

He heard the bullets move closer, growing louder.

Then he heard Sergeant McGuire's voice over the radio, and Noel-Len knew that Andrew would not make it in time. If Noel-Len moved, he would lose his best chance of neutralising the targets.

Heavy footfalls rang throughout the room. The gun felt warm in Noel-Len's hand, but he did not think much of it, nor was he aware that the tiny bands around the bullets would reach temperatures high enough to pierce steel. Then, from around the bend, Sergeant McGuire emerged.

Three profusely armoured alien soldiers were behind him, firing their weapons. Noel-Len had not come across their other enemies within the last few minutes—in fact, he had almost forgotten they were at war with aliens. Sergeant McGuire ran to the desk where Noel-Len hid and slid over it; at the same moment, Noel-Len aimed and fired. He shot every alien in the head before he glanced at Curt.

"Targets neutralised, Sir."

"Where were you?" Curt growled, as he and Noel-Len dropped behind the counter to shield themselves from potential enemies.

"Here," Noel-Len replied, and Curt studied Noel-Len for a moment. Andrew's voice swept between them over the radio. Then, from around the corner, he emerged. "There you are."

"What? I got here as quick as I could."

"Found anything?" Curt asked, climbing to his feet, his eyes and rifle pointing around, scanning the area. Without another thought, the soldiers moved to secure the rest of the building.

"Dead civilians," Andrew replied. Noel-Len did not answer. His eyes drifted over Andrew's face. He recognised the grimness there. Noel-Len could not blame the man. He and the soldiers in Sergeant McGuire's team had that same look on their faces when they realised, they had to kill the human civilians that attacked them. They knew they could justify their actions in court, but it was a narrow escape. Even now, he felt like he wanted to throw up. Instead, he forced the images of their dead faces from his mind. He knew he had to be strong if he wanted to survive.

"Dead how?" Curt asked. Both Andrew and Noel-Len knew what Curt McGuire meant.

"Dead, dead. They all had bullets in their foreheads, sir."

Noel-Len and Curt watched him with a steady gaze, waiting for a better explanation. He sighed.

"They appeared like the civilians that we had first encountered when we initially arrived."

Noel-Len asked,

"How so?"

When silence greeted the men, Noel-Len glanced around. He was not certain how, but he felt odd.

"What's the matter, Ignatius?" Curt asked.

"Nothing, Sir," Noel-Len recovered. "How were they different?"

"Well . . . it's hard to explain. They're strung up, among other things. It's easier if you see it yourself."

When Noel-Len and the others stepped into the room, they were uncertain of what to expect. What they saw was something Noel-Len would never have thought possible. The perfectly polished porcelain tiles, which once reflected the figures that strode upon them, were now uneven and destroyed. Earth splintered through the tiles in spikes. The lights overhead remained without current, leaving them in darkness at first. It wasn't until the morning sun flooded through the blinds that Noel-Len managed to make out the figures strung up against the walls and hanging motionless from the ceiling at odd angles.

Noel-Len recognised the small bullet holes in between their brows. There was a bullet hole on every man or woman he saw.

"Strange isn't it?" Andrew asked from behind Noel-Len as he analysed the woman's expressionless features. She hung upside down, her face paler than what he would have expected. There was no sign of life and the familiar bullet hole between her brows.

Noel-Len waved his hand before her face. He recalled the girl that James had killed at the last scouting site. Her black eyes flashed behind his eyes as he stared at those same eyes. This time they were lifeless. All the monsters' eyes were black but not all stayed open.

"What are they?"

"I . . ." Curt began, ". . . We don't know."

"So, they can be killed?" Noel-Len asked.

"Obviously," said Andrew, tapping the chest of a man hanging upside down by one leg. His light blue buttoned shirt was splattered with dried blood. "I don't think they're getting back up."

"We don't know that."

"They're not zombies," Andrew said evenly. "Otherwise, we'd be dead."

Noel-Len turned from the strung-up bodies and regarded Curt.

"We should probably get out of here."

Curt glanced at Noel-Len, then back at the bodies.

"Move out."

# Chapter 18

WHEN CURT MCGUIRE AND his team returned, the room was filled with thick silence and grinding anticipation. The apprehensive soldiers and terrified civilians relaxed in their presence.

"Did you get them?" Leandra asked Noel-Len.

"Not all. One got away." Noel-Len replied. It was when those words left his lips that he questioned whether he believed his words. The way he'd been attacked by the woman in the abandoned school made him question how many enemies he had. At first, he originally believed Anaphora to be the monster, but now—he was not too sure.

"That's good," Michael said. "I really didn't want to shoot them." Everyone glanced at Michael, uncertain of where his loyalty lay. "They wear the same uniform. It's weird."

"Just because they wear the same uniform," Curt declared, "doesn't mean they're on the same side. Sometimes, the people we think we know are entirely different from the people they really are." Michael nodded while everyone in the room took in his words. A small number of civilians stepped forward, inquiring about the safety of the environment outside the room.

Unfortunately, Sergeant Curt McGuire knew that if they continued to stay here. They would all be killed. Caprice stayed hidden beneath the desk, her hands over her mouth, as Curt relayed what they knew about their number of enemies. She had no idea that they had three types of enemies. Now, she understood how dangerous her home had become.

Lost in her thoughts, she did not feel or see Noel-Len crouch beside her.

"Caprice."

Her pale blue eyes flickered over to him.

"How are you feeling?" he asked, with a kind smile. A mixture of emotions surfaced in her at the sight of him, and she could not help but smile in return. They were both unaware of Michael staring at the ground, desperate to find anything else to focus on.

"Better," Caprice whispered.

Michael climbed to his feet, breaking Noel-Len's train of thought and halting his next words. His eyes assessed his friend. Noel-Len understood Michael's reaction, but before he could say anything, Michael turned away and walked over to Curt, Leandra, and Andrew without glancing back at either of them. Caprice and Noel-Len shared a concerned look before they heard Constable Mark Roberts's voice.

"Noel-Len. Can I have a word with you?"

Noel-Len followed Mark to the furthest end of the room. He could make out the tension in the man's shoulders and the stress lining his middle-aged features.

It was in that moment that he understood the impact the invasion was having on him and potentially everyone in every part of the world. Not until now did he feel the dread cling to his bones, pulling him deeper than any quicksand.

"I see. You're as scared as I am," Mark said, failing to ease the grimness carved into the young man's features.

Noel-Len's dark eyes coasted over the bare, cracked walls of the office before finally replying,

"Don't worry. I won't say a word."

"It's not that I'm worried about. Some people still haven't been evacuated." Mark's gaze coasted to the men and women clad in modern clothing that would have been once fashionable to wear throughout society. Now, it was torn, battered, and stained with blood both dry and fresh. He watched as soldiers knelt to tend to their wounds.

The wide eyes of the office men and women regularly flicked to the doorway, fearful of both another alien surprise and the weapons gripped in the soldier's hands.

Noel-Len could make out the hesitation in the civilians' body language towards the service men and women alike. Some even refused to have their wounds tended to. His frown deepened at the sight. *They do not trust us anymore*, he thought.

"They should have been evacuated," Mark continued. "Instead, they were trapped in this building, surrounded by those inhuman monsters. You did see the bodies of those detectives and other officers outside." Noel-Len nodded, grimly. "We responded to a distress call. Luckily, everyone departed with the other evacuees. So, a handful of us worked to try and safely remove the remaining survivors from this building. By the time we did, we had to retreat inside. The number of monsters grew. It was weird, they were like zombies, but they were not at the same time. I mean, they weren't eating each other."

"Maybe that's only in movies."

"Maybe." Mark remarked, unamused. "Or maybe . . . I'm thinking about it too much. I just can't help but draw similarities to that prisoner we saw two days ago. First that, then—well I can't say. This. . . " Mark ran his hand over his face and around his neck.

"What happened before?" Curt inquired, overhearing Mark and Noel-Len conversation. His suspicion grew when both men became uncomfortable at the question. Mark was unaware his voice that his voice had echoed in the destroyed office room.

Noel-Len scrutinised Mark, then Curt.

After a moment's silence, Mark described the most recent event before the re-invasion to the whole room. Everyone's features shifted from curiosity to horror. It was not until he described what had happened at the coroner's officer that Noel-Len began to confirm his suspicion.

"As I was saying before, I cannot help but draw similarities. These people that are trying to kill us don't have any need to survive because they're already dead and have been for a while."

Everyone in the room gasped while others remarked how impossible it was. Noel-Len eyed Curt, waiting for his reaction, but when none came, Mark continued.

"Dr. Martin Aaen proved his theory when the most recently-dead bodies had their organs removed. Many did not have any left. This explains why shooting them in the chest doesn't work."

Curt's eyes narrowed. His mind resurfaced with frightening images of when their vehicles were attacked, moments after leaving the base. Shooting the monsters in the chest did not slow them down.

"How do you know all this?" Curt asked.

"I'm a Constable with the Territory Police. I worked alongside the Major Crimes detectives who investigated the case of the prisoner with similar characteristics to the walking dead," Mark replied. Curt continued to eye the man with suspicion as his eyes drifted over the navy-blue police uniform.

"Okay, say I believe you. Then explain why we were only able to kill them by shooting them in the head."

"You may or may not believe this, but their brain has been . . . pilfered," Mark said, a serious tone in his voice. The other soldiers' disbelief made Mark uncomfortable. "That's what we call it. I'll tell you the rest later, but we need to get out of here before we're all dead."

"I think we can keep you alive a little longer," Andrew said.

"Knowing how they work will prove to be useful." Leandra added.

"Really?" Mark shot back. "Have any of you fought them single-handedly? As far as I know, your orders are to take out the hostile aliens."

"No," Curt argued. "Our orders were to secure the scouting sites and take out any hostile that prevented the completion of our mission. Without the scouting sites, they are not able to communicate. Without commands and intel, they are a useless army."

"So, I repeat my question: have any of you specially trained soldiers come across a walking corpse?" Mark asked. Noel-Len could tell Mark was losing his patience. When none of the other soldiers responded, Mark added, "They're stronger than we expected and faster too. Even though their cells have been dead for a long time. Yet they've managed to calcify their bones and increase their muscle mass. But it's what's on the brain that has everybody freaking out."

A brunette civilian woman asked doubtfully,

"What are you saying exactly? Something is on their brain. As in, on top of it? That makes them faster and stronger?"

Mark stood his ground.

"That is exactly what I am saying. And theoretically, they're programmed to kill. The organism controlling the deceased humans is alien. Similar in biology to those of the aliens sitting high in the sky." Then Mark gasped, horrified by the figure in the doorway.

Everyone followed his gaze. The soldiers pointed their rifles. In the doorway stood an Xzandian, who slowly began to reveal itself as the element of invisibility faded. Everyone fired at once. Despite being practically as close as Noel-Len had been to the aliens in the lobby, these rounds had nowhere near the impact on this alien as the others had.

Suddenly, a sword pierced through the alien's back and out its chest. The sword had a similar design to a katana but was smeared in a green liquid. Everyone continued to fire, even Noel-Len, until Curt gave the order:

"Hold your fire!"

Abruptly, the sword was removed from the alien. The frozen alien fell to the ground, revealing a woman clad in a black combat uniform Noel-Len was unfamiliar with. A black helmet concealed her head, exposing only her lips.

"Leave now," she said coolly. "More are coming."

Curt aimed his rifle.

"Who are you?" he asked, his finger on the trigger.

The woman did not respond and only stared him down.

Noel-Len recognised a silver swirl on her shoulder; then a small fire burst out on her uniform. It started from the centre and spiralled outward, before travelling up towards the ceiling. Within an instant, a thick smoke clouded the room and the woman vanished.

"You guys saw that, too right?" Curt asked, tentatively.

"Yeah. We saw that," Mark replied, relieved.

It did not take long for the men and women sheltered within the building to escape. To their relief, no one was outside. However, the daunting silence made the soldiers and the Constable alert.

The civilians scattered, running in random directions from the building. Curt and Mark called for them to stop, but it was too late. Horror marred their sweaty faces as they saw two aliens round a corner right near some of the women.

At first, it appeared they had not seen the women—but the women's screams caught the aliens' attention. The two women stopped and sprinted towards Noel-Len and the others. When their backs were turned, the echo of the alien firearms stunned the onlookers. The women fell to the ground. Noel-Len and Michael opened fire on the aliens, along with Leandra, Andrew, and Curt.

Mark and Caprice squatted behind the rear of a car under fire. The *ping* of bullets against the metal caused Caprice to shriek in fright and cover her head.

"What are we going to do?" she yelled, terrified. "They can't keep shooting forever." She watched as Leandra and Andrew reloaded while Curt pulled out his pistol.

Mark paused, then said,

"We have to retreat. We're too far away to do any real damage." Mark yelled at Curt repeating what he had just said to Caprice. Curt appeared not to have heard him, his focus solely on the approaching aliens. Mark shouted louder, his throat sore from the strain.

THE GROUP REMOVED THEIR combat boots and placed them by the door before heading further into the house.

The stone beneath their feet was cold and the hall, lit by fiery lanterns, gleaming in gold. In the open space sat a kitchen and a dining room that faced an open living room area.

L'Eiron was seated at the table with a bowl before him.

"You guys aren't allergic to anything right?" Aurelia inquired; her warm brown eyes lingered over the group.

"They're not. It's basic screening," L'Eiron answered.

Aurelia, dishing up a bowl of soup, smiled and retorted,

"As you say, but it's always polite to ask." Everyone smiled at her words, aware of the comfortable yet peaceful atmosphere drifting over them.

"Is that magma soup? I haven't had that in so long!" Demetria squealed, reminding Gothalia of an excited child. *It's not that exciting it is just very spicy-sweet soup*, she thought frowning.

"What? Not impressed?" Danteus questioned from beside her.

"What are you talking about?"

"You're glaring at Demetria and Asashin."

"No, I'm not."

"Sure, whatever you say. Just don't frown too much. When the wind changes, that look on you face will stay the same," he teased before joining the others.

"How can I not look annoyed when you say stuff like that?" Gothalia muttered to herself, then smiled as she admired his strong body. "And the wind can't freeze my face," she added before walking towards Aurelia, and picking up an empty bowl.

The last few hours felt was like a bad dream; however, her tender body and tired eyes made them more real with each passing second.

Later that evening, tranquillity calmed the silent night. Sitting in a room that was both serene and hospitable, Gothalia anticipated Danteus's return.

On the bed, her fingers tightened around her short dagger, deep in thought. She didn't notice the satchel Danteus carried over his shoulder when he entered the room.

He dropped the bag on the wooden floorboards, catching Gothalia's attention. Her eyes were distant but lit up with recognition at the sight of him. A small smile graced her lips.

"Back already?" She felt the cold blade rest on her knuckles, a reassuring reminder.

"I am," he responded, and she dropped the dagger. Then she ran into his arms and kissed him as hard as she could. After a lengthy kiss, Danteus asked, "Are you okay? I was really worried."

"I'm better now." She placed her head on his chest and relaxed in his arms, admiring his strength.

"I have something for you," he said with a small smile. "It's a gift from Michalis."

He handed her the bag and she opened it.

"It's my gear!" she said. "It's been so long, I almost forgot that I owned it."

"It hasn't been that long."

"No, it hasn't."

Danteus wrapped his arms around her.

"There have been no causalities, just a handful injured so far . . . every attack that occurred was in the city. We are certain it had more to do with their objective than killing off random civilians, but you did good. You kept them from assassinating the Prince."

Gothalia eyed him, determined.

"What do you mean?"

"You know what I mean," He took the bag from her hand and pulled out a computer chip, her helmet, and a small disc, and handed them to her. "These won't activate until Kronos recognises you."

Danteus withdrew and walked to the door.

"Where are you going?"

"To check on the others. They're probably discussing what to do."

"Probably."

Danteus stepped back to her and took her chin, stroking her jaw with his thumb.

"Keep your head up." With that, he parted and Gothalia felt herself blush.

"Danteus," she whispered into the shadows before moving over to the bed.

Danteus moved through to the furthest end of the hallway, where voices loudly resonated, deep in conversation. He paused in the hallway, out of sight, and listened.

"You've seen how she is. Something's not right," Demetria insisted, with a resoluteness to her tone that Danteus almost found offensive.

"She's fine!" Levi remarked tensely. "You're just over-critical, probably because she kicked your butt."

Demetria pulled her feet from the table, allowing her boots to thud against the wooden floorboards.

"That's so not what happened, and besides, we all know you're biased."

"Excuse me, since when?" Levi responded, refusing to flinch beneath Demetria's scathing gaze.

Normally their behaviour would not have bothered Danteus, but there was something about this situation he did not like. Stretching his neck and rubbing his shoulders, he moved from the shadows of the halls and into the chandelier-lit living room before their conversation could execute.

L'Eiron observed him with an indifferent expression, ignoring Levi's curiosity and Demetria's unexpected hostile gaze.

"You heard, didn't you?"

"Maybe, maybe not. Does it matter? I was going to hear all of this eventually." Danteus pulled out a chair and sat down.

"And you agree . . .?" Demetria questioned, hopefully. Danteus returned her gaze steadily.

"Should I?" he pressed, exhausted by her expectation. "She seems fine, to me. A little shaken, but alright. It's not something she can't bounce back from; she's taken worse. She'll be alright."

"She killed people! What makes you think we're not next?" Demetria pressed. "Or would you prefer she took us out one by one?"

"She wouldn't do that!" Levi growled, his fist thundering against the hard-oak table and, at that moment, Danteus was appreciative of him. "You make it seem like she can't control herself. She's not some mindless monster. You know that for a fact! Science even proves that it was not her fault, yet still you condemn her. They took advantage of her weakness and exploited it because they're nothing but cowards."

"Or they're geniuses," L'Eiron interrupted, and everyone turned to him. "Anyone who'd recognise her potential would either stop it before it becomes something more or take out two birds with one stone—as the saying goes."

"So, you think that they were after Gothalia to benefit themselves?" Danteus asked. "That makes a whole lot of sense."

L'Eiron ignored Danteus's sarcastic comment before sliding a disc along the table. After a few beeps, a holographic projection of Anaphora hovered above the table.

"Looks like you made it out alright and in one piece," she said. "How's Gothalia?"

"All right," L'Eiron answered. "Or so I've been told."

After a heavy pause Anaphora queried,

"Is it true? There were . . . causalities?"

L'Eiron ran his hand through his hair and rubbed his neck.

"As much as I'd like to believe that she's innocent, I have seen the bodies. Many were not recognisable, but they were there. It's only time until forensics confirms it. His Highness may have placed his confidence in her, but this is almost naïve, no offence."

"Offence taken," Levi muttered, glancing away.

"Don't you think that was a little uncalled for, my lord?" Demetria asked gently, and Danteus crossed his arms, observing Levi, searching for a larger reaction that never arose.

"Regardless, if she committed a crime, why is she free? Shouldn't she be publicly executed? What's stopping the Grand Elders?" Anaphora questioned, her tone even; Danteus fought back a shudder at her words. "It's traditional law: one must not ever go unpunished. However, you're right that our enemies are hoping we kill her in place of them."

L'Eiron held her gaze, sharing a message no one else understood. Anaphora continued,

"Well, that's something we'll have to deal with later. For now, we are going to need your help, Gothalia's included. The surface world is under siege and considering how everything has played out; I can see why."

GOTHALIA CONTEMPLATED the information Kronos delivered to her.

"So, what do you think?" he asked her, from where he stood as a virtual projection. "What are you going to do?"

"I'm going after her," Gothalia declared, like it was the most obvious thing in the world. "If she's connected to Betheous—the gladiator in the arena—I need to find out how."

"Let's go before someone notices," Kronos prompted, and Gothalia, dressed in her combat uniform, stepped further into the hall. Behind her, the grinding of a chair against floorboards caught her ears; footfalls followed, from the living room into the hall.

Quickly, Gothalia darted into an adjacent hall and pressed her back against the door so the frame hid her from view.

The shadow approaching grew under the lanterns, until she spotted L'Eiron striding the hall. Glancing from where she was to the window, she whispered,

"Do you think I can get out without breaking it?"

Honestly, Kronos replied.

"It's an old window with one horizontal frame. I'm sure there's a latch, just flip it up, push the window up then climb out."

"You don't need to be sarcastic."

"You don't need to ask a question you already know the answer to."

She moved to the window.

"You really have a distinct personality for an AI."

"Thank you."

She climbed onto the roof. Gently, closing the window, she snuck further down the building to where she knew the hall would end—there she paused, seeing through the window that L'Eiron had Aurelia in an intimate embrace.

"And that's our queue to leave," Gothalia muttered, and Kronos eagerly agreed. She travelled further along the roof, careful to make sure that L'Eiron did not notice her. Hidden from sight, she moved from the roof and to the house next door.

Gothalia advanced along the stone streets using the rooftops, alert to both the Customary and Centurion Peacekeepers who patrolled the city streets in groups or two-person teams.

Her uniform was as dark as the artificial sky, from which shone a sliver of moon.

"Their numbers are unusually heavy tonight," Kronos noted.

"I'm not in my cell. They're probably looking for me right now."

"What makes you think they're after you already?" he remarked, and Gothalia did not reply, only moved from one roof to another. She paused when a shadow shifted at the corner of her eye.

Out of sight, she observed a figure off in the distance, on the streets below. A woman was speaking to one of the Peacekeepers; but Gothalia paid no further mind, not even when she shoved one of them.

Gothalia pressed on until she was away from the tall buildings, where the city began to fade away into a countryside landscape along the massive cavern.

She mounted the horse that she found at the edge of the fields and continued along the grassy countryside before stopping at the edge of the crater, just before a long drop into the magma below. Dismounting the horse, she patted it, before walking along the bridge that connected her home to the other countries.

"Looks like we're here. That was easier than expected," Kronos announced proudly, as if he'd made the journey himself.

"And yet, I'm the one with real legs," Gothalia retorted and walked towards the "docks" as most of the Centurions called it.

It was a small town outside of the Fire Reserve that ferried other Excelians to and from countries by the vast underground boats. Gothalia eyed the largest ship.

"Of all the advancements we've made, I never understood why we still use boats."

"It's to give jobs to the water and air-users, not to mention those with other unique abilities," Kronos replied.

"Good to know. Okay, so now what?" Gothalia inquired, striding through the evening market, and passing the smell of various spicy soups and other foods, including merchants who called for customers. At the same time, her ears caught the conversations of excited travellers who could not wait to enter the Land of Fire. Gothalia tactfully avoided border security draping the hood attached to her cloak over her face.

"Now, we meet Betheous," Kronos declared and Gothalia observed the buildings she had become so accustomed to over the years, admiring the old architecture, the various edifices. Houses, office buildings, hotels, and even brothels were stacked along the walls. With her faceplate on, Kronos locked onto the building where she expected to meet Betheous.

# Chapter 19

BY THE HIGHEST TOWER, lit by fiery torches beneath the full moon, Gothalia knew where any person with the appropriate information would hide. Her faceplate pulled away from her features as she moved through the crowd of people, dodging Peacekeepers, and other Centurions from different areas, who returned from other countries or were on their way to their next missions.

Successfully, she slipped by unseen and travelled through the more silent section of the small town to an area that housed a brothel.

She grimaced, not because she would look down on such place, but because of the type of men within.

"You can wait until you're ready if you want to," Kronos commented, feeling her heart rate rise with her anxiety.

Gothalia brushed off his concern.

"It's not like I haven't been in one before it's just—"

"—Not your scene."

"Something like that."

"Try not to think about it," Kronos encouraged when she climbed the steps.

"How can I not think about it?" The open doors filtered out music and a mixed smell of sugar and mint. Extensive security guarded the inside and outside of the buildings. Their eyes watched her with interest, and one stopped her.

"You're the new replacement for tonight's entertainment?" he questioned, and Gothalia realised what Kronos had done—forcing herself into character.

"I am. What shall I do first?" Gothalia asked, in a deep, seductive tone.

The guard cleared his throat and stepped back while others smiled.

"Follow me, your client awaits." He moved past her, and the men behind her stared; she forced a wink and a smile at them as she walked away.

"Well played, very convincing," Kronos congratulated her.

Betheous sat at the far end of the room, with a glass of wine in hand.

"Have a seat, *bella*." He gestured to the seat beside him. Gothalia smiled and moved towards him, only to pause and sit opposite him without breaking eye contact.

He frowned.

"Your defence could use some work, especially considering he beat you that day."

Betheous' eyes narrowed.

"You're not accompanying me, tonight, are you?"

"No. That's not in my job description." At that, she tapped the side of her headset twice, permitting the digital disguise to disappear, leaving her full suit tactical gear exposed. Then she sat cross-legged, across from a shocked Betheous.

"Lieutenant, I . . . um . . ."

She raised a hand. "I'm not concerned about this particular embarrassment on your part. Where's Numitora?"

Betheous raised a brow. His lips twisted in thought as he stroked his grey-peppered beard.

"I heard you have beef with her, and I wonder why that is? Is it because of that day? Or is it because she killed your cousins in cold blood?"

"We should retreat," Kronos advised.

Ignoring Kronos, Gothalia pressed,

"All of the above. That's why I was surprised that you had an affiliation with a traitor."

"I have no affiliation with her. She requested something of me, with a high price tag, and I delivered." Betheous seemed disinterested. "If the price is right, I always deliver, no matter who the client is." Gothalia frowned, disapproval seeping from her pores at his arrogance. "What will you do if I tell you? Will you go after her?"

Betheous stood, unconcerned that the towel slid from his waist into a heap on the floor.

Gothalia's eyes remained on his, holding his calculating gaze, before she stood as well.

"I will." She refused to let her disgust surface. "But I get the feeling you won't just give away her location without an exchange of some sort. What would you have me do? For your sake, it had better be appropriate."

"It is. I need you to get something for me. It is in the caves not too far from me. You retrieve it, then we talk."

Without another word, Gothalia turned her heel to leave, but she heard him clear his throat expectantly.

"Leaving now would only raise suspicion, since no one can see who you really are unless Kronos provides them access to such sensitive information. Imagine being cornered, with no escape."

Gothalia remained quiet for a moment before saying tentatively,

"How so?"

"Oh, I don't know—by you not doing your job."

"I am! I'm protecting my home!"

Blankly, he stared at Gothalia before scanning the rest of her. She glanced down at herself and saw that Kronos had reactivated the disguise without her knowledge.

"I apologise, my lady," he said and Gothalia inhaled deeply before seeing Betheous nod to the cameras.

"I suggest you act convincingly."

And so, for the next hour, she did. She pampered him with massages and gentle tones, periodically pinching him hard, as a reminder for him to watch his hands before he lost them to the sword on her hip. When she vacated the area, the security guard stopped her.

She felt her heart leap into her throat, though she did not waver.

"Can I help you?"

"Yes, you can," he informed her, abruptly. "Come with me."

As the security guards guided her through the building and towards another room, she grew suspicious.

"In here," the guard said and Gothalia frowned. The way the guards moved was not like other Peacekeepers. Their stance and their footwork looked like some she had seen somewhere else, but she could not remember.

She entered the small room, as they held open the door. Within were just chairs, a table, and an empty bookcase. She regarded the sight of it with distrust but ensured she kept her disguise up. The guards closed the door.

Then, from within the shadows of the room, a figure shifted, going from invisibility to visibility.

"You," she gasped.

"I'm sorry, you recognise me?" he asked, his golden eyes searched her false green ones.

"No, sorry." Gothalia shook her head. "I think I got you mixed up with someone else."

He was silent for a moment, then gestured to a chair.

"Sit, you must be tired after your challenging work. Betheous can be a lot sometimes."

Without a word, Gothalia sat in the chair.

"Who are you?"

He sat in the chair opposite her, separated by a wooden table.

"My name's Altair. You are an extremely dangerous being, aren't you, Gothalia?"

FRUSTRATED, CURT GAVE the order to retreat. He threw a grenade a few feet in front of the aliens. The shell landed beneath the bonnet of a car. A few seconds later, there was a violent release of energy, accompanied by a shock wave's familiar blast.

Quickly, they hurried away from the enemy and rounded the building they exited. Andrew and Leandra scanned the surroundings while Noel-Len and Michael fumbled with a car door. Within the car sat a headless human. Blood sprayed the windshield. Noel-Len heard Caprice and Michael gasp at the sight of the body.

"Looks like someone shot him," Mark said from beside Noel-Len. "We won't take this car."

Noel-Len closed the door. His eyes lingered over the empty car park.

"We need to return to base," Noel-Len reminded them.

"Looks like we're going there on foot," Sergeant Curt McGuire and his squad, with Caprice, Mark, and two other civilians headed south, away from the city centre. Luckily, they stumbled upon two cars parked on the side of the street. The civilians and Mark took the first car while Sergeant McGuire took Leandra, Andrew, and Michael. "Hop in," he told Noel-Len. Noel-Len glanced at the lack of room before his eyes moved over to a red bike, similar to his motorcycle.

"I have a better idea," Noel-Len said. His eyes drifted to the rider, who was several feet away, wrapped around the base of a tree. Noel-Len picked up the bike. "Sorry about this mate." He hotwired the bike and mounted it as the engine rumbled to life.

The city was silent as they drove down the streets. Occasionally, stumbling upon an alien or an inhuman. Not once did they engage in a fight unless they had no other option. When the empty highway finally divided into two directions, Curt stopped his car.

"This is where we leave you," he said. "Keep heading down the Stuart Highway, and you'll be out of the city in a few hours."

"Are you sure you don't need me to stay?" Mark asked. "I do have weapons training, Sarge."

Noel-Len smiled, but he knew what the Sergeant would say.

"That's why you can't come. *They* need you." Curt's eyes fell on the civilians in the back of Mark's car, then he pulled away down the road. Noel-Len rolled his bike up beside the car, aware of Mark watching him in the side mirror.

"Stay alive, kid." Mark said.

"Sir," Noel-Len responded. He pulled away as well and followed Curt back to base.

As expected, base was filled with the bodies of dead soldiers. Noel-Len felt his insides twist as he recognised several faces.

When Noel-Len pulled up beside Curt's car, he saw the horror in Caprice's eyes and heard Michael promise it would be okay. Noel-Len glanced away and climbed off his bike. He had one thing at the forefront of his mind: they had to survive.

The group entered the closest building and was met by Anaphora and the SAS soldiers.

"Look who's back." said a woman. Noel-Len regarded the sandy-haired woman. She was carrying the patch of the SASR unit.

"You sound disappointed, Maria," Andrew muttered, taking off his helmet.

Noel-Len suspiciously eyed the rest of the office room.

"Where is everyone?" he asked Anaphora, who had been examining the whiteboard covered with numerous battle strategies.

Her conflicted gaze drifted to the back of the room. Noel-Len had never been inside this building, but he knew it was much bigger than the area they currently occupied. No one moved as he crept towards the darkness at the back of the room, which everyone else was avoiding.

Noel-Len moved to the verge of the chilling shadows. It was as if they beckoned him closer, while the expression on his fellow soldier's faces slowed each of his movements. His heart thundered in his tender chest. The pain from his injuries and stiff muscles resumed with his slowly increasing adrenaline rush.

Beneath his feet, the ground felt softer and stickier. Noel-Len froze. Lifting his boot, he recognised the dark wet colour of the blood on his beige combat boots. His eyes made out soldier's feet, inches from his boot. He stepped back.

"Noel-Len, what's wrong?" Caprice asked, moving towards him, but was held back by Michael. Caprice glanced at Michael and saw that he and Noel-Len knew something she did not. "Something's wrong isn't it?" she asked again, her eyes searching Noel-Len's back.

Noel-Len swung around, facing Caprice.

"We're in a war. One we might not be able to win," he said, his brows creased in frustration and worry. He muttered under his breath, "Seems like history is repeating itself."

A hush filled the room. His words filled the soldiers with both shame, remorse, and anger.

"That may be the case, but at least we have a fighting chance," Curt said.

Noel-Len's held his gaze.

"How?"

"We're still alive, aren't we?"

"Even if that's the case," Michael began, "We have no idea what to expect. This is a new enemy. One we've never encountered."

Anaphora, Curt, and James Michaels shared a look, one that caught Noel-Len's curiosity.

"What do you know?" he asked, cutting Michael off. He received a sharp glare from his old friend, but Noel-Len ignored Michael and Caprice's building anxiety as he studied his superiors.

"It's complicated," Anaphora deflected. "However, these aliens, as you know, aren't new."

"I know." Noel-Len studied Anaphora. His jaw tensed as he fought the images of his mother's premature demise from his mind. "But it can't be that complicated."

"It's more complicated than you give it credit for," Anaphora responded. She informed Noel-Len and the others who recently returned to the barracks about the immediate military response to the invasion, and the preparations to mark Darwin and the surrounding smaller towns as a war zone.

Noel-Len knew this news would reach the public; it was only a matter of time. Most of Darwin's residents had already vacated the city due to their lack of sense of security.

The government attempted to remind the rest of the Australian citizens, residing within the rest of the untainted cities, of the natural beauty the Northern Territory possessed, and was criticised for its disregard for the traumatised citizens and its insensitivity.

Soldiers were set up several kilometres around Coolalinga, a country town with more bushlands than the rest of the higher-populated areas, to ensure that civilians wouldn't enter the dangerous regions, and to tend to the survivors with minor injuries or fly out those with severe injuries.

This was the General's attempt to keep the invaders from breaching the rest of Australia, or so he hoped.

Due to this, Anaphora declared that their next mission was to observe and eliminate as many threats as possible with the help of the advancing soldiers. She informed Curt McGuire that his team would be briefed further before deployment.

While he waited for briefing, Noel-Len was tended to, with new bandages around his chest and arm. The pain diminished a little. He hadn't felt the effects of his injuries until his body had completely cooled down and the adrenaline didn't rush as vigorously through his veins.

Even within their command post, he felt he was not safe. He was still discreetly peering over his shoulder, waiting for the next assault. The lack of safety was only reinforced by the deceased soldiers at his feet. Finally, the newly arrived soldiers removed their remains.

Sergeant Curt McGuire guided his combatants to their lodgings in a building further away from the command centre and across the mowed green grass, untouched by blood and shells.

The building was silent, as were Noel-Len, Leandra, Michael, Caprice, Dave, and the members from Sergeant James Michael's unit. They followed Sergeant Curt McGuire into the large open room, which had once been an office.

Curt pointed at the blue carpeted floor, marked by the moved office furniture.

"Make yourself comfortable. You finally get a rest."

Noel-Len and Michael did not respond. Without a moment of hesitation, Leandra, Caprice and Maria moved to one side of the room, while Dave, Noel-Len, Michael, and the rest of the men moved to the opposite side of the room.

The division was merely to ensure Caprice, as a civilian, was comfortable; Noel-Len knew Leandra did not care. He was con-

fident she stopped caring when she was stuck in a room with
Michael and the other men during their year-long training. Maria,
like Leandra, would have been through the same thing.

Oddly, he was a little envious of their mentality. Sometimes,
Noel-Len did not want to be in the same room as Michael when it
came to sleep. He had a habit of keeping Noel-Len up until the early hours of the morning or talking in his sleep.

Noel-Len silently hoped Michael was too tired to talk tonight.
When he peered over at his friend, he was surprised to find Michael
lying on his sleeping bag, already asleep, his boots and gear set neatly at his feet. Noel-Len did the same and scanned the room.

By that time, everyone else was already asleep. His pain had become more bearable, thanks to the medication. Lying down, Noel-
Len's heavy eyelids drifted shut. He curled and turned in his sleep,
his mind twisting over the memories of the recent horrors and the
last memories of his mother.

After three hours of drifting in and out of an unsatisfying sleep,
he finally climbed out of his sleeping bag. His breathing was quick
and his skin clammy. His fingers tugged at his hair, an action he was
not consciously aware of.

"Can't sleep?" Sergeant James Michaels asked. Noel-Len
looked over and saw Curt beside James. He sat fully upright against
the wall, his eyes closed, with a knowing smile on his lips.

"Yeah," Noel-Len said. "How long as he been like that?"

"Not sure," James said and glanced at his watch. "I didn't exactly check the time when I walked into the room. Maybe an hour or
so."

"Looks uncomfortable," Noel-Len commented, his brow
raised.

"You get used to it," James said. "How are your injuries?"

Noel-Len flexed his tender arm and ran his hand over his sensitive shoulder, bandaged beneath his murky green shirt.

"Sore."

James did not say anything. Noel-Len climbed to his feet.

"I'll be back." With that, Noel-Len exited the room and headed outside.

The grass was still green, but he knew it was only a matter of time before it became colourless and dead, like everything else around him. Clutching his chest, he moved to the fence and watched as the silent trees danced in the calm breeze.

Closing his eyes, he felt the wind trace its gentle fingers against the light stubble beginning to form on his face. He glanced up and observed the dark skies overhead, clouds darker than any brewing storm thundered towards him, especially at this time of year.

"Shouldn't you be resting?"

Noel-Len glanced over his shoulder and regarded Anaphora standing behind him, a meter away. She remained sharp and clean, as expected. It appeared as if the battle for their home had not had any effect on her. Her eyes, though, were empty. Seeing her blank look, he hoped she was as shaken as he was.

"I should be, ma'am."

She raised a brow at his tone.

"Then why aren't you?" she inquired, marching to him. "It's not safe out here."

"You're welcome to leave." Noel-Len turned away from her.

"You're worried, aren't you?"

"Are you ordering me to answer? . . . Ma'am?"

Anaphora did not speak, studying him. Her eyes were stern.

"No. You may be a soldier, but I'll only ask questions that need to be asked. There is a psychologist on base if you feel you require it."

"No thank you, ma'am."

"Private. That wasn't a request."

With one last look at her, he marched away. His mood changed within a blink of an eye from scared to worried to frustrated. Each one swirled like a brewing tsunami within him.

He stopped, his eyes on the other soldiers in the distance who had recently returned. Their uniforms were dirty, torn, and some covered in blood. Several were minorly injured, others severely injured. He glanced away; he knew there would be more casualties. By the amount that returned, he knew that they had suffered another massive loss.

He recognised two men, the Marines he'd met on base, what seemed like years ago. Their shaved heads did not hide the dried blood nor the dirt on their tanned skin. Noel-Len was surprised when they caught his eye. The looks that had flashed across their faces when they saw Leandra and Tracey had vanished, replaced with pure horror and distress. Noel-Len swallowed.

He needed to find Tracey.

Noel-Len marched to the infirmary with Michael at his heel after he had woken him up, both curious to see if Tracey had survived the attack.

Entering the infirmary, Noel-Len scanned each injured soldier in bed or walking past him.

However, his attention was caught as a man with a rank equal to Anaphora graced the room.

The man did not glance at Noel-Len as he passed, leaving both Michael and Noel-Len confused. They still hadn't found Tracey anywhere.

Walking further inside, he caught wind of a familiar voice drifting through the tense environment.

He followed the sound.

"You need to calm down," said a voice. Around the bend of the curtain, Noel-Len peered down at Tracey's battered and bandaged body. "I'm not the enemy." Noel-Len recognised the voice;

his attention fell on the doctor at the side of the bed. Dr. Thornton, with his crew-cut strawberry-blonde hair and thick jawline, happily tended to her injuries.

"You're right. He's not," Noel-Len announced and stopped at the end of her bed. "What happened?" He stared at her arm. The white bandages tightly wrapped around her upper arm and elbow; beneath that, nothing else remained. His attention returned to her stunned expression as she tried to hide her handicap from him. Shame shadowed her features as she glanced away.

"We were ambushed. Even though we were certain it was safe to pass through. The buildings tumbled, and trees were uprooted. A huge metal beast is all I remember. I remember choking on dirt and hearing the loud echo of the Para Minimis firing from the other people of my unit. No matter how close anyone got, the beast was impervious to our bullets. It was the largest human thing I have ever seen, over eleven feet tall. Don't get me wrong, I've seen bigger creatures, like those drop-bots but. . ."

"Drop-bots?" Michael asked, from beside Noel-Len.

"It's what most of us are calling them. Those machine monster things that climb out of the pods." Her voice grew heavy. "That–thing–picked us up and threw us around as if we were nothing. Some died in an instant. Others were burned or were chopped to pieces with its weapons."

"What type of weapons?" Michael asked, and before he could receive an answer, Dr. Thornton ended the conversation, implying that Noel-Len and Michael leave Tracey alone. Even as they walked away, Noel-Len was aware of Dr. Thornton watching them.

Tracey scrutinised Dr. Thornton with concern.

"You believe me, don't you?"

Dr. Thornton remained silent, critically selecting his next words, before declaring,

"You didn't lose blood when your forearm was removed. I'm sure that scorch mark alone says it all." With that, he left Tracey alone. Relaxing against the pillow, she forced her mind to shut out all the sounds and attempt to sleep, even though her tired mind repetitively replayed the horrifying memories of the past few days.

A few feet away, Michael paused.

He studied the infirmary behind him.

"What's wrong?" Noel-Len asked. Michael regarded the soldiers positioned outside the doors of the building. He knew that the injured soldiers should be protected, but he also knew those that were seriously injured would not be able to fight back, let alone make it out alive, if they were attacked.

They would be easy targets.

"That officer who exited the infirmary before . . . do you recognise him?" Michael's eyes returned to his friend.

Noel-Len considered his words for a moment; his expression was calm and reassuring. With a hand on his friend's shoulder, he said,

"I'm not sure but try not to worry about it." Even as Noel-Len uttered those words, he could not deny his own concern about a high-ranking infantry officer entering the infirmary.

Without another glance at Michael, he sped away, hoping the movement of his legs would wipe away the concern he felt twist in his stomach.

# Chapter 20

AN AIR OF UNDERSTANDING shifted between them and Gothalia regarded Altair for a moment longer.

"Come on, how much longer are you going to pretend like I don't know who's really being kept hidden beneath your disguise?"

Gothalia removed her cloak and narrowed her gaze. Altair smiled.

"That's better, now I can actually talk to you—properly."

Gothalia sat in the chair before him, and something shifted around her wrists. Shocked, she tried to move.

"What is this?" she asked, panicked. Silver metal had oozed out of the chair and melted over her wrists before moving to her hands and solidifying.

"It's called morphella. It can, as you see, capture its prey by crawling over its skin and shackling it. Quite clever; it saves us the trouble. The Xzandians are very smart if you ask me. This invention is perfect for now. Anyhow, Gothalia, isn't it? I'm quite glad I've finally gotten the opportunity to meet you. I've heard so much. It feels like I already know you. Which explains, why I have to do this." Without a second thought, he pressed a cloth over her mouth and nose, forcing her to inhale its scent. Within seconds, she passed out and he folded the cloth back into his utility belt and removed the morphella from her wrists. Then he threw her over his shoulder and left the room, with guards outside in tow.

He travelled down the vacant halls and towards an electric vehicle parked outside the back doors of the brothel. A homeless man regarded Altair for a moment and Altair handed the Gothalia to a guard.

He strode over to the homeless man and declared,

"Tell no one and you might live." With that, he handed the man a couple of hundred dollars, then moved to the car.

They placed Gothalia in the backseat, using morphella to again secure her in place, before climbing into the front. A second later, they were on their way.

AN HOUR LATER, AFTER the group discovered Gothalia's disappearance, they retraced her steps and stumbled upon her latest location.

L'Eiron and the others cornered Betheous as he stepped out of the brothel.

"Hey, guys," he said with a casual smile. "Here to get your fix? I heard there are a few party favours for the women too." He eyed Demetria who pulled her lips up in disgust before asking,

"Where's Gothalia? And don't lie, if you don't want to become a popsicle for the rest of your life."

"How am I supposed to know?" he asked. "You sure you have the right person?"

L'Eiron stepped forward; the tracking device he had placed on Gothalia's uniform Michalis' request had provided them with all the information they needed. But he wasn't about to explain that to Betheous.

"We're sure. Now, where is Gothalia? Don't make me ask again."

Betheous smirked, and Danteus pinned him against the wall.

"We know she was here."

"Then you must know what she does in her spare time," he remarked with a sly smile and Danteus slammed his head against the closest glass window, then pinned him back against the wall.

"Unless you want me to find another way to hurt you, you'll talk," Danteus threatened.

"There is nothing you can do to me that can ever scare me," Betheous retorted with an amused look on his face.

"Want to bet?" L'Eiron asked

"They're really angry," Demetria hissed to Levi, concerned. "And Betheous may be dead soon."

"Yeah, he just may be." Levi sighed. "It's not like we need another reason for the Peacekeepers to be after us." Then Betheous screamed, startling Levi and Demetria, as L'Eiron used his elemental abilities.

"You don't need to be with us, Your Highness," Demetria declared. "We all still believe it's best you go home."

"As I said before," Levi replied, "I'm helping Gothalia. She saved me. I will save her. There will be no further discussion."

"Okay. But it will get messy. Are you prepared for that?"

There was a moment of silence before Levi replied.

"I am."

"Good. You need to be in a job like this."

When Betheous' screaming died down, L'Eiron threw him to the ground. He climbed to his knees.

"Okay," Betheous began, "I've never been the one to kiss and tell, but . . ."

"But—*what*?" Danteus growled, impatient.

"Simmer down." Demetria put a hand on his shoulder. "If you kill the guy, he won't tell us where she is."

"That's the thing. I don't know where she is. She spoke to me, then left," Betheous confessed his hands in the air. "I swear."

L'Eiron pressed,

"What did these guards look like?"

"I don't know, I didn't get a clear look, but . . .They seemed to know her."

"Do you think it's the Order?" Danteus asked L'Eiron.

"It has to be," Levi interjected. "Or why else would they take so much interest in her? Did you see which way they went?" he asked Betheous.

"No. Maybe . . . yes—actually. They went further down the hall—inside."

L'Eiron released Betheous, who then guided them inside, down a few corridors, before retracing his steps towards the room where he'd last seen Gothalia. Danteus's frown deepened as he eyed the comfortable room.

"This is where we were. I saw them take her that way," he said, pointing towards an adjacent corridor that led to only one room.

"Thanks. You've been an immense help," L'Eiron acknowledged.

"You're welcome." Betheous' grin faltered when he caught Danteus's dark gaze. Then the group parted from Betheous and entered the room. There was a table and two chairs. One was knocked over, but the place appeared otherwise untouched.

"There's nothing really here to indicate a struggle," Demetria commented.

"Aside from this chair," Danteus declared and kneeled before it. His hand slid over the wood while his gaze dissected it.

"That chair won't tell us anything," L'Eiron said.

"But this might." Levi walked further ahead and towards an emergency door that led into an open car park. It was empty.

"Good job," L'Eiron commented, then stepped outside. "But it looks like a dead-end."

"I don't think so," Levi said, gesturing to the homeless man not too far from them. Levi and L'Eiron shared a look and approached the man, who ran at the sight of them. They chased him down easily and L'Eiron caught hold of him.

"Why would he run?" Levi asked.

"Because he knows something," L'Eiron replied as the others joined him.

"I know nothing!" the man yelled, holding up his hand to reveal a several hundred-dollar bills. The man regarded the money and L'Eiron's heavy look.

"You better think very carefully about what you say next. It may be the last thing you ever say," L'Eiron warned, his voice dark. "Who paid you?"

"No one," he responded.

"You can't get money out of thin air. Where did you get it?" Demetria asked from beside L'Eiron and Levi.

L'Eiron's hand erupted in small sparks of electricity that, bit by bit, began to crawl towards the terrified man.

"You have three seconds to tell me who paid you or you'll suffer by my hand."

Demetria and Danteus were stunned by the intense expression L'Eiron bore but did not say anything.

"One . . ." he began, then skipped to, "Three."

"Okay!" the man yelled, before L'Eiron could electrocute him with blue lightning. "A man with golden hair and eyes took her."

"What else did he look like?"

"Like he was from the Northern Reserve. He had russet skin and sharp features. He took her with the other guards and put her in a car, then drove away." At those words, Danteus's and L'Eiron's heart sank.

WHEN GOTHALIA WOKE, she was in the back of a car. Her mind felt groggy. The car stopped and Gothalia did not move. She attentively listened to the voices, distinctly hearing one ask,

"Do you have her?"

"We do," a man said. "It was almost too easy."

"As long as you have her, that's all that matters," the voice responded. Then the sound of coins permeated the air. "Here's your payment. Open the boot." There were footfalls and Gothalia closed her eyes. Moments later, light shone through the open boot and skimmed over Gothalia's unmoving body. "Get her out and take her to the doctor. We'll gather what we can from her blood."

Gothalia felt arms pull her out of the vehicle but not once did she move, allowing her limp body to be thrown over a thick shoulder. She was carried some distance. Then there was a familiar voice.

"So, you finally have her, I see."

"Yes. Your services are no longer required, Numitora."

"Bummer," Numitora declared with spite. Then footfalls approached Gothalia once more. Numitora gripped her hair and pulled her head up. "I would have enjoyed killing her slowly." The other woman, Gothalia could tell, pried Numitora's fingers from Gothalia's hair and smacked her hand away.

"You'll not touch what's mine," she warned, in a dark tone. "Or you'll end up back in that prison. And I promise, I'll put you there myself."

There was a moment of silence.

"I understand," Numitora said, forcefully.

"Do you?" she queried. "Last I checked, you went off and attacked her in her own home when that wasn't a part of our plan—then you got captured and if it wasn't for Altair you would still be rotting in their prisons. I suggest you tread very carefully—if you don't want to end up like your friend."

With that said, the man carrying Gothalia continued moving, following the woman out of the garage and into an unsecured area lit with lights. Finally, he paused.

"I have a gift for you. Doctor," the woman said. Gothalia could hear her smile.

"Well done," the doctor said. "Set her down." The man carried Gothalia from the edge of the room and towards a metal table in the centre, not too far from where the old doctor stood in his bloodied lab coat and thick black gloves. The man set her down and the doctor said, "Well done, for acquiring such a specimen. I trust it was no easy feat?"

"Unfortunately, it was. We just set out a rumour of Numitora's presence and she came running like a lap dog. Not that I care. I'm glad the final phase will be complete soon."

"Patience child. We have yet to extract this demon at the right time. Until then, keep looking for Midnight Eclipse. I'm sure Arthur will tell you all he needs to, if he doesn't want to endure further torture."

"He continues to remain silent. Nothing's working. Why don't you just extract the information, as you'll do with the demon?" she queried.

"Again, *patience*. We did not spend twenty years preparing to conduct our plan to search for Midnight Eclipse, only have you mess it up because you cannot be patient. We will lose everything we worked hard for within seconds if we do not take the necessary precautions. And besides, I'm kind of interested to see how long he lasts."

"You're more sadistic than the rest of us. Fine, keep preaching patience like a priest. But if this does not work, he will have your head before he has mine or Altair's," she warned, then was on her way, the guard in tow.

Gothalia, who had peeped at the scene, closed her eyes quickly when a shadow towered over her.

"You're not going to enjoy this. Good thing you're asleep."

When she sensed that the doctor was close enough, Gothalia's eyes snapped open and her fist struck the doctor in the face. He jumped to his feet once more and scrambled for a needle.

Gothalia swung her legs over the edge of the table and kicked him in the face, knocking out him cold as he moved to inject her. Then she rushed towards the door.

At the threshold, she cautiously cracked the door open and peeked through. Soldiers walked past and a camera watched the room. Gothalia returned to the doctor.

"Kronos, scan the doctor."

Gothalia held out her wrist and a light scanned the doctor's body.

"Done, my lady."

"I'm surprised you were quiet that whole time," Gothalia commented with a smile.

"I figured you had something in mind. You weren't scared. Not even when he placed the sedative on you. Why is that?"

"He gave me the impression I was too valuable to be killed—for now anyway."

"And you gambled with your life?" he questioned. "That was risky."

"It was," Gothalia responded, sneaking out the door and down the hall. "But I had to. If I'm going to get answers."

"Answers for what? The attack?"

"Yes."

"What if we don't find them here?" Kronos questioned. "What then?"

"Then we keep looking. We can't just give up because it gets hard."

"I admire your grit, but what happens if there's nothing here?"

"There has to be something here, Kronos," Gothalia said. "There has to be." Gothalia paused at the end of a hall where a cleaner regarded her.

"Doctor Legato," the cleaner said. "How are you? Going for another walk?"

"Yes, I am," Gothalia replied and walked away. "Do you think I just blew my cover?"

"Maybe. We won't know until later," Kronos responded. "Keep moving, there is another room up ahead. It's the largest on the map."

"You've accessed the blueprints."

"It wasn't easy."

"Interesting," Gothalia said, not listening to him.

"What?"

"That room, there are machines." Gothalia saw the machines through the glass panel on the door; it swung back in place whenever someone exited or entered the room. Gothalia moved inside and noticed the sound of drills. The room was filled with the sounds of power generating and charging. Gothalia was amazed by the sight. She walked down the stairs and regarded the massive clock above the machines.

"Doctor Legato," a man called. "Glad you're here. The bombs are almost ready to be launched. On your order."

Shock consumed Gothalia, but she composed herself.

"Good. I'll let you know when they're to be dropped," Gothalia declared, with little emotion to her voice.

"Still I wonder, is it necessary? The surface worlds don't know of our existence, maybe if we waited—"

"—Waited for what?" another woman interrupted, walking towards them with her steps quick and her shoulders pulled back. Gothalia recognised the woman's voice, but not her face. "Waited for them to send in more reinforcements? They attacked the city of New Icarus, setting their filthy feet on our soil. They did the same thing in New Eorthen. What makes you think they will not come here? Our people would be endangered." She stepped before Gothalia and her gaze narrowed. "I thought you were taking care of that demoness."

"I've sedated and prepped her. I figured I'd stretch my legs a little and see how everyone was doing," Gothalia responded. "Is there a problem with that?"

"No. I'm just wondering why you're taking your time."

"We must be p—"

"—I swear to our ancestors, if you say the word patient again, I'm going to break something," the woman commented, with a scornful look.

Gothalia regarded the woman, evenly.

"Still that doesn't change my perceptive on things. I'll be the lab if you need me." With that said, Gothalia turned and walked away. "And—"

"Carolina," the woman reminded. "How you keep forgetting my name is more irritating than this 'patience' you possess."

"*Right,* Carolina," Gothalia declared evenly, with her hands behind her back and her back to the others. "Patience *is* a virtue. Remember that." Gothalia exited the room and paused outside the doors.

"Kronos, we have to do something," Gothalia said, at last, once she was clear of everyone else. "Those bombs, we need to find out what they're going to do with them."

"I'll guide you back to Legato's office. We may find some answers there."

When Gothalia arrived at Doctor Legato's office she was not surprised to find that the doctor had information stored on his computer about the bombs and the plans they had for her. The computer Gothalia used had an encrypted password, but Kronos helped her decrypt it.

"That's the experiment," Kronos said in her ear. "They were planning on using your blood to create super soldiers."

"What?" Gothalia exclaimed. "That's not possible and it doesn't make sense. Why create super soldiers? Excelians are naturally stronger and faster than Humans." An image of a large Xzandian crawled onto the screen and Gothalia regarded the thumbnail, then played the video. The largest Xzandian towered over a few Excelian Centurions and threw the Excelians to the side as if they were nothing, before destroying everything in the area. The Xzandian was massive and controlled elemental abilities of its own while wearing layers of unfamiliar armour. "How is this possible?"

"Excelians aren't invincible."

"I'm aware of that," she said. "But it still doesn't explain what that thing is."

"That could be what they're trying to match. Code-name: Behemoth."

Gothalia was certain that the Excelians could match the Xzandians, but she wondered about the Alastorians and the humans—what was their part in all this?

Then, in amongst it all, she found a file on herself: all her elemental abilities, the slaughter of her clan, whether she had had any children, information on the demon... Among all the files that she regarded there was one word on her file that the others had not had. It was the word 'upgrade' with a question mark beside it.

"Kronos, what do they mean by an 'upgrade?'"

"I don't know," he answered, after some time. Gothalia closed her file and moved on to the rest of her team's files. All the files were in-depth and included everything about them: their elemental abilities, their family trees, their ranks, and their clearances. "But I do know one thing. There must be a mole—otherwise how else did they get this information?"

Gothalia pushed herself from the computer and stared at the screen, conflicting emotions flashed across her eyes as she took in the information on everyone. Their positions were compromised—they themselves were compromised. There was a small red flashing light on the desk, not too far from the computer beneath it, reading: Lab AB. Gothalia's finger grazed over the button but did not press it.

"I wouldn't," Kronos warned.

"I know." Then Gothalia heard a noise. It was faint, but it was there. She moved from the desk down a corridor lined in cabinets and towards a red door. When she arrived at the door, she turned her attention to the keypad beside it. Gothalia removed the card she had confiscated from the doctor and swiped it along the keypad. The door opened, and she stepped inside. The noise grew, and what she discovered left her breathless.

Excelian bodies were stacked behind transparent glass tubes, each lit with green light and wired with oxygen masks and cords. She moved from the top of the stairs and towards the base, then walked along the centre where each body floated in green water.

"Are they're alive?"

"They're alive, just asleep. They must be sedated," Kronos responded. "I've recorded all the information we've found. I suggest we get out of here."

"Where's here and how much time do I have?" Gothalia asked as she made for the exit.

"Not long, Dr Legato will be waking up soon. And news of your escape will spread. We're currently on the outskirts of the Fire Reserve, in a small town called Armandale."

"I know where that is," Gothalia responded. "Kronos, bring up a blueprint of the facility."

"Give me a moment."

Then there was an explosion. As she moved throughout the building, further explosions permeated the far end of the room, shaking the ground beneath everyone's feet, and setting everyone off balance. Some fell upon each other like dominoes, while others managed to keep their feet planted by holding on to a machine; those closest to the wall were thrown across the room.

Suddenly, Gothalia's heart leapt: the explosions were caused by Danteus and his team! Quickly, she ran to them and the entire group pointed their swords at her. Gothalia held up her hands and removed her hood. "It's me."

Everyone relaxed and Danteus's eyes glittered.

"Are you okay?" he asked.

"I'm fine."

"Then let's go."

"We can't go just yet." Gothalia insisted. "There are bombs set to be dropped on the capital cities of the surface world; we need to dismantle them. Now. Otherwise, the Fire Reserve will be at war with the Surface Countries."

L'Eiron regarded Gothalia.

"Alright tell us what we need to do."

An ear-piercing yell resonated throughout the room. Then Numitora rushed at Gothalia and kicked her in the face, throwing her from the raised ground where the others stood. In moments, she'd taken out Danteus, Demetria and Levi—but L'Eiron stepped in.

Lightning erupted from his palms as he rushed at Numitora, who leapt onto a machine, and flipped off it. L'Eiron halted just in time to avoid her.

"Just when I thought you'd fall for that," Numitora taunted.

"I'm not so naïve," L'Eiron responded, his fists up.

Numitora shrugged,

"It was worth a—" Before she could finish, Gothalia tackled her to the ground and started throwing punches. Numitora held up her own, blocking the attacks. She caught both of Gothalia's arms and pushed them aside, then struck her in the head with her fist. Stunned by the attack, Gothalia pulled away and Numitora hit her again, hard. Gothalia's vision distorted as she climbed to her feet, cradling her head, and holding onto a nearby handrail.

Across the room, the woman who had spoken to Gothalia before entered, holding a rifle.

"You're a Centurion," she cried, and fired at Gothalia, who shoved Demetria to the ground in time to avoid the bullets. The others leapt out of the way and hid behind scattered desks—shielding them from the shots. "How did you get inside? I thought—"

"The doctor was taking care of me?" Gothalia taunted. "I took him out first."

Demetria crouched behind the desk with Gothalia.

"Try not to piss off the armed crazy lady, will you? Now go left." Gothalia nodded. When Demetria ran around the desk, Gothalia ran around the other side and tackled Carolina to the ground. As she removed the rifle from her grip, Demetria punched her hard in the face.

"Look at us, working as a team." Gothalia commented.

Demetria gave her a deadly look.

"I'm still mad at you, so don't make me hit you."

Gothalia held up her hands in a silent surrender. Her attention returned to her comrades; they seemed to have Numitora well in hand, so her and Demetria's attention shifted to the Human and Excelian mercenaries that charged out of the hall. Gothalia and Demetria met each other's eyes and nodded. In mutual agreement, they launched themselves at the soldiers.

"How did you guys find me?" Gothalia called to Demetria as they fought.

"L'Eiron said there was tracker of your uniform."

"You're messing with me."

"Nope. That's the truth."

Numitora's shriek caught everyone's attention, as L'Eiron used his lightning to throw her across the room.

"Again, that looks like *that* hurt," Demetria quipped. At Gothalia's confused look, she added, "Inside joke."

The mercenaries dispensed with, Gothalia jogged over to Danteus and Levi, who were climbing to their feet.

# Chapter 21

"ARE YOU GUYS ALRIGHT?"

"Never better," Levi responded.

"Good to hear."

Her eyes locked with Danteus and she gratefully smiled—he was alive.

"How did you guys get here?"

"We followed you," L'Eiron said joining the group once the action died down. And Numitora lay unconscious on the ground, L'Eiron contemplated killing her but thought against it. She would be better left alive to provide enemy information.

"See told you," Demetria commented. Gothalia did not say anything. Instead, her gaze drifted to the bombs.

"We have to shut that down somehow."

"We know, but how?" Levi asked. "We don't know their systems. We have no idea what software they've used."

"I do," Kronos declared. "It's the same one as on Dr Legato's computer."

"Kronos does," Gothalia repeated to her team.

"What's he saying?" Demetria asked. Kronos connected with their individual AIs. "So, all we need to do is overwrite the command sequence. Should be easy enough." At his words, more mercenaries and soldiers entered the laboratory, including the giant Xzandian that Gothalia had seen on the computer monitor.

"Oh no," she said and stepped back fearfully. The large room fell dangerously silent and still.

"My lady that's a . . ." Kronos began.

"I know!" she yelled, as the Behemoth charged at her. Its thundering feet echoed against the tiles it cracked beneath its weight.

"Separate!" L'Eiron ordered and the group scattered, running for cover as the Xzandians and the soldiers fired their rifles.

Gothalia took down a few soldiers, then avoided the hand the Behemoth threw at her, slipping out of the way and under it.

L'Eiron directed the team to take out the soldiers and Gothalia to battle the Behemoth.

"You want me to what?" she demanded, barely avoiding its strikes.

"Don't argue. Just do it. We'll hold the others off." L'Eiron took out a few soldiers and Gothalia growled as she leapt onto the Behemoth's hand and ran up its arm. Taking her opportunity, she sliced the Behemoth in the neck. The beast screeched, but the cut was not deep enough to do real damage. Gothalia cursed and flipped off the Behemoth.

She landed on the ground, and the Behemoth towered over her. Its eyes burned with rage. Earth, fire, air, water, and lightning erupted into the room, shooting out of the Xzandians' scaly hands.

"I swear, these aliens enjoy making us miserable."

"I'm sorry you're miserable." Kronos commented with genuine concern, catching Gothalia by surprise. She did not answer and avoided the earth attacks the Behemoth threw at her. Did he genuinely feel sorry for her? Perhaps. He was an AI. He was a computer, wired with the algorithms for empathy and sympathy, but he could not begin to comprehend how Gothalia must feel, especially in the middle of a fight. He knew she never wanted to become a Centurion—it was a fate she was forced into. "I apologise that was not a proper question."

Gothalia ducked and avoided another strike.

"It's okay... It's not your fault." Then the demon within pulsed, halting her movements. The Behemoth took its opportunity, hurling her across the room with a wave of water.

"Gothalia!" L'Eiron and Danteus yelled, as she was thrown violently into the wall. Danteus slipped by the soldiers, avoided the Behemoth, and ran to Gothalia. Her skin had become dotted in black and red markings. When she opened her eyes, they were red as blood. Shock engulfed Danteus, but she didn't notice; instead, she charged at the Behemoth. Her movements grew faster, and her strength increased as she battled the Behemoth, avoiding its attacks or slicing through the earth with her sword that materialised in her hand. Fully in her power, she dived towards the Behemoth, her red eyes burning with fury. She leapt from its large chest onto its head, and her sword pierced its skull.

Gothalia felt her energy she dissipate as she climbed from the Behemoth. She fell to her knees, but before she could hit the ground, Danteus caught her. He pulled out his pistol and shot at the remaining soldiers. As they fell, Gothalia woke up.

"Are you alright?" Danteus asked, kneeling behind the table, firing his pistol. When he took cover again, she responded:

"I'm fine. What happened?"

"What happened? You took out the Behemoth." When his pistol ran out of bullets and his energetic levels a little low, Danteus pulled the earth from the walls and across the floor, throwing all the soldiers that ran towards them across the room. Gothalia didn't say anything further; now was not the time to be thinking about what she could and could not remember.

Climbing to her feet, she vanished and reappeared behind the line of foot soldiers that moved towards them, firing their rifles. Explosions of fire erupted within the cloud of smoke, blinding, and taking out the enemies within. Demetria spotted Gothalia and how fast she moved.

"Two can play this game," Demetria muttered, then tossed her rifle aside and summoned an ice sword.

The soldiers caught in a sea of explosions never stood a chance. Gothalia narrowed her gaze on the ones furthest away.

"Gothalia, take out the snipers!" Danteus ordered through her earpiece, spotting them on the upper level. Without hesitation, Gothalia allowed the élanocytes of the Valdis clan to permeate her cells as they had before.

Her muscles expanded and she crouched, ready to sprint. Energy gathered around her feet, swirling in dust and dirt. Her eyes glimmered blood-red beneath her helmet. She launched herself at the alien soldiers and Excelian mercenaries, as fast as her body could take her. Smoke blew behind her, as black as ash and electric with explosions. It followed her and left behind only the screams of her victims.

No matter how swiftly Gothalia moved, no matter how hard she drove to eradicate their enemies' numbers, they remained numerous.

"There's too many," Gothalia gasped, yanking her sword from where it was embedded in the tile floor. Then ran at the next alien and deflected its attack, before shoving her blade through his chest. Pulling it out, she focused her attention on her next attacker. Her combat helmet that had once concealed half of her features now concealed it entirely while Kronos counted the enemies' numbers, their distance, and their weapons.

"Hold your position," Danteus ordered. "I'm on my way." The ground shifted beneath Gothalia, and she leapt out of the way as the earth split, causing the aliens to fall into the deep dark crevasses.

Her eyes lingered over an Alastorian in the distance and paused. There was nowhere to hide. Energy bullets fired at Gothalia, and she leapt out of the way, firing her arrows from her crossbow at the enemy before throwing the weapon aside and picking up a pistol from a fallen soldier.

She shot down several aliens, only to scream in pain when the Alastorian she had seen threw her onto her back.

"Gothalia!" Demetria cried through the radio. "You better be alright, Gothalia. Danteus, I can't hear her!"

Gothalia glared up at the Alastorian as it stared down at her, taunting. Then the Alastorian screamed as the alien bullets pierced its skin, irradiating it with only a few shots. Gothalia stared at the sight, stunned. Her arm ached, and her thoughts filled with fear. She was stranded in the middle of a battlefield and her shoulder burned. She suddenly recalled L'Eiron's voice from when she was much younger:

*"You carry the flame of the Ignatius. They weren't just excellent soldiers, but excellent healers."*

Closing her eyes, she concentrated on the ache in her shoulder. The shoulder numbed bit by bit. Eventually, her wound healed, and her eyes shot open as she rolled onto her feet. She stared at the heavily armoured alien; its black armour gleamed beneath the overhead lights and its black hair barely hid its scaly black skin.

The Alastorian did not speak, and neither did she. He spun his spear around in hand, preparing to strike. They launched themselves at each other, and Gothalia slipped past him in time for Danteus to throw forward sharp mounds of earth that only missed Gothalia's attacker by centimetres.

A cloud of dry ice concealed Danteus and Gothalia, hiding them from the eyes of the enemy and Gothalia ran her sword through the Alastorian. Then the entire battle was over. Gothalia observed the soldiers at their feet.

"Did they honestly think they were a match for us?" Demetria remarked. Gothalia gave her a look. "What? You know it is true. We're awesome."

Gothalia moved over to the computer, there she began to type in the codes to deactivate the bombs, following Kronos' instructions while the others stood guard. After, L'Eiron destroyed the computers and overheated the circuits, causing rapid explosions to go off throughout the laboratory. Then Gothalia regarded the tele-pads like the ones they had back in New Icarus.

"Isn't that—?" she asked L'Eiron.

"It is," he said. "Everyone on." Quickly, Levi, Gothalia, Demetria and Danteus clambered onto the tele-pads while he punched in the coordinates. Before the next round of soldiers could enter the area, they vanished and reappeared in the war-torn streets of Darwin.

"Why are we here?" Levi asked. L'Eiron set his jaw, determined.

"Because Anaphora needs us."

ALTAIR AND NUMITORA judged the platforms upon which they vanished, with vivid contempt.

"They've gotten away," Numitora spat before wiping her bloodied jaw. "That entire family will fall."

"Your hatred for them is a little—*odd*." Altair declared nonchalantly, walking over to Numitora with confidence to his stride. "It's not like Gaius died."

"No, it's not," Numitora admitted, spitting the blood from her mouth. "But I still hate—*her*."

"I know and in time, you'll have everything you ever wanted. Next time don't run away," Altair warned, his golden eyes landing on hers.

"I wasn't running away. It was a strategic retreat," Numitora responded. "Besides, you were right, L'Eiron does possess elemental lightning. Where he inherited that is another question."

"No, it's not. He's distantly related to the Barack clan. It's been several centuries since they've been united and bore an heir, but he must be one of the few who've activated the gene for that ability." Altair stepped past the cracked ground and the shards of ice embedded in the floor, then wandered towards the Behemoth on the ground. He regarded it with little surprise, then pressed the button on the device on his wrist. The image of the Behemoth vanished.

"Why did you not send out a real Behemoth?" Numitora asked. "Wouldn't it have been easier to take them all out if there were a real one present?"

"It would have been easier, but I wanted to see, with Dr. Legato, if there was a chance, she had accessed it."

"Accessed what?"

"The other level of her abilities. From what I've seen, she's barely scratched the surface. This war will eat her alive."

"Not if I have anything to say about it." Numitora's eyes glistened beneath the light of the bonfires throughout the room; then the emergency generator kicked in and power returned to the room.

"That's if you get to her first. But like Dr. Legato once said—"

"—Patience will win this war." Dr. Legato declared, entering the room brushing his shoulder as if there were specks of dust on it.

"I was wondering when you'd wake up," Altair greeted him. "So, is it true? Did she find out about project X?"

"She did."

"And?"

"I don't know. I wasn't awake to see her reaction. But I did notice one thing: if we keep pushing her, she'll access her demon more frequently. With its cells, we'll be able to finish the final stages; then our buyers can use it as they see fit. How are the weapons, are they still being sold to the Humans?"

"They are," Altair confidently said, brushing his well-manicured fingers through his slick golden hair. "I've made extra arrangements to have them moved."

"Excellent." Dr Legato said. "He should be pleased with that."

*"BECAUSE ANAPHORA NEEDS us."* Gothalia had never heard those words before.

To her, Anaphora never needed aid and never needed comfort. But she was aware that Anaphora and L'Eiron had known each other for a long time and meant the world to each other.

So, they walked together through the streets, moving past the bodies that lay untouched throughout the streets. They group regarded them with disgust and sadness.

"Some were only children," Demetria commented, glancing down at a body before her. "How cruel."

"Let's keep moving," L'Eiron ordered and the group cautiously executed through the deathly silent streets, until they stumbled upon a few Xzandians in clusters. Their armour gleamed beneath the moon, highlighting their subtle movements.

The group moved through the streets, closer to the Xzandians.

They were cautious. Careful. As such, the Xzandians did not notice their presence until it was too late. Swiftly and quietly, the Excelians began to take out the Xzandians. When only a few remained, L'Eiron gave the final order and the group took out the rest. Then before they could do anything else, a bullet grazed Gothalia's arm. The group scattered and ran behind abandoned cars and buildings for cover.

Gothalia recognised the sniper in the distance, and she ducked as a cloud of black smoke whipped around her. Avoiding the bullet in time, she vanished from the sniper's view.

The sniper sat hidden above, on the roof. Its scope scanned the demolished buildings and ruins below, searching.

With Kronos's help, Gothalia silently closed the distance between her and the enemy. Gothalia reappeared above the man; pulling out her crossbow, she fired. Gothalia turned her attention from the fallen sniper and regarded his uniform and the flag on his shoulder.

"That's an Australian."

"Why were they firing at us?" Kronos exclaimed. "You're not wearing the colours of the Xzandians and you don't have scales for skin." Gothalia's eyes lingered over the body. There was something off about the soldier, but she could not place it. Then her ears caught the sound of feet behind her. Quickly, she turned around to find a soldier behind her. Immediately, he launched himself at her with a knife. She caught hold of his wrist and disarmed him, but he avoided her kick with lightning speed.

They wrestled and she blocked and deflected most of his attacks, until he threw her to the floor and tried to pin her down. Gothalia held his wrists as he climbed over her, and she threw her head forward and head-butted him in the jaw.

He rolled from her and pulled out a pistol; Gothalia launched herself at him, avoiding the bullet. She leapt, threw her legs around his arm, and twisted. An explosive pop sounded, accompanied by his scream. They collided with the ground and Gothalia kicked him in the jaw before climbing to her feet.

Gothalia recognised him as the man she'd seen the day Argos died. He was dressed in the uniform of the Australian soldiers and Gothalia read the name on his chest. Walker. Then disarmed him before he could point his rifle at her.

"You!" Gothalia growled, pointing at the man.

He smiled at her.

"I'm sorry, do you know me?"

"You killed Argos!"

The man fired his pistol that he'd pulled from his holster. Gothalia threw a device at her feet and a steel shield was formed, which she crouched behind. A fire erupted in her fingers as she attempted to control her rage. She pushed the shield forward. Then with as much force as possible, she threw the man across the room. His weapon slid across the floor and, blood spilled from his head. Then his injury healed, and he climbed to his feet and ran.

"Excelian," she muttered, her gaze narrowing.

"See if you can catch me, little lady."

Gothalia chased after the soldier as he ran down the building's stairs and towards the lower levels, then out into the streets. Gothalia was suddenly surrounded by men. She pursed her lips and glared at the man she had chased.

"We have you surrounded. What will one woman do but submit to defeat?"

"I don't care for your numbers nor my impending demise. You killed Argos; I saw you that night, and for that alone, I will not submit," Gothalia proclaimed confidently, without an ounce of fear in her voice.

"You will," he growled. "Kill her!"

Gothalia glowered at the enemy, even as they ran to her while others pulled out pistols and fire. She avoided the bullets than took out the men one at the time, using their weight, power, and speed against them and allowing the sparks of the flames to ignite into a string of explosions that outlined the forms of each man. With a snap of her fingers, they were burnt alive. Among it all, the man she had pursued vanished.

"Where did he go?" she wondered, scanning the buildings. Then she entered one.

"Gothalia report, where are you?" L'Eiron asked.

"In a building," Gothalia responded. "About five-hundred meters south."

"I'm sending Danteus," he promised.

An Alastorian moved through the shadows of the abandoned office sites, watching Gothalia as she chased down her target, searching. Its eyes shimmered beneath the crescent moon and falling dusk. Its jade eyes locked onto the circle sketched in blood on a nearby wall. Gothalia regarded the ground, then paused, aware that she was no longer alone. She turned on her heel and disappeared from beside the corridor leaving the Alastorian searching for her.

Gothalia stepped out from the shadows. and walked up behind the Alastorian. She unsheathed her sword. As she approached, the scent of blood lingered in the air, along with the stench of rotting flesh. There had to be a body nearby.

Her eyes landed on a child's small form. Disgust twisted within her and her anger burned. She turned back to the monster only to freeze as it faced her.

It held an eerie smile upon its twisted features. Sharp teeth lined its mouth, and its red lips were coated in blood. Stunned, Gothalia stood motionless and slowly breathed in through her nose and out through her mouth. It was on her third breath . . . that the Alastorian attacked.

Its sharp claws cut the air, and Gothalia stepped back, deflecting the attack with her forearm guard. The deflection of the attack rang in the air.

Gothalia held up her arms to protect her head as the Alastorian continued to attack with its sharp claws. It kicked Gothalia's stomach, forcing her to stumble back and fall on her rear. The Alastorian leapt and pinned Gothalia to the ground by the arms. Gothalia knew she was in trouble and pressed the smooth button on her palm. Suddenly, electricity shrieked, and the Alastorian jumped from Gothalia a split second before electrocution.

"Clever," Gothalia muttered as she flipped to her feet. "You seemed to have smelt that before it happened."

The Alastorian let loose a gurgling scream, and Gothalia heard hurried footfalls approaching. She did not turn over her shoulder; she knew who it was. Suddenly, the Alastorian's arms wrapped around Gothalia. The Alastorian lifted Gothalia into the air and squeezed.

A FEW HOURS LATER, Noel-Len and the others were required to return to the battlefield. With new food rations, armour, uniform, packs, and weapons, Noel-Len felt different.

Noel-Len, Michael, and the rest Sergeant McGuire's team huddled in the back of a small truck and listened as the Marines and Diggers spoke with trembling voices and curled fists about the massive monster that Tracey had spoken about. They also spoke of a woman dressed in black, accompanied by two others in a similar uniform. Noel-Len heard Andrew ask Curt on what to do, and, for the first time, Curt did not know.

"Ignatius," Sergeant McGuire said. Noel-Len's dark eyes flickered to his team leader. "You still with us?" There was a hesitation to his words. Noel-Len's mind was distracted by the roar of the engine and the pulsing vibration of its machinery beneath his boots.

Curt bumped Noel-Len's helmet with the back of his fist. "Don't think about it. Remember, everyone's relying on us." Noel-Len nodded, and once again, silence filled the truck.

When they re-entered the battlefield, Noel-Len found the once-even tarmac roads almost torn from the ground, accompanied by scorched buildings, and melting ice spears. In the past few days, Noel-Len had seen grenade explosions; and what he witnessed opposite him was not damage from a grenade.

He followed Curt, with Leandra, Michael and Andrew following on his heels as they moved through the city to meet up with other Commandos and SAS.

Sergeant Curt McGuire's squad moved cautiously; their eyes vigilant. When they recognised the energy blasts of the enemy's rifles, they stopped and silently watched.

A man with red-orange hair stood at the end of the road, waiting, as the Xzandians approached him. He held a bow in his right hand and a quiver of arrows hung off his opposite bicep. The uniform he wore was identical to the woman who had saved them.

His dark eyes assessed the approaching drop-bots moving toward him. It reminded Noel-Len of an Old West standoff; the Xzandians waited for him to react before they launched themselves at him.

The stranger was impossibly fast. Noel-Len had seen that speed once before, with Anaphora, but assumed she was the only one who could move that fast. The man flipped out of the way in time, slipping past the giant alien robots.

He released an arrow, and a wire connected to the arrow lodged in the foot of the robot. He twisted around and wrapped the wire around its other ankle, then yanked.

The robot tumbled back.

Noel-Len heard Michael mutter 'shit' but did not pay him much mind as he watched the man leap high into the air. His body twisted around like an ice skater, and Noel-Len recalled seeing Olympic skaters perform the triple revolution on his television when he was younger. When the man released his next arrows, he took out both robots before they could reach him and landed perfectly on the chest of the first robot he'd tripped up. Pulling his bowstring back, he fired and walked away.

"Stay on guard," Curt ordered. "Move out."

# Chapter 22

NOEL-LEN MOVED IN THE formation his team had been trained to fall into when encountering a threat. His stomach twisted. In his mind, the stranger did not do anything wrong. He was only protecting himself. Before Noel-Len could utter his thoughts, Curt pointed the rifle at the man and demanded he freeze.

The stranger, with his back to them, held up his hands. Most of his face remained hidden. However, his red hair remained exposed, as did his lower jaw.

Curt demanded the stranger's name, but even with the rifle aimed at him, the man remained silent.

"Fine. Don't want to talk? You're coming with us." Curt ordered.

"Sir, what about the others?" Michael asked. "They need us."

"Don't worry. *He* may help us with that." The man ignored Curt and remained still, even when Noel-Len cuffed him with Flexi cuffs. The stranger was shoved forward to the front of the group. Curt made a threat or two, but it was not those threats that made Noel-Len uneasy. It was the way the man watched him.

A soldier that recently joined them was Jason who dragged the man, they acquired away and towards the shadows of the demolished buildings not too far from a crashed helicopter. As they passed, soldiers regarded him with perplexity but did not question or stop him. He tossed the man on the hard ground and pulled out a pistol, aiming it at the man's knees.

"Now, are you going to tell us who you are? Or do I have to shoot? Which is it?" he threatened.

Curt glanced at Jason, concern, and fear marred his expression. Andrew with Leandra turned away. This was not something they wanted to see.

Even Noel-Len had trouble accepting this . . . interrogation. It was inhumane. Sure, the man was the enemy, but he did not necessarily need to be shot, let alone in the knees, which would render him inadequate to save his own life.

"Is he the enemy?" Noel-Len muttered not expecting anyone to answer, let alone anyone to listen.

Leandra glanced at him from over her shoulder.

She too assumed the same thing. If this man were the enemy, he would not have fought the aliens as he did.

Jason fired a round at the man's feet.

"I'll count to five. One." He counted slowly. "Two . . . Five."

Everyone cringed at the echo of the gun, including Curt. However, they were stunned by the silence, and the lack of screaming. Then they saw a woman crouched in front of the man, with her sword impaled the ground, leaving no hint of the deflected bullet.

Jason collapsed.

Everyone pointed their rifles at the woman.

Curt rushed to Jason's side while blood pooled along his neck, soaking his uniform.

The woman climbed to her feet and regarded them. Anger hummed in the air between them, and a deadly snarl lined her pink lips.

Everyone felt the tension in the air gyrating at their trembling nerves. Curt held up his hands, then slowly reached for Jason.

"Take the man. We will not harm him. Let us tend to our own."

Curt and Andrew curled over Jason, placing pressure on the wound they feared had nicked his jugular.

Blood spilled through Andrew's fingers as he applied pressure. The emptiness in Jason's eyes made Noel-Len's stomach curl and Andrew painfully pull away. The distress of failure blanketed his sweaty features.

"He's gone."

THE UNNATURALLY ALASTORIAN screeched, then gargled like bubbling acid. Gothalia heard hurried footfalls approach. She briefly turned her attention from the Alastorian and to the person.

It was Danteus.

"Gothalia!" Danteus called, as he entered the corridor within the building, sprinting towards the demon and slicing at the Alastorian's arms. The Alastorian shrieked, and dropped Gothalia; Danteus ran to her, "You all right?"

"I'll be fine," she declared, her tone stoic as he helped her to her feet.

Danteus stepped back and placed his sword on his back. He held a handheld electronic crossbow, flicking his combat cloak away he watched the Alastorian began to morph, becoming something almost unimaginable. Its limbs extended and grew as did its body. It appeared stretched yet disproportional.

"Strange," Danteus muttered.

"Gee, you think?"

"How does it have so much energy?"

"Hold him off," Gothalia ordered him.

"What are you doing?"

"I need to find that assassin, if he's still around."

"The chances of that are slim to none; he's out of reach."

"Not with Kronos."

Gothalia sprinted by Danteus, and the ground uprooted behind her, exploding across the path of the Alastorian.

"I see you've scared everyone away," Danteus taunted.

"I'll. End. You," it managed.

"Oh, you talk. Just my luck," he said sarcastically. At that, earth flew from the ground and at the Alastorian; this provided Gothalia enough time to track the assassin. He'd run over the throughout the building.

He eventually slowed and faced the area he had run from. He calmed his breathing, then, with a smug smile, turned and walked away.

Gothalia's scream surprised him and he rolled out of the way to face her in combat.

"You killed Argos! I saw you!"

"Does anyone else know?" he asked casually, throwing her to the side. Gothalia moved out of his way and climbed to her feet.

"Why does that matter?" she asked. Their swords clashed throughout the silent office building.

"Because it means I get to kill you first!" he growled. Gothalia parried, avoiding his blade.

They battled for several moments longer until finally, Gothalia won. By some luck of the universe, she had survived yet again. Kneeling beside the injured man, she placed her knee on his wounded shoulder, and he screamed.

"Your arrogance is your downfall," Gothalia declared with a blade to his throat. "Now tell me, why did you kill the General?"

The man laughed, blood splattering everywhere.

"Because I was assigned to, idiot."

Gothalia punched him hard, not caring how the blood spattered across her armour and uniform.

"Why?" she pressed.

"Why does it matter?"

"It matters. Trust me." She pressed her knee harder into his shoulder and he screamed. "How did you get past the wards? And who do you work for?"

"Simple, I was let in," he said. "Not everyone in your home is perfect as you'd like to think. And not everyone agrees with the system your people have built. Your kind once stood for something. Now, you hide beneath our feet and keep your technology and your knowledge all to yourself, while pulling the strings of our society. You think your doctrine is so great that nothing can be corrupt.

"What did you think would happen when the surface world found out about your people and the purpose of their existence? Did you think they would be so welcoming? No. They would ridicule you for your abilities and your technology. And remember, I work for the Order of the Rukh, the most honourable of Excelians, Humans, and Xzandians working toward a better world, before you get any ideas about slitting my throat."

"Only fools would ridicule what they do not understand," Gothalia responded.

"That may be so."

"Tell me about the Order. What are their plans with the super Excelians? And before you lie to me, I've seen the files and I've seen the bodies." *Super Excelians* the words sounded odd falling from her lips. *Super Excelians.* They were—impossible to imagine.

"I don't know. All I know is that I was sent to assassinate your General and was paid a hefty sum in return." He coughed. Blood pooled at his lips and he smiled a crooked smile. "And in my eyes, he deserved his death, as does Arthur."

"What are you talking about? What about Arthur?" she asked, and he smiled.

"Arthur is long gone, and you'll never find him. Or the Fragments of Midnight Eclipse." Unable to hear any more, Gothalia climbed to her feet and walked away. Aware his injuries would bleed out.

Later, she stumbled upon Danteus, cleaning his sword. He glanced up at her with a glint in his eyes.

"What's wrong?" he asked.

Gothalia sighed.

"I know who killed Argos."

"Who?"

Gothalia glanced behind her.

"He did."

"The assassin? You found him?"

"I did, and I didn't like what I heard." Danteus' communicator beeped and Gothalia waited as he answered it.

"What is it?" he answered the video call.

"We need you back," Demetria told him. "Human soldiers almost killed His Highness."

"I'm fine," Levi called from behind her.

Gothalia peered over Danteus' shoulder.

"There's something else too," Demetria continued. "We need Gothalia to show us the Fragment she acquired back in New Icarus."

"Sure," Gothalia answered. She patted herself down, ensuring she still had it—and was thankful she did. She turned back to Demetria. "Where do you want us to meet you?"

"We'll send you the coordinates," Demetria said. "And Gothalia, just so you know, we have . . . unexpected reinforcements."

Gothalia and Danteus shared a look, before returning their attention to Demetria.

"What kind of reinforcements?"

"The Peacekeeper kind. You should stay out of sight."

"Done."

Then, as quickly as she had made the call, she was gone. Gothalia stepped away from Danteus, deep in thought.

"What's up?" he asked.

"I think you should go on without me."

"What do you mean?" Danteus asked. "Gothalia, I—" he began, then paused, with hesitation in his voice. Gothalia understood the reason for his hesitation and walked up to him. She tenderly kissed him on the cheek, hoping that would make up for everything.

"I'm not leaving forever. I'm just collaborating with you from a distance," she declared, hoping he'd understand.

"Okay." he said, and she had a rush of gratitude.

"What are you going to do?" he asked.

"I'm going to fight for my home and search for answers, as well as the Fragments of Midnight Eclipse."

"That's a lot to take on board. Will you be okay?" he asked. "On your own, I mean?" *Caring as ever*, she thought, and smiled.

"I'll be fine. I'll manage. I always have." She understood what she had to do.

He vacated the grounds soon after, heading towards the others, while Gothalia lingered in the street. Then she glanced down the hall for the assassin—only to discover his body had vanished, and she cursed.

AFTER SERGEANT MCGUIRE'S team had providing the young Lieutenant's body with the necessary respect, the first and second regiment of remaining soldiers moved to Sector Z, far from the front lines and hidden beneath a building. *I didn't know there was an underground bunker in the city filled with special forces?* Noel-Len thought and took a seat, with Michael, at the front, in one of the many empty seats that lined the room. A large projector screen had been set up against one wall. Once everyone was seated, high ranking officers like Anaphora entered the room, including a man with black and silver armour, concealed by a sleek black cloak.

The room tensed as they observed the stranger. He remained unmoved by the scrutiny and kept his eyes ahead, never drifting to the soldiers in front of him.

Soon enough, General Nathan Gunner entered, followed by Military Police.

His eyes drifted over every individual in the room. Under his piercing gaze, no one dared to speak nor move.

"Several of you know why you're here. Most of you don't."

"It has come to my attention that these Xzandians are here in search of a powerful relic called 'Midnight Eclipse'. It is something that has been hidden in this world for centuries. Something that many have worked to keep secret. It has been proven our enemy wants it bad enough that they are willing to wipe every individual off the face of this planet to find it. As such, our allies are working hard to aid our country in this dire situation, but we must do our part to protect our home and its people." General Gunner paused for a moment, searching every expression before continuing. Images flashed behind him of the Xzandians and the last time they invaded. "Midnight Eclipse was last seen in the hands of Captain Natalia Ignatius, the first female accepted into the Australian special forces."

Noel-Len sat up straight, staring at the image of his mother's security photo. Her face was harsh yet soft. Her eyes—empty and deadly.

"As such, it was her mission to ensure the safety of a relic. A relic with the power equivalent to that of thousands of nuclear warheads. Captain Natalia Ignatius was not like you or me; she was like Lieutenant Colonel Anaphora Valdis and Squad Commander L'Eiron Valdis, the two soldiers you see standing beside me. They are what many call Excelians. Some of you have, by now, run into these special types of Humans; some of you have not. They, like the Americans and the United Kingdom, are our allies and the only card we have to match the Behemoths." A blurry image of a Behemoth was shown on the screen.

"With supplies running low, we have devised a plan, one that Lieutenant Colonel Valdis has relayed to the units of Excelians at our disposal. Our goal is to cut the supply chain the Xzandians have. To get close, every special forces and SAS member is required to wear breathers to avoid the parasitic infection known as 'stylap'—a significant ingredient for the manifestation of Alastorians. These viruses have no preference of gender, size, age, or ethnicity. We've learnt that the élanocyte count found in every human determines their immunity to such infections." An image of a girl in a white, blood-stained dress with dark eyes blanketed the screen.

"The infection enters the nose and sits in the brain. Over time, it grows and devours the human brain, immediately killing its host. Then it reboots the body and substitutes itself as the brain, thereby making the human body a puppet. To prevent this, the breathers you all are expected to wear have been trial-tested since the first invasion and have proven to be effective against this infection. Any questions?" A video played of the breather they were expected to use, explaining how to wear it.

Noel-Len glanced at Michael, who looked concerned. He raised his hand. General Gunner glanced at him.

"Private Williams?"

"So, are we to work alongside these Excelians as allies?"

"Exactly," General Gunner declared turning to another soldier's question. "Our allies have volunteered to provide supplies. We'll continue to fight until they arrive." General Gunner dismissed the group before stepping to out of the room with his guards at his heels.

Noel-Len felt an apprehensive air replace the General's reassuring one within an instant, and every soldier in the room silently deliberated Anaphora's next actions as she stepped forward, organising each soldier into small tactical units. This time, Michael and Noel-Len were not on the same unit, to Noel-Len's fear. The subliminal concern he felt for his old friend was something that would forever go unspoken: *Stay alive, Michael.*

Each unit had two experienced Excelians to accompany three other Vulgarians—humans with no Excelian traits. In other words, regular humans. That term alone rubbed Noel-Len the wrong way. Curt made a sound of displeasure as he stood beside Noel-Len, observing the Excelian's reactions to their presence.

"I think they're afraid of you?" Curt asked.

"I don't think so. Might be something else," Noel-Len replied. The laborious silence echoed around them as Curt and Noel-Len observed the Excelians. Within a single breath, heavy footfalls replaced the silence separating the unit before Squadron Commander L'Eiron Augustin-Valdis marched towards the two men.

He was a man with an acute stare. His high cheekbones were complemented by his strong jaw and tight lips. Noel-Len and Curt shared a look as they wondered how the foreign soldier would see past the hair concealing half of his features. L'Eiron scanned each man from head to toe before running his eyes over them once more to meet their confused expression. With a single glimpse, Noel-Len felt as if the Squadron Commander did not approve of him. L'Eiron turned away.

"Where are your units?" he asked.

The two men glanced at each other.

"We thought we were with you, sir?" L'Eiron shook his head slowly and did not say anything as he watched the two men leave.

L'Eiron placed his hand to his ear.

"Left Lieutenant Valdis, respond." A voice broke through; however, it was not loud enough for Noel-Len and Curt to hear from where they remained standing. "Over."

L'Eiron turned to Noel-Len.

"Who was your mother?"

"Excuse me?" Noel-Len regarded L'Eiron strangely. Out of all the things that the man could ask him . . .

"Your mother, Ignatius."

Noel-Len had a bizarre feeling he already knew the answer.

"Natalia. Natalia Ignatius." If the man had known, he did not show it.

His eyes flickered behind them and Noel-Len followed his line of sight. A woman with mixed features and fair skin like Noel-Len stood a few feet away. Noel-Len recognised her from when they were pinned down; she showed her recognition of him for a moment, but quickly dismissed it. She stood off to the side with the red-haired man she'd saved.

Both Curt and Noel-Len observed the woman's almost discourteous mannerisms with confusion as she strode by Noel-Len and Curt. L'Eiron put on his helmet and vacated the area, ordering: "Move out".

CAPRICE SAT ON A FOLD-out chair with a warm hot choco-late in her trembling hands. Her head ached, while her leaden body refused to respond. Tiredness streaked her colourless features and dried cuts and blue-black bruises graced her once-healthy skin.

Silently, she watched the soldiers move about as she waited for the vehicle that would escort her and the others away from the city. She glanced at the man and woman not too far from her; they were smaller than her but held more years of experience than she did. Caprice watched with mild envy as the husband comforted his ter-rified wife in his arms. Her thoughts returned to Noel-Len, but she shook her head. *We need to get out of here. We are not soldiers.*

Getting to her feet, Caprice moved to the closest soldier, a brunette woman.

"Excuse me?" Caprice began. The soldier glanced at Caprice and scanned her dirty clothes. "We need to get out of here. Is there a vehicle that we could use?"

Observing her surroundings, the soldier eventually responded,

"I'm sorry, the ones available you are not authorised to use. But if you are waiting for someone, it is best to wait for them. They're most likely on their way."

"I know, but it's been a while," Caprice said, hoping she did not sound selfish. The woman held Caprice's gaze, calculating her mo-tives. After another once-over of her clothes, the woman nodded.

"Give me a moment. Don't wander off."

Five minutes later, the soldier returned.

"Come with me. Are they with you?" she inquired, nodding to the couple a few meters away. Caprice did not know them from a bar of soap.

"They are."

Swiftly, the woman led Caprice and the couple to a civilian car, one of many parked in the lot on the far side of the base. She opened the car door and glanced at Caprice.

"Get in."

"You're taking us to—?"

"—the place where the aliens haven't reached. For now," she said, her tone even. "Name's Jasmine. Nice to meet you." Jasmine climbed into a car.

Once everyone was seated, she urged them to put on seatbelts. Caprice wanted to retort that the police wouldn't bother them nor pull them over, but Jasmine added,

"If I suddenly stop the car, I don't want to have to explain what happened."

Everyone listened, fastening their seatbelt before Jasmine pulled out of the driveway and exited the military base.

Soon enough, they were travelling down the Stuart highway.

"How much longer until we reach the safer area?" Caprice inquired, once they had been on the road for an hour.

"The Safety Zone? Not much longer."

"Thank you." Everything that had happened to Caprice since Noel-Len saved her flickered through her mind. Despite her fear, she was grateful to be alive. "For driving us, I mean."

"No problem. You look like you've been through hell. It's the least I could do." By her tone and sincere smile, Caprice knew she was genuine. Caprice felt her stress roll off her shoulders as she stared at the barren highway before her.

Another hour later, Caprice and the elderly couple noticed a black speck in the distance. With the heat waves of the midday sun, Caprice was not too sure if they were close or if it were the outback playing tricks on her.

Her attention drifted from the distant vehicles to Jasmine as she grumbled an inaudible response in the back of her throat. Caprice followed her dark gaze in the rear-view mirror before peering over her shoulder, curious about the car that behind them. Caprice was not too sure who they were, but they kept their distance. Eventually, they arrived at the Safety Zone. Caprice glanced around; she recognised the area. *This is Adelaide River,* she thought, *the Safety Zone's here?*

When Caprice and the others climbed out of the car, a soldier debriefed with Sergeant Jasmine Rodriguez, then escorted them to a bus. The man who spoke to Jasmine could not be seen from where Caprice sat on the bus. All she could was make out the rank of Captain on the front of his shirt. Moments later, the bus departed for Adelaide, the capital city of South Australia.

"Thank you for escorting the survivors Sergeant," a male voice uttered.

"Not a problem at all Lieutenant." Within a few moments, Jasmine climbed back into her vehicle and headed back to base. As she vacated the area, the Captain quickly scribbled down her details, with a click of his tongue through his puckered lip. His gaze shifted back to the bus and he pulled out his radio.

"The eagle is soaring."

"Roger," a voice called on the other end. Putting his radio away, the stranger turned his back and vacated the area.

# Chapter 23

HOURS LATER, NOEL-LEN scanned the area he was set to guard. He heard his allies over the radio considering the potential hostile outcomes. The non-Excelian soldiers were, without a doubt, concerned about Xzandian surprise attacks that Noel-Len did not believe were possible. However, he remained silent.

A few moments later, he spotted the outline of an Xzandian. It was larger than the rest, grotesque per usual and utterly frightening. The largest stood tall and at the front of the group; it was a 'Scouter'—aliens that weren't just the pack leaders, but also responsible for the communication from their ground position back to their command ship.

Noel-Len did not say much as he mentally counted the group. There was a layout of expected numbers, but Noel-Len had a strange feeling that it might change.

Within the blink of an eye, it did. Two additional Xzandian members of the Scout team stalked the streets. Noel-Len swiftly relayed this information to his team as he moved from one part of his post to another.

From the closer position, Noel-Len pulled out his binoculars once more and zoomed in on the leader, scanning his attire from head to toe, then the others. He was searching for the device that the enemy used to communicate.

"Delta concealed," Noel-Len announced into the radio.

"Roger," L'Eiron answered. "Squad A. Move out."

Noel-Len watched as a group of Excelian soldiers hurry towards the group. Noel-Len glanced over at Curt, who returned an equal frustrated glance. His look said, *we are soldiers too . . .* The distant echo of bullets in the distance reminded Noel-Len of the battle raging on the harbour.

Noel-Len waited and watched. He was not certain if his allies would win or if they would lose, but a part of him knew he had to remain confident in his fellow soldiers, regardless of how thin his hope was. And, if they were to die here, they would be proud to know they did the best they could for their country.

It was very patriotic. *But that doesn't mean I'm not scared*, he thought watching his comrades fall one by one, after initial contact. When L'Eiron gave the order, Noel-Len and Curt fired their rifles from a distance, dropping low on the roof. Noel-Len felt the return spray of bullets hitting concrete on their office building and worked to draw further attention, while Curt climbed to his feet and rushed to the opposite end of the building.

Noel-Len recognised the sniper rifle strapped to his Sergeant's back as Curt leapt from the office building and clipped himself to the zip-line they had set up. Curt rolled over his shoulder as he touched the lower roof, then crawled to the wall. Pulling out his binoculars, he watched as Noel-Len continued to draw their fire. Only two of the aliens had been eliminated.

Curt's determination narrowed on the aliens as he armed the sniper rifle and aimed it at the aliens. Using the scope, he scanned the thick armour on their chests, shoulders, and abdomen.

"Fucking covered from head to toe," he muttered, frustrated. Then, he saw an opening between the helmet and the upper section of the chest armour. "But you do have necks." He fired two bullets, then a third. He took out the aliens crouching behind invisible shields that could only be spotted when the bullets from his comrades touched the shields.

"Ignatius! Reposition!" L'Eiron proclaimed through the comm-link. Curt continued to fire, then dropped the moment a spray of blue light entered the corner of his vision.

It confused him at first. Then he felt the heat, glancing at the door several meters from his feet. Shock replaced his curiosity as he saw the melted door. *That would have been me*, he thought, his heart hammered, rebounding with the terror that coursed through his veins.

L'EIRON HAD PROVIDED Gothalia with her next task. She regarded the abandoned battlefield as the stench of death, carnage, and ash filled her nose. She frowned at the sight.

She had separated from Danteus hours ago, but she could not help but feel an emptiness within the pit of her stomach. Pushing it aside, she focused on the task at hand and pulled up the map of the Fragments on her faceplate. The city of Darwin was circled on it and she wondered where it would be. Then she heard footfalls approach.

Her lips pursed into a thin line. Her brows lowered in concentration as her gaze narrowed on the bodies in the distance. She could not find the Fragment as soon as she would like to. It was only a matter of time before the Xzandians retrieved all the Fragments.

The footfalls continued than a distant sound caught her attention. Her map disappeared, and she followed the noise before stumbling upon a man. Cautious, she placed her hand on the holster of her crossbow before pausing. Then she pulled out her pistol and pointed it at the man. As she inched closer, she noticed he was curled over something.

Her brows furrowed in confusion.

Uncertain of what he was doing, she slowly approached. Then she noticed that the man's hand was covered in ice.

With his hands on his head, he slowly turned and faced her.

"Look what we have here. Gothalia, finally we meet."

Gothalia was stunned to find that a stranger knew who she was.

"Where are you from?" she questioned.

"The Northern Reserve."

"What are you doing here?" she grilled. "Surely, you recognise a battlefield when you see one."

"That I do," he said, stepping away from her. Gothalia brandished her weapon.

"Don't move," Gothalia warned. Then she ducked out of the way when a shard of ice flew towards her. She avoided the next string of attacks, only to curse when the ice impaled her cloak on a wall. Detaching herself from the cloak, she avoided the next attack and asked Kronos for the man's weakness. Exploiting it, she gained an advantage—until his ice sharpened into blades and he lunged at her.

The battle raged on until the man slipped out of Gothalia's next attack and ran up a wall, kicking her away. She fell on her back. By the time she'd flipped back to her feet, the man had climbed a car, hopped over a fence, and scaled a building, before disappearing.

Gothalia's side ached. Tapping the side of her headpiece she queried,

"Kronos what was that all about? Tell me you know him."

"No, not personally but I have run a data scan and discovered he descends from the Crystallovis clan."

"Does Demetria know?"

"Potentially."

Removing her cloak from the wall, Gothalia wandered the streets again, attempting to distance herself from her attacker. Then she paused.

"What's wrong?" Kronos questioned, sensing a change in her.

"I know you said it's in this general area, but where exactly is it? It's like finding a needle in a haystack." She had no idea how many Fragments there were and how many the Xzandians had acquired over the years. Gothalia glanced at the ship above.

"What are you thinking?"

"I'm thinking we need another advantage."

"How?" Kronos questioned.

"I'm not sure, as of yet, but we need one if we're ever going to win this war."

"Well, if you find that advantage, please let me know."

"You'll be with me when I find it," Gothalia responded.

"That's pretty much how it goes." Then Kronos alerted her to an oncoming attack seconds before an explosion blew up at Gothalia's feet and she was thrown into a concrete wall. An Xzandian hovered in the air on a platform. Gothalia climbed to her knees. Her eyes lingered over the Xzandian.

"Next time, a little warning," Gothalia muttered climbing to her feet.

"The Fragment," the Xzandian declared, with a handout. "Hand it over and I'll consider sparing you."

"Sure, you will," Gothalia remarked.

He pulled back his hand and his gaze narrowed on her. His pale features gleamed beneath the moon like marble, while his scales and silver armour shimmered with each of his movements.

"Why are you Humans so difficult to negotiate with? Do you want your entire world destroyed?" he asked casually.

"No," Gothalia responded before pulling out her sword. "And I'm not Human," she declared, rushing at him. The Xzandian leapt and flipped over her from his platform before landing on the ground, avoiding Gothalia's attack. She pivoted and ran towards him. The Xzandian stood in mid-air.

"You're an Excelian. It explains why you smell different."

"What are you, a dog?" Gothalia inquired, glaring up at him.

"Hardly," he responded, unamused.

"Why don't you come down and fight?"

"Because I'm giving you an option to surrender."

"Or else what?"

"Or else you'll regret taking such a tone with me."

"And what would you do if I chose to not surrender it?"

"Then you'd be another waste of talent," he answered.

"As if you know me."

"I do. I have seen and heard a lot about you. The young demoness who fought off most of my enforcers. Few Excelian women have the strength to do that and few are as talented with the sword as you are."

"Are you threatened?" Gothalia challenged.

"Me? Never. I'm impressed." Then he leapt from the platform and towards her. She rolled out of the way and avoided the sword he impaled in the ground. Gothalia pulled out her own sword and blocked the next attack, then deflected it and pushed him from her. As they fought, Gothalia deflected, parried, blocked, and countered his attacks, but it was not enough to avoid the cut to her arm he delivered.

"That could have been avoided," he said.

"I doubt it."

He ran his fingers along the blade, barely touching it. Then he turned his attention back to her and sheathed his sword. Injured, Gothalia ran at him and he kicked her in the stomach, forcing her on her back, winded. He walked over to her and removed the fragment from her utility belt.

"I'll be taking this." Before she could climb to her feet, he was on the platform and hovered out of her reach. "Oh, and another thing. My blade is laced with a bane. Not as lethal as some, but lethal enough to render you . . . immobile." At his words, Gothalia's vision clouded and darkness washed over her. She collided with the ground and passed out.

"Gothalia!" a man called. "Child, please don't run off too far." Gaius Ignatius paced through the rowdy streets of Lower Plerrolt District with his clan emblem on his back.

The district itself was calm and quiet.

"I won't, Father," Gothalia happily responded.

"I'm holding you to that."

She ran through the streets with her arms wide, mimicking a bird. Gaius admired her free spirit and lack of fear. Gothalia's imagination never ceased, and his other child was just as adventurous and imaginative. Gaius paused. Speaking of his other child . . .

"Noel-Len?" Gaius scanned the streets behind him to find no sign of his oldest. "Noel-Len," he called, a little more loudly. Noel-Len never answered. Concern and fear washed over Gaius. "Gothalia!" he called and noticed she had already made her way back to him, no doubt hearing him call out for her brother. Gaius returned Gothalia's concerned expression. Gothalia's scream startled him: there on a steel box stood Noel-Len with a makeshift mask. He growled and Gothalia ran behind her father.

Noel-Len laughed, but Gaius was not amused.

"What? It was funny!" Noel-Len attempted, removing his mask.

"No, it wasn't. You scared your sister," Gaius answered, trying to calm Gothalia. "You know better than to behave like that." He walked over to Noel-Len and lifted him off the box, setting him on the ground. "You promised you wouldn't scare you sister. She is not supposed to be afraid of you, she is supposed to look up to you. Remember our deal?"

Gothalia peered around her father. Noel-Len crossed his arms and pouted before looking at his sister.

"I remember. I'm sorry, Talia."

"Are you?" she mocked, with her hands on her hips.

"Gothalia," Gaius reprimanded.

She tried again, this time, genuinely.

"Are you, really? You promise not to do it again?"

"I promise," Noel-Len proclaimed and grabbed his sister's hand as artificial fireworks lit the afternoon sky. "The festival. Let's go!" Both children ran off, hand in hand, and Gaius raised a brow. How his children were able to change moods so quickly was beyond him.

When Gothalia opened her eyes, the sky overhead was a subtle lavender, a reminder of the oncoming morning. Crawling to her feet, she discovered that her body ached in places she had never thought possible. A sharp twinge caught her side and she gasped. Then feet padded over to her.

"You're up."

She eyed the voice, cautiously. Then she relaxed, recognising it as Sergeant Curt McGuire from the Human infantry.

"What are you doing here?"

"I was sent to find you," he responded.

"By whom?" Gothalia climbed to feet, holding her arm.

"Does it matter?" he responded, regarding her. "Word has it the aliens are retreating." He saw she was in no shape for a fight. But as quickly as he noticed her injuries, they vanished in wisps of smoke.

"Why do you think they would retreat?" Gothalia questioned.

"Because they found the Fragment."

"Most likely. If we're lucky, they're only employing a tactical retreat."

"Why do we need the Fragment so badly?" Curt asked, not that he wasn't briefed but he wondered why not destroy them rather than preserve them. If they were so powerful.

"How did you know about . . .?" Gothalia began but cut herself off. "Since you're so clever, why don't you explain why you think we need it?"

"Because it's a powerful weapon, one that can match any nuclear weapon or more when combined to form Midnight Eclipse."

"And why were nuclear weapons harshly criticised?" Gothalia pressed.

"Because they didn't just destroy an area once, but also affected the environment after."

"And that's why we need it. If it's any consolation, it does not matter how strong an Excelian is—or how secure a Human is—If we have an uninhabitable world, what do you think will happen to us?"

"We'll die."

"If we're lucky." Gothalia walked past him. Curt called after her,

"What do you mean by that?" A few moments later, Gothalia walked the streets alone, past the demolished buildings, the abandoned cars, and the fissured roads. There was a pungent smell of ash and rotting flesh in the air. Then the smell of ash and burnt flesh greeted her nose. In the distance she noticed that the flames engulfed a building. Smoke permeated the air and reached Gothalia's nose and as she took in the smoke, she couldn't help but worry about who was within. Gothalia ran towards the building. "My lady, there could be some soldiers inside," Kronos commented.

"That's what I was thinking," Gothalia muttered and stopped before the building where she noticed outlines of soldiers. They were not Humans but Excelians. She could tell by their uniform. Though as Gothalia approached, she had never known that when she reached the building her comrades were within. Smoke and fire permeated the edifice consuming it in raging flames.

"Asashin!" she called. Running over to him.

"Gothalia!" he greeted, in a panic. "The flames. Demetria and Danteus—they're inside."

"Wait here," Gothalia declared. "I'll go get them." When she entered the warm flames greeted her and her Excelian cells deflected them as much as the smoke, so not once did she cough and gag on its toxic fumes.

When she rushed within, she called for Kronos to identify the location of bodies. As he did, one by one, she pulled them from the flames. Her tender body ached, and her mind was consumed with worry and fear, though she worked hard to not allow it to consume her like the flames that consumed the building. Bit by bit, the building weakened, until eventually the entrance she had used collapsed.

Gothalia stared at the enemy that she observed didn't retreat with the others as she had expected them to. Instead, the Xzandian watched the building engulf in flames and from this distance she couldn't tell if he was smiling or if he was not. Though she assumed the latter.

"Danteus?" she queried turning her attention back to him and observing his closed lids. Aware of another presence, Gothalia glanced up and regarded the man who descended towards them. Gothalia turned back to Danteus. "Wake up. Danteus!"

The man approached and Gothalia knew she was in danger. She had so many questions. What was going on? Who was this man? And why did he attack Danteus? Gothalia stared at the man as he inched closer. She climbed to her feet and faced the enemy.

"Who are you?" she demanded.

"Why does it matter? You'll be dead soon," he declared and raised his broadsword in the air and Gothalia leapt out of the way before the sword could strike her. "I see you're fast."

"I am."

The alien remained silent. His green eyes gazed upon Gothalia, who glared back at him from where she crouched.

"You look so much like your mother," he articulated with a sombre expression. Gothalia's eyes widened at his words. The stranger smirked. "No matter. You will not get away—heiress of Valdis Clan. None of you Excelians will touch that Fragment."

"Run!" Asashin blocked the first attack.

Asashin kicked him away and continued to battle the dark-scaled man. Gothalia watched as Asashin fought off the man, then crawled over to Danteus.

"Please don't be dead," she whispered. She could tell he'd lost a lot of blood and he was not healing. She began to panic. "Danteus?" She noticed no burns but cuts, as if someone had used a sword. Then her eyes lingered over his face.

No response.

"Danteus!"

"Gothalia!" a voice called, and she looked up.

An injured Asashin ran towards her.

"Asashin!" she shouted, and he vanished from sight with lighting speed. Surprised, Gothalia glanced around. "Asashin?"

She felt a presence behind her and loudly heard the *clang* of two swords making contact. Gothalia turned around. Asashin held off the alien man's sword. She glanced over at Asashin as he fought the enemy.

"He's able to multiply?" Gothalia regarded the man, confused. "Asashin! Danteus and Demetria are injured."

"I know."

Gothalia knew she had to get Danteus to safety. She had to make sure he was still alive. She crouched and lifted him, dragging Danteus away from the fight, then did the same with Demetria.

"Don't give up on me," she said to both. Blood mixed into the dirt and dust that covered the city floor. Gothalia regarded the sight of the enemy. *He's busy*, she thought, *this is our chance.* Then she froze as she felt Danteus move.

He was prying her hands free.

"Danteus?"

"I'm fine."

"No, you're not. You're bleeding."

"I know." His blue eyes rested on the alien man.

"Then don't move," Gothalia growled. Danteus smiled a small smile.

"They have it. Gothalia, they have the Fragment."

"I know." Gothalia responded, with a mournful expression.

"Get it. We'll join you soon," he promised. She held his gaze for what seemed like an eternity. Then a flash of crimson splashed before Gothalia's eyes. The first thing she saw was the spear in his chest, covered in blood. She heard Danteus's shriek of pain pierce her ears and she knew the spear had stabbed him.

Gothalia's scream filled the abandoned street, reaching everyone's ears. Astonished by her reaction and the spear through Danteus's chest, Asashin turned to move towards his fallen comrade, only to be stopped by the enemy.

Tears brimmed in Gothalia's eyes and she did not care that the tears made her weak or that the woman laughed. The woman held up her hand and the spear flew from Danteus's chest and into her hand.

Gothalia ran her fingers through his hair and whispered his name repeatedly before muttering,

"This can't be the end."

"It's the end little girl," Melissa McGuire said. Her straight blond hair fell to her waist and her dark eyes landed on Gothalia. "And you're next."

Something fragile snapped within Gothalia.

The next thing she felt was complete control. She was calm. The tears stopped and her breathing was meticulous as she removed her arms from around Danteus. Gently, she placed his head on the ground. The woman watched as Gothalia climbed to her feet and glared at her. Gothalia's red eyes locked onto the woman.

"You're going to put up a fight, are you?" the woman teased, and pointed the spear at Gothalia. "Come at me."

With the sight of the golden spear smeared in Danteus's blood, Gothalia did not need another reason. Gothalia launched at the woman and struck her; she had no time to react to Gothalia's speed. The woman was thrown across the street and into a building's wall. The men froze, staring at Gothalia's unnatural strength. Blood lined the women's lips and she stared at Gothalia with shock.

The alien man turned his attention from Asashin and hurled himself at Gothalia, who recognised his presence at the corner of her eye and vanished and reappeared behind him in a cloud of black smoke that dispersed quickly.

"Witch!" he barked.

Asashin stared at Gothalia. Her eyes were empty, her expression blank, and her movements controlled and calculating. Gothalia vanished once again and reappeared behind the alien man, delivering a tornado kick that sent him fifty meters away. His feet locked into the ground as his arms blocked the attack. When she landed, Gothalia held her leg in the air and gently placed it on the ground with utter control. Then she ran at him, producing a series of punches and kicks that were both powerful and quick.

The Xzandian man could only block. When Gothalia paused, she stared at him for a moment and he threw a punch. His fist connected with Gothalia's jaw; ignoring Asashin's cry, Gothalia did not move. Her eyes locked onto his and he removed his fist. Slowly, he backed away.

"What the fuck are you?" he asked, shocked. Red mist flowed from her pores, making her red eyes glower in anger.

Then Gothalia vanished and reappeared in front of her comrade, moving with such speed it shocked Asashin. Gothalia hauntingly walked towards the Xzandian man and his companion. With each step, she left indentations of her feet in the ground. When the man ran at top speed and vanished, so did Gothalia.

"Gothalia!" Asashin cried. "What was that?" He ran into the streets, able to sense her dangerous presence.

# Chapter 24

GOTHALIA COULD SMELL it. The blood she was after. She craved it and she was going to get it. Gothalia leapt from building rooftop to building rooftop as she chased after those monsters. She was closing in, and fast, but she knew that this was not enough. She was going to tear them apart with her bare hands—slowly. She could not remember why she was so angry, but she just knew she was. She heard the woman whisper,

"What are you doing?"

"Corporal Melissa McGuire. Stay here," she heard the man reply.

"You can't!"

Gothalia was close now. SShe leapt off the edge of a building and landed on the ground, forming a large crater beneath her.

There they were.

Gothalia could smell them. She could hear their frantic heart beats and sense their fear. Her eyes locked onto them.

"She's here. Thanat!"

"You have to leave. Tell *him* she is tapped into the power Natalia had. Tell him she is dangerous! Go!" Thanat cried as Gothalia walked towards them.

"But . . ." Melissa McGuire began and Gothalia saw it. The woman was helpless and vulnerable.

Gothalia disappeared and reappeared behind Thanat. Her sword in hand, she drove her weapon straight into the air as she sliced off his head. She vanished once again from the clearing before dashing after the woman.

She was not going to get away. Gothalia would not let her.

Gothalia heard her scream and continued ahead. Gothalia considered the sight of the scared woman as she rushed through the city. Gothalia's altered vision could see the veins within the woman's body, her muscles as they relaxed and contracted, her blood vessels, and her entire skeletal system. Within an instant, Gothalia knew which arteries to hit.

Gothalia closed in on the terrified woman, who had fallen over in her hurry.

Then she smelt it, a familiar presence. Gothalia froze.

"Gothalia!" a voice called. Gothalia scanned her surroundings until she noticed a man running towards her in the distance, with his familiar red hair and green eyes. He froze once he closed in on her.

Fear flooded through him as he took in the sight of Gothalia glowing red eyes.

"Gothalia?" Levi asked.

"Your highness!" Asashin called as he ran into the abandoned intersection. "Get away from her!"

Gothalia's unreadable eyes skimmed over to the woman. Without even thinking, Gothalia walked over to the woman, who sat frozen on the ground. Suddenly she felt something wrap around her entire body. With her limbs restrained, Gothalia fell to the ground. Asashin yanked at the wire as he dragged her toward him.

"What are you doing?" Levi demanded.

"Saving your arse."

"But she wasn't going to hurt me." Levi did not sound so convinced himself once he turned his attention back to Gothalia, who still stared at the woman with predatory eyes.

"Maybe not, but she might, and that's a chance I can't take."

"Wait, before you do something drastic, let me try something." Levi approached a restrained Gothalia, who chomped her teeth like a monster trying to escape captivity. Her inner demon growled. Gothalia was going to tear that woman apart.

Melissa McGuire stood, and her eyes bore into Gothalia's.

"This is going to be easy," Melissa said, and approached Gothalia, spear in hand.

Levi spun around and fired an arrow from his bow that shot through Melissa's wrist. Melissa McGuire dropped the spear and screamed, as she held her wrist.

"Stay away from her!" Levi seethed, glaring at Melissa McGuire before turning his attention back to Gothalia. "Are you alright?"

"Mine," she growled.

"What?" Levi asked, confused.

"Mine," Gothalia repeated with a deadly growl. Gothalia's eyes locked onto Melissa McGuire and she watched the blood trickle down her wrist.

"What happened to her?" Levi asked Asashin.

"I think I know what happened," Asashin said. Gothalia continued to stare at the blood. She could see the energy flowing throughout the woman's body, and that was everything she needed. She was going to destroy her. Gathering her energy, she channelled it along the wire and, sure enough, it snapped.

Gothalia launched herself at the woman, and Asashin appeared between them.

"Gothalia! Stop!" he yelled.

She had not seen Asashin move so fast in her life.

Her flames paused centimetres before reaching Asashin's throat.

It was only when Gothalia observed him with blank calculation that he understood she did not recognise him.

The demonic appearance Gothalia faded and her fangs retracted.

Asashin tossed a small pill-like device at Melissa. Electricity shot through her body, knocking her unconscious.

Asashin's eyes drifted over Gothalia on her knees as she mourned for Danteus, then Asashin picked up the sound of his faint pulse and hope leapt within the chests of the Excelians.

Hastily, Gothalia and the others ran back to Danteus before carrying him back to the Excelian barracks and he was taken by the Excelian medics to the Excelian tent. Soldiers rushed back and forth, shouting orders, while others returned from their recent battle or mission.

Gothalia could not stomach it, as Danteus was placed onto a spare bed. She stroked his forearm and whispered,

"You'll be okay. You'll be okay." But his pulse was now silent.

The Excelian doctors pushed her aside and rushed him into the farthest part of the tent where they tried to revive him. Gothalia stood there, unable to move as she watched them restart his heart.

At that moment, she realised that no matter how strong she thought she was, as strong as she knew her people were, they could still die. It had never dawned on her how quickly death could come.

The Excelian doctors and nurses tried to move her out of the way, but Gothalia fought back.

"I'm not leaving him," she responded, determined. When the doctors did not listen, she roared, "I'm not leaving him."

Levi said,

"You don't need to see this. Let's go." He ushered Gothalia out of the room even if she'd struggled to leave. "Are you okay?" he asked her once outside. Gothalia paused and her heart ached, she didn't believe Danteus was dead, she heard his heart's faint beats. Then a soldier rushed to them and pointed at Gothalia.

"That's her," he said to a Peacekeeper. Gothalia's stomach sank. "She's the one who was responsible for the attack on the Cetatea."

Gothalia's eyes narrowed upon the man who called the Peacekeepers towards her. She stepped back, and Levi stepped forward protectively.

"How do you know it was her?" he asked.

"I was there, and I'd never forget *her* face," the man exclaimed, with such rage it scared the young prince. "She must pay for her crimes." Guilt splashed across Gothalia's russet features as Levi glanced upon her with equal pain.

"I understand," Levi declared and Gothalia felt her heart sink, deeper than it had ever sunk—if that were even possible. She was not certain what Levi would do, though she trusted he would do what was right. Even at the cost of that which she'd always taken for granted—her freedom.

"He's right. He understands, as do I, the consequences of my actions," Gothalia articulated carefully. Then she recalled the words of her AI, words she thought she had long forgotten. "But as much as I understand, dearest sirs, I have other things to do."

Gothalia turned on her heel and ran from the Peacekeepers as if a ghost were at her heels. She rushed by the other soldiers and out of the barracks, into the dry and barren bushlands where silence greeted her.

Once she was certain of her safety, she stopped to catch her breath. In the distance, from behind a tree where she hid, she identified an Xzandian deliberately searching the ground.

"Kronos, what do you think they're after? Another Fragment?"

"Potentially, but we won't know unless we get closer."

Gothalia moved towards the Xzandian, careful to avoid large piles of dry leaves that would give away her presence.

The digital map that Arthur had provided was displayed across her faceplate and she regarded it carefully.

"It is a Fragment," she identified.

"What are you going to do?"

"I'm going to get it first." Then she felt a presence beside her and without thinking, her fist swung at the person that stood behind her. Surprise bloomed within her when the presence caught her fist; she gazed up at the man, only to find it was none other than Asashin.

"What are you doing here?" she asked him.

"Helping you, what else?" he answered, like it was the obvious thing in the world.

"Um, thanks," she said, pulling away. "You don't have to. This mission I can do on my own."

"Honestly, I believe that, but I'm wanting to help, so let me." He crossed his arms.

"Okay."

Together, they followed the aliens as they moved through the bush. Their scales gleamed under the sun.

"So, what's the plan?" Asashin asked, beside Gothalia.

"Not sure yet."

"Wait . . . so you're planning on attacking them with no plan."

"I'm working on it," Gothalia replied. "And besides, with you here, it'll be a little easier."

"What do you mean?"

"You're going to be my decoy—once they secure what they're after."

"*Okay*," he said, slowly. "Then what?"

"I take back the Fragment. I'll come support you after."

"So, I'll be doing all the heavy lifting. Nice." Asashin remarked sarcastically and Gothalia shrugged.

"Since when do men not like heavy lifting?" Gothalia joked.

"Um, since one has realised that you are scary when you lose control. You could probably take out the whole group, if you just allowed that demon of yours to possess you."

"What do you mean by *possess*?" Gothalia queried. "I'm not some sort of vessel. It's genetic and I can't control it when it happens."

"Right, so you become possessed."

"I don't become possessed."

"Sure, you don't."

They paused and observed the aliens as they travelled downhill. Eventually, they paused and Gothalia observed them closely as one pointed at an area in the ground.

"I think they found something."

"Me too." Gothalia glanced at Asashin and nodded.

Without another word, they split up and Gothalia hid out of sight while Asashin crept closer to them. One alien kneeled on the ground and began digging up something. Asashin heard footfalls in the distance and hid behind a tree. The Peacekeepers that were after Gothalia stopped at the edge of the sharp drop overlooking where the Xzandians stood below. Then they opened fire on the Xzandians while some Xzandians took cover and fired back.

"There's my distraction," Gothalia declared and rushed from the tree, towards a boulder. Racing to another tree, she crouched to avoid the bullets the Peacekeepers fired. When the bullets died down, Gothalia and Asashin noticed that all that remained was one Xzandian that waited for the Peacekeepers to leave before quickly, taking it down. Asashin climbed out of his hiding spot.

"That was easy," he responded. Than his gaze lingered over Gothalia.

"What?" Gothalia asked, realizing he was staring at her.

"Nothing."

"It can't be nothing you were staring."

"You noticed?"

"How could I not?" She questioned and kneeled where the Xzandians had started digging. She paused and regarded aliens' weapons that were buried within the ground. Gothalia picked one up. Asashin, a little skittish, regarded her carefully. Then she smiled and dropped the weapon.

"I was thinking about . . ." he began.

He took a deep breath and tried again.

"I was thinking about what happened back at the Cetatea. Everyone said it was scary when you lost control. I saw what you were capable of, and I was scared."

Gothalia faced Asashin; she had no idea what had brought this on, though she understood his reasoning.

"Do you fear me?" she asked, with an even tone but a flicker of sadness in her dark gaze.

There was a long pause on Asashin's part until he said,

"I'm not sure."

"Do you trust me?"

"I'm not sure."

"Does anyone else trust me?"

"Honestly . . . I'm not sure."

Before they could continue, a woman with black hair, accompanied by two men, entered the clearing. One man wore a mask covering his lower features while the other wore a black headband around his forehead. Gothalia saw the woman's eyes burn from brown to crimson.

"There you are," she said, stalking before the men as their leader.

"You know me?" Gothalia asked, aware she had never seen her before. She gripped her rifle, ready to fire.

There was a brief pause before the woman replied,

"You have no idea what you've got yourself into, do you?"

"No. But it doesn't matter," Gothalia coolly replied.

"Oh? Is that so?"

"Yes."

She laughed.

"Such a shame you ended up in this dump. No matter, without Dragon Core, you're outnumbered and alone. You're an open target with a high price on your head."

"She's not alone," Asashin responded. The woman barely noticed him, her eyes solely on Gothalia.

Gothalia stared them down and observed the woman pull out silver weapons from behind her back; they were two short-swords. The men did the same but remained a few feet behind her. Gothalia and Asashin were shocked and glanced at each other. They recognised the scales crawling along their enemies' skin beneath their armour.

"Get her. We'll freeze her and hand her over" the female announced to her comrades.

The men pounced on Gothalia, like lions on a gazelle. They knocked her rifle out of her hand, and she cursed.

Asashin attacked, only to have his sword knocked clean out of his hand by the mace attached to a retractable whip, which the woman manoeuvred. Asashin groaned and rubbed the back of his hand; he dodged her first strike, then evaded the second attack, before jumping to avoid being swept off his feet.

He was thrown into a nearby tree when the woman summoned a shield that sent a mighty wave. Winded, Asashin lost consciousness, and Gothalia called out,

"Asashin!" Having defeated the men, she turned on the woman. "You'll pay for that."

Gothalia evaded her first attack and dodged the next.

The men climbed to their feet and ran at her. Gothalia kicked one away, then blocked the next punch and head-butted the man. Grabbing his wrist, Gothalia turned her back towards him and stepped closer, before effectively flipping him over herself.

She deflected the next attack from the next man. With a summoned sword, he threw his weight behind his strikes and Gothalia avoided them, waiting for an opportunity. Without a second thought, she caught his hand, kicked him in his stomach, then retrieved the blade before slicing his arm in one move. He fell to one knee, and she kneed him hard in the face; blood spurting from his nose, he fell unconscious. The hostile woman sneered and snarled,

"Morons! She's just one woman!"

Asashin groaned and climbed to his feet. He glared at the woman.

"That hurt," he said, with malice.

"I'm glad," the woman responded, with a slithering smile.

Without another word, both Asashin and Gothalia ran at the woman and threw a string of attacks. The woman effectively and quickly evaded both of their attacks. Even working as a team, it was not enough. The woman was determined and talented—a deadly combination. When the woman paused, she said,

"I see you haven't forgotten how to fight. Excellent."

"Why do you continue to speak as though you know me?" Gothalia demanded.

"How can I not? You hail from the Ignatius-Valdis clan. That demon blood of yours is something many will pay a high price for."

The woman closed the distance between them. With several quick kicks, Gothalia evaded them all. Asashin swept at the woman, and Gothalia kicked her in the face, leaping to avoid her counter-attack.

The woman tumbled to the ground, then climbed to her feet and rushed at Gothalia and Asashin.

She became agitated as she swept at Gothalia, who tumbled to the ground and rolled out of the way, avoiding her foot as it shattered the ground where Gothalia was moments prior. The woman kicked Asashin in the head, sending him to the ground.

Gothalia felt her blood race beneath her skin. The woman flung kicks towards Gothalia, who rolled away from her. Asashin wiped his jaw and dashed at the woman. The woman pulled out a wire and wrapped it around Gothalia's neck. The cord yanked Gothalia from her knees to her feet. Gothalia stomped her foot onto the woman's and whacked the back of her head against the woman's nose. The woman staggered back, clutching her bleeding nose and Asashin smirked.

"Nice shot."

"Thanks." Gothalia pulled the cord from around her neck and turned to face her, tossing the wire on the ground. "You think that'll work on me?"

Casually, the woman shrugged; blood pooled over her lips but as quick as it came, the blood vanished. Gothalia glowered at the woman. The men pulled themselves to their feet and ran at Asashin, weapons in hand.

The woman ran at Gothalia, who used her forearm that held her armour to deflect the attack. Gothalia was too slow to evade the next attack from the woman and was thrown into a nearby tree. Pushing away from the tree, Gothalia ran up the side of it, then leapt off it to a neighbouring building, where she watched as Asashin battled the men.

By the time the enemy reached Gothalia, blood was racing beneath her skin. The masked male threw his blade towards Asashin's head, and he avoided it just in time. The man with the headband jabbed at his stomach, and Asashin deflected the attack with his forearm blade, before kicking him away.

The woman jabbed both blades at Gothalia, who brought up her forearm guard. Gothalia spun around, deflecting the blades, and swept at her ankles. She jumped in time and easily avoided Gothalia's attack. The battle continued, and Gothalia was confident the woman was running out of stamina. *I must finish this quickly*, she thought.

Gothalia glared at the woman, her hair parting as her gaze narrowed on the woman with dangerous hostility.

The woman leapt and summoned a sword, pulling it from an unknown void. She surged towards Gothalia, who froze in fear when she recognised that she could not evade the attack in time.

Suddenly, a dagger speedily zipped through the air, stunning the woman's attack, and grazing her arm. She paused and glared at the shadows, carefully eyeing the towers in the distance.

The men were defeated by Asashin, who joined Gothalia on the roof of the neighbouring building. He noticed the attack and, just like Gothalia, understood; the attack was too quick and too precise to be Human.

Several more daggers gleamed through the air, darting from several directions. Gothalia searched the buildings in the distance but did not spy any movement.

She turned her attention to her enemy, only to find that the woman had disappeared along with the men. Gothalia and Asashin shared a look of confusion.

"They vanished," he said, walking to the edge of the roof. "There's no trace left. I doubt the trackers could find them."

Gothalia did not respond but instead recognised a fire emblem on a distant building; Asashin regarded her puzzled.

"What is it?"

"That emblem." Gothalia pointed. "That's not the Emblem of the Fire Reserve, is it?"

Asashin regarded the emblem.

"It looks similar, but I doubt it." Before Asashin could say anything else, Gothalia leapt from the building and onto the street below. She ran towards the military structure that sat hidden within the bushlands; she would not have noticed it if not for her keen eyes. Asashin followed but did not question her alacrity.

The structure was old and abandoned, but the building had a fire emblem carved into the open and ruined eaves. Gothalia approached with caution. She pulled the door from its hinges and walked inside. Half of the building was destroyed and open to the bushlands, while the old dwellings within were overgrown with shrubs and insects.

"There's nothing here," Asashin said. Gothalia was a reluctant to leave until she recalled the map she had borrowed from Arthur's study. She pulled it out. She observed the map and identified the emblem that she had seen on the building on the map. "What did you find?" Asashin asked, after some time.

"The map has the same insignia." Asashin peered over her shoulder and at the map below. He recognised the emblem and the markings of crosses and fire emblems on the Northern borders. "What does it mean?"

"It means we're going to find answers." Gothalia tucked the map away after she had read the runes on the side, written in Arthur's handwriting. Gothalia moved deeper into the building and towards the far corner protected by the rain and the sun.

In the corner was the same emblem and Gothalia tapped it. Nothing happened.

"Maybe you have to push it?" Gothalia placed her palm against the smooth carving and pressed. Still nothing. She frowned—then, after a moment, her hand lit in fire, and she placed her hand against the emblem, and the ground shook beneath their feet.

They were both silent as they watched the ground open beneath them. Gothalia and Asashin shared a look of concern and curiosity; without another thought nor word, they marched down the stone stairs. Gothalia's hands ran along with the earth before she recognised the sensation of smooth metal.

Kronos automatically activated the lights on her uniform and commented,

"This is very old."

"The metal, it's smooth. There's no sign of oxidation," Gothalia responded. Asashin followed Gothalia deeper into the ground and noticed something move. "Did you hear that?"

"Yeah. I did," he answered once they reached the landing. The stone ground was smooth beneath their boots and untouched by dirt or dry shrubs. Gothalia heard the sound again, this time, as if something slithered along the ground.

Gothalia reached for her rifle.

"Maybe we should go back," Gothalia said, her back accidentally bumping into Asashin's chest.

"What's the matter? Scared?" he teased, and she glared at him. He stepped around her and followed the noise. With his sword, he stabbed the ground and picked up something: a massive snake. "He can't hurt you now."

Gothalia did not say anything, contemplating snake, which would have been big enough to strangle them both. She suppressed her fear and walked over to Asashin, ignoring the look masking his features. Then noticed a cave opening.

She walked ahead and into the darkness, just out of earshot of Asashin's comment:

"She's scared of snakes but not the dark, huh?" He sheathed his sword and followed.

They did not say a word until Gothalia paused at the edge of a cliff; the darkness below almost made her lose her footing. She steadied herself and searched for any paths.

"Kronos, where are we?" she asked.

"It appears to be a chasm," he responded. "From what I measure, it's a fair way down."

"Scan for vitals." After a moment, Kronos responded that there were no vitals. Gothalia glanced at Asashin, and he asked:

"What are you up to?"

# Chapter 25

"I'M SEARCHING FOR ANSWERS." With her back to the darkness below, she fell backwards, allowing the dry, cold air to brush through her hair and graze her exposed features. As she fell, Kronos calculated the distance until she reached the ground; when he warned her of imminent impact, she flipped and landed on the ground. The force of her impact shattered the ground beneath her boots. If it were not for her Excelian heritage, her bones would have broken under the sway.

She climbed to her feet and scanned the trees around her. She recognised a fire emblem on the top of the cave. Then heard Asashin land behind her, his impact much more significant than hers.

"There's another emblem," she said.

"The same as before?" he asked.

"Yes."

"That can't be a coincidence."

"Agreed."

They walked into the second tunnel and darkness surrounded them. They turned down a few corridors here and there, following the fire emblem . . . until Gothalia and Asashin stopped and stared at an ancient city.

Beneath the old ruins, there was a large fire emblem in the middle of what once would have been an ancient courtyard.

"Where are we?" Asashin asked.

They caught sight of a statue of Leonardo Da Vinci reading a book. Gothalia glanced at Asashin, confused.

"Leonardo?" she questioned.

"That's him, but these ruins look so much older than when he was born," Asashin said. As they ventured further into the ruins, they came across an almost-untouched building. A skylight far above displayed more statues of ancient men and women; some were soldiers, others were architects, diplomats, scientists, and hunters.

"They're Excelians." Gothalia wandered through the buildings and passed shattered ground. Her boots crunched on something, and she stopped, staring down at the bones near a shield and sword. "There was a war."

"Not just any war. It looks like they were trying to protect something," Asashin said recognising the way the buildings were situated. They surrounded other buildings, as if forming a castle wall.

"They didn't go down without a fight."

"With an indomitable spirit, as any Excelian." Gothalia regarded the walls and the ancient writing. She understood them and knew Asashin would too. It was the language of the Fire Reserve. "This was a colony."

"It's about time you found this place," a voice behind them said. "I was beginning to worry."

SWALLOWING HIS FEAR, Curt crawled away from his position and pulled out his binoculars. Spotting Noel-Len relocating closer to the enemy, Curt muttered, "Use your brain kid."

Noel-Len allowed his rifle to hang over his shoulder. He cradled two smoke grenades, as well as a few explosive grenades. Several meters away, Curt noticed an Excelian Lieutenant crawling closer to the enemy, one of her swords drawn as she watched Noel-Len. *She's waiting . . . but for what exactly?* Curt wondered.

Noel-Len tossed the grenades; they smoked and hissed around the enemy, momentarily stunning them. With the protective mask concealing his nose and mouth, he rushed into the grey abyss. The infrared vision goggles outlined two aliens, that he struck down by severing their necks with his hunting knife.

Shock and frustration consumed Noel-Len as his final target disappeared. The smoke faded and the alien raced at him. Within a single breath, a sword pinned the monster against a nearby brick wall. The sword targeted the alien's eye precisely.

Noel-Len struggled to drag his eyes from the sight and managed to follow the sword's initial trajectory.

The Excelian woman pulled out a handheld pistol and fired. Noel-Len froze, feeling the heat of the bullet and the force as it moved passed his jaw. A gargling sound drowned out the sound of his own racing heart.

Another alien dropped to the ground; its head severed from its body. Noel-Len's attention eventually rested on Lieutenant Crystallovis, who watched him with expectation before placing her pistol into her waistband behind her back.

"Thank you?" he attempted. His throat was dry with fear and stiff with hesitation.

Lieutenant Crystallovis's brows lifted in surprise for a moment, before they returned to their intimidating arch. She hurried past Noel-Len, declaring,

"Keep up. I may not save you a second time."

Swiftly, the group vacated the area. They needed to complete the mission if they had any chance of surviving this battle, let alone the war.

On the roofs, the aliens revealed themselves to the squadron on the ground. Demetria fired her weapons and moved—fast.

Noel-Len hid behind a wall and curled away, feeling the concrete shatter and splinter, ricocheting off his skin.

The aliens continued to fire their weapons. However, in a few seconds, the rain of bullets ceased, and Noel-Len slowly glanced around the corner: the aliens that had been stationed on the roof now lay motionlessly on the ground.

"Um, Lieutenant?"

"Keep moving."

"But . . ." he began.

The woman narrowed her gaze on him.

"I said. *Keep moving.*" Without another word she stalked on ahead. Noel-Len regarded the woman strangely but said nothing further.

"What's wrong?" Curt questioned, from beside Noel-Len. Noel-Len glanced at his commanding officer. There was a curiosity and gentleness in his gaze. "Is it the war?" He was aware that the young man had already endured more than any his age. Curt never doubted he could not take it—it would knock him over, it would make him cry, but it would never consume him. Or so he hoped.

The group continued further down the street, searching for their next enemy. Demetria heard a noise off in the distance and her stomach curled. She ordered for the men to stay behind.

"But . . ." Noel-Len began, and Curt cut him short. Demetria's stomach twisted as she entered one of the buildings. Her features darkened into a scowl as she took in the Alastorian staring at her. Its uncanny smile spread across its stained black lips.

Demetria pulled out her crossbow and fired, piercing the Alastorian in the heart before noticing another. She flipped out of the way and pulled out a handheld pistol. Firing at the second one, the men behind her set themselves into position.

Once Demetria drew one Alastorian out, the men fired—they did this one after another, until Demetria was certain the building was safe to enter, or as safe as it could ever be.

"Let's go." When she entered the building, one Alastorian waited in the centre of the room, sitting on a crate, cuddling a small teddy bear. Demetria held up her hand and the soldiers waited. Slowly, Demetria crept forward.

The Alastorian turned and smiled at her.

"I'm going to wipe that smile off your face," Demetria said, placing another arrow on her crossbow and firing.

The Alastorian's lustrous crimson eyes egged her on, while its smile hauntingly remained.

"I bloody hate Alastorians," she grumbled, then turned her heel and sprinted. The other soldiers drew the Alastorians' attention, only to be cut down by that same creature or slipped by as it chased Demetria.

She peered over her shoulder as she bolted out of the room. The Alastorian paused, watching her, before it moved at an unnatural speed. Demetria's heart leapt as she rounded a corner and darted into a room, slamming the door behind her.

She backed away from the door and noticed the room was pitch black, but her eyes could make out every little detail. She could see the machines behind her, and many boxes filled with the unknown. Realising she was in a large storeroom, she discovered there were plenty of places to hide. She shrouded herself in the darkness behind a large crate.

She waited, and leaned forward on her knees, yanking out her sword. Peering around the corner, she noticed the door remained untouched. She was unaware of the Alastorian that stood on the highest box above her.

Its eyes raked her in, and the monster's smile never wavered. It leapt and dropped. The ground cracked beneath the demon's landing; Demetria rolled away instinctively, and her eyes widened at the sight. The Alastorian landed on all fours and its head turned to her. The sight of it petrified her.

The Alastorian rushed to her. Demetria stood and ran. Terrified, she ducked under a machine and the Alastorian leapt onto it, its claws digging into the metal to keep it from falling. Its hands swiped at either side of the machine, blocking off her escape. She heard another machine starting and realised that it had started all on its own. A forklift moved towards her; its metal plates were ready to slice her in two. She moved under the machine and away from the forklift, but as she did, she noticed the demon's beady eyes on her.

A spark flared and the forklift caught fire; it exploded, and the explosion destroyed the machine above her, sending the Alastorian flying to the far steel wall. The Alastorian was unable to move, crushed between the wall and the shrapnel that scattered the room. Catching her breath, Demetria pulled herself to her feet and sprinted out of the room and down the corridor, glancing behind her to make sure she was not followed. As she turned back, she collided into someone and fell flat on her back.

Gunfire echoed and Demetria flipped to her feet, catching sight of Noel-Len who regarded with a humorous glint to his eye.

"Yes?" she questioned once she discovered that the final Alastorian was killed. Sheathing her sword, she observed him, curiously.

"Nothing," he shrugged, with a smile.

Without another word, she walked by him and lead the group to clear out as many Alastorians and Xzandians as they could find. Once their numbers began to dwindle, it was time to conduct their plan. They knew that, with the Xzandian numbers dropping, they would send in reinforcements.

They travelled the streets for a little longer, working to draw out the enemy. Demetria observed the Xzandians from where she stood under a tree near the harbour.

"What do we do now?" Noel-Len asked her.

Demetria eyed him steadily for a moment.

"Take your positions around the perimeter. Group B will draw in the enemy, while your team will flank them from either side. That should be enough to distract them." Noel-Len turned to leave with Curt before Demetria added, "And don't be afraid to use explosives. We need to make a lot of noise."

"Ma'am," both Sergeant McGuire and Private Ignatius responded.

ASASHIN PULLED OUT his sword, and Gothalia placed her hand over his, lowering his weapon.

"What are you doing here?" Gothalia questioned.

"Hadn't I made that clear? I'm here to help," said the white-haired man, who had appeared behind them. He stared at her for a moment before continuing. "My name is Bilack. And these are old ruins of an early Excelian society that was built well before the Renaissance period. Isn't it a beautiful sight? These buildings were built to last."

"What happened?" Gothalia asked, aware of Asashin regarding her with confusion.

"There was a massacre. Some of these people were different, and because of that, they were feared. So, the Southern Earth Reserve wiped them out, every one of them."

"How were they different?"

Bilack held her gaze.

"They were like you young one."

"Me?"

"Yes. They had unstable élanocytes. Yet, they were different from you; your condition creates a variation of abilities. Members of the Valdis clan were known to disappear and reappear as they choose. The Ignatius clan were known to bear fire and be the Fire Reserve's first guardians. Those of the Brutus clan are known to be skilled at hunting, tracking, and weapons. Your clan lord, Brutus, is a powerful one, even if you are of Caligati blood."

"How do you know so much about me?" Asashin questioned.

The man smiled.

"I don't know so much as you think. I am just a little informed. Follow me. There's something I wish to show you."

Bilack turned from them and wandered deeper into the destroyed city. Gothalia followed, and Asashin trailed after her, deep in thought. Gothalia, equally deep in thought, did not notice Bilack stop. Catching herself, she paused, waiting for his revelation.

They had entered a building. Half the roof was sliced open, providing a filtering in of the light of day from above. Gothalia recognised the runes on the walls and the Fire emblem in the centre. It was covered in carvings of people, objects, and activities that told a story. She stepped into the room and recognised the symbol of her mother's clan etched beneath the fire emblem.

She walked over to it and placed her hand against the cold stone wall. Beneath the light, she stared at it, deep in thought, her fingers tracing the insignia and her heart hammered in her chest.

"There is so much you don't know," Bilack said.

"So much, I don't know?"

"Why your family was slaughtered, why your mother disappeared, and why your brother was separated from you."

Asashin studied Gothalia and recognised the flash of emotions flicker across her face: contempt, anger, and hurt. He knew she had been on her own for a while, even when they were children. He never knew why. Based on Bilack's words, there was more to it.

"Why is my mother's family crest here?" Gothalia asked.

"Your mother hails from the Valdis clan, who were one of the guardians of this colony."

Then there was a grumble and a growl. A large shadow towered over Gothalia and both men pulled out their weapons, ready to take on the threat.

"Gothalia get out of the way!" Bilack yelled.

Above Gothalia's head was a giant serpent with black scales and beady red eyes. It stared her down and growled once more. Fear flashed across her features as she stepped back away from the monster.

"What the hell?" she muttered. "What is that?"

"The second guardian," Bilack said. "And we're not welcome."

Gothalia slowly backed away until she was closer to the door and the serpent lifted its head and crawled closer to Gothalia. Gothalia felt its hot breath against her skin and smelled rotting flesh between its teeth. Her stomach dropped, and she stared into the eyes of the monster, hypnotised. Fear left her body, and she felt practically relaxed in its presence.

"Gothalia!" Asashin called.

Bilack rushed forward and grabbed Gothalia by the wrist and yanked her out of the way before the serpent could devour her.

"Don't look in its eyes!" he yelled and dragged her after him. Covering his eyes, Asashin sprinted after them as they ran into a hallway and down a set of stairs.

Sparks of red and black flared around the serpent, lighting up the lane. Asashin, Gothalia and Bilack soon realised that the sparks were coming from the serpent.

"So, what's the plan?" Gothalia yelled as she ran after them while the serpent's tail smashed the walls of the halls.

"Not sure yet," Bilack answered, his hands consumed by dark clouds. Gothalia saw the power in his hands, almost mesmerised. She pulled her gaze away and fired her rifle at the serpent—but she'd run out of bullets. Throwing the weapon aside, she pulled out her sword while Asashin threw knives at the serpent, who grew angry that Asashin's blades had pierced its skin.

Gothalia leapt into the air and thrust her sword forward, aiming for the monster's head, only to be stunned when it threw her into a building with a flick of its tail. She heard Asashin and Bilack call out to her, but she could not move. Darkness consumed her.

Gothalia's unconscious form lay in the pile of bricks as the serpent approached. Asashin ran at the monster—a monster that was larger than the tallest building in the ancient city and thicker than any great waterfall. There was a hiss and the baring of its teeth as it moved towards Gothalia. Asashin tossed a grenade that stuck to the stomach of the serpent; but when the explosion rang out, the monster remained standing.

When Gothalia came to, she spied figures surrounding her. Before one man could stab her, she rolled out of the way and locked her legs around his arm. She knocked his sword out of his hands and grabbed it before kicking him in the face. Gothalia avoided the strike and blocked the next attack. With her newly acquired weapon, she frowned.

Gothalia ducked to avoid the next strike, spinning around on her knees she sliced at his ankles. He fell down and she kneed him in the head. The next man attacked her. She deflected each attack before stepping in and kicking him back. Gothalia caught him and held him by the front of his armour.

"Who are you?" she demanded. "What are you doing here?"

The man held up his hands and called,

"I surrender."

Gothalia was surprised and stared the man down until she heard Asashin cry out in pain. Her gaze fell on the serpent, and Asashin caught under a pile of rocks. *He will heal,* she thought. With a new plan forming, she pressed her blade to the man's throat.

"What is that and how do we stop it?" she demanded. When the man did not answer, she repeated more forcefully, "The serpent, how do we stop it?"

He held up his hands.

"You can't stop it with mere attacks; it's intended to withstand them."

"No, it's not. My comrade stabbed it with his knives," Gothalia responded, with a dangerous glare.

"If it happened over thirty seconds ago, it has already healed. It's designed with the similar make-up of . . ."

"Of what!" Gothalia pressed the sword against his throat. "Well?" She saw that Asashin could not move from his position and that Bilack was doing all he could to keep the serpent at bay.

"Of Excelians. It's designed by us—like us—to protect us."

Gothalia pulled the blade from his throat. A silent exchange of understanding shifted between the two and Gothalia regarded him carefully, before dropping the sword on the ground.

"Then how do we stop it?"

"You don't attack," he said.

"What?"

"You heard me. If you want your friends to survive, do not attack. Tell your comrade to fall back. Now." Gothalia regarded the man for a moment before agreeing to his terms and hearing Kronos confirm her next course of action. She climbed over the guard from the top of the building, dropped to the ground, and sprinted to where Asashin stood, caught under thick stones. He would heal, she knew, but she could not waste time.

She sprinted to Bilack, where he battled the serpent, who shattered buildings, overpasses, and statues. Bilack was throwing black knives at the serpent who became more agitated at his attacks. Before the snake could throw him into a building, Gothalia forced Bilack to the ground.

She felt the impact of the serpent's attack by the wind rushing overhead and throwing her cloak into the air. Its tail had just missed them both, and they were meters from Asashin, who struggled to free himself.

Though he was managing to free himself little by little, he would not be able to move in time. Climbing to her feet, Gothalia stared up at the serpent, unafraid and determined. Bilack did not move from where he lay on the street, watching her.

Before the next attack, Gothalia took a deep breath and held up her hand. The next attack paused in front of her hand. She felt the force run along the tips of her fingers, up her arm, and through to her cloak and hair. The serpent did not move its red eyes, reverting to its natural black colour before retreating. Gothalia gasped and sank to her knees. The fear that owned her body until that moment had finally been released. She had never felt more tired and relieved in her life.

The sound of approaching footfalls caught everyone's attention, and Gothalia noticed the men that had attacked her before. She stepped towards them.

"We're not here to fight," one said.

Cautiously, the men regarded Gothalia and lingered, waiting for her to react incorrectly. They did not engage but did not disengage either. Instead, they waited for Asashin, Gothalia and Bilack to believe their words. When they finally did, the group revealed that they were Excelians of another colony not too far away, where only a few remained. With questions on their tongues, Gothalia, Asashin and Bilack followed them down a few dark corridors and hidden passageways lit by fire lanterns. After a few turns and passing a canal, they arrived. The city was tucked away into the crevices of walls lined in the earth.

The group halted before the gate. The soldiers punched in their passcodes after requesting that Gothalia and her friends turn away. Gothalia rolled her eyes at the notion, before turning her back on them with the others. Once the soldiers finalised the code, Gothalia and the others returned their attention to the men.

Gothalia understood these people hidden behind thick walls were hidden away for an exceedingly long time, but it did not mean they did not trade. She kept those thoughts to herself then paused, silently observing the gates as they opened.

Within the city, the architecture reminded her very much of the Fire Reserve. On the outside, it blended with the environment, but on the inside, it was large, beautiful, and healthy, with blue skies and green grass as far as the eye could see.

She glanced at the symbol on the doors, where three fires overlapped each other to form a larger fire, and Gothalia recognised the insignia.

"You're from the Eastern Fire Reserve," Gothalia said, with awe and fascination. The man, their leader, stopped beside her.

"That we are. It's because of our ability to forge intricate diamond steel that we've survived as long as we have."

"But the city?" Gothalia questioned. "It's destroyed."

"It is," he said. "Though our ancestors built that city with their bare hands. It reminds us every day that we have not forged any kind of allegiance with the Southern Earth Reserve and never will. Well done in taking me down. It was awe-inspiring."

He walked confidently by Gothalia who hesitated.

"Um . . . you're welcome?"

He glanced back at Gothalia with a genuine smile, then gestured for her to hurry inside with the others before they closed the gate.

Inside, Gothalia smelled the cool breeze, and felt the warm, artificial rays of the sun on her skin. The grass crunched beneath her feet, and the water in the stream could be heard trickling not too far from where they were. The village sat quietly within the secured walls, and many citizens moved freely throughout the Reserve.

# Chapter 26

AFTER GOTHALIA AND the others were cleared to enter by the Peacekeepers, the happiness and laughter grew louder, and Gothalia could not help but smile as she gazed upon the civilians.

As she strolled with the men through the streets, she saw children run by her while merchants worked to sell their products or services.

The man who guided them introduced them quickly to the city; the people were cautious at first, but recognised the emblem of the Eastern Fire Reserve symbol on their uniforms and relaxed, recognising that no danger would befall them while their Centurions were around. The man guided them to the centre of the town and Gothalia paused outside a large manor.

"Tapila, open the doors, we have guests!" he growled, pacing back and forth within the courtyard.

"My name is Volvomich," the man said to Asashin and Gothalia, "and it is nice to meet you."

"It is nice to meet you too," Gothalia said. When the doors opened, the man ushered the others and his soldiers inside along with Bilack; Asashin did not move and only crossed his arms. His gaze lingered over Gothalia.

"Come in, come in. Don't be shy," Volvomich said, and Gothalia walked into the house. The glossy wooden floorboards were smooth beneath her boots and gently echoed beneath each step; she couldn't help but feel, for the first time in a long time, relaxed. "Your reputation precedes you," he said to Gothalia. "*You*, my dear, are exceptional! After what happened in the Northern Reserve and with the princess, including what you did for the Prince of your Reserve, All of the Excelian underworld knows of you and your team."

"Okay, are you sure you're not over exaggerating?" Asashin asked, both curious and honoured.

"I don't exaggerate, and I don't lie," he said, pointing a stiff finger at Asashin. "Now, let's introduce you to the others. We have a lot to do."

"What do you mean?" Gothalia asked. "We haven't been here long, and we don't—" Then, from around the corner, stepped Anaphora and L'Eiron. "What are you two doing here?"

"Meeting with our allies."

"Allies?" Gothalia asked, flabbergasted, "Since when?"

Volvomich stepped confidently forward.

"Since those Xzandians mongrels conspired with Human mercenaries. The Xzandians set the plan for those bastards to infiltrate the Fire Reserve and kill the Seers, leaving one wounded and in a critical condition. Even to this day, no one knows when he'll wake."

Gothalia and Asashin stopped before Anaphora and L'Eiron with Volvomich joining the circle.

"That means that this was an inside job. We need to find the person or people responsible for opening the wards," Gothalia said. "And who thought it was okay to use me as a distraction, the bastard."

"There's more. The Grand Elders were taken or killed—not sure, but Grand Elder Michalis is in hiding and under guard. The Royal Family has declared they will step in until the Grand Elders have been found, and until they do, the city is vulnerable."

"There are hundreds of Excelian Centurions. I'm sure the city will be secure a little bit longer," Asashin said confidently.

"It will be, but we don't know how much longer," Volvomich confessed.

"In any case, Asashin, you are to return with Danteus, Demetria and Noel-Len to the Fire Reserve and help the forces. Gothalia, you need to hunt down the rest of the Fragments and ensure the Xzandians do not find them first. Arthur's map will guide you."

"Wait, that Human is going to the Fire Reserve?" Asashin questioned, confused.

L'Eiron and Anaphora shared a look before L'Eiron declared, "Noel-Len is not Human. Is he, Gothalia?"

Asashin regarded Gothalia, surprised.

"No," she said simply. "He's my brother, but he doesn't remember."

"Did – did I hear that right?" he said. "Noel-Len, that *Human* soldier, is an Excelian. And your *brother*."

Gothalia stared Asashin down.

"He is."

Asashin held up his hands.

"I'm not doubting you or anything, I'm just surprised. I don't recall there being another member of the Ignatius-Valdis bloodline existing. It actually explains a lot, like that spike we felt, and the fact that he looks a lot like you."

Gothalia wondered to how her brother had forgotten her and how he had survived on his own for so long. These were questions she wanted answers to, but questions she did not have the time to find answers to, yet.

"Anyway, I'll send word to Danteus," L'Eiron said and stepped away from the group.

"It looks like you'll have to complete this mission on your own, and you will encounter resistance. Remember this: you are the

KALVERYA JOHANSSON

heiress of the Ignatius-Valdis clan who has naturally inherited your mother's traits. Use that to your advantage," Anaphora said placing a hand on Gothalia's shoulder. "The road may be long, but you'll always be in my thoughts. You'll need to protect the Reserve while you're away, in whatever way you know how."

Gothalia regarded Anaphora for a moment longer before declaring,

"I understand."

"Good. Don't forget your training."

"I won't."

"I'll see you a little later, perhaps." Anaphora turned away.

"Where are you going?" Gothalia asked Anaphora.

"To return to the battlefield. The Humans have drafted a plan for how to exploit the Xzandian weaknesses."

"I understand. Be safe."

"You too, young one. You too." With that, Anaphora walked away; even with Asashin beside her, in that moment, Gothalia felt utterly alone.

Later that day, Volvomich guided Gothalia to the outskirts of the small town, where lush open fields filled the countryside. Long, thin grass flowed in the wind just below her waist while thick, scattered trees danced in the meadows. She glanced at the small buds of flowers curving in the long grass and smiled.

"It's so pretty," Gothalia said, as she plucked the little flowers, which were no bigger than her smallest finger. She felt the sun light her chilly cheeks and the wind slide through her thick curly hair, running its gentle fingers over her scalp.

"It is. Isn't it?" Volvomich asked from beside her, as his eyes scoured the pasture before him. In the distance, they could see sheep being herded by a dog. "This is a large town, but they use the fields around them as a source of income."

"So, they're pretty much ranchers?" Gothalia asked, as she watched the black and white sheepdog. She had always wanted a dog and never was given a chance to have one.

"Almost. They do have animals, but they also grow crops further out. It's one of the towns that's under the protection of the Colonial Lords."

"Interesting." Gothalia glanced behind her and saw a large mansion in the distance. "Is that where he lives?"

"Yeah. How did you know?" Volvomich asked.

"Because it might be the biggest building in the whole town," Gothalia said, as if it were the most obvious thing in the world. She contemplated the appearance and architecture of the other buildings. They were not in bad shape, but they were large enough to fit a lot of people.

Volvomich pulled a piece of paper out of his pocket and handed it to her. She assessed the folded paper in her hands.

"What's this for?"

"Read it and find out," he said, as he walked away from her and sat down on the grass. Cautiously, she unfolded the paper. Gothalia stopped and stared at the man sitting on the grass, then back at the letter. "What?"

She folded the paper up and walked over to him.

"So, you're the prince of this Reserve, and you're also a—" Gothalia was cut off by the sound of ear-piercing screams.

Immediately, Gothalia and Volvomich climbed to their feet and ran towards the sound. They saw men and women clad in unusually-designed leather clothes. Gothalia turned to Volvomich; his lips were pulled into a snarl as he glared at the men.

The hostile strangers rode on horses through the streets, their swords bare and pointed at the vulnerable.

"Volvomich!" she called. "Who are they?"

"They're a band of thieves."

Gothalia followed the men, while Volvomich chased after her. They paused before the group and Gothalia spotted the advanced weapons they carried. One of the men, Gothalia saw, held a woman by the front of her dress before throwing her to the ground.

"I'll ask you one more time. Give us all your money or else."

Gothalia noticed that the woman they had forced to the ground wore regal clothing. Gothalia stormed over to them but her wrist was held fast in Volvomich's grip.

"Don't," he said.

Gothalia glared.

"Am I supposed to sit by and watch?"

"No," he said and stepped forward. Gothalia saw the bow in his hand and the tattoo on his opposite wrist, a tattoo she knew was not there moments ago. He took aim and fired, pinning the wrist of the man who had assaulted the woman to the stone wall. Everyone's attention fell on Volvomich.

"Back away from her," Volvomich warned, while Gothalia prepared herself for an attack.

All six men watched Volvomich. It was not fear that filled their ragged features, but amusement.

"What do you want, commoner?" the man asked, the one who Gothalia assumed was the leader. He wore a brilliant red sash around his waist.

"I already told you," Volvomich said, growing impatient. "Back away from her."

The leader's dark, unreadable eyes bore into Volvomich's while the sleeve of his left wrist remained pinned to the stone wall by a gleaming silver arrow.

"Don't make me repeat myself," Volvomich warned, and Gothalia marvelled at his strength. Without thinking, Gothalia rushed over to the woman on the ground and kneeled before her.

"Are you hurt?" she asked.

The woman inspected Gothalia's outstretched hand. The woman shook her head and climbed to her feet, accepting Gothalia's aid.

"I'm fine, just a little shocked," the woman announced.

"Who the hell do you think you are?" the leader demanded, as he pulled his arm free of the arrow, tearing at his sleeve. Gothalia felt the rushing wind behind her before she realised what was happening. Another arrow flew from Volvomich's bow and locked into the wall a few centimetres behind the leader's head. Volvomich reached for another arrow.

"I'm the one you must answer to, if you even consider touching her," Volvomich warned and Gothalia spun around to find that the leader had frozen, his hand outstretched to grab her. Changing tack, his hand moved to the hilt of his sword. The men surrounding Gothalia and the regal woman began to unsheathe their swords. Gothalia judged the leader. Her mind rapidly worked to identify his weak points and what attacks would be most effective.

Gothalia's eyes narrowed on the one who had reached for her and she stood up, with her fists raised. Suddenly, there was a loud shout, then the clanging sound of hooves bashing the ground.

Gothalia glanced behind her and saw men in gleaming Centurion armour rushing towards the group. The men surrounding them grew uneasy and several demanded that their leader give the order to flee, but Gothalia knew that was not going to happen. She could see that the leader was a prideful man, one that caused her skin to crawl.

The thieves turned to face the oncoming Centurions holding large wooden crossbows. It happened too fast for Gothalia and Volvomich to react as arrows flew and Gothalia watched in horror when men fell from their horses. Screams filled the air from the nearby citizens and Gothalia froze.

The arrows struck their chests and heads. Gothalia saw Volvomich fighting the leader. Several of the leader's gang were preoccupied with the men on horseback, so Gothalia figured it was time to make her escape; she would come back to help Volvomich later.

As Gothalia ran down the battle-filled street, she knew she would have to get her and the woman to safety. Once Gothalia and the woman were away from harm, Gothalia glanced through the crowd to catch sight of Volvomich, but there was nothing.

"Thank you," the woman said, as she fought to catch her breath.

"You're welcome." Gothalia forced a smile. At the corner of her eye Gothalia caught sight of a drawn blade soaring towards her. Quickly, Gothalia pushed the woman away and disarmed the man. He pulled out a long stiletto, but the long knife that threatened to destroy Gothalia, was blocked by a silver sword. Her gaze followed the length of the blade that held of her attacker and found Asashin wielding it.

"Weren't you supposed to leave?" he asked

"Are you trying to get rid of me?" Gothalia retorted.

"No, but finding Midnight Eclipse is important, you must ensure no one else will get it."

"I know."

Asashin disarmed the attacker. Steel clashed throughout the area and she knew more Centurions and Peacekeepers had arrived. Gothalia pushed out her leg and swept her attacker off-balance, so Asashin could knock him unconscious.

"Then why are you still here?" he asked.

"Volvomich had information for me."

The clash of swords rang throughout the area. Behind the thugs, Gothalia noticed in a man dressed like a Human soldier, sprinting away. It happened so fast she was not certain if she had imagined it or not.

At the front of the group of Centurions was a man clad in expensive clothing. He rode a majestic white horse and the first thing Gothalia noticed was the large flags behind him. His long brown hair tossed in the air as he rode towards Gothalia and the others. Quickly, he dismounted his horse and rushed over to the woman.

"Ellena!" he called as he ran to her side. "Are you alright?" His attention fell on Asashin and he forced Ellena behind him, drawing his sword on Asashin.

"I'm fine, Alastair!" Ellena barked. "He's not our enemy!"

"You don't know that, dear sister," Alastair rebutted gently. Asashin turned from the man and to Gothalia, expressionless.

Gothalia's eyes skimmed over the soldiers behind her and down the bloodied street. Some were dead, others severely injured. In the distance, the remaining soldiers and thugs fought. Then she saw it: the red sash wrapped around the waist of a man who ran from the arrows.

"Don't," Asashin suggested. "Let's see what he's got."

Eventually, the battle between the leader and Volvomich ended. Volvomich stood victorious before the man, who fell to his knees. Gothalia and the others ran to him. Sweat dripped from his jaw and soaked his golden hair as he smiled at them.

"Are you okay?" Asashin asked.

"I'm fine."

"Good work," Gothalia added.

"No, not good work," Volvomich corrected. "One's got away and he wears the uniform of the surface world."

Before Gothalia could say anything, she had heard Alastair say,

"I thought I noticed a stranger in the distance, but I was solely focused on this mongrel." He pushed the thug leader before him in the chest. He coughed and sputtered, but still winked at Gothalia.

"Hey, beautiful."

"Not interested," Gothalia responded, coldly.

"Suit yourself."

Asashin crossed his arms, less than impressed.

"Anyway, thank you for saving my sister, your majesty. She does have a habit of not being vigilant." Alastair placed a hand over his heart and bowed. "Lieutenant Valdis, at long last we meet."

"Glad to meet you . . . Alastair."

Volvomich laughed, and Asashin looked pale when Gothalia glanced up.

"What?"

"Gothalia," Asashin whispered, "That's the Colonial Lord."

"Oh . . . um . . . Sir."

Alastair laughed.

"Rumour has it you're on a journey," he said. Gesturing for the Centurions and Peacekeepers to take the thieves to the cells below the Grand Elder building.

"I am, but how did you know?" Gothalia asked.

"Your General informed our General, who in turn informed me, the royal family, and the Grand Elders. As such, you were granted permission to enter our lands."

"How did you know I'd be here?" Gothalia asked, walking beside the Colonial Lord as he wandered the streets back to his building.

"The map given to you by your scientist led you here. From the video footage we found, we suspected you must have had a good reason for coming here, especially when you tried to stop your General's killer. We realised, there was more to it and helping you could help us all. The map was first acquired by one of our Centurions before it was sent to the main Reserve for deep analysis.

"It contains a map of where all the known Fragments are and the suspected areas the others. However, because the Human world is quick for coin, they have a habit of selling and purchasing items that they may or may not know hold value. Meaning . . ."

". . . Meaning, the Fragments could have exchanged hands one too many times." Gothalia finished.

"Exactly."

"What of the man?" Asashin asked, on the other side of the Colonial Lord. "The soldier in the Human uniform. Where is he?"

"My men are searching the city for him now. He couldn't have gotten too far on foot, especially being human. He won't be able to outrun our trackers. We'll find him in time."

"Where are we going?" Gothalia asked.

"To our Cetatea. We need give you something before you conduct your journey. The Fragments come in many different shapes and sizes, but the overall colour and texture remain the same as I'm sure you know."

They arrived at the Cetatea after a short walk. The building was a similar design to the Cetatea in the Fire Reserve. Automatically, Gothalia felt comfortable. When they entered the Cetatea, she recognised the Fire Emblem of the main Fire Reserve.

"This way," Alastair said, guiding them down a hall, stairs, and out the back to where the courtyard lay. They reached a central fountain, with a statue of a Centurion woman that was the same as the fountain at Gothalia's Cetatea.

Not thinking too much of it, they stopped before the statue, and the Colonial Lord punched in a code. The ground opened beneath them, and they walked down into it. The guards stayed outside while the Colonial Lord, Volvomich, Gothalia, and Asashin entered. When they reached the bottom of the stairs, they paused.

"This is what we wanted to show you," Alastair said.

"Is that a . . . ?" Gothalia began, ". . . Fragment?" She took in the sight of the Fragment, shaped like a diamond, hovering in the middle of the room. Gothalia could see that around it were four pillars on a platform that controlled and harnessed its power.

"It is. As you can see, the black texture of the metal allows the absorption of energy, explaining why it is hovering. Others may be this size while others may not be. When you get close enough, this one will release energy of its own, reacting to the presence of the others."

"Wait, what are you saying?"

Alastair moved towards the Fragment.

"What I am saying is that you need this to find the other Fragments that haven't been found—that much I'm sure you're aware of. You'll take this one with you on your journey."

"But wouldn't it be safer here?"

"No. Word has gotten out that there's a Fragment here. To avoid what has happened on the surface world, I am handing it over to you. With the permission of the Royal Family and the Grand Elders, of course. It'll be safer on the move." He placed his hand on a monitor before the four pillars that surrounded the diamond. After a flash of light, Alastair removed his hand and walked towards the main pillar where the Fragment lay.

He gestured for Gothalia to follow. When she climbed another set of stairs, she paused on the landing. He handed her the Fragment. The flat diamond was smooth beneath her fingers.

"How am I supposed to carry it?"

Alastair ran his finger over the side of the Fragment and the Fragment shrank down to the size of her pinkie. "No way."

"Way," Volvomich commented. "It may be small now, but it still carries the amount of power it would in its original form." Then before Gothalia could utter another word, the entrance to the underground tomb exploded. Volvomich and Alastair pulled out their swords. "Let's take 'em."

Gothalia hid the in her utility belt and armed herself. When the sound of footfalls grew near, Gothalia spotted the first enemy and threw a knife. The person plunged to the ground, dead, with the knife protruding from his head.

The enemy fell one by one to Gothalia and Asashin's throwing knives, as each rounded the corner. One used a body as a shield and closed the distance to Volvomich. As Volvomich and the stranger fought, Gothalia and Asashin engaged in close-quarter combat to keep the Fragment safe, fighting off the last of them.

When the battle ceased and the last of the enemy was defeated, Gothalia, Asashin, Volvomich, and Alastair ran out of the sanctuary and into the courtyard, where the sound of clashing steel and war cries rang in the air.

# Chapter 27

"LORD ALASTAIR!" A CENTURION cried. "They've come for the Fragment. We'll hold them off." The overcast sky swallowed the soldiers in the shadows, while Gothalia searched the crowd for Bilack.

"There you guys are," he called as he reached them, his sword in hand and his usually clean clothes smeared in dirt and blood. "We should move. Now." He ran and the group followed. The man that had initially run from them cladded in military attire, no replaced in casual Reserve clothing.

"Isn't that—?" Gothalia began and ran inside after the man with the others following. They heard the pop of a rifle and everyone ran behind pillars, ducking for cover. "Where did he get a rifle from?"

"Who cares! Take him out!" Bilack cried and Gothalia glanced around. They were pinned down by the fire while the man walked towards them.

When the bullets ceased, he reloaded and pointed the armed weapon at the pillars embedded with bullets.

"Hand over the Fragment," Captain Ethan Wilson declared. "And you can all live."

"Not happening," Gothalia declared, her voice echoing around the foyer.

"Does this woman speak for all of you?" Ethan asked.

"She does! You sorry excuse for a soldier!" Volvomich yelled, his voice shrieking and breaking beneath the strain. "You wouldn't know a real woman if she crawled between your legs, you bastard." Gothalia realised he was feigning emotion as a ploy and could not help but smile. Peering around the pillar, she could see the anger cross the Ethan's face and knew the distraction was working.

He moved towards Volvomich and Bilack. Beside Gothalia, Alastair pulled out a nine-millimetre pistol.

"Where were you hiding that?" she whispered. Alastair smiled then then aimed the weapon at the soldier.

He fired, but Ethan evaded the bullets in time and ran behind another column. Gothalia sprinted from the pillar where she waited and towards the door. Ethan made to pursue but was stopped by Alastair, who continued to fire his weapon. "Get to the tele-pads!" he yelled, to Gothalia, who sprinted down the halls, passing Centurions on their way to the battle.

Gothalia glanced at the map carved into the wall and recognised the area she needed to get to; she raced down a corridor and a set of steps before stumbling upon the room that she needed.

She paused outside the door, which was locked.

She punched numbers into a keypad and groaned when the passcode was rejected.

"Really?" she muttered. "Why can't the pass-codes be the same?"

"Where do you think you're going?" a familiar voice questioned and Gothalia spun around to find Numitora leaning against the wall with her arms crossed. A look of mockery flashed across her features. "Trying to run away? I wonder why?" Her eyes were calculating but Gothalia kept her cool.

"What makes you think I'm running away?" Gothalia asked and kicked Numitora. She caught the kick and threw Gothalia into a wall. Gothalia shoved off the wall and kicked again, aiming for Numitora's head; she narrowly avoided the blow.

Gothalia threw a few punches, blocking Numitora's counterattacks. They continued to fight along the hall and towards the stairs. Gothalia kicked at Numitora's knee and she buckled. Gothalia kicked her down the stairs and ran back to the room—just in time, the door opened by itself after there was a beep and a voice declaring "access granted". The door opened and Gothalia ran inside, past the workstations.

A voice called over the speakers,

"Get on the platform. I will set the coordinates for Russia. When you arrive, search for the rest of the Fragments. Kovac will provide you with latest information and anything else you may need."

Gothalia ran to the platform and glanced up. There was Volvomich playing with the controls. He was battered and bruised with blood trickling down his mouth. Noise permeated from where the control room was and Gothalia recognised the soldiers trying to get into the room.

"Good luck."

With that Gothalia was teleported to Russia.

Noel-Len regarded the area he was set to guard with an air of trepidation. From beside Curt he asked,

"Will this work?"

"I'm not sure," Curt responded cautiously. "But we need to make sure that it does." His eyes lingered over the accessible. Through his binoculars, he observed the soldiers on the other side of the street. They crouched low and out of sight, just like Noel-Len and Curt. To their left, further down the street, Demetria waited with her squadron and the squadron of others, forming group B.

A few moments later, more Xzandian soldiers entered the abandoned street. Every soldier on the rooftop stayed hidden and out of sight until given the order to open fire. Finally, Group B fired.

With their shields up, the aliens remained standing, even as bullets that ricocheted around them. The Xzandians moved towards group B with their shields up, so the human bullets could not graze their armour. Noel-Len knew if they were not careful, this would be the end of them. *Could flanking really cause enough of a distraction?* he wondered. *Why not, drive them right down the middle?*

They were driving the enemy into a corner, rather than wiping out their numbers, to ensure that it caused more reinforcements to arrive. How long they could keep up the distraction, he didn't know.

When it was time, he fired his rifle with the others and took down the aliens who only had their shields focused on the front. When their numbers dwindled, another group poured in and Noel-Len dropped to the ground to hide behind the wall. Noel-Len pulled out a grenade from his pack. Removing the pin, he tossed it at the aliens—the intense explosion eliminated the enemy and silenced the battlefield.

After a moment of stillness, he peered over the wall and down at the Xzandians on the ground. Their bodies were mangled and spattered along the ground.

Other soldiers piled out of their hiding places, and Noel-Len heard his earpiece buzz to life.

"Squadron C moved to sector 5D," the General ordered. While Noel-Len and Curt climbed to their feet and rushed to the others down the emergency stairs to Demetria.

"Let's move."

Demetria led the group down the streets of Darwin and towards the vehicles that were left for them by the other soldiers.

Everyone climbed on board while Noel-Len drove. His mind buzzed with the different possibilities and outcomes of their plan.

More orders were provided through the comm-link and Noel-Len listened to the open channel as some soldiers secured their position behind enemy lines.

When Noel-Len parked the vehicle, all the soldiers stared in wonder at the aliens in the sky and the largest ship.

"They're on board *that*?" Noel-Len asked, uncertainly.

"They are," Demetria responded.

"We can't just leave the response team up there," Curt declared. "Is there a way we can help?"

"Yes," Demetria declared. "By sticking to the plan. We've already created the diversion. Now it's time for the second phase." Noel-Len regarded the battlefield before him, where bodies littered the harbour and explosions from grenades and aerial strikes disfigured the natural landscape. The ocean remained black underneath the evening sky and Noel-Len could barely make out the Xzandian camp in the distance. Curt handed him night-vision goggles; Noel-Len put them on and observed the layout before him.

It was as he suspected. There were many Xzandians who guarded their base from any frontal assault.

"Alright it's time," Demetria declared and climbed off the vehicle. Noel-Len felt deeply apprehensive; they were only human, what good could they do against the Xzandians?

"Don't look so worried," Curt remarked and climbed out of the vehicle, patting Noel-Len on the shoulder. "It won't be as bad as it looks."

"You sure about that?"

"Yeah, pretty sure."

Noel-Len followed Curt out of the vehicle and moved into position. The main attack which, he was a part of, would move around the battle and towards the camp, drawing the attention of other

Xzandians while the others dismantled their weapons and supply chain. He didn't yet know how to dismantle the weapons, but there was no time to ask. Demetria gave the order for the minor attack to conduct the plan.

Men and women, armed in modern tactical gear and wearing Australian and American colours, ran forth with a loud war cry. They threw grenades and opened fire on the enemy; with their tactical shields up, they hid from the enemy bullets. Explosions burst across the battlefield as the Xzandians rushed forward and towards the soldiers. Quickly, Noel-Len, Curt, Demetria, and the rest of their team moved through the shadows and around the battle.

In Russia, Gothalia strode the streets, searching for Kovac. After questioning, eavesdropping, information-digging, she finally found him, in the Irkutsk city of Yerema.

With her hood up, Gothalia as any other woman as she knocked on the blue door. Beneath the disguise was armour, weapons, and her uniform. The door opened, and a woman spoke in Russian. Kronos translated her words.

"Yes?"

"I'm looking for a Kovac. Kovac Rusakova," Gothalia declared.

"And you are?" the woman demanded, with vivid hostility and a sharp tongue.

"A friend of a friend," Gothalia responded, "Forgive me but I don't have much time. I'm hoping you can help me out." Beneath the hood, there was a genuine glint to Gothalia's gaze that caught the woman's attention.

Convinced, and the woman called for a man and stepped away. The man moved to the door and said,

"I'm Kovac, what do you want?"

"Gothalia Ignatius-Valdis," Gothalia replied with a bow and a hand over her heart. "I was hoping you could help me with the Fragments. A mutual friend Volvomich referred me to you." Kovac brows rose at the sound of her name and his mouth gaped at the word 'Fragments.' With a steady nod, he asked:

"You're of the Ignatius-Valdis clan?"

Gothalia concurred, setting a hand over her heart, and Kovac stepped aside. When Gothalia entered the modern house, she admired the architecture, but saw that the interior was not on-par with the buildings in the Fire Reserve. Her stomach clenched at the thought of her own home that she could not return to, but she pushed the feelings to the back of her mind.

Kovac led her to his office and pulled out a chair for her.

"How did you get here? The Fire Reserve is far away."

"Tele-pads. And I wasn't in the main reservation. I was at the Eastern Fire Reserve."

"I see. How did you know where to find me?"

"I have my ways."

"Like interrogation and eavesdropping perhaps?"

Gothalia shrugged.

"When we meet next, I'll be a little more discrete. Everyone knows this face I wear."

"I understand, and you're welcome to take off that disguise. You're among friends." Kovac moved from the chair. The woman entered the room and leaned against the wall. She watched Gothalia remove her hood.

"So, you're really not a blond?"

"Unfortunately, no."

"That's not a dreadful thing."

"Amelia, would you inform the others we have a guest?" Kovac asked.

"I've been told," Gothalia said to Kovac, "That you can provide the latest information about the Fragments, so we're one step ahead. We know that they may have been sold or bought within the past twenty-four to forty-eight hours in stores or at auctions."

"Yes, I figured you'd need some help." Kovac turned on his computer. "Volvomich always said that I had a keen eye and ear for these kinds of things."

"Does Volvomich meet with you often?"

"Not often, why?"

"No reason."

Kovac eyed Gothalia with uncertainty before brushing off her question.

"The last known locations of the Fragments are here." He pulled up a map of Russia and Gothalia noticed only two markers in Russia, one in St Petersburg and the other in Moscow. There was another marking on the screen and Gothalia asked:

"What's that?"

"That's where we last caught wind or encountered the members of the Order of the Rukh. After Sir Arthur's disappearance, I was told to track their movement."

"I see. That's handy."

"Would you like this information?"

"Yes, and every known location or recent incidents that they could be linked to. With the Fire Reserve vulnerable, I doubt Lord Michalis would send anyone after Arthur."

"Good thing you're here, then."

"It's why I'm here, among other reasons."

Kovac printed off the map and handed it to her.

"These are the most recent locations of where they've been sighted in Russia but keep Arthur's map on you just in case. From what we have gathered, there's roughly twenty-five Fragments."

"Roughly?" Gothalia questioned. "Can't you be more certain?"

"Not at this point. But we do believe that they're pieces of a complete puzzle."

"Arthur told me that too.".

"We only found out yesterday. How long have you known?" he asked.

"Since before Arthur was taken. I need you to keep track of all the sightings of the Order. Their movement, their communication, their safe houses, the works."

"That'll take forever."

"Make it faster," Gothalia said, then moved to the window. Down below in the street were two men, clad in black and white suits and holding nine-millimetre pistols. "We got to move."

"What—?" Kovac questioned, then moved beside her.

"You know them?"

"No, I don't." Kovac moved back to the computer and began typing in codes. "Amelia!"

Footfalls thundered down the hall and Amelia returned with a smile, "Everyone's here—"

"—Code Red," Kovac declared and Amelia's face dropped in horror. "Get everyone out. Take the kids."

Amelia nodded and Gothalia watched her run down the hall and to the children's room. Gothalia turned her attention to Kovac.

"They're here for me," she said.

"No, they're here for me and if they find out an Excelian is here, things will get a whole lot more complicated. Take this and go." He handed her a USB drive and she took it.

"What did you do?" she asked.

"It's a long story, but I'm not the bad guy. You have to trust me."

Gothalia held his gaze for a moment and agreed.

The armed men pounded on the door. Amelia returned with the children and led them to another room with bags. Amelia handed Kovac a bag. The children kept asking what was going on—Amelia attempted to calm them down by saying they were going camping and travelling for a bit.

Gothalia bit the inside of her cheek, her jaw clenched. She did not like this one bit, but she knew she had to do something. Kovac grabbed the bag and made for the exit.

"Come on. We can't stay here."

"Go on ahead. I'll try and buy you some time."

Kovac nodded and led his family out the back door.

As Gothalia made for the front door, Kronos asked,

"Got a plan?"

"Well, improvise faster, they're going to force their way in."

"Disguise now and translation *automators*."

"As what?"

"Amelia."

Gothalia had no idea what to expect when she opened the door. When she did, she detected weapons on the men, concealed beneath their jackets.

"Can I help you?" Gothalia asked, with a pleasant smile.

"Sorry to bother you, Mrs. Rusakova," one man said. "We're searching for your husband. We were hoping he'd be home."

"My husband isn't home. You have to come back another time," Gothalia stated and attempted to close the door. One of the men held it open.

"We need to come in now," he declared, with a dangerous, sinister smile and Gothalia pressed her weight against the door, forcing it to close. Both men groaned, and one shouted,

"Keep it open!"

Gothalia punched the closest man in the nose, hard enough that he stumbled back, and she slammed the door in their faces before locking it.

Without another thought, she turned around and ran into the hall. The ricochet of bullets permeated the air as they shot at the lock and Gothalia pressed her back against the wall when they forced their way into the house. She made to pull out her sword, but instead reached for an umbrella. The men pressed on, their guns drawn, making for the kitchen.

Gothalia snuck around the kitchen and towards the back door, only to circle around and hide in the living room. When one of the men discovered her, she attacked.

Using the umbrella, she stabbed the man in the foot, before shoving the umbrella into his stomach and swinging it around so the handle hit him hard in the head. He fell back and collided with the glass table.

Gothalia dropped the umbrella and ran for the other man. Before he could train his gun on her, she pushed his hand up into the air. Reflexively, he fired his weapon, and she kicked him the stomach and again in the head, knocking him unconscious.

When she was certain no one else was around, she walked through the living room and to the front door. As she vacated the premises, she realised the family was long gone, but she knew she could find them again.

After a few hours of walking the streets of Moscow, she heard a scream not too far from her.

Quickly, she peered over her shoulder and saw a ten-foot-tall muscular alien with black hair shove a man out of the way. Gothalia and several other people watched in horror.

One man helped the victim to his feet and Gothalia glared at the large man.

"How rude," Gothalia mumbled beneath her breath. "He's not even wearing a shirt."

They were only a hundred feet in front of her, but she could hear their conversation clearly as she saw their lips move.

"Are you sure she's here?" the smaller man asked.

"Positive. I'd never forget that scent," the larger one grunted.

At the same time, they glanced at Gothalia through the crowd and their eyes met.

"There!" the smaller man growled and pointed at Gothalia who turned on her heel and ran, forcing her way through the growing crowd, who pulled out their phones to record her.

"Move!" she growled. Though it had taken only a few seconds to exit the swarming throng, to Gothalia it felt like hours. When Gothalia was free of the crowd, she spotted another bridge that stretched over the highway below. She ran along it and darted to her right and around a nearby wall, then flattened her back against the stone wall. Several moments later, the men appeared and glanced around.

"Is this where she went?" the smaller one asked.

The larger man sniffed the air.

"Yeah. She went this way alright."

Gothalia's blood raced through her veins. They were closing in, she knew, and there was nothing she could do except to run.

"There!"

Gothalia peered over her shoulder and continued running.

Gothalia entered a wide, clean alley, then ducked in time to avoid the fireball that was thrown through the alley. She was cornered. The men caught up at the end of the alley.

"It's hard to believe it's her. Are you sure it's her, Yogic?" The smaller man called.

"I'm certain," Yogic announced. "I never forget a scent, Karim."

"Your nose is as sharp as a dogs.'" Karim's eyes narrowed on Gothalia while his pale lips curled into a dangerous smile. "We'll be rewarded greatly if we deliver her head."

"I thought they want her alive."

"Well, we could always tell them there was an unexpected complication."

Gothalia glared at both men. She was not in any mood to deal with them. Time was running out.

"You work for Numitora, don't you?" she asked.

"We don't answer to you," Yogic spat. "Nor to anyone of the Valdis clan."

Gothalia's glare narrowed.

"I maybe a descendant of the Valdis clan but that doesn't mean I'm any less than Excelian."

"Sure, girlie, you keep telling yourself that." Yogic pointed at her. "Get her."

# Chapter 28

THE LARGER MAN RUSHED to Gothalia and she leapt out of the way, allowing her energy to take over. An explosion burst in the air behind her, and Karim stumbled, growling in pain as the explosion seared across his exposed back.

"I'm warning you, back off," Gothalia snarled, satisfied with the painful look on Karim's face. "I don't want to hurt you, but I will if I must."

"We're not going anywhere. Have not you been informed? There's a bounty on your head. We want that reward."

"Let's see you try to get it."

Seconds after they came at her again, the men collided with the ground. Gothalia smiled with satisfaction, as she regarded their prone forms. Then she summoned Kronos.

"My lady."

"Where are we?" Gothalia asked.

"We're five kilometres south-east of Mr. Rusakova's residence."

"Thanks. And Kovac?"

"He's out of the city. On his way to Moscow," Kronos replied. "He's hacked into our main server. As long as he's logged on, I can keep track of his whereabouts."

"Good. Keep me posted." Before Gothalia left the area, she pulled out her map and regarded its contents. She was certain another Fragment would be nearby and, hopefully, she would find more information around the Order. For now, she knew she need-ed to be careful; there was more than one person hunting the Frag-ments, that much she knew.

Gothalia wandered the streets of Moscow, deep in thought, as everything that had happened began to weigh in on her. She could no longer return home as Michalis had long-ago instructed. But was she supposed to acquire all the Fragments on her own?

No, she thought, I'm not a fully-fledged Centurion yet.

Deep in thought, she did not hear the thudding of boots be-hind her until someone bumped into her. She glared at the back of the man then realised her utility belt had been taken.

"Hey!" she called out. "Get back here!"

Gothalia pursued the man realising that the maps leading her to the Fragments had been taken. As she sprinted after him, she wondered, *how did he take my belt?*

The thief sprinted down a street, cut across a road, then turned down another street, which led to a quiet warehouse.

"Why do they always run?" Gothalia groaned and followed him.

When she entered the warehouse, she was on guard. Darkness surrounded her. Beams of light filtered through open windows and holes in the roof. Where the man had gone, she had no idea.

"Kronos. Thermo-print now."

"As you wish," he said.

The footprints Kronos projected led her to the enemy; she found him attempting to unlock the far door of the warehouse.

"There you are," Gothalia said. "I understand you have your reasons, but they're not good enough to take something that isn't yours."

"What do you know?" the man growled. "Have you ever lived without?"

"Maybe we can get you some help," Gothalia attempted, and the man laughed harshly.

"Help?" he queried. "You can't be serious."

"I am."

"I'm not going back to the shelters and I sure as hell am not going back to the slammer."

"You speak English?" Gothalia asked him.

"Yeah, and?"

Before Gothalia could become too distracted, she stepped forward with her hand out.

"I won't report you to the police. Just hand back what you've taken, and we'll call it truce. What do you say?"

The man still seemed determined to deny to her—but suddenly he saw an Xzandian appear behind her, with silver scaly armour and thick limbs. The man stammered and pointed. Gothalia eyed him with confusion. When she finally glanced behind her, the man ran for his life.

"Shit," she muttered. She sprinted after the man as the Xzandian fired its weapon. Bullets ruptured more holes in the abandoned warehouse walls, while she and the man ran for cover. She dropped beside him where he hid behind a forklift. She held out her hand to the man and he relinquished her belt. "Thank you."

"Don't thank me yet. That thing is going to kill us."

"Not if I have anything to say about it." Gothalia pulled out her crossbow.

"Where did you get *that*?" he asked, wide-eyed.

"You might want to run," Gothalia encouraged. The man did not need telling twice. As he fled, Gothalia fired her arrows at the alien; several pierced its sternum and the Xzandian screamed. Gothalia avoided the next attacks the Xzandian threw at her, before pausing when he said,

"Hand over the Fragment you've recently acquired, Excelian, and I'll spare your life."

"I don't think so." Gothalia rushed at the alien, determined to take him down, but the Xzandian avoided most of her attacks and threw her to the ground. Gothalia groaned and rolled out of the way as he leapt. Barely missing the blade attached to the rifle. The Xzandian pulled the blade out of the ground and Gothalia avoided the next strike before flipping away and kicking the alien in the head.

Throwing all its weight forward, the Xzandian threw her through the wall, then carried her across the open carpark and towards an electric fence. Gothalia allowed flames to consume her body and the Xzandian relinquished its hold. She slipped from his grip and between his legs before kicking him into the fence. Electricity shook his body and the Xzandian fried, his body parts burned and melted into an ichor of guts, bones, and flesh.

Gothalia sighed in relief and climbed to her feet.

"My lady, the police are on their way," Kronos said.

"Understood."

Before she could leave, though, she spotted the Xzandian man she had seen in Darwin, hovering above the ground, watching her.

"The soldier from the Southern Island. How interesting," he mused.

"Who are you?" she asked.

"My name is irrelevant, but yours is familiar. Gothalia. The name that bears resemblance to Golgotha."

"How do you know who I am?"

"Simple, I wrung it out of a couple of your soldiers. 'Give me the name of the woman who withheld the Fragment of Midnight Eclipse from my unit, or I will kill you.' Some refused to cave, while others did, but I killed them all anyway. There was really no point in keeping them around. They're nothing but insects."

Gothalia narrowed her gaze on the monster before her and felt the desire to tear him apart with her bare hands, but she knew his strength rivalled hers.

"So, you know everything about me, but I can't know anything about you?"

"That's exactly it. Now, I'm asking you nicely: hand over the Fragment and the map."

Gothalia braced herself for a fight.

"And if I refuse?"

"Your head will be the one I sever next."

"Bring it."

WITHIN THE SHADOWS of the night, Demetria led her group around the battle, conscious of the enemy presence in their vicinity. Her movements were silent as were her accompanying soldiers. They worked their way past the Xzandians and towards their temporary base. When Noel-Len and the others entered the grounds, he was cautious.

Suddenly, though, smoke engulfed them. Demetria called,

"We're surrounded!" Swiftly, she disappeared in the smoke, and Noel-Len fired his silenced rifle at the closest shifting shadow he knew was not any member of his team. As his fellow soldiers behind him strode to keep their backs to each other, their rifles set on the enemy. Noel-Len listened as the Warrant Officer gave their next order. The group moved through the smoke carefully.

Noel-Len eyed the smoke around him, perspiration lining his features. He heard thundering footfalls and witnessed enemies with electric swords that glittered in the light.

His team opened fire, and Noel-Len rolled out of the way, avoiding one strike from the electric blades of the enemy. Noel-Len fired his rifle, but a barrel was severed in half. He tossed it aside, pulled out a pistol and fired at the enemy. The enemy looked too far away to have cut his rifle; *How did he do it?* Noel-Len wondered.

Noel-Len jumped back when the closest enemy jabbed his blade at him. Noel-Len stared at the burnt ground three feet deep. *So that's how. Energy.*

He avoided the next few attacks while he fired at the aliens. Under the stress, he didn't notice his increase in perspiration nor the rapid increase in his heart rate. No one else noticed either, until Noel-Len started to smoke as if he were heating up.

He ran at the alien nearest him. Noel-Len managed to get the upper hand and placed the barrel of his gun alien's jaw. He cackled.

"Ignatius, your clan will fall, and we'll have what is rightfully ours."

"Shut up," Noel-Len responded. The echo of his pistol sounded in the battlefield, and he stepped away from the fallen enemy.

When he battled the enemy, he could see the cold calculation of its gaze even if it were shrouded in a helmet. There was a determination to the enemy's hostility and intelligence that made his skin crawl. Putting his thoughts aside, he re-joined the group and to carry out the mission.

They forced the way through the battlefield.

They finally made it to their goal, and abandoned building, and moved in quickly to secure the alien room.

"Are you seeing this?" Noel-Len asked Curt.

"I see it, still trying to believe it."

Noel-Len paused outside the door. His ears perked, listening for any movement before entering the building, careful of any hostiles within. He walked inside, passing a lecture room and a hallway before walking further into the carefully-situated office rooms. There was silence and no further movement.

"How's it looking?" Curt asked from behind him.

"Clear," Noel-Len responded.

WHEN DANTEUS AWOKE, he was in the infirmary, surrounded by doctors and nurses. He glanced at one of them, confused. *Why am I here?* he thought. His memories were hazy, and his mind recalled someone screaming his name.

"Gothalia," he mumbled, feeling the IV in his arm. Doctors ordered him to calm down and he called, louder, "Where's Gothalia? Where's Demetria and Levi?"

"I'm here," Levi assured him.

Danteus heard his voice but could not see him. The doctors stepped away, and Levi finally got a look at his friend, alive.

"Don't get all teary eyed on me. It's weird," Danteus insisted and Levi laughed.

"I see you haven't changed."

"Where's Gothalia?"

"I'm not sure. The Peacekeepers. . ." Levi began, uncertainly.

"The Peacekeepers, what?"

"They took off after Gothalia."

"Is she alright?"

There was a moment of heavy silence.

"I'm not sure." Levi replied. Worry was etched into Danteus's features. "She'll be fine. She's tough."

"I know. But I can't help but worry about her, Demetria, and everyone else. I'm especially worried about how we're going to win this war."

"We'll acquire Midnight Eclipse. It's what they're after. If we can secure that . . ."

"—Then what?" Danteus interrupted. "If they're desperate enough, they wouldn't hesitate to wipe us all off the face of the planet."

"I know. I don't like it either, but that's the best plan we've got."

"I'm aware of that," Danteus affirmed. "It doesn't mean I have to like it." He climbed out of bed and regarded his uniform, which had been sliced open when the doctors had needed to use the defibrillator.

He picked up the shirt folded beside him instead. It was one size too small, but Danteus slipped it on anyway and clipped on his weapons and his gadgets.

"What are you doing?" Levi asked.

"I'm going to find the others. They'll need us."

"You've just been taken out by an Xzandian. Don't you think you'll need some more time to recover? I know we're different from the Humans, but all your injuries wouldn't have completely re-healed by now."

"They're good enough." Danteus walked past him and out of the tent.

"Wait," Levi uttered, hurrying after the other man and into the cool evening. "What's your plan?"

"I'm not sure, but we'll be fine." Patting Levi on the back, Danteus walked off.

THE ENEMY BEFORE GOTHALIA was tall, and dressed in black, otherworldly scales. Casually, he strode towards her and she stood ready to fight, ready to defend the Fragment at all costs.

The alien paused before her.

When his helmet was removed, she noticed his human-like features. Black scales ran beneath his jaw and over the rest of his body. He was a man; she could tell by the broad shoulders and narrow waist. She thought about the conversation she had with Kronos.

"It's like they're not even aliens," she whispered.

"What's the plan?" Kronos asked hurriedly.

"Survive."

"Survive?" the alien before her responded. "What an odd thing to say." He held out his hand. "I was playing nice, before but I'm out of patience. You humans have proven to be stubborn like the roaches of your world. I won't make the mistake of kindness a second time."

"Newsflash: I'm not human," Gothalia responded and threw a smoke bomb before her feet. She vanished in the smoke, activating her hood's camouflage mode.

The alien scanned the area as the smoke dispersed.

"Are you still here?" he called, and Gothalia held her breath as he walked towards where she hid, behind the electrified Xzandian, whose body still glittered with electricity. She stepped out of his way, slowly and carefully, trying not to make any noise against the loose gravel.

He was inches from her, and he watched the alien crackle in electricity.

"You did well my friend," he said, to the deceased alien. "But not well enough." When he was convinced, she was no longer present, he took to the air and cursed. "I'll find her," he promised himself.

Once he was out of sight, Gothalia released her held breath as the tension slowly subsided. She glanced at the alien and covered her nose—she now noticed the smell. The alien was cooked, and it smelled like steak.

"I think I'm going to be sick," she muttered, and Kronos laughed.

"It's a good thing I can't actually smell anything."

"Aren't you lucky?" Gothalia sarcastically retorted. The sound of the sirens grew loud and quickly Gothalia burnt the body of the alien to ash, before vacating the warehouse grounds.

A couple of hours later, Gothalia paused outside of a hotel. On the top, there was the crest of the Fire Reserve, blended into the gold and silver that lined the hotel's architecture. She glanced at the map she had uploaded into her headpiece.

"Am I reading this right?" she asked Kronos, her voice low to avoid any odd looks she would receive when appearing to talk to herself.

"It looks right," he said. Gothalia turned and walked away. "What are you doing? The crest is the other way."

"If the entrance is anything like the previous one," Gothalia said, "We're going to open something up. I'd prefer not to have witnesses." She wandered down the road and Kronos did not speak further on the topic. An hour later, Gothalia returned. This time it was much darker, and the air was cooler. There were fewer people on the street, and she relaxed.

"So, you think there's a Fragment," Kronos said.

"I'm not sure." Once she was certain she was free of lingering eyes and curious minds, she stepped into the hotel garden and towards the fountain. The fountain was tall, white, and majestic, and at the base of the fountain was the Fire Emblem, hidden behind carved gold and silver flowers. "Talk about extravagant."

Gothalia knelt and brushed her fingers along the crest and the roses. In the distance, with her Excelian hearing, Gothalia heard footfalls approach and knew security had noticed. Glancing at the security camera in the corner, Gothalia allowed her hand to light up in a brilliant flame pressed her palm against the emblem, as she had the last time. The fountain gently pulled away from her, almost folding into itself. It was loud but quick.

"Now if I go down, my question, Kronos, is: How will I get out?"

"There may be another way out. We won't know until you go." So, unhesitatingly, she entered the darkness.

The security guards who had noticed her trespassing found that she had vanished, both in person and off the camera recording. The fountain opening was never shown on the camera, leaving many to believe had they only imagined it.

When Gothalia entered the darkness, lights lit up on the walls. She descended further into the earth, until she finally found the landing. She paused at the landing and scanned the area around her; the hallway was narrow, much like the one beneath the Eastern Fire Reserve. The room was bare and old, and appeared to have been built before the city itself.

Gothalia travelled down the hall and came to a steep drop where there was once a bridge. It was destroyed, and deep waters ran below her.

"Care for an evening swim?" Gothalia asked Kronos.

"You're the one going for a swim," Kronos declared. "I'm just watching."

Gothalia scanned the walls and found Fragment in the middle of the room on a pillar. To get to it, she would have to jump or leap up a series of ledges. Her brows narrowed as she thought it over. She knew she could do it, but her utility belt was heavy and bulky; it would weigh her down when she jumped. Then there was the water. How deep was it? Could she jump into it or would she have to ease herself into it?

"Thinking about something?" Kronos whispered in her ear.

"How did you know?"

"You've gone quiet."

"I was wondering how to do this without injuring myself or . . ." she began, and then she heard a growl.

Her stomach tightened at the noise, her mind alert. She couldn't figure out where it was coming from.

"My lady, you hear *that*?"

Gothalia rolled her eyes beneath the helmet and shifted her weight.

"I do now." She scanned the left, the right, in front of her and behind her. Something sticky and wet dripped onto her shoulder, and she realised there was one place she did not check. Up. Slowly, she looked up, just as the monster clinging to the ceiling drooled on her shoulder once again. "Gross!"

The monster screamed and Gothalia jumped out of the way as it leapt at her.

"It appears to be the guardian of this Fragment," Kronos informed her.

"Kronos," Gothalia said, avoided the monster's claws, "This is not the time to—" Gothalia ducked as it swiped at her and she rolled over her shoulder and between its four legs. She ran up the wall and pushed herself off, slicing the monster's shoulder with her sword. She flipped over its tail.

"Aside from the growling, what do you hear?" Kronos asked impatiently.

"You," Gothalia responded, avoiding another attack before sliding behind the monster's back legs and slicing its ankles. The monster screeched and Gothalia grinned. *I can get out of this alive,* she thought.

"That noise: can't you hear it?"

"All I hear is you!" Gothalia shouted. She leapt and sliced the demons head off his body. The head rolled across the ground and fell into the water below. "About time," Gothalia muttered relaxing.

"So, you really can't hear it?" Kronos asked again. Now that Gothalia was not distracted, she noticed the light hum in the air. I grew the closer she walked to the edge of the cliff-face. The Fragment was calling out for another Fragment. Gothalia glanced up to ensure the cavern ceiling was high enough, then jumped.

She landed in the centre of the platform, where the hum grew even more. Picking up the Fragment, she examined it. Then, out of curiosity, Gothalia unfastened the Fragment from her utility belt and enlarged it. The closer it came to its fellow, the louder the hum grew.

She placed them together, and a wave of energy pushed her back a little. She realized the Fragments were beginning to wrap around her arm. Quickly, Gothalia tried to pry the metal off her hand, but it had already wrapped around her hand and forearm guard.

"What in the world?" she gasped. "Kronos, are you seeing this?"

"I am. The Fragments have become armour. And appear to fit quite well."

The ground trembled beneath her feet and she glanced up: the chasm was about to cave in. She leapt from the centre of the room and onto the cliff. Turning on her heel, she sprinted out of the room. For a second, she thought there was no other way out—then she spotted a lever, and cranked on it. A door opened, and she rushed out of it and into the night.

Gothalia observed her surroundings with confidence in her stride. She felt the power in her walk, and on her arm. The power in the palm of her hand. There was a flash of images before her eyes: a woman and a city lit up, then vanished. Gothalia gazed down at the armour.

It was telling her something, she knew. Though it was not something she could decipher, she knew and understood one thing: this weapon was more powerful than she had ever expected, and she had to get the rest of the Fragments as soon as possible. And if someone else got them first, she would have to take them back.

She paused, thinking everything over. The Fragments were scattered all around the world. Her home was attacked because of the Fragments and the surface world was also attacked. She wondered who the mastermind was behind the attacks, whether it the alien man she'd battled or if he was under someone else's orders. Taking a deep breath, she cleared her head. *First things first*, she thought, *I must find Arthur, and Kovac will help me.*

So, on her search she went.

The next day Gothalia searched the city for Kovac with Kronos' help. Gothalia wandered the suburban streets of Saint Petersburg, stunned Kovac had covered so much distance in a short amount of time. As she strode down the street, Kronos declared,

"He's dropped off again."

"But you were able to finalise his location."

"Yes. Sending it to you now." Gothalia's faceplate concealed her features and she saw an icon on the screen before her of where he would be. She marched towards the beacon.

She was certain Kovac would be in an old inn. When she reached it, she climbed a wall with her hood up, conscious of the security cameras, then dropped into the patio below in the back garden. There sat Kovac with his wife and children.

Kovac noticed the shifting of bushes and requested his wife take the children to the pool. She left and Kovac walked over to the shrub where Gothalia was camouflaged.

"I know you're here."

Gothalia removed her hood and her presence was revealed.

"What are you doing here?" he asked her.

"I'm here to find out where they last had Arthur."

"He was last seen in Saint Petersburg."

"Whereabouts, what district?" Gothalia strode around the garden. It was so peaceful.

"He's in District Three, the Kalininsky District," Kovac said, "It's on the right bank of the Neva. I suggest you start your search there."

"Thank you, Kovac. I'll call upon you again when I'm in need of something." Then Gothalia vanished.

# Chapter 29

LATER THAT DAY, GOTHALIA found Kalininsky District, passing buildings along the silent road, where no car travelled the street, and no person wandered the footpath. The sight of it put her on high alert. Out from behind a building stepped out a strange man. He strode towards her assertively, yet cautiously, and eyed her. "So, you're Gothalia," he commented.

"And you are?"

"Sorry, you're right. It is customary to introduce one's self." the man said. "My name is Ethan Wilson. I heard you have the Fragments and Arthur's map."

"So, what if I do?"

"I'll politely ask that you hand them over. I really don't feel comfortable raising my hand against a woman."

Gothalia rolled her eyes beneath her hood.

"Thank you for being such a gentleman. As for the Fragments, unfortunately, I cannot surrender them and never will."

"Yes, you're on a mission, aren't you?" Ethan Wilson said. He watched her closely, torn between amusement that she'd made it this far and awareness of her deadly combat skills.

"Why should it matter to you?"

Two more men revealed themselves and Gothalia placed her hand on the throwing knives at her thigh. They were Excelians, she could tell, and she glowered at the men.

"Because unlike you, I actually *need* Midnight Eclipse."

"Fine." Gothalia said, her eyes on Ethan, alert to any sudden movements. "I'll hand it over. On one condition."

"My lady, no," Kronos exclaimed. "You can't hand over the Fragment."

"Tell me where Arthur is. *Exactly*," Gothalia demanded, ignoring Kornos. "Or I won't hand over the Fragment."

"She's lying," a female voice declared. Then before Gothalia's eyes was the woman she had seen at the café so long ago. The woman held something in her hand—it was a trigger. "Come with us and hand over the Fragments, unless you want me to blow up a school."

"You're bluffing." Gothalia smirked.

"You should know by now: I'm an Xzandian. I will take life to further our cause. So, I'll say this once. Hand over the Fragments and come with us. Or do you want to risk it?" The woman's thumb moved closer to the red button at the top of the device and Gothalia knew one thing for certain: she could not risk it. Not if there were other lives on the line.

She pulled out the Fragments and released them to the men.

"And that's how that's done," the Xzandian woman said to Ethan. The group set off, with Gothalia in shackles.

They led her down the street and into a large house, then down another set of stairs to a basement. Gothalia eyed the architecture and the armed men guarding a door and glaring at her.

"Open it," the woman said, gesturing at the door.

"But . . ." one man began, in a thick Russian accent.

The woman responded in Russian and Gothalia understood: "No excuses." The man opened the door and stepped aside to show a bare room with a concrete floor and a single light overhead. The woman removed Gothalia's shackles and threw her into the room with strength that even surprised Gothalia.

"Watch her at all times," the woman instructed a man standing within the room. He crossed his arms and narrowed his gaze on Gothalia. Gothalia in turn snubbed him. *Really?* she thought, *you are not scary. Not one bit.*

Then she heard a voice, one she had thought she would never hear again, at least for a long time.

"Gothalia, is that you?"

Gothalia followed the sound of that voice and, within the shadows, found a man.

It was none other than Arthur Cicero.

Sweat dripped down his forehead and soaked his clothes. His hollow cheeks and limbs were too fragile to take his weight.

"Arthur?"

"It's me," he answered.

"You look terrible," Gothalia couldn't help herself saying, then added apologetically. "How are you feeling?"

"How do you think I'm feeling?"

"Not so good, I assume. But you're alive, that's all that matters."

"For now," he said. "There's something I need to tell you."

"Stop talking!" the guard ordered.

The woman stepped back into the room with more men, who chained Gothalia to a pole beside Arthur.

"Hey guys, surely I'm not that dangerous," Gothalia joked, attempting to distract them. They regarded her evenly. "You know I'm a girl. Right? You shouldn't treat me like this."

The woman walked over to Gothalia and slapped her.

"That's enough out of you." The woman turned back to Gothalia, shooing away the guards. "Try anything funny, and I assure you there are things worse than death that you'll be acquainted with. Get the machines ready." Then she vacated the room, though left one guard in place who stared down Arthur and Gothalia.

"Machines?" Gothalia asked once they were gone.

"Yes, that's what I'm trying to tell you. That's the reason the Order captured me. They knew I was the only one that could decipher the ancient dead language."

"What Latin? Every Excelian knows Latin, it's hardly dead in my eyes but—"

"No, another completely different language. I mean, it wasn't of this world. And they wanted me to build something—a weapon of some kind. They had me working hours, slaving away for them, and I now know that my creation is going to harm thousands, if not millions. It has to be stopped."

"First thing's first." Gothalia declared starting to heat her metal handcuffs. "Let's get out of here. Then you tell me the rest."

NOEL-LEN OBSERVED THE room cautiously. The enemy was smart: so far, they had localised all their soldiers but not their supplies. Noel-Len was not certain of what to expect when this far behind enemy lines, and he could not afford time to worry. And, to be frank, he could not afford to distract himself.

There was a loud crack. Through the glass ceiling above, Noel-Len regarded the ships and saw lightning stretch through the sky striking a few of the ships. Noel-Len could not believe his eyes until he heard Demetria declare,

"Well . . . well, looks like the Lord of Lightning has finally made his arrival." She turned to Noel-Len and Curt. "Keep your eyes sharp, this could get messy. Start setting up," she said to the other members of the team, whom Noel-Len recognised as the bomb squad.

"Aren't they supposed to dismantle bombs, not set them up?" Noel-Len asked Curt.

"Yup." His eyes drifted to the glass ceiling above and Noel-Len followed his gaze. The ships that hovered over the city began to fall from the sky.

Noel-Len stepped towards Demetria.

"Ma'am, what do you need us to do?"

"Keep an eye out. There'll most likely be more Xzandians patrolling this camp."

Noel-Len nodded and observed the area in which he and Curt were set to guard. It was silent, not a soul to be seen. Noel-Len could only hope it would remain that way.

Within moments, though, an Xzandian on casual patrol entered the room they guarded. Before the Xzandian scout could notify his people, Curt fired his silenced rifle. Down the body fell and Noel-Len jogged over to it. He and Curt dragged the Xzandian body out of sight and into the room where the waited for the bomb to be armed.

"That was close," Noel-Len said.

"Too close," Curt agreed. "I don't like this. It feels like we've entered a hive."

"That's exactly what it is," said one bomb squad member, who had finished arming the device. "And we're going to blow it up." He handed Demetria a device and she took it carefully.

"Alright, everyone move out."

As they exited the building, it happened: they heard an explosion from the ships above as they came crashing down. The alien base was ensnared and under siege. Quickly, Demetria worked to get her team out of the alien base and into the shadows of the ruined city. From a distance, crouched low, they spotted the Xzandians as they worked to put out the flames. Then another explosion ripped through their camp, setting of the bomb they'd set up which destroyed everything.

"Time to go," Demetria ordered, but a voice from the shadows halted everyone's movement.

"I don't think so," he said, coolly. "You've caused quite a mess. Just like that Excelian woman whom I took the Fragments from."

Everyone turned their attention to the Xzandian that stood on a hovering platform. He gazed upon the group with an indifferent expression before his helmet covered his face and he threw his hand forward, sending a flame towards them.

Demetria brought up an ice shield to protect them all. The soldiers opened fire from behind the wall of ice and the Xzandian man leapt from the platform, landing on the ground behind them. He launched himself at them.

THE SHACKLES FELL FROM Gothalia's wrist—then it was Arthur's turn.

"You ready?" she asked, aware that the heating of the metal while attempting to be incredibly careful conscious that her flames would burn him down to the bone if she wasn't careful. She had given him the end of her cloak to bite onto. She took a deep breath, allowing the élanocytes to consume her hands, then there was fire.

Arthur's muffled screams echoed in the air, and Gothalia cringed, but did not stop until the metal was severed, freeing his hands. Arthur dropped to his knees and rubbed his wrists in shock.

"Are you alright?" she asked, concerned, noticing the blistering of his skin, the blood that stained the shackles and his clothes.

"I'm alright . . ."

"We need to move."

"Where are we going to go?"

"Somewhere that isn't here," Gothalia said.

"And where's that exactly?"

"I'm not sure."

"Great, so you don't have a plan."

"I do. It's called improvising."

Gothalia glanced around the room. It was not a cell, per se, but the window was tiny.

Arthur's eyes widened.

"You do realise how small that is? Only a child could fit through that. I doubt we could."

"No, you could. I couldn't."

"What?" Arthur exclaimed, distressed. "I'm not leaving you."

"You're going to have to. This isn't up for discussion." Gothalia moved to the small barred window. She burnt through the metal with her fire than with her cloak covering her hand, she smashed the glass and cleared out any shards that remained. "Quickly, while you have a chance."

"What are you going to do?"

"There'll be another way," Gothalia assured him. Arthur regarded Gothalia for a moment, then nodded. He understood the sacrifice she was willing to make. "Besides, I have to take out those machines, right?"

"They're in the central part of the manor."

"Understood." Gothalia smiled. "See you soon."

Arthur returned the smiled.

"Very convincing." With that, Arthur crawled through the window and slipped into the midday streets.

Gothalia turned from the window, and towards the door. She knew there would be armed guards outside the door. With Kronos activated, she scanned the walls around her. With thermal imaging she outlined her enemies and was able to make out the two men on the opposite side of the door.

Yanking the handrail from the wall, she moved to the door, then whacked the pole against the door loudly.

There was movement outside the door, and Gothalia quickly moved out of the way as the door opened and hid behind it. The men entered the room, and she closed the door behind them with a smile.

As they swung back around, Gothalia hit one of the men across the face, then launched herself at the other one. She struck him in the throat before he could yell, then hit him across the face.

"Well done, my lady!" Kronos cried

"It could have been smoother," Gothalia hissed. "They could have been smarter too." She walked into the bare hallway.

Her footfalls were silent as she shifted along the halls. She began searching every room she could find looking for the machines. That she knew would be heavily guarded.

"If I were a machine where would I be?" Gothalia wondered aloud.

"Someplace with a lot of power."

"And where exactly would that be?" Gothalia stopped moving. "Wait. The basement."

"The most likely place to have a generator."

Gothalia began searching for the lower level. When she finally came across it, it was heavily guarded by men in Kevlar vests. Gothalia cracked her knuckles and walked towards them confidently.

They rushed her, Gothalia disarmed them, then promptly knocked them unconscious and dragged their bodies out of sight.

Entering the basement, she noticed a lot of noise and a lot of steam.

"What is this, a boiler room?"

"No, it's most likely from the machine," Kronos corrected. "They're burning fuel rather than relying on electricity."

"Why?"

"To keep their power usage to a minimum. Any unusual spikes will cause suspicion." Gothalia ducked behind a wall and peeked around its corner. People guarded two colossal machines. Her eyes traced the outline and the forms of the security guards that walked back and forth. The basement was as large as a hangar bay. Kneeling, she waited, then hurriedly moved to another wall, and hid behind a large crate that was within the blind spot of the cameras.

"My lady, we need to get to the security room."

"Understood."

Gothalia scanned her surroundings, searching for a way to the security guard office, until she saw a small security cart drive towards where she waited. She pressed the button that connected her cloak to her uniform and waited as her cloak retracted. When the cart was close enough, and Gothalia was confident the security guards were not looking, she threw herself under the cart and clung to the bottom of the vehicle. The heat would burn her skin if it weren't for her heritage, and she could feel her hair dragging on the ground.

Once the engine ceased, the men climbed out of the cart. They conversed casually, and Gothalia waited until words they moved away before she rolled out from under the cart and onto her knees.

Her black-and-silver helmet covered her features as it zoomed in on the men in the distance and the security cards at their waists.

"Looks like we're not going in the front door," Kronos commented.

Gothalia ignored him and moved through the internal carpark, which lead to the outside off in the distance. Except her attention drifted further inside where she heard a door opening and closing in the distance, and hid behind one vehicle, she noticed a cleaner enter the carpark and walked over to his car.

Opening the van, he pulled out extra cleaning supplies then returned to the entrance. Gothalia smiled, quickly catching up with him, and knocked him unconscious so she could remove his security card.

She towed his body away, placing it in the van, and then closed the door. Gathering his supplies, she allowed her cloak to extend and pulled up its hood so she would now appear as a cleaner in the same uniform.

Gothalia walked to the door with the supplies and entered the building, scanning her card with the photo-ID based entry. The security guards greeted her when the doors opened, and one said,

"Where's Jeremiah?"

"He's feeling a little under the weather," Gothalia responded, with a smile. "I'm just stepping in for him."

"Normally, we need to be called in advance about this," the security guard said. Then he shrugged. "But since you're here, you might as well get to it. The staff rooms are horrendous."

Brushing Gothalia off, he turned back to the camera monitor that observed the carpark which Gothalia noticed, he was not too concerned about. Gothalia frowned. *What a lazy person*, she thought.

She pushed the supplies further down the corridor. After a few turns, Gothalia found a vacant room, where she disposed of the supplies.

"Is there a way you can pinpoint the power usage in this manor?" she asked Kronos.

"I'll try. Standby."

Later, Gothalia crouched behind a wall as two mercenaries walked by after she removed her hood. Kronos provided her with the blueprints of the building, and she was on her way, waiting for Kronos to pinpoint the exact location of the device.

"In the lower section of the garage," he said at last. "The garage is using high amount of electricity. We'll start there after you dismantle the security."

"On my way." She entered the main section of the security room. Men observed the monitors and Gothalia smiled. Closing the door behind her, she locked it and whistled. The men faced her, and immediately attacked. Moments later, the men lay unconscious.

Gothalia muttered,

"This was too easy."

"Don't let your guard down my lady. They are Human, but they still carry weapons that can kill you."

"I'm aware of that, Kronos."

"I'm glad. Just reminding."

Gothalia rolled her eyes. Regaining her energy, she moved to disable the security and hide the unconscious bodies. Gothalia knew she would have a limited time to dismantle the machines before she could escape—that is *if* she could escape. She was in one of the Order of the Rukh's hideouts, and she could not risk them capturing her again. As swiftly as possible, Gothalia vacated the building in search of the machines. When she stumbled upon them, she was surprised by their compact size; she had expected something bigger, the way Arthur had spoken about them.

"I guess size doesn't matter," Gothalia muttered.

"My lady?" Kronos queried.

"Nothing. How am I going to dismantle that?"

"Try searching for a computer. There should be a reboot protocol in the system. When you find it, I'll guide you through it." Moments later, Gothalia found it. Kronos guided her through the next steps on what to do. Once the machines were wiped of intel and shut down, Gothalia's hand lit up, and fire erupted into her palm. She threw it at the computer.

"Good," Kronos said. "That should prevent them from restarting the machines."

"That'll last only so long," Gothalia declared. "I need to destroy the machines. Prevent them from rebuilding for a while."

"Sounds like a plan, Lieutenant."

"You should know, I'm no longer a lieutenant. I'm no longer anything, Kronos. I don't even have my title anymore."

"So? You're still a soldier and still a lady of the Ignatius-Valdis clan. Even if you can never return home. Let us remind them why we shouldn't be underestimated."

"Roger." Gothalia made her way over to the machines. With sharp edges and hard lines, the metal was sleek and clean. It was like it had not been touched. Gothalia glanced at her reflection in the glass, and hardly recognised herself. She lit an enormous fireball in her palm and threw it at the base of the machine. She watched as a fire grew, sparking and burning the cords. She did the same thing to the next machine, then heard gunfire.

There were bike keys by the computer which she found odd, and glanced around, there were bikes in the distance. Quickly, Gothalia rushed out of the open space and behind a crate. She cursed. Pulling out her pistol, she fired, then ran for the exit. Security personnel chased her, and she sprinted away, luckily coming across a security motorbike. Climbing onto the bike, Gothalia kicked up the stand, started the bike with the key and was on her way. Down the streets of Russia, she rode, turning down new roads to avoid being shot by the Humans in large black cars. The cars travelled down the road and after Gothalia.

"Kronos, find Arthur," Gothalia ordered as she rode across an overpass, avoiding bullets and twisting around cars. When Kronos identified Arthur among the Russian crowd via satellite, she saw that he had made it extremely far on foot.

Men, on bikes and in cars, tried to stop her passage, but she managed to lose them. She continued further down the road until she was sure she knew where Arthur would be—but she could see him. Gothalia leapt from another overpass and onto the road below that would lead her straight to Arthur.

Suddenly, she noticed that two black vans trailed Arthur.

"My lady, those are not friendly."

"I assumed that much." Men were attempting to force him into the vans, so she rode onto the footpath and screamed for everyone to move. When she made it close enough, she spun the bike on its front wheel and hit a man in the face with the rear, before shooting at the remaining men with her pistol. "Get on," she demanded, and Arthur leapt on the bike without hesitation. "Hold on." He wrapped his hands tightly around her waist, and she was off.

Then she heard sirens.

"Shit," Arthur muttered. "What are we going to do about them?"

"Avoid them."

"And if we can't?"

"We will."

Gothalia rode haphazardly through the streets, careful of other cars and pedestrians. She heard Arthur's worried mutters behind her but ignored him forcibly.

Thinking they'd outrun the police, Gothalia pulled up and hopped off the bike with Arthur. They abandoned the bike in the middle of a partially-empty carpark.

But sirens grew around them immediately, and police cars surrounded them. Gothalia noticed a helicopter in the distance and knew that was how they had tracked her.

Pushing Arthur forward, she threw a fireball at the bike. Engulfed in flames, it exploded, throwing the policemen from their motorcycles and onto their backs.

Gothalia and Arthur rushed through a shopping centre, leap-ing past security guards.

Then there was another explosion. Gothalia knew it was only a matter of time before they were captured, and that she needed to use this distraction to her advantage.

"My lady, we have a problem," Kronos declared.

"What's that?" she asked.

"You're out of camouflage élan."

"Got it." Gothalia said before she glanced at Arthur. "It's best we split up," she said to Arthur.

"Why?"

"I'm out of camouflage élan. So, I can't camouflage anymore more and I'm fearful that my presence, dressed the way I am, is causing many to not only fear us, but remember us as well. You head east. Search for Kovac Rusakova, he's a well-known hacker." Before Arthur could say anything else, Gothalia pushed him to run, while she worked to distract the police until she was sure he was gone.

"Does she have to run off before I get a word in?" Arthur mut-tered, then sprinted away.

# Chapter 30

GOTHALIA BATTLED THE policemen and security guards, careful to not severely injure them. She had to escape, but she didn't know where to go.

Then, out of nowhere, images flashed behind her eyes: Pictures of herself covered in blood, the face of a dragon. She heard a whisper: *Gothalia*. Gothalia froze as her eyes landed upon the woman she'd seen before at the Cetatea, in a lab coat—but as she took a closer look, the butt of a gun struck her in the head, hard.

Between the bursts of darkness, hands turned Gothalia on her stomach, and there was a click of shackles around her wrists. Then darkness washed over her.

When she came to, Gothalia was in the back of a police vehicle. Her head hammered, and her mind continued to flash with images of blood and bodies. Frightened, she sat up.

Gothalia glanced at her waist. Her weapons and utility belt had been seized, as well as Kronos.

"Shit," she muttered. "How are you going to get out of this one now, Gothalia?" Her wrist ached from the cuffs, and she cursed. Then worked to heat the metal cuffs but the police grabbed her by the shoulders and threw her into the back of the car before slamming the door. Gothalia finally burnt through the cuffs, rushed towards the door, and started banging on the door. "Hey! Let me out!"

The police car halted. Gothalia glanced through the barred panel. She noticed two figures standing in the middle of the road. Then her eyes widened in horror: it was the Xzandian man that she had escaped from before. His dark eyes rested on the car, and beside him was another man she had never seen before.

The policemen climbed out of the vehicle. Gothalia called, "Wait! No! Stay away from them!" No response. Gothalia felt her élanocytes rush through her body.

She sat on her rear and started kicking at the car door—on her fourth kick, the door tore off its hinges and she climbed out of the car. She moved to the front of the vehicle and saw that the police had already been killed by the men standing in the street.

The two men marched to her and Gothalia stood, ready to fight. They were huge and very usual in appearance.

"You. Gothalia. Where are the Fragments? Don't make me ask—" Then his eyes darted to Gothalia right forearm, where the Fragments wrapped around her. Fury laced his features as he took in the armour. "You dare defile that weapon with your filth!"

"And you dare speak to a lady like that!" Gothalia retorted.

The men rushed towards her, desperate for revenge and desperate for the Fragments of Midnight Eclipse.

THE ALIEN RUSHED AT Noel-Len and the others as Demetria's ice wall crumbled. The Xzandian was faster and stronger than the Humans, and Demetria could barely keep up with his speed and strength. He managed to strike her a few times—though she fought desperately he managed to defeat her. She lay with the other soldiers who had been fatally wounded. Curt rolled onto his back from where he lay on the once-green grass and fired his rifle at the

Xzandian, certain to deter him. But the Xzandian moved so fast that Curt's bullets missed him.

Noel-Len climbed to his feet and rushed at the Xzandian, as if his feet were on fire. He lunged at the Xzandian, firing his rifle wildly. The Xzandian sliced the rifle in half and Noel-Len pulled out his combat knife. Rapidly, he slashed at the Xzandian, who dodged with ease and punched Noel-Len in the stomach, winding him.

"Your armour isn't enough to withstand my attacks," the Xzandian said and kicked Noel-Len away. He wandered back to him, ever so slowly—ever so tauntingly. "You have spirit. I will give you that. Normally, you Humans would have run in fear by now. But you lot do not, which surprises me," he said. Then he kicked Demetria, who was still unconscious, in the face. "*Excelian.* You Excelians have been a pain in my arse since our first encounter, and as much as I want you to run away, you never do." A weapon materialised in his hand and he pointed it at Demetria's throat, about to strike.

Noel-Len climbed to his feet and lunged at the Xzandian, throwing him to the ground. Noel-Len's fist began to heat—and, within seconds, an explosion went off in the clearing, catching the attention of all the soldiers. Throwing the Xzandian away from him, with fire licking the grass around him, Noel-Len stood in the centre of charred ground.

"What the hell?" the Xzandian hissed. Noel-Len paid no attention to what had happened, his eyes solely on the Xzandian.

"This isn't hell. Not yet," he said. "But I'll be damned if I don't put you there myself."

"Cute," the Xzandian said, wiping blood off his jaw. "A Human who can match me—*interesting.*" Exhausted Noel-Len watched as the Xzandian climbed to his feet. "That is . . . if you are Human."

"I am."

Then, as quick as this mysterious power appeared, it vanished, and the Xzandian threw Noel-Len into a tree, landing awkwardly on the ground.

"Noel-Len!" Curt cried.

"Just dumb luck," the Xzandian declared.

Demetria, awake again, tried to climb to her feet. But before she could, the Xzandian man walked over to her, grabbed her by the throat and squeezed.

"I will eradicate you Excelians from the face of this planet."

"You can't . . ." Demetria began, struggling to breathe and attempting to pry his hands from around her throat. "You'll have to . . . wipe out every human."

"Now that's an enticing idea," he declared, with a wicked smile.

"Lieutenant!" Curt called. Curt fired his rifle once more, but he was out of bullets. He clicked the trigger a few times, then threw the rifle aside, pulled out his pistol, and fired at the Xzandian. He let go of Demetria and retreated, after being recalled.

Curt relaxed and Demetria climbed to her feet and wandered over to Noel-Len, who had not moved.

"Private Ignatius," Demetria called. Her injuries ached, but she knew she would heal fast—unlike the Humans. "Private Ignatius." Demetria dropped beside him on her knees and checked him. "Private?" Then she saw the blood pooling out of his helmet.

When Noel-Len did not wake up, she called for a medic. He rushed to Noel-Len and scanned his injuries before removing his helmet and searching for other obvious injuries.

Curt climbed to his feet and regarded his friend.

"Noel-Len?"

"He's still alive," the medic declared. "But most likely has a severe head injury."

"He'll be fine right?" Curt responded.

"I saw the strikes he received from the enemy, how hard he hit the tree and I saw how he landed," the medic replied. "I doubt anyone could survive such blows without injury."

Demetria told the group to return to their makeshift base as soon as possible while the medic pulled out a portable stretcher and demanded another soldier help him placing Noel-Len's body on the bed.

"It's best we set up camp," the medic declared. "That way I can provide him the appropriate support."

"I understand," Demetria replied. "But not here."

"Then where?" Curt asked.

"Some place the enemy won't look."

GOTHALIA AVOIDED THEIR attacks as best as she could, before disarming them. She used one of their weapons to attack the larger Xzandian. He threw Gothalia to the ground with a kick and she slid along the street, tearing up clumps of road in the process. Gothalia groaned and rolled onto her side.

"You think you can just waltz right in here and take what isn't yours? *Really*?" the larger Xzandian spat. He picked Gothalia up by the front of her uniform and lifted her into the air. "Now little lady, you're going to tell me where that Fragment you have is."

"News flash dumb-ass, I don't have it." Gothalia retorted.

"Why you Excelians would employ disrespectful females in your ranks is beyond me," the smaller Xzandian piped up. "I would have had you all culled."

"Of course, you would," Gothalia responded. "You filthy barbarian."

"Where are they?" the Xzandian asked, shaking her.

"I wouldn't tell you, even if I knew. And I don't know where they are."

After a long pause, the Xzandian said,

"Leave her."

"But—" the other Xzandian said.

"You will do as I say."

There was a heavy moment of silence between both men as they closely faced off.

"I understand," the other Xzandian declared and dropped Gothalia. "Wouldn't feel right to kill for no reason, anyway." He paced after the other man. "We're here for one thing and one thing alone and that's the Fragments. Then we can kill them—all of them."

Their platforms picked the Xzandians up and they shot into the air, climbing into the back of a hovering ship.

Gothalia sighed.

"What just happened?" she asked herself. "I'm alive," she repeated as she climbed to her feet. She hobbled over to the police car and listened to the radio. There were more units arriving and Gothalia knew that she would not have much time before they caught her. She scanned the police car for her gear and found her utility belt and gear in between the front car seats.

Sirens rang and Gothalia quickly grabbed everything and ran into the shadows of the buildings, before limping further down the road. Observing the flashing lights of the police vehicles, she rounded a corner and kept moving.

Eventually, Gothalia paused to catch her breath, and put on her cloak, utility belt and Fragments.

"Kronos," she called, between hefty breaths.

"My lady, you're back! Where did you go? Your heart rate has spiked."

"I'll explain later," she said. "I need to you provide the fastest route out of here."

"Roger," he responded and Gothalia followed the route he provided for her. Instead, of the streets, Gothalia stuck to the roofs, jumping from one to the next until she was certain she was free. Then she heard a helicopter in the distance. "We won't be able to get away with that following us."

"And how am I supposed to stop it?"

The helicopter light scanned the area but Gothalia remained frozen and camouflaged. With the light directly on her, a shadow stretched along the wall behind her. "Do you see that?" the man in the chopper declared over the radio.

"See what?" the other said.

"The shadow?"

"Kronos," Gothalia whispered, "The shadow. They still see me."

"Understood." The shadow faded.

Police cars surrounded the area and men spread out, scanning the area for Gothalia. She shifted ever so slowly towards the shadows. Then one police officer stepped before her without noticing her. She watched him, drawing out a blade just in case.

The officer scanned his surroundings intently and Gothalia never moved an inch.

"Clear," he finally declared and moved on. At that, Gothalia released a breath she did not know she had held and hurried away.

Feeling fortunate for her mild success she moved from the area and down another street. She avoided the police cars that slowed down at each intersection while their drivers scanned the streets for her. Before she knew it, she was out of reach and beyond them.

She crouched in an abandoned building, resting briefly, though knew she had to keep moving.

"We have a problem," Kronos told her

"What kind of problem?" Gothalia asked, glancing behind her.

"Your blood sugar levels. They've dropped too low."

"I thought the suit doesn't require me to eat often."

"It doesn't, but you've exceeded the amount of days you can go without food and water. Do you feel different?"

"Different how?" she asked.

"Do you have a headache? Your heart rate has increased."

"What does that mean?"

"You're dehydrated. You need to find some food and water. Now."

"But the Fragments—" Gothalia began.

Kronos cut her short.

"—Aren't as important right now. You know that. You can't afford to become weak."

"I understand." Gothalia left the building and hurried down the street. As she walked, she noticed her dry throat and mouth. As she walked past a glass window, she spotted herself in the reflection, and noticed her sunken and tired eyes. Quickly, she pulled her attention from the glass window and kept moving.

"PLACE HIM THERE," DEMETRIA ordered, and left Noel-Len's rifle beside the makeshift cot. Her pale blue eyes scanned the area around them; there was enough shrubbery that they could be concealed in the shadows of the night. However, she knew with their technology the Xzandians could still find them.

Demetria glanced down at Noel-Len. He still had not woken up and everyone was beginning to worry he was lost. Demetria blinked and, in the darkness, she saw the images of fallen soldiers and the Alastorians rushing at her. When she reopened her eyes, she appeared startled.

"You okay?" the medic asked.

"I'm fine," Demetria responded. "Just keep an eye on him."

"I will. Maybe you should rest a while."

"You're giving me orders?"

"No. Merely a suggestion."

Demetria turned away from him and towards the edge of their little camp. She could not rest, not now, not when her anxiety was the highest it had ever been in her whole life.

Her back to the medic, she asked,

"Will you take the first watch?"

"I will."

"Good," Demetria said. "I'll be over here if you need me." Demetria walked to a clear area in the shrubs at the base of a tree and sat down. Her back felt the lines of the bark, and the soles of her feet ached in places she had never thought possible. She pulled up her AI.

"Eva."

"Good evening Lady Crystallovis, how may I be of service?"

"I need you to do a complete internal analysis and see how much longer I have left."

"No problem." Moments later, Eva declared, "You have two hours before your blood sugar level drop too low. Please be mindful of excessive strain."

"I understand." Demetria replied. Eva disappeared from her faceplate and Demetria closed her eyes.

Demetria's sleep was full of nightmares. She was alone on the battlefield, and no matter how much she cried out to Danteus and Gothalia, they could not hear her, the sound of bullets drew, and Demetria ducked, cowering in fear.

Her dream changed, and she was back in the Fire Reserve before the attack and before Gothalia's demon was unleashed. She ran down the halls, searching for Gothalia, then heard Danteus over the radio. She felt immense pain as she collided with an Alastorian. Then she woke up, panting.

"You okay?" asked Curt, near her.

"I'm fine. How's Noel-Len?"

"He's fine. He's been stirring since you've fallen asleep," the medic told her. Then everyone heard footsteps trudging through the unsecured area. Slowly, Demetria moved to her knees and pulled out her sword.

DANTEUS AND LEVI WANDERED the streets of Darwin, searching for their team.

"How much longer do you think they'll be gone for?" Levi asked.

"Gone? They're not out on a trip," Danteus frigidly responded.

"You know what I mean. How much longer until we run into them?"

"Not sure," Danteus answered after some time. He saw the tiredness in Levi's gaze and felt the heaviness of his own body as he walked. In the distance, they both spotted large sparks of lightning illuminating the dark sky.

"What's *that*?" Levi asked, halting beside Danteus. Every lightning strike was gold, not white, and Levi realized it was an Excelian causing it. He also knew that there was only one Excelian who could cause so much damage. "Lord Berith!"

"Looks like it," Danteus responded. "But we won't know for sure until we get a closer look."

"Wait? We're going to *that*?" Levi declared pointing at the alien ships in the sky. "We might as well be walking to our own deaths."

"Do you want to come or not?"

"I do, I'm just thinking about our odds."

"Our odds are not good."

"No, they aren't."

"But that doesn't mean we should give up."

"No, it doesn't mean we should give up," Levi concluded.

"So, you're staying."

Levi crossed his arms.

"You need someone to watch your back."

Danteus stifled a laugh. After some time of walking down the road with their weapons drawn, Danteus and Levi made it to the battlefield. The now-deathly-silent battlefield.

GOTHALIA UNWRAPPED the hamburger she'd swiped from a nearby café table and devoured it in the park. Her eyes were alert for danger, trailing over any and everyone she considered suspicious.

"You need to calm down," Kronos warned in her ear. "This isn't healthy."

"I'm fine."

"That's not what your heart rate's telling me," he answered. "Are you alright? I'm no Excelian, but you're too hyper-aware."

"I'm fine. And besides, it's kind of what happens after you've been in danger a few times."

"A *few* times?"

"You know what I mean." Her tone was harsh, so Kronos switched topics, hoping to distract her.

"What are your plans?" he asked.

"Plans? Wing it I guess."

"Since when has that ever kept you out of trouble?"

"Since never."

"It's good to see you have your sense of humour back." Kronos responded. Then he was silent. Gothalia waited for him to say something else, and continued to eat.

When she finished the burger, she wiped her fingers clean, grateful for the meal. She had drunk some water too and knew that it was enough to keep her going for now.

Gothalia travelled the streets once more, on the hunt for Kovac, and wondered what she was going to do after she found him. If she were honest with herself, she knew that she would have a tough time trying to find the Fragments on her own but if she had Kovac it might be a little easier. Or so she hoped. She glanced at her arm, where the Fragments lay connected, wrapped around her forearm, hand, and fingers.

They were like gleaming black scales and she knew innately that these Fragments were too powerful. She tried to remove the armour, but it would not budge.

"What are you thinking?" Kronos wondered. "You've been quiet for quite some time."

"I'm just thinking," Gothalia confessed. "What if the Fragments were separated for a reason and us just bringing them together is probably a bad idea? Like, for starters, I can't get it off my arm."

"Kovac or Arthur may know a way to remove that," he said. "I wouldn't worry about it for now."

"But I am," Gothalia declared. "I know it doesn't help my current situation, but I'm worried that they'll have to cut off my entire forearm."

"They won't."

"How can you be so sure?"

"Because a whole soldier who can protect the Fragments is better than part of a soldier." Gothalia fell silent. Her mind turned at the memories of the battles she'd fought. She had not had time to process everything until now and she felt sick.

"All that death," she murmured. "Is it worth it?"

"Don't know, but I guess we're going to find out," Kronos replied.

Gothalia shut out the memories and climbed to her feet. She had to keep moving; wallowing in sadness would not save her. Kronos brought up where Kovac was last logged in to their main server for only a split second before logging out. He pinpointed the exact location and then Gothalia was on her way.

Gothalia travelled through the large park and paused. Her eyes scanned her environment. Then she glanced up and saw an Xzandian on a platform. He hovered in mid-air and Gothalia slowly backed away.

Next to the Xzandian was none other than Altair. The man she had thought was innocent. He observed the surroundings with a searching gaze, and Gothalia slowly moved around the tree and out of sight.

The Xzandian man and Altair muttered to one another, in deep conversation.

The Russian citizens glanced up at the group, some eyes were curious. Others glinted with horror. Their faces became pale at the sight of them and ran as if they'd seen a ghost. Others stared at the Xzandians and pulled out their phones to record the incident.

"This isn't good," Kronos remarked.

"I know."

"My lady, they're getting closer."

"I know," Gothalia replied once again.

"What are you going to do?"

"Survive."

Then the Xzandian spoke loudly to the crowd clustered below him.

"Some of you are quite surprised by my presence. And yes, I am an alien."

The crowd collectively inhaled at his words and he continued.

"Some of you are aware of the war that befell your home, while some of you don't know what has happened at all. Some of you are happy that your streets have not been painted with blood, while some of you are wanting a war. However, this is not about *you*. There are a few among you that are not Human. We seek these exceptional Humans out. They wear many faces and are not like you. They are much stronger, much faster, and much deadlier. If you desire your home to not be burnt down, then I suggest you seek her out." Then an image of Gothalia's face was projected on a holographic screen behind the Xzandian and the man. "Seek out Gothalia of the Ignatius-Valdis clan and I shall keep your home from burning. And if you do not believe me," he said, and held out his hand so that the ground before him erupted, demolishing a nearby building. "I shall destroy every part of this city until you find her or until I find her."

Gothalia ran from the alien and the man. She hid a little longer and moved from one tree to another and another until she was certain she was safe than sprinted. Then a loud *thud* hit the ground beside her and Gothalia glanced in the direction of the noise. She ducked in time to avoid a blow from one alien, cursing as she flipped away. As she battled the aliens, Gothalia ducked, blocked, and countered all attacks. She stunned the alien, but before she could deliver the final blow, he grabbed the Fragment on her forearm and turned to dust.

"What in the—?" she questioned.

The other Peon soldiers regarded her carefully, hesitant to approach.

"If you don't wish to . . . disappear," Gothalia said, more confidently than she felt, "I suggest you leave."

"Sorry, that's not going to happen," one Xzandian replied, pointing a sharp finger at Gothalia. "We must take back what you have stolen."

"I didn't steal anything."

"Liar. Your people and you Humans take what isn't yours, and for what? The pathetic coins you carry that someone once upon a time considered valuable. Pathetic."

The alien fired its energy bullets at her. She turned on her heel and ran, avoiding the bullets and hiding behind a tree.

Gothalia ducked to avoid a sword that cut through the thick tree. Shocked, she flipped away and tossed smoke grenades at the Xzandian's feet. She put on her face mask and ran through the smoke, with Kronos guiding her away. As she sprinted through the park, Gothalia noticed a circular robot floating in mid-air and following her. Then she heard a roaring crowd. A voice cried,

"That's her, folks. That's the one with the Fragments. Let's see if she can survive this, ladies and gentlemen!"

# Chapter 31

GOTHALIA TRIED TO SWAT away the annoying device, then pulled out her gun and shot it down.

Wind picked up in the middle of the park. Gothalia was silent as she listened intently. Gothalia felt the Sibyl as she flipped backwards and out of the way. The ground beneath her split. Gothalia landed with her legs spread over the fissure in the ground. She stepped off to the side and was startled as a large, unexpected voice called,

"Fe Fi Fo Fum, I smell Excelian scum." Out of the trees crawled a giant. "And I'm hungry."

The giant picked up a few humans and devoured them, while Gothalia watched horrified.

"What in the hell . . . ?" Gothalia's gaze lingered over the scaly, oversized man who stood taller than the trees. Blood pooled over his lips and Gothalia stepped back away.

"Let's not make this difficult, Gothalia," the Xzandian on the platform declared. "We know you're here and we'll let people die one by one,"—Gothalia watched as the giant devoured another human—"And no matter where you go with those Fragments, I will find you and take as many lives as I can in the process."

"He's playing you," Kronos whispered in her ear.

"I know."

The silver-armoured Xzandian regarded Gothalia from beside Altair. He nodded at Altair and leapt from the platform and onto the ground before Gothalia.

"Gothalia, how are you?" Altair asked.

"I could be better."

"Aw, what a shame," he replied. "I'm sorry I have to do this, but you . . . well, you leave us no choice. Kill her," he ordered, and the giant growled a terrifying growl.

"Excelians are so yummy." The giant licked its lips. "I'll have you in my hungry tummy." He reached for Gothalia, who leapt out of the way. She hid behind a tree, but he sniffed her out, he pulled the tree she hid behind from the ground and threw it across the park. "There you are."

He caught a hold of Gothalia, and she squirmed within his thick hand.

"Let me go!" she yelled, fighting the monster as much as she could.

"No." He held her up to his single eye.

"Yes."

"No," the giant pouted. "I'm hungry."

"And I'm tired of you," Gothalia responded. At those words, the giant growled, unhappy with her. The air from his lungs reeked of rotting meat and Gothalia coughed. "What is that smell?"

"That would be the giant's digestive tract," Kronos muttered.

"Not helpful."

"Sorry."

"Who are you talking to?" the giant asked.

"No one," Gothalia replied.

"No, you're talking to someone," the giant said and grabbed Gothalia by the wrist and held her several meters in the air. Gothalia glanced down, held onto the giant with her other hand for dear life.

"You're funny," the giant said, with a crooked smile.

Altair sighed.

"Will you stop playing with your food?" He brushed the dirt from his black skin-tight uniform that mimicked the scales of a snake. "I'm growing bored."

"No," the giant replied. "I will play with my food as much as I want to." Altair rolled his eyes and glanced at the Xzandian on the platform a few hundred meters in the air. The Xzandian, Xaviaius, regarded Altair, less than impressed. Altair sighed as the giant threw Gothalia in the air before dangling her over his mouth.

"Tiresome," Altair responded and sat down on a fallen tree.

"You're going down the choo choo tunnel," the giant told Gothalia, with a beaming smile.

"What are you, a child?" Gothalia yelled, clinging to his fingers.

"He probably still is," Altair replied. "You know they are a little 'slower' than Humans. Quite underdeveloped. Hurry up and finish her."

"I'll finish her when I want to," the giant replied, glaring. Gothalia reached into her utility belt and pulled out a grenade. Aiming carefully, she dropped it into the mouth of the giant. The giant glanced ahead, stunned, with a hand on its stomach, as he felt the grenade she'd dropped.

Without thinking, Gothalia focused as much as she could on the grenade, sending her energy towards it. Then the grenade exploded within the giant, tearing it open from the inside. Blood and guts pooled across the ground and Altair jumped far away.

Gothalia landed in a pile of blood, then ducked when skin and other tissues began to fall towards her. Bloody flesh covered her, and she pushed against the skin, desperate to find an opening. She began to panic, and Altair looked on amused.

"Well, that's one way to end her."

The Xzandian on the platform landed beside Altair.

"Search for the Fragments." Altair nodded and hopped onto the green grass, now coated in blood. Altair's golden eyes searched the earth, deep in thought, lingering over where Gothalia had fallen. A smile curled his thin, lips highlighting his straight nose and long black lashes.

Carefully, he stepped onto the blood, which soiled his boots.

With his spear tip pointing at the ground, he searched for Gothalia. Then she appeared, gasping for air, and he pointed the blade of the spear towards Gothalia.

"I'm surprised you didn't suffocate."

"I was close," she remarked and pushed her hair out of her face, covered in blood. Before she could stand, Altair twisted the spear around to the blunt end and whacked her across the jaw.

"You'll have to forgive me. I'm normally above harming women, but in this instance, it can't be helped," he said and wandered over her. He removed the unsecured Fragments from her belt and smiled. "I'll be taking these."

Gothalia's arm shot up and she desperately held onto the Fragments.

"Not if I have anything to say about it," Gothalia replied. There was no desperation in her voice. Instead, it was filled with a confidence that he did not expect. He regarded Gothalia for a moment, stunned by her words, then he yanked the Fragments from her and hit her. Gothalia lay within the ruins of the giant.

He walked away from her and to the Xzandian, handing him the Fragments. The Xzandian's face lit up beneath the midday sun.

"Glorious isn't it? We've secured the rest. I can't wait until I show *him*." His eyes intently regarded the Fragments, then his hand rested on the Fragments still on her arm, linked together. They gleamed brilliantly beneath the sun and he smiled. "Bring her with us. We will remove those Fragments, even if we have to cut off her entire arm."

WHEN NOEL-LEN WOKE, silence greeted him, and nightfall surrounded him. He went to sit up and a hand rested on his shoulder.

"Don't move too quickly," the medic admonished.

"I'll be alright," Noel-Len responded.

"Are you sure?" Curt asked, opposite him.

Noel-Len nodded.

"I'm sure." The medic relinquished his hold, Curt returned to cleaning his rifle, and Noel-Len sat up. He glanced around the clearing at the shrubs and the grass and a nearby building. "Where are we?"

"A temporary camp," Curt replied, his eyes on the barrel of his gun. "Don't worry. We'll get back to everyone else soon."

"I'm not worried."

"Good."

"Are you worried?"

"No."

"You sure?"

"Positive."

Then Noel-Len heard footfalls approach and pulled out his knife, cut with a serrated edge and a clean edge, sharp enough to make him comfortable as he carried it. He wondered, when had carrying a weapon become comfortable?

There footsteps paused. Demetria placed her finger to her lips and Noel-Len nodded. Then his gaze drifted to the entrance of their little camp. A hand poked through it.

Demetria grabbed the hand and yanked the body into the camp, where it landed with a thud on the ground and a yelp. The man that Demetria had pulled through pointed his rifle at her and Demetria placed a knife to his throat.

"Wait!" Curt called. "I know him."

Demetria paused.

"You do?" she asked.

"I do." he responded. "He's one of us."

"He is . . . " Noel-Len agreed. "he's one of us."

"How do you know?"

"He helped me with the Scouting sites. That's James Michaels. He's with the S.A.S."

"Glad you remember me," James declared with a smile, his white teeth gleaming.

"How could I forget?" Noel-Len replied.

"Considering all that's happened, I thought you would." James scanned every face, then nodded at Curt, before his eyes drifted to Demetria. She was cautious and hesitant to release him, but she did. James commented, "About time. And here I thought you were going to kill me."

"I was considering it," Demetria replied before adding, "Except you were human."

"So, you'd kill non-humans?"

"If necessary."

"Interesting." James replied and Curt cut him short reminding him that they were on the same side. Noel-Len shook his head and regarded them with mild disbelief. It was the middle of a war and they were cracking jokes. "What? Don't like jokes Noel-Len?"

"In the middle of a war, not particularly."

"It's the only way to cope. Trust me."

"SO HOW MUCH LONGER?" Levi asked Danteus, as he strode the edges of the battlefield with his bow and arrow drawn. He regarded the battlefield diligently, eyeing anything and anyone he considered dangerous.

"Not much longer," Danteus responded as he glanced up at the sky. Berith was close, closer than he expected, and he watched as the alien ships dropped from the sky while others retreated.

"I never knew he had that much power," Levi commented, staring up at the dark sky that clashed with golden lightning.

"Neither did I," Danteus replied without thinking. Thankfully, Levi hadn't heard him.

"Did you say something?"

"Nothing. We need to keep moving."

"I understand, but you do realise that there could be Alastorians lurking around? Just saying." Levi's eyes darted to every corner and behind every building.

"I know. Stay vigilant but stay close. I don't need to lose you too."

"Aww, you really do care."

"Don't make me throw a boulder at you," Danteus retorted. He paused and so did Levi. They both looked over at a demolished base, then their eyes lingered over the trees in the distance and a hill littered in bodies. From the shadows, Danteus noticed a few Alastorians clustered around something that he couldn't quite make out, even with his Excelian eyes.

"What's that?" Levi asked, and took aim. "Alastorians?"

"Yeah," Danteus declared. "And a lot of them."

"What are they doing?"

"They're after something or someone," Danteus responded, then moved down the hill and towards the Alastorians with Levi following him. As Danteus inched closer to the Alastorians, he noticed they were very fixated on something. "Did all the teams make it out?"

"Not sure, why?" Levi asked.

Then they noticed something even stranger about the Alastorians.

"Danteus," Levi commented. "We're kind of out-numbered," With his arrow taking aim, his gaze narrowed on one Alastorian. "Let me know when you want me to shoot."

Danteus regarded the Alastorians as the grass beneath their feet flattened and stone paths shattered. "How strong are the Alastorians?"

"They're not too much stronger than us," Levi responded. "Why?"

"Because their feet are creating cracks in the ground." Levi felt Danteus's back against his, and realised they were cornered. Back to back, they watched as the Alastorians clustered around them.

Danteus gently pulled out his sword and regarded them carefully. It was like they were ready to pounce. He knew one wrong move and it'd be the end of him; there would be nothing anyone could to do save him or Levi.

"You have any ideas?" Danteus asked.

"Just one," Levi responded. "On the count of three."

"One," Danteus said.

"Two," Levi muttered, then took a deep breath and pulled his arrow back as far as the string in his bow would allow.

After one final breath, Danteus announced,

"Three."

Then the earth beneath Danteus's feet shifted and moved, throwing the Alastorians off balance, while others leapt to avoid the earth that threatened devour them like the waves of an ocean. Danteus brought up his sword and blocked an attack from an Alastorian, then pulled out a pistol and fired—shooting it in the head.

When the Alastorian fell, Danteus focused his attention on another and another until he was certain there were none left. After the fighting ceased, Danteus turned to Levi. He was battered and bruised and barely escaped with his life, but he had to ask:

"How about that? We didn't do too bad."

"Yeah, you didn't." Levi rubbed his injured arm. "That thing almost took off my entire arm."

"And it's my fault."

"No, it isn't." Levi's attention drifted to the makeshift camp camouflaged within the shrubs. He pulled out one arrow from the head of an Alastorian crumpled on the ground and knocked it into the bow. He saw an Alastorian round the camp and put its head into the door of the tent.

"You think can hit that?" Danteus asked.

"Just watch." Levi glanced at the Alastorian that has been wandering around the tent before sticking its head inside. Levi released the arrow, and it pinned the Alastorian's head to a nearby tree. Then both Levi and Danteus cautiously moved towards the camp.

DEMETRIA SAT UP STUNNED when she heard the thud of an arrow. She climbed out of the tent and regarded the men who'd saved them.

"Danteus? What are you doing here?"

"Searching for Gothalia, but we somehow stumbled into *this*. But, you're alright?"

"I'm fine."

"Good to hear," Levi commented, exhausted, as he sat down on the grass. After their recent fight, his feet felt sore.

Out of the tent piled Noel-Len, James, Curt, and the rest.

"So, what were you guys doing?" Levi asked.

"Taking a break," Curt joked, and Noel-Len elbowed him in the arm. "What? It's true."

Demetria stepped forward.

"After a rest and waiting for Noel-Len, we were planning on returning to the barracks, as we've successfully completed our mission."

"Sounds like a plan," Danteus replied.

"Did you find, Gothalia?" Demetria questioned. "She was with us. Then she vanished. Do you know where Asashin went?"

"No, I don't, unfortunately."

Curt glanced at James.

"What are you doing here?"

"We were searching for survivors."

"Who's we?" Noel-Len asked.

"You'll see."

"It's best we get moving," Demetria said.

"Agreed," Danteus declared. "There could be more hostiles around." Danteus placed his hand to his ear. "Lieutenant Valdis, do you read?"

There was no response, only static.

"Maybe she's out of range," Levi offered.

"Maybe," Danteus muttered.

The group vacated the grounds of their temporary camp and moved across the battlefield, passing their dead comrades. Their stomachs clenched at the sight, but they kept moving. There was no alternative.

Then the group stumbled upon another unit of soldiers with their rifles drawn and pointed.

"Now, let's be smart," Curt began. "We're on the same side."

The soldiers regarded Curt carefully. He had never seen them before; they were from the first and second regiment. The soldiers dropped their rifles and relaxed.

"Noel-Len?" a familiar voice called.

"Michael?" Noel-Len cried back, seeing the man covered in dirt and sweat just like him and the others. "You're alive!"

"Obviously."

"Alright, ladies. Let's move," the lieutenant of Michael's group declared. The larger group of soldiers moved through the streets. Carefully, they trudged the streets of Darwin towards their base. When they had arrived at the second untouched base, it was busy, with many different soldiers moving about, and everyone in the group sighed with relief.

"We're alive," Curt muttered.

"I know," Noel-Len replied. "I'm surprised."

"I'm just glad," said James.

"So, you're the Excelians," Michael's lieutenant stated, standing straighter. He strode over to Danteus with an air of hostility. "You don't seem that strong to me." He glanced at Demetria. "And letting a woman on the front-lines. Stupid."

Demetria moved to attack but Danteus held up his hand, stopping her.

"At least she's tamed," the lieutenant remarked.

"You're a soldier too," Danteus retorted, "Doesn't that make you tamed, as well?"

The soldier placed his hand on his gun.

"Let's see if I can tame you."

"Try it."

"Hey now," Noel-Len interrupted. "We're all on the same side, fighting for the same thing. We shouldn't fight among ourselves."

"Don't waste your breath," Michael hissed. "I've been trying to convince him that since the war began, and his stubborn arse doesn't want to believe that there are beings stronger than us."

"You want to try me?" the lieutenant asked Danteus.

"I'm not going to try you; I'm going to own you." Danteus removed his cloak and handed it to Demetria. "Especially, in that get-up."

The lieutenant eyed the uniform Danteus and Demetria wore, lined with weapons and a utility belt.

"Hey," Noel-Len began.

"Let him learn." Michael glanced at Noel-Len. "He needs his ego deflated."

"You're lucky you're not on my turf, boy." Danteus said. "Children like you wouldn't last in our ranks."

The Lieutenant pulled out his gun and pointed it at Danteus.

"Interesting. You didn't even flinch."

"Let's go little man. Let's see how you stack up."

Then a voice broke through the tension.

"Gentlemen, I hope I'm not interrupting." General Gunner approached and every soldier besides Danteus and Demetria stood up straight, saluting. The General wasn't amused. "These are our allies, Lieutenant Mathews, and will be treated as such. If you don't wish to be court-martialled, I suggest you tread *very* carefully."

"Sir!" Lieutenant Mathews replied.

"That goes for the rest of you," General Gunner declared. Immediately the group responded with "sir." The General's stare drifted to Noel-Len. "Private Ignatius. If you don't mind, along with Lieutenant Crystallovis and Squadron Commander Nero-Drausus, I'd like for you to follow me. We have much to discuss." He turned on his heel and vacated the premises, while Danteus, Demetria and Noel-Len followed.

Tension remained even after Danteus vacated the area.

"You're going to have your arse kicked," Michael said to Lieutenant Mathews.

"Whatever," he said and strode from the group.

Danteus, Demetria and Noel-Len followed the General through the base, where soldiers ran back and forth, some yelled orders, and others quickly mounted a vehicle and exited the base. Then they entered a tent that was larger than the rest, where other soldiers either lined the tent or were bent over a map.

Noel-Len's eyes lingered over the map of Australia and the map of Darwin. Then the man pulled out a computer and began typing.

"Sir," they greeted. Everyone paused and saluted.

"At ease," he said. "What do you have?" he asked the soldier beside the computer.

"The Xzandians are retreating, but they're not leaving our airspace," he said.

"And what of Lieutenant Colonel Valdis?" he asked.

"She's warned the underworld of the potential alien invasion and is due to return."

"Underworld?" Noel-Len asked the General.

"You have a lot to learn Private, but I guess it's our fault that we've kept the Excelians a secret from the rest of the world. Our allies—where do you think they're from?"

"The Underworld."

"Exactly," the General responded. "And why do you think they've only been with us during the invasion?"

"Because our goals run parallel. Sir."

"Smart boy," the General declared. His hazel eyes drifted from Noel-Len to the map. "We've cut off the Xzandian supplies and launched our attack. They shouldn't be able to keep on fighting for much longer. Regardless, I trust everyone will be on their guard." The General picked up an object and placed it on the table with the maps. The black surface covered in other worldly markings stared at Noel-Len. "They won't stop until they get every last one of *these*."

"What's that?" Noel-Len questioned.

"Something that you wouldn't normally be given permission to see, considering everything that has happened. You've been given special permission to see such items. This is a Fragment of Midnight Eclipse, and it's what the Xzandians want."

"And they're willing to kill to get it," another soldier said. "It doesn't matter who. They want this badly. So, we've put together a team that will be made of up Excelians and Vulgarians. You're on that team."

The soldier walked over to Noel-Len and handed him a badge and a computer chip.

"What's this?" he asked him.

"The information of your next mission," the General said.

"What about the others? I can't just leave them," Noel-Len declared, "Sir."

"I understand that you want to help but you'll be more helpful by finding these," the General declared. "The sooner we have them, the sooner we could probably negotiate a peaceful treaty with the aliens."

"A peaceful treaty?" Danteus questioned from beside Noel-Len. "No offense, General, but I doubt they want a peaceful treaty. What are you really up to?"

"I'm not at liberty to say."

"Why me, sir?" Noel-Len asked, uncertain, after a heavy moment of silence. "There are plenty of other soldiers capable of completing this mission."

"That is true," the General said. "However, I've gone over your stats and your experience. You have what it takes to conduct this mission. Even if you don't believe in it yourself. Besides, there is one other major factor that you haven't considered that will make you successful."

"What's that?"

"Your heritage."

# Chapter 32

GOTHALIA WOKE TO THE darkness, voices whispered around her then a bright light lit up the room. Gothalia groaned when footfalls walked towards her as she hung in the air with her limbs apart. Something kept her up, she knew but it defied the logic of gravity, she believed but didn't say anything. Her wrists and feet restrained by circular discs holding her upright. Gothalia stared up at the approaching figure and her jaw dropped. "No way," Gothalia muttered. "But you're—"

"Surprised?" the vicar examined.

"What are you doing on an alien ship?" Gothalia questioned. "You should be back at the Reserve."

"Oh child," he said, running his fingers over his lengthy beard. "You still think I'm on your side. Surely, you can't be that naive."

"You're the man who let the enemy into the Reserve but how?" Gothalia concluded, then her gaze narrowed. "It was all you. You killed the Seers." Gothalia stared the vicar down then her gaze drifted from him and to the man behind him.

Altair.

Casually, he leaned against the wall and silently observed the interaction. "Most of them. One unfortunately got away but no matter. It's not like he saw my face." Gothalia regarded him for a moment and he continued, "And it's not like anyone could tie me to the slaughter."

"That's what you think, the Peacekeepers will find something. They always do." Gothalia replied.

"By the time they found out what had happened, I'd be long gone."

"That's why you're so confident."

"Hardly," he said, "I'm angry."

"That's a shame." Gothalia remarked and electricity shot through her body. Gothalia shrieked in pain and the vicar smiled.

"You don't need to be so disrespectful." he replied. "I'm trying to have a proper conversation with you. Anyway, as I was saying . . . before you rudely interrupted me. It was all too easy." Then the doors opened and an Xzandian entered the room his gaze was hard but Gothalia recognised the face. It was the face of the man she had long but battled. He smiled up at her in her restrained state and Gothalia glowered back at the man.

"Gothalia, what have you been up to since I last saw you?" he proclaimed, as if they were old friends.

"Oh, you know this and that. The Fragments you know how it is," she declared. The Xzandian smiled. She racked her brain for his name, and she recognised the name that he had. It was Xaviaius and the other one that entered the room was Prometheus. Where their parents got their names was beyond her.

The Xaviaius smirked and ran a hand through his dark hair. "You are troublesome you know that, but it can't be helped I guess it's genetics."

"What are you talking about?" Gothalia queried.

"Oh nothing," he replied.

"Why are you here?" the vicar asked, his eyes on Xaviaius.

"Calm down, Augustus. I'm not going to ruin your fun."

"Fun? You think I enjoy this?" Augustus responded.

"I think you do," Gothalia remarked before being shot with another bolt of electricity and all the men smirked.

"She's a keeper, don't kill her." Altair observed and everyone turned to face him. "If that's what you were intending to do."

"Why is that?"

"Simple, she could be a valuable asset couldn't she, Prometheus?"

Prometheus responded, "I'd like to see her dead, but I see your point."

"What point?" the vicar, Augustus, declared confused. "Keeping her alive would not do us any favours."

"No, it would," Xaviaius said. "Remember, Natalia of the Valdis clan was able to bare the power of Midnight Eclipse. What makes you think that she won't."

Gothalia wasn't following. "What are you talking about?"

"Has it ever occurred to you why the Fragments are enveloped around your arm and no one else's?" he queried.

"Because no one else found as many Fragments as much as I have."

"No," Xaviaius said. "It has to do with your heritage. I mean there's a reason why the members of the Valdis clan have unstable élanocytes. Your people are the perfect accommodators of Midnight Eclipse. Without your people no one could wield its power. We'll for now that is."

"What do you plan to do with me?" she asked, staring him down.

He smiled a deadly smile than declared, "Simple, we're going to make you one of us."

"MY HERITAGE?" NOEL-Len queried. "How does my heritage have anything to do with Midnight Eclipse?"

"You don't know, do you?" a soldier questioned from beside the General.

"Know what?" Noel-Len examined.

"That some Excelians aren't at their full power because of their unstable élanocytes."

"Élanocytes are energy cells that provide Excelians their elemental abilities, strength and speed and what not." the General cut in.

"And what does my heritage have to do with this?" Noel-Len queried. "I understand my mother was last seen with Midnight Eclipse, but that still doesn't explain why my heritage has to do with it."

"Noel-Len, you have unstable élanocytes."

Noel-Len crossed his arms. "You're implying that I'm an Excelian."

"Yes, I am," the General answered. Noel-Len regarded the General and acknowledged the seriousness in his expression. "You don't believe me, do you?" The General sighed and glanced away from the young man before he began once again, "Think about it." Turning away from the maps and his back to Noel-Len. "When it came to the training you didn't just pass but you excelled and that's natural for Excelians who haven't completely awoken."

"I could just be lucky," Noel-Len remarked.

"Luck wouldn't have gotten you into the Special Forces, now would it?" the General queried.

"No, Sir," Noel-Len replied.

Noel-Len regarded the General and declared. "I can't be an Excelian. I'm Human."

The General stepped aside and never uttered a word. A medic Noel-Len was unfamiliar with stepped forward and asked, "Give me yourself." In a thick Italian accent.

"Excuse me?" Noel-Len queried, confused yet shocked by her question, unfolding his arms.

He regarded the General who nodded. "Just do it."

Noel-Len held out his arm and the doctor pulled up his sleeve and withdrew an unfamiliar device. She tapped the butt of the device against his skin. Not once did it puncture his skin and not once did it hurt. Moments later, the device turned red and a number popped up. Noel-Len regarded it cautiously and the woman released her hold on him and held the device before the General to view what was written.

"What is it?" Noel-Len asked.

"The device is an élanocyte detector and it detects that you have élanocytes but for some reason your levels are quite low." The General declared.

"Is that a bad thing?" Noel-Len asked.

"It isn't." Danteus put in.

"It's just rare," Demetria cut in. "All Excelians have a high élanocyte count but depending on the gene expression in our DNA which can determine what elemental abilities we have it can also determine if we are born with little élanocytes and unstable élanocytes."

"It's not just your élanocytes," the General declared. "But your unstable élanocytes that bothers me. It's quite high."

"Should I be worried?" Noel-Len asked.

"Yes." Danteus and Demetria replied, at the same time.

"Why?" he asked them.

"Unstable élanocytes have a tendency to cause . . ." Danteus trailed off. "A way of bringing out the worst in us, to put it mildly."

"Let's just say there are certain diseases that can occur and sometimes there are some that are hereditary," Demetria began, and Noel-Len thought he saw her shiver but it was so subtle that he thought he imagined it, "Can cause a type of side-effect."

"What type of side-effect?" Noel-Len queried.

Danteus and Demetria regarded the General, uncertain. He nodded in approval and the Demetria continued. "You can become . . . not like yourself."

"What do you mean?"

Danteus stepped forward, "What Demetria means here, is that you could become what we call a demon and that's if you're lucky."

"How?" Noel-Len questioned.

"You sure ask a lot of questions. I don't remember you being this talkative when I last saw you," Anaphora declared and entered the tent with L'Eiron at her heel.

"Lieutenant Colonel. Commander." The General greeted. "Glad you could make it."

"Wait so you know she's an Excelian, but she wears our uniform. Why?" Noel-Len questioned.

"You're right, he does ask a lot of questions." L'Eiron said, crossing his arms and turning to Anaphora who shrugged at the comment.

"Of course, I'm asking a lot of questions." Noel-Len continued. "There is a war at our door and you're telling me that I'm an Excelian. You do realise that's a lot to take in."

"Can you manage it?" the General queried.

Noel-Len fell silent and contemplated his words. After a moment, he said, "I can."

"Good. No more questions, for now anyway. Just trust, we're trying to help."

Noel-Len never stated his concern but regarded the sight of the General, Anaphora, L'Eiron, Danteus and Demetria. There were more Excelians in this room then there were Humans and he wondered how many walked beneath their feet.

ALTAIR KEYES WALKED the halls of the alien ship that hovered over the city of Moscow, hidden from view. Its technology allowed them to camouflage with the clouds. Though, he'd seen the broadcast of their presence on the news with the title reading— '*They live among us*'. Altair smirked at the idea that the humans were used to this idea that only they existed, but it was no longer the case and will never be the case from now on. Not that it ever was.

He entered a room and passed a familiar Excelian woman.

He was certain that the humans would crumble beneath their fingers and his smile grew at the thought. Then beside him he felt a hand on his shoulder, and he removed the hand. "What's wrong?" Numitora asked, with a little purr to her lips.

"Nothing," he commented. "Have you found the rest of the Fragments?"

"No."

"Then what are you doing here?"

"I wanted to know how many we have so I have an idea of how many to chase after," she uttered like it was the obvious thing in the world. Altair frowned.

"We have six so far. The rest you'll have to find, with your team."

Altair glanced at the two other men. Yogic and Karim. They regarded Altair with an air of hostility. It wasn't like they were going to kill him not without the Council's approval. "You two, instead of glaring at me why don't you go and do something else worth your time?" Altair prompted and Numitora crossed her arms and shifted her weight.

"You heard the man. Time to leave boys." Yogic and Karim regarded each other for a moment longer before they turned their heel and exited the door Altair entered. The room was silent and filled with the two of them. "Now that we have some alone time," Numitora purred and Altair wished he were anywhere else. "Let's talk. What's going on?"

"What do you mean? I'm hunting the Fragments as you should," he uttered when her hand stroked his chiselled jaw.

"That's not what I mean," Numitora affirmed resting her hand on his chest. "You know I only joined this cause because you asked me to. Not once have I seen you hesitate for this cause and yet you did, why?"

Altair turned to her and regarded Numitora. "I didn't hesitate."

"You did with Gothalia," Numitora uttered, wrapping her arms around him.

"I did not." Numitora stepped away and Altair felt a little grateful for the space.

"Sure, you didn't." Numitora remarked, glancing away refusing to believe his words. "Let's pretend the all-powerful Altair doesn't hesitate and doesn't feel fear." Numitora's sarcasm was evident and Altair's frown deepened. "Remember, as high as you may think you are. You don't stack up to *him*. If he wanted, he'd kill us all and because we don't want to die, we're aiding him with the Fragments. Maybe you should think a little more." Numitora asserted, with a seriousness he'd never seen before. After a moment of thick silence, she uttered. "So, is it true? Xaviaius brought Gothalia back. What does he intend to do with her?"

"Brainwash her, make her one of us," Altair remarked.

"He can do that?" Numitora asked then frowned. "I still want to kill her."

"You'll do no such thing," said Xaviaius as he entered the control room. Other Xzandians sat at the computers and worked while

Numitora and Altair stood on the bridge overlooking them and the city of Moscow below.

"Sir," Numitora declared. "I um . . ."

"Have a vengeance you'd like to cull. I understand. I would have enjoyed killing her mother slowly. Especially, after what she did but I guess that will not happen. If I can't get what I want, neither can you."

"Is it true?" Numitora asked. "You intend to make her one of us?" Numitora stepped forward and observed the Xzandian man and his otherworldly features that glittered beneath the lights and appeared to glow. It wasn't obvious at first, but she noticed it a little more every day.

"I do."

"Why? What purpose will she serve?" Numitora asked, heatedly.

"She'll acquire the Fragments since someone failed more than once," he remarked, with his hands behind his back. He observed Numitora carefully, "you and your band of troublemakers have done nothing we've asked. When we said find the Fragments—you fail. When we say kill—you hesitate. When we say slaughter countless—you don't. I wonder why that is? Regardless, Aragor has declared that she will replace you."

"What?" Numitora questioned. "So, you'll kill me."

"If we have to yes but not right now," Xaviaius declared. "We still have use for you. Don't fail anymore, or you won't exist anymore. *Understand*?"

Numitora swallowed. "I do."

"Good."

Altair regarded Numitora for a moment. Then his attention drifted to Xaviaius.

Numitora regarded Altair and Xaviaius one last time then turned her heel and exited the room leaving Altair and Xaviaius behind. "Do you trust her?" Xaviaius asked.

Altair regarded the older man. He'd become a veteran at war and knew that he had to choose his words carefully. "Honestly, I don't trust her, but I trust the anger she has towards the Ignatius-Valdis clan. She'll aid us for as long as she sees she has a purpose."

"And when she no longer has that purpose. I will end her personally."

"I look forward to it," Altair replied than turned his heel and exited the room.

He had only entered the bridge to have a look at their progress and nothing more.

When Altair exited the room, he passed a few other alien soldiers who regarded him differently. *Typical,* he thought. *Even if I bring them a powerful asset, they're still ungrateful.* He entered another room, further down the hall then paused. Gothalia's unconscious form hovered in the air before him. Two guards were stationed before her limp form and Altair had no idea why they had kept her like that but never commented. Quickly, Altair dismissed them.

Then he approached Gothalia and said, "I wonder how long you'll last." Before he pressed a button that opened another door where the good doctor stood. Dr Legato entered the room and he regarded Gothalia carefully, "She'll be an asset. Thank you," he said to Altair.

"No problem," Altair responded. "Make sure she can't remember."

Dr Legato stopped before the controls and began his experimentation.

NOEL-LEN, ANAPHORA, L'Eiron, Danteus and Demetria listened to the next phase of the plan and that was for Danteus and Demetria to guide Noel-Len to the Fire Reserve at the request of the General.

"This human will accompany you?" the female AI asked. There was a hesitation to her voice, Noel-Len noticed but didn't say anything.

"Yes. Set up the coordinates Eve." Danteus said, glancing at Noel-Len than away.

"No problem." Eve responded. Danteus pulled out a disk seconds later a holographic woman appeared, cladded in unfamiliar clothing and Noel-Len was stunned by the sight yet intrigued by the advancement of their technology. "Since there's been a bit of a situation. We're going to have to return to the Reserve through the old route."

"Okay?" Noel-Len declared. Then faced the General who was covered in bandages with cuts and grazes lining his jaw and nose. "General Sir."

"Travelling back to the Fire Reserve will be difficult without knowing the paths you can be lost but from what I see, you have an Earth user, no doubt you know the route back."

"I do." Danteus proclaimed.

"Then I suppose getting there is no problem. We'll hang onto the Fragment while Lieutenant Valdis acquires the rest." he said.

"Wait what?" Noel-Len questioned, uncertain as to why, but he knew he didn't like the idea of her going alone to acquire the Fragments. "Is anyone going with her?"

"Lieutenant Valdis understands the risks that comes with her travelling alone as an Excelian Centurion. She's trained her whole life for a mission like this." Danteus declared. "We all do."

Noel-Len regarded them for a moment, there was a determination in their gaze that he knew would remind anyone of their courage. With a nod, "I understand." He didn't press the matter, but he couldn't help if it were a good idea, and how would she find the Fragments, he wondered. Did she have a map or a general location? He pushed the thoughts aside and focused on Danteus.

"Let's get going." he said, and Noel-Len nodded. With that, the group vacated the barracks.

Noel-Len knew, when he wandered beside Danteus and Demetria as they lead him down a dark cavern, he should be concerned and a part of him was. "So, where are we?" Noel-Len questioned, after some time.

"We're on route." Demetria declared. After a they borrowed a vehicle that lead them north to the ocean. Danteus had directed them to an old war tunnel and from there they entered an old tunnel that was sealed shut by an old metal door. It wasn't until a day later, that they Noel-Len started to notice a change in the sediment against the chasm floor and the smooth walls of the caves.

It was almost unnatural.

Though, he could not understand why but he recognised the walls narrowed into tunnels. The tunnels they walked down almost made him feel claustrophobic as the walls wrapped around him, Demetria and Danteus. "How much longer?" Noel-Len asked, after several hours of walking.

"We're here," Danteus said and stepped aside when he did light shone through the vines that covered the entrance.

Danteus stepped through, then Demetria who muttered, "Thank the Elders we're home. I'm starving." Noel-Len was hesitant first to follow both Demetria and Danteus were too deep in conversation to notice until when he stepped through, they stopped and stared at the gaping look on his face.

Danteus smiled and readily mocked. "What? Never seen an underground city before?" Demetria sternly elbowed him.

Noel-Len moulded his features into a blank expression and stepped onto the green grass and strode to where the others stood on a hill overlooking the City of New Icarus. "How did we get in without being caught?" he asked, without thinking too much about it.

Danteus gave him a quizzical look. "This isn't New Icarus. We're outside. We need to get inside the gates over there and we have permission." Noel-Len regarded the intimidating gate and slowly nodded. He wasn't too certain if this was a good idea. Then he wondered when he saw Anaphora take out the drop-bot he wondered if all women in New Icarus were as strong as her. Slowly and with caution, he regarded the woman beside him.

*Can she throw me through a wall and easily too?* He thought then gulped. When they eventually arrived at the gate there were other Excelians cladded in a different type of uniform. It was completely red from head to toe and deep in colour as blood. "The peacekeepers," Demetria muttered to Noel-Len and he nodded.

"We have permission to enter." Down a zip line several Excelian dropped to the ground faster than Noel-Len had ever expected and with ease. The closer they walked to him, the sooner he recognised their armour was different and advanced. They stopped before him and one man held out his hand.

"Welcome back. Danteus. Demetria." He took one look at Noel-Len and didn't say anything but turned away when Danteus handed him a transparent card. The man placed the card into his forearm and a holographic projection of a woman who appeared like Anaphora who uttered a passcode then a few other verification codes until the peacekeeper was satisfied and the codes were confirmed.

Noel-Len followed Danteus and Demetria to the entrance and the man allowed them passage. He watched Noel-Len for a moment with a confused look before he nodded, accepting Noel-Len's entrance but recognising he was an outsider.

When Noel-Len, Danteus and Demetria entered the city Noel-Len was surprised to find that the city was clean, beautiful, and completely different in architecture than to what he expected. His jaw dropped at the culture and the vehicles he could tell didn't use any bad fuel to power them.

Danteus and Demetria guided him through the city, and he couldn't help but gawk in awe at the city and the diverse people cladded in the colours of the city or their element. After what felt like hours, they finally paused outside a red door, one that reminded him of the door back at the prison, but it was different at the same time.

On the outside, Danteus and Demetria looked calm but there was an unspoken silence that lingered between them when the door opened. A man stepped forward, and he looked displeased at the two of them but allowed them to enter before asking, "Who is this man?" Grand Elder Michalis questioned.

"Forgive us, my lord." Danteus proclaimed. "But he is Noel-Len of the Ignatius clan." Michalis's eyes shifted to one of understanding but there was a caution in his gaze that kept Noel-Len on his toes. Michalis stepped aside and Noel-Len entered the large house.

"Tell me what brings you two back especially after I had given strict orders to have you accompany Gothalia in search of the Fragments."

"There's been an unfortunate change of plans, my lord." Demetria proclaimed. She was hesitant at first to provide Michalis the reason Noel-Len noticed but she didn't hesitate too much after she'd gathered her courage and stepped forward and handed him a transparent card where he'd placed it into his forearm guard and a holographic projection of Anaphora was revealed once again and this time her words were different. They were stern and unfortunate. Noel-Len heard his name come up and he realised that Anaphora had relayed that he was the daughter of Natalia Ignatius and Gaius Ignatius which made him the sibling to Gothalia.

"Wait. Hang on. I'm what now?" Noel-Len questioned, and the man Michalis had stopped himself from saying anything while Demetria and Danteus remained silent. "I am the son of Gaius Ignatius and Natalia Ignatius, but I have no biological sibling. I only have my half-siblings that my father managed to acquire with his recent marriage."

Michalis didn't say anything and only walked over to Noel-Len with a welcoming and hospitable smile. "Why don't you get settled? You look like you've been through a lot." Michalis walked away and narrowed a glare at both Danteus and Demetria who followed him.

Before Noel-Len could say anything Danteus silently gestured he don't say anything. Then, a woman arrived with a polite smile. "Follow me sir. I'll see you to your quarters."

"But . . . I need to speak to . . ." Noel-Len began confused and unsure why the man he wanted to speak to walked away.

# Chapter 33

WHEN NOEL-LEN WOKE, he was surprised to find that he had slept and when he slept there was no scary dream that woke him. There was nothing but he knew that he had a strange dream but couldn't remember what it was. Instead, he brushed the thought aside and threw his legs over the edge.

When Noel-Len climbed to his feet he had never understood the ache at his side and dropped back onto the bed. He cursed at the pain not understanding where it'd come from and the door opened to reveal a woman, she recognised the blood pouring through the bandages and ran to him. "Please sir, you mustn't move. The wound's been reopened."

"What wound?" Noel-Len questioned, sharply. Then he re-membered when he fought in the war. After he'd had his arm cut. Noel-Len didn't remember much when he woke, the war was noth-ing but a blur, but he saw it now his hand covered in blood and the woman frantic to save him. She moved him to the bed and lifted his shirt, where the blood pool and quickly provided first aid.

"You may not remember the wound, but I do," the woman said. "It had coagulated and had been tended to but when you went to clean yourself up in our baths, the wound reopened, one of men saw you, unconscious and unable to move. We realised you had lost a lot of blood and the wound was susceptible to infection." she said as she tended to the wound.

"You've been out for quite some time and missed quite a lot but considering what you've been through. No one can blame you." She continued.

"I'm exhausted." Noel-Len proclaimed, not physically tired but felt as if he'd been hit by a train.

"You must rest both your mind and your body. It's endured a lot."

"But I'm not tired."

"You don't always have to sleep to rest." she wisely said.

"Where am I?" Noel-Len asked.

"You're in the eastern quarters of master Michalis's estate. You came to visit him with your friends. Don't you remember?"

"I remember." He groaned when she cleaned his injured side with a disinfectant she'd pulled out from the bedside table before re-bandaging him up. "He wouldn't talk to me. He just passed me off."

"Lord Michalis is a busy man, but I can understand why you're a little angry. When you're feeling better you can join your friends when it's their turn to meet with him."

"When are they meeting with him and why?" he asked.

"Soon," was all the woman said before she vacated the room to tend to her other duties. Noel-Len gently pulled himself from the bed, careful not to open the gash as flashbacks of the war and the injury wrought his mind. Moving to the door, he exited the room.

He wandered down the halls of the estate and felt out of place, cradling his injured side he attempted to recall when he'd been injured and why hadn't he noticed. *The adrenaline*, he thought. *I must have been so focused on surviving.*

The voice of children in the courtyard, caught his attention, bringing with it a flicker of happiness and sadness. They sang a song and danced around in a circle above the mowed lawn and beside the rose bushes.

He eyed them for a moment with a smile and recalled a time when he was a child with a little girl. The same girl that would flash across his features, catching him off guard. She called out his name and he was surprised, "Len," the voice said.

"Noel-Len." Danteus said. Noel-Len blinked, the memory vanished and Danteus stood before him with worry, "Are you okay?"

"I'm fine."

"Are you sure?" Danteus asked, watching Noel-Len lean against the stone wall, his features were damp and almost distraught.

The children stopped playing and glided over to Danteus and Noel-Len. "Are you okay mister?" A young girl questioned, with bright eyes.

Noel-Len straightened himself, "I'm fine. Thank you for your concern."

"No problem," the child beamed before beginning another game of tag. Their squeals echoed down the hall before their feet padded away. Demetria rounded the corner and smiled at the sight of both men.

"There you are," she hailed. "I've been looking for you—" She began until her eyes lit up upon Noel-Len. "Ah, Noel-Len glad you're up. How are you feeling?"

"Sore but good." There was a moment of reflective silence that befell the group before Noel-Len questioned, "So when are you guys going to meet Michalis?"

"*Lord* Michalis." Demetria emphasised.

"*Right*?" Noel-Len responded, a little reluctantly.

"We're meeting him in a bit." Danteus acknowledged. "For starters let's get you into some clean clothes." And, flagged down a nearby maid requesting that she provide clean clothes in Noel-Len's size. Within a few moments, she vanished into the halls of the estate afore returning with a new set of clothes.

Once Noel-Len changed into a new set of clothes he was relieved. The clothes were black around the arms and legs but red around his chest and waist. It was snug around his tender body but loose enough to not be uncomfortable. Accentuating the worn muscles beneath. Before he'd realised, he uttered the words faster than his mind could stop them, "Where are my weapons, my pack and my utilities?" Noel-Len inquired, holding Danteus's gaze.

Danteus turned his eyes from Noel-Len's filled with guilt. "They're safe."

"Where?" Noel-Len questioned. He was certain Danteus wouldn't respond and as such Danteus didn't respond.

"In a secure location." he rebutted, folding his arms over his chest. He didn't like what Noel-Len was implying, Demetria knew, but never uttered a word. Instead, she waited for the men to work out their differences. When they finally did and Noel-Len was satisfied with the answer, he proclaimed:

"When are we going to have this meeting?" Noel-Len held Danteus's gaze a little longer searching for deceit. Then a woman joined the group, one that strode with elegance and a proper air.

"It's time." Danteus proclaimed. Then the group turned and walked away.

Noel-Len regarded Danteus, not impressed about their acquisition of his weapons. When Danteus stepped aside and ushered Noel-Len forward, Demetria held back a laugh at the look searing upon Noel-Len's face.

The group followed the woman, down the winding halls and to a large study. The woman bowed upon entering and upon departure before closing the door behind her, leaving the group within and Noel-Len dazzled by the unique architecture. "Lord Michalis." Danteus and Demetria greeted, with a slight bow and a hand over their hearts.

Michalis's eyes fell on Noel-Len who didn't offer the same respect as the other members of his group and Michalis felt no need to scold him for his surface world teachings. "So, now that you're cleaned and feeling a little better, mind telling me what it is that you're doing returning home?"

"With all due respect Lord Michalis. We're here for protection as lady Anaphora explained."

"That she did," he said. "Though, I'm not too please about it. She's implying that our current soldiers are no match for what's about to come? Our city—no—our home has remained standing for centuries and we're not about to give it up because a few outsiders entered its vicinity." As Danteus continued to persuade Michalis, Noel-Len glanced out a nearby window, his eyes curious about the new world and his mind reeling with so many memories before his attention paused on a distant man running towards the building.

Baffled, Noel-Len stepped closer, the conversation in the room drowned out. His eyes peered at the sight of another man running towards the building followed by ear-piercing screams. Noel-Len gaped at the large larva monster standing tall above the wall. Fire balls were thrown through the air and towards the city, smashing homes and offices, before landing collectively in the streets and burning to pieces Excelian flesh.

"Our home is a sanctuary!" Michalis growled. "The Fragment we have here is safe!"

"With all due respect, my lord. . ." Demetria began, "We don't know what the enemy is capable of."

"We do! The Rangers have—"

"Guys." Noel-Len began, and everyone's gaze landed on him.

"Young man, we're having a serious discussion it's rude to—"

"—I know," Noel-Len countered. "But you might want to see this." Michalis stepped towards the window with Danteus and

Demetria following. Alarms ignited around the city and explosions permeated the air. Though the rest never touched the city but the barrier surrounding the city.

"We're under attack." Demetria declared, with stunned shock.

"Your orders sir," Danteus waited as did Demetria.

Without a second thought or hesitation to his words he commented, "Get rid of that monstrosity before he brings down the *ward*." Demetria, Danteus and Noel-Len vacated the room and ran down winding halls until they were in the front courtyard that overlooked the city and spotted the largest monster that Noel-Len's ever seen. The monster towered over the buildings with skin that cracked yet filled with larva and eyes that glowed a dangerous fiery red and orange.

"What the hell is *that*?" Noel-Len questioned, shocked. Never in his life had he seen such a monster.

"We don't know." Demetria replied staring back at it in shock.

"You guys come from a different world, so I assumed—" Noel-Len began, and Demetria glared muttering: "you fought aliens and you think that's weird".

"Enough! We need to find a way to stop it from entering the city." Danteus proclaimed and scanned the streets below. Everyone began to evacuate the southern gate and the surrounding areas.

Rangers, Centurions, Knights and so many different branches of the Upper Echelon of the Order of the Phoenix arrived and climbed onto roofs with torrents, bazookas and many different weapons Noel-Len was familiar with and unfamiliar with at the same time. His wonder was halted when they heard a voice. Then noticed several anti-tank guns crawl through the streets and form a line and turrets.

"That's a lot of fire power." Noel-Len commented and glanced around, "So when do I get mine?" Danteus relayed an incredulous look and Noel-Len wasn't fazed. "Well . . ."

"Hey!" A voice called. And everyone followed the sound of that voice to find a man with golden hair and eyes. Electricity sparked around him. He stood on the adjacent roof and glanced down at the group. "Give him whatever weapon he wants. We have a bigger problem." Berith Barak declared.

"Lord Barak?" Danteus questioned, confused.

"Do it. Now. The ward isn't going to hold much longer." Berith said and dropped down to where they were. "And besides, he has the right to defend himself."

Danteus scowled at the thought then uttered, "Demetria. Show him where his weapons are." Demetria nodded and urged Noel-Len to follow her.

Danteus turned to Berith, "Happy?"

"A little." he said, then Danteus frowned the sighed.

"One thing after another isn't it? Talk about no reprieve."

"It'll be over soon." Berith said.

"How do you know?"

There was silence before Berith proclaimed, "Honestly, it's just a hunch."

When Demetria revealed the weapons to Noel-Len. He grunted in displeasure. "Why are they caged up?" he responded, with an ebbing frown.

"Just a precaution." Demetria declared, almost amused by his reaction before unlocking the steel cage. Noel-Len pulled out his rifle and his pistol, including his hunting knife.

Then checked the bullets. "Not much left."

"Here." Demetria offered, tossing him a sword. The straight edges carved with an ancient language gleamed under the light and balanced easily on his palm. "Satisfied?"

"Very. You guys must have a good blacksmith." Noel-Len commented, eyeing the craftsmanship.

"All our blades come from the Eastern Fire Reserve." Demetria tossed him a sheath and something he hadn't ever seen before. She regarded him for a moment and watched as she fiddled with the straps that held the weapon to his upper body.

"You loop your arms through there and clip the front." Demetria pointed out. Once Noel-Len got it he muttered his thanks after he sheathed his sword, something he's never used in his life, but he figured now was a better time to learn.

Then, they were on their way.

When they returned Danteus was no longer on the balcony but in the courtyard below the balcony and Noel-Len threw himself over the railing and onto the roof before pulling out his rifle. He fired at the larva monsters and watched as several fell to his weapon only to not stay down. So, as fast as he could, and as accurately as possible, he aimed for their heads. They never rose again after that and Noel-Len climbed down into the courtyard where Danteus cleaned his sword.

"How come that didn't melt?" Noel-Len asked.

"Not sure." Danteus proclaimed.

"Hey guys." Demetria said, as she stopped before them. "The largest one can't get into the city, but his little guys can."

"We've noticed." Danteus uttered. "Your point."

"My point is . . . the Fragment is safe. For now, but . . ."

"This maybe another diversion." Danteus finished.

"Diversion?" Noel-Len began, and watched as Danteus spoke into his headpiece and declared for all beta squadrons to follow him to the Cetatea while the delta squadrons remained fighting the lava monsters.

"Let's go." Noel-Len and Demetria didn't argue as they ran through the streets and towards the Cetatea while taking down all the larva monsters Demetria had seen with Gothalia at the southern caves.

Their journey was a slow yet rigorous task until Danteus proclaimed, "Beta hold them off and draw a perimeter when we reach the Cetatea."

Once they reached the Cetatea, the Earth users and the water users, created a moat around the building causing several monsters to fall into the water creating steam and smoke. A scene that gave Danteus, Demetria and Noel-Len enough cover to vacate the area.

When they entered the Cetatea, Danteus ran into Arthur's study and began searching for the Fragment. "It's not here." he concluded, after some time.

"Where would . . ." Demetria began.

"Gothalia." he recognised in understanding.

"No that's not right. Gothalia found a Fragment in the southern caves, she didn't steal it." Demetria defended.

"I'm not saying she stole anything I'm just saying it's not here and Gothalia may know where it is."

"It's still an implication." Demetria concluded.

"Hey, what are the monsters doing here if the Fragment isn't here?" Noel-Len asked.

"If they haven't retreated. The Fragment must still be here." Demetria began. "What about the Council Chamber?"

"We'll try there" Danteus felt inclined to say but confirmed it nonetheless, guiding his group to the Council Chamber where the Grand Elders sat upon their chairs forever looking over the city or upon the people who were deserving of criticism and judgement.

Upon arrival, the partially opened doors held a haunting call and Danteus glanced at Demetria with an epitome of concern.

They both knew the doors were to always remain closed and guarded by soldiers who were nowhere to be found. The partially opened grand door, was forced further open by Danteus who ground his teeth as the door slid against the marble floor. The doors revealed an elegant room with black marble floor and an extinguished bonfire that sung an eerie song.

As they climbed the black marble stairs, uncertainty danced along his already anxious skin. Demetria's lips folded into a grim line and Danteus's gaze was hard, determined like the soldier he was. They climbed the stairs, each to their own fear and uncertainty but remained calm and collected on the surface.

When they reached the top, the stairs were stained in blood and the chairs that once held the Grand Elders were vacant. Bodies of the Cratians spanned the floor, and blood smeared the walls. "What happened here?" Demetria questioned.

Noel-Len ran his finger over the blood. "It's dry. Whatever happened here . . . happened a while ago." There was no yellow tape, and there most definitely wasn't any form of any other presence being there prior to theirs and if there was, there was no knowledge of it.

Demetria rushed to the door, and forced it open, the door without a handle. She slid her card over a black sensor and the door responded with an "access denied" in an emotionless and computerised tenor. Demetria tried again, and it responded once more with the same words that Noel-Len could tell ground at her patience.

"Here let me," Danteus declared. Demetria stepped out of the way and Noel-Len watched as Danteus produced a card and moved it over the sensor. There was the sound of a blot being pulled across and the computer declared, "Access granted. Welcome Squadron Commander Danteus Nero-Drausus. The Grand Elders are waiting for you." The automated voice declared when Danteus stepped inside and Demetria followed along with Noel-Len.

With mild trepidation Danteus, Noel-Len and Demetria entered the room. Yet, on guard, they examined the small study then made their way up the marble stairs where the Grand Elders sat.

Blood stained the ground and the walls left their chairs empty and bare. Noel-Len gasped at the sight, the tapestry that hung behind the chairs was torn as if someone had sliced it, the walls were etched and carved in cuts and scratches that would not have been against the wall before. "They're all gone." Danteus said.

"Does Michalis know?"

"I think he does; it explains the excessive security surrounding his estate. Though, if that monster outside is after the Fragment. . ." Danteus began.

"Then there was that invasion on the surface world for a Fragment which was secured and is no on its way to a remote location." Demetria declared.

"The Alastorians. . . I think they're called, what do they have to do with this?" Noel-Len asked. Not entirely certain what they were getting at.

"But they were almost aiding the Xzandians." Danteus declared, recalling a time when the Xzandian never fired at the Alastorians. "The Grand Elders were taken because of the wards that means there's only one remaining."

"Because of Grand Elder Michalis." Demetria declared.

"The Alastorians that entered the city had accompanied the Humans when Gothalia and his highness was attacked." Danteus declared unaware that Noel-Len had ventured from them and into another room. His eyes widened at the sight.

"Guys. . ." he called. Danteus and Demetria followed Noel-Len's voice and stumbled across a sight that startled them. It was one word, written in blood across the windows.

"Rukh." Danteus said then shared a knowing glance at Demetria. "They were after Gothalia and are most likely responsible for all of this."

"For what reason?" Demetria questioned.

"Whatever the reason," Noel-Len began, "It can't be good."

Noel-Len regarded the blood on the wall carefully, it had said only one word and Danteus crossed his arms, almost defensive and this caught Noel-Len's attention. "You okay?" he asked Danteus who nodded at his words.

"I just don't like this." he confessed. "A lot has happened including the abduction of Arthur."

"Arthur?" Noel-Len questioned.

"He was our engineer and scientist. The head of the science and engineering department. Specialising in producing, manufacturing, and designing our weapons, vehicles—the whole nine yards."

"He sounds really smart." Noel-Len commented.

"He was." Danteus proclaimed, with an awe to his voice. "The Order of the Rukh had taken him. We don't know where but last we heard he was in Russia. Then vanished almost into thin air."

"And this all happened while your leaders were taken or worse?" Noel-Len questioned.

"Yeah."

"It's all too coincidental."

"We agree." Demetria declared for Danteus who silently observed his surrounding searching for any clues that might lead them to the Order. "But I'm still trying to figure out why the Peacekeepers hadn't discovered this place before us."

"Because someone wanted them not to discover it. Think about it, when Gothalia was not herself, it was a big enough distraction that all combat trained personnel within the building to abandon their posts. The guards would have no doubt, tightened security around the room. Except . . . his eyes trailed to the window. Except here," Danteus proclaimed, his long strides closed the distance to the window in seconds. Then his eyes drifted out of it, there was a long steep drop into the larva below. But a few meters from it was land, green grassy land of the Contor district where defence was minimal due to the Dragon Core building not too far away.

"Wait are you saying the bad guys entered here and slaughtered the Grand Elders."

"Not slaughter there's no bodies and too much blood."

"So, then what." Demetria asked.

"They tried to force the Elders out of the room, without being seen but must have been spotted and the Cratians who would have responded as fast as any Centurion. Explaining the markings on the walls and the blood. Where are their bodies, I'm unsure but I did notice as we walked in a lot of dust?"

"Dust?" Demetria proclaimed. "As in ashes."

Grimly, Danteus nodded.

"Are you saying the report Gothalia had written up about what happened Maximus and Anton is the same thing that happened to these guards? You mean Numitora."

"I'm not saying it's her but I'm not denying it could be. Grand Elder Michalis had believed Numitora was in the city when the attack occurred on the Prince and Gothalia, but the Grand Elders may have been taken before leaving the wards open."

"Are you saying it's an inside job?"

"It's a possibility."

"Who would betray our country like that?" Demetria questioned.

"Anyone with a vendetta against it." Noel-Len finished. "Looks like you guys have more to worry about than just the Xzandians." Then, there was a loud bang and that reminded everyone of the monster outside the final ward. The wards were held up by the Grand Elders and the number of Grand Elders always determined the number of wards available around the city, aiding to keep it hidden and protected. The bang rumbled and the ground trembled beneath their feet.

"Search the room." Danteus said. "We need to find that Fragment."

# Chapter 34

"WHAT?" DEMETRIA BEGAN, "You expect it to be casually lying around?"

Danteus gave her a look. "It has to be somewhere." Noel-Len said, helpfully and Demetria groaned.

"We don't even know what we're looking for." she proclaimed, a little reluctantly and Danteus sighed.

"Of course, we don't know what it looks like, but look for something that is out of the ordinary."

"Like this." Noel-Len said and both Demetria and Danteus clamoured around him. With stunned expressions.

Noel-Len regarded the object that he couldn't begin to describe, with an air of confusion. It looked like nothing it important and he wondered, was it because it looked like nothing important that it was what he thought it was. Though it was black and had indention of square scales, this one he noticed was shaped like half a donut.

Danteus's gaze lingered over the object carefully. He was aware of that the Fragments could appear as any shape, but the Fragment was always of one design. The design they were looking at. "That's it." Danteus confirmed.

"How do you know?" Noel-Len asked.

"The Fragments are always shaped differently but are always black with an otherworldly design."

"That makes sense." Demetria proclaimed. Then the ground shook beneath their feet and Demetria glanced at Danteus alarmed. "That monster, it's still out there!" Demetria declared as she glanced out the window that was a perfect view of where the monster had smashed its large hands against the last ward that everyone—including Noel-Len could see would eventually waiver.

"What are we going to do?" Noel-Len asked.

"We get the Fragment out of here."

"Is it only one?" Noel-Len queried.

"We don't have time to find out." Danteus proclaimed.

The ground trembled again and Danteus gripped the wall beside him for support. Once the tremor ceased, Demetria glanced at Danteus before turning her gaze out the window where the monster stood, smashing his fists against the ward that caused the ground to tremble beneath each strike and Noel-Len said, "We got to move."

It wasn't until they heard a female voice that everyone stopped, "I don't think so."

Noel-Len glanced at the door where the woman stood while Danteus's gaze narrowed. He recognised her and knew her from the live feed he'd seen Gothalia provide on her mission the night she'd ventured into Lust-us, it was that same night when Maximus and Anton died. A grimace formed upon Danteus's features and the woman smiled at his expression, content she had such an affect.

"Look who it is." she purred. "The Captain of the Alpha squadron of Dragon Core. Tell me, does the Duchess of Excretion still live?"

"Who's she talking about," Demetria muttered from beside Danteus.

"Gothalia," Danteus responded while Noel-Len aimed his pistol at the woman.

"I wouldn't do that if I were you." she said and held out her hand. In the palm of her hand was a grenade, without a pin. Tightly, she held onto the lever like her life depended on it and it did. So, did everyone else's and Danteus scowled—he didn't like their position, not one bit. "You all know what this is." she concurred. "Hand over the Fragment and I'll consider not blowing you up."

"You'll die too." Demetria articulated.

"That's not my concern. If I don't get what I want, I'll take you all out. So, I'll ask again, hand over the Fragment if you value your lives and besides have you forgotten what family my father hails from." Demetria recalled as did Danteus, but Noel-Len never knew what her bloodline was, and he figured he'd ask once he was free of this predicament.

Numitora held onto the grenade and Danteus scowled at the woman. She merely smiled at his reaction, almost smug to see him at a loss for words. "Slowly hand it over and no funny business."

Noel-Len glanced at Danteus, who nodded. Noel-Len slid the Fragment along the ground and towards Numitora. Not trusting her words but left with no other alternative.

"Thank you." Numitora proclaimed. Slowly, Numitora backed away and towards the door, leaving the room where Demetria, Danteus and Noel-Len were.

"Why did you let her go?" Demetria proclaimed, glaring at Danteus. "Even if Gothalia wasn't here. I could have at least frozen her. Why didn't you let me?"

"She's an ice user as well," Danteus declared. "Your attack would have cancelled."

"What?" Demetria began. "Since when?"

"Since she battled Gothalia back at her estate." Danteus moved over to her old friend, recognising the turmoil in her eyes. Placing a hand on her shoulder he said. "She's not getting away." Then spoke into his earpiece of his imminent threat. "Let's go." Danteus began then lead the group of the Council Chamber and into the lower levels of the Cetatea. "I don't care. Find Numitora!" he shouted into his earpiece. "She's got the Fragment!"

Danteus with the others ran down the halls of the Cetatea and out the front doors. The moat that was created now filled with solidified magma and the Excelians battled the monsters that were only ever told in legends among the people of the land of Fire.

"Where is she?" Demetria yelled, freezing a larva monster beside her.

Noel-Len fired at the monsters and was stunned when he found that he missed a few times. Then cursed. He panted then aimed his rifle again and fired, the piercing the head of one lava monster. He turned his attention to the next one and fired then the next one.

With this sword, Danteus ran at the closest alien then sliced off its head. The heat burnt against his skin, but he regenerated as any Excelian. Though, he was certain he'd be finished if he weren't careful. "Not sure!" Then a voice called over his earpiece. "East. She's headed east, out of the city!"

Danteus lead Demetria and Noel-Len down the street and there further down the road was a crackle of lightening and a massive explosion. Not too far away, Noel-Len could see when the cloud of smoke settled there was a man. He wore the Excelian combat uniform and when the group ventured closer Demetria called out, "Lord Barack!"

The man didn't glance at her when the group finally descended on the fight. Numitora battled the man while throwing shards of ice at him and freezing the ground, icicles shot into the air and Berith cut through the ice with a string of lightening. "Whoa." Noel-Len said and realised he wasn't much help in a fight between Excelians.

Lightening sprinted along the ground and towards him, missing Numitora who leapt out of the way in time. Noel-Len watched in horror, as the lightening flew towards him and he moved to run but it travelled faster than he could move. Not even Berith could stop it.

Then he was out of range. He glanced up and Demetria curled over him protectively. "You okay?" she asked, and he nodded, surprised she'd gotten him out of the way in time. His gaze returned to Numitora and he aimed his rifle once Demetria parted.

"You're not getting away Numitora, so stop fighting." Berith proclaimed.

"That's what you think, *Berith*."

Berith looked less than impressed, "That's *lord* to you." Then electricity crackled around them before Noel-Len covered his eyes when the ground Numitora stood light up in lightening and not from his hand or from the air. Noel-Len noticed, he merely looked at Numitora and lightening appeared.

It sent chills down his spine.

Danteus manipulated the earth creating jagged spikes where Numitora was and enclosed her in a cage made of earth. Ice melted over the earth and with her hands she shattered the bars.

Noel-Len watched on in both wonder and horror until his eyes were pulled to the monster several blocks away towering above the city smashing his palms against the wards. He noticed the wards appeared to have holes in them and they grew. Noel-Len regarded the sight in shock, "Um guys," he said.

Demetria looked at him and followed his gaze. "Oh no."

"The wards are dropping, why are the wards dropping!" Noel-Len proclaimed hysterically.

"It's done." Numitora said and Danteus narrowed his gaze.

"What do you mean by that?" he asked.

"The last of the guardians have been removed. The legendary impenetrable city is now penetrable. Congratulations." Numitora said.

Berith's temper rose and lightening stuck Numitora's shoulder who shrieked out in pain. "Bastard!" she screamed. Her face and eyes were red in agony as her shoulder had a small hole in it right through and she fell to her knees.

Berith walked over to Numitora and knelled, "Now you're going to tell me something or I'll send another current through you and it won't tickle I promise you." Numitora held his gaze. She shook under the pain and Berith, Noel-Len could tell as he joined the group, they were not bluffing. "What did you mean by it has been done? Where are the Grand Elders?"

She smiled, blood poured from her lips and Noel-Len realised Berith must have hit her in the torso more than her shoulder. "Far from here and Michalis is no more."

"You're lying!" Demetria said as she pulled ice out of thin air and formed it into a sword. "Let me remove her head. This snake will tell us nothing."

Noel-Len regarded the wards. They were breaking but they weren't completely dropped. He recognised Danteus noticed too if they're lucky Michalis was alive but severely injured. Though it was enough for the monster to stick his hands through and when he did, lava dripped onto the streets below and screams permeated the air in the distance, and he realised that not everyone had evacuated. "That thing's going to get in."

"We know." Danteus said.

"What do we do?" Demetria asked, Danteus.

"Try not to get killed." Berith answered.

"It's not *us*, I'm worried about." Demetria responded, regarding Berith. "I'm worried about *them*!" She gestured to the screaming civilians that had yet to escape the area.

It was in the tone of her voice, Noel-Len recognised the fear there. The terror there. It couldn't be explained, and it couldn't be escaped. Though there was a growing crowd, he knew that the civilians needed to be removed from danger.

In the distance, everyone observed the lava that spewed down the street and Danteus regarded the sight of the threat with an almost cool manner. He glanced at Demetria and nodded. Quickly, she ran forward and threw her hands up as if she were throwing an upper cut and a large ice wall thicker than any Noel-Len had ever seen, appeared in the street and continued to widen down either side of the street. "Holy cow." Noel-Len muttered, feeling a chill in the air.

From the sky, dark clouds gathered, and lightening glittered in the sky. Then the largest bolt of electricity shot towards the ground and the larva solidified before more larva rounded it. The lightening skipped along the ground, towards the citizens and Berith crossed his arms and narrowed his gaze. Then amongst it all, the lightening never touched the citizens or the ground beneath Noel-Len's feet. Instead, it skipped along an invisible dome that Berith had created and along its surface before dying out. "Okay, that was cool." Noel-Len said, admiring Berith who didn't even move like Demetria had.

Then it was Danteus who placed his hands on the ground and allowed the earth to roll in waves before shooting up behind the thick ice. Even wider than the ice wall, shattering the houses that couldn't withstand the impact. Once Danteus was certain everyone was safe, they turned their attention back to Numitora who amongst it all—escaped.

"Shit." Danteus muttered and Noel-Len regarded the man a moment longer. Then stepped out of the way to avoid being bumped into by the fleeing citizens who slowed a little once they were certain the lava couldn't touch them.

Noel-Len's attention shifted from the absconding citizens and to the cracking ice and splintering earth. When the last resident vanished from the sight, the ice that had kept the lava out crumbled a little, with loud cracks permeating the air and the solidified earth began to dwindle Noel-Len asked:

"Now what?"

"Now, we hunt down Numitora." Danteus proclaimed, with a hard gaze.

"For the *Fragment*?" Noel-Len asked.

"Yes. For the Fragment." Danteus declared. Though, Noel-Len had a feeling there was more to it than just the need to hunt down the Fragment.

On the ground, Noel-Len noticed a shiny object and wandered over to it. Picking it up, he scrutinised it. It was the same object he held in his palm not too long ago. "Isn't that?" Danteus began, wandering towards Noel-Len.

"I think it is." Demetria said, peering at the object.

"Did Numitora, deliberately forget about it?" Noel-Len questioned, not impressed. His gaze on the Fragment. The texture was smooth beneath his fingers, regardless of the scale like indentations.

"It's very unlike her to leave precious items behind." Danteus said. "Maybe it was an accident and she most likely didn't have time to retrieve it."

Berith declared, "Does it really matter. We have it now. Hang on to it and let's get the others to safety." Noel-Len handed the Fragment to Danteus while Berith ran from the group, his silver and black cloak flew behind him, as did, Demetria's and Danteus's. Noel-Len watched the group run from him and ran after them.

He sprinted down the roads after the others, though he couldn't keep up with their speed, he noticed, someone as he ran past. A man dressed in a brown cloak with a hood. The man watched him run by. Not thinking much of it, Noel-Len rushed after Danteus and the others pulling his eyes from the man that watched them run ahead.

The group halted, with tension to their strides, as ice shards grew from the ground. It stopped their venture and hovered in the air meters from them. Danteus regarded the style of the ice, aware that every elemental user was different, and it was something he had seen before. Clasping the Fragment, he threw it at Noel-Len who caught it, surprised it was thrown to him. "Take it and go."

"But—" Noel-Len began and was cut short by Danteus's urgent request, to get the Fragment out of there. Noel-Len nodded, and turned his heel as he ran from the fight, while Demetria held off Numitora. Whose long black hair was unkempt and messy from the lack of direct attacks Demetria deflected and blocked. On the contrary, Demetria's hair was well maintained and smooth regardless of her swift movements.

"Protect Noel-Len." Danteus ordered Demetria, who nodded. Numitora leapt from a large ice burg and towards Demetria with a sword in hand. Sword and sword clashed, as Demetria held off the attack, permitting an energy wave that threw Noel-Len from his feet. Then he felt, an impact on his wrist, where he held the Fragment. Glancing at the pain, he noticed a foot crushing his wrist against the hard-concrete road and shattered glass.

The man he'd seen before, commented, "I'll be taking that." Noel-Len reached for the Fragment with his other hand but was kicked in the face hard. The world spun, and blood pooled around his mouth. "*Hmm*, and you're an Excelian. Pathetic." With those words, the man vacated the battle ground and Noel-Len climbed to his feet to chase after the hooded Human man.

Noel-Len rushed quickly after the man, determined to catch him. However, what he didn't expect was the man to run so fast. Noel-Len continued but felt his muscles ache in pain before he groaned in anger. The man ran over obstacles of abandoned vehicles before running along the width of a building wall fast enough it caused Noel-Len to pause. Taking in the sight, Noel-Len gaped. "How the hell?" he muttered, and the man flipped and landed, sliding along the ground with his hand catching his fall. The stranger easily climbed to his feet and smiled at Noel-Len's expression.

"What? Can't keep up?"

"That's not possible. Excelian or Human. That's not possible."

"That's because unlike you, I'm not soft." Then removed the cloak he wore. Noel-Len stared at the man, with metal arms, legs, and a torso. The top of his head was engineered with metal while it held his brain within a sturdy container. Multiple internal extracts shifted and moved according to his movements—almost like muscles. Confidently, he strode towards Noel-Len then halted. "You don't remember who you really are, do you?" he asked, as curious as Noel-Len. "No matter. You'll be the end of the Ignatius-Valdis clan."

Then there was a searing noise, as if a saw had cut through metal, and the arm that reached for Noel-Len was severed. "I don't know who you are, or what you are. *Leave*." Berith declared and Noel-Len eyed the man grateful. "I won't tell you again." And lightning permeated his body and pulsed in a dangerous warning that made the hairs on Noel-Len's neck rise.

"Oh lightning, how *scary*." The man mocked. "You Excelians really piss me off. Walking around, as if you're high and mighty, while the ordinary ones that aren't like you suffer. Sometimes at the hands of your own kind. Tell me, with you flexing your power, are you any better than me."

"I'm *not* flexing." Berith declared. "I'm *warning*."

The man turned from Noel-Len focused on Berith and muttered beneath his breath, "Cocky and stupid." Then marched towards the lord of lightning. "You forget Excelian. You're just as soft as the Humans because of that, I'll cut you open where you stand."

Lightning slithered along the ground in hot waves and Noel-Len leapt out of the way. Electricity singed the air and the ground crackled.

"It's time you leave." Berith said to Noel-Len.

"I have to get the Fragment." Noel-Len reminded.

"Over my dead body." The stranger responded.

Berith growled beneath his breath, when the man reached for Noel-Len who leapt out of the way in time to prevent being zapped and in that moment, lightning struck the cyborgs hand and Noel-Len watched as the man shuddered under the lightning. "Your circuits run of a little thing called electricity. Your technology isn't like ours and as such is vulnerable under my touch." Berith proclaimed and shot another string of lightning from his form where it sparked against the metal of the man and his body trembled beneath the lightest touch of lightning.

The man crumbled to the ground, then moments later, he rose again, his armour and mechanical limbs glowed a brilliant blue. Berith regarded the man. "You know. Lightening recharges my circuits. So, what will you do?" the man mocked.

And Berith pulled out his sword, "Then I'll sever your limbs the old of fashioned way."

The robotic man regarded Berith with an evil grin. "Let's see you try it."

Noel-Len observed the battle, absolute that Berith would have his hands full with his current opponent. Then, he noticed the Fragment, knocked from the cyborg's grip and Noel-Len leapt for it before slipping the square-shaped Fragment into his pocket. "Get out of here, now!" Berith called, blocking an attack from his enemy.

Without a second thought, Noel-Len ran past the battle and towards the buildings. He didn't know where to go until he heard a voice, "Stop!" Noel-Len on guard, gripped the pommel of his sword eyeing the man who stood before him. In the alleyway, the man stepped forward from the shadows and into the light. Noel-Len cautiously questioned:

"Who are you?" Noel-Len asked.

"L'Eiron." He said, then his eyes were gentle before asked, "Noel-Len?"

"That's my name," Noel-Len responded. "What are you doing here? I thought you were supposed to be in Darwin."

"We were but—"

"We?" Noel-Len questioned.

Then from the shadows ran Anaphora smeared in blood. Both Anaphora and L'Eiron appeared to be tattered in cuts and bruises while Anaphora's anxious eyes drifted to him. "We were in Darwin, but our home is under siege, we returned immediately to provide aid. Do you have the Fragment?"

"Yes."

"Good. We need to keep moving," Anaphora said. Then turned to L'Eiron. "Let's go." With Anaphora and L'Eiron, Noel-Len ran dodging all the larva monsters and the lava that threatened to burn his feet. "We head south." Anaphora had instructed. Slicing down on lava monster with L'Eiron and Noel-Len found himself separated from them. His mind alert as he took in the monsters surrounding him. "Noel-Len!" Anaphora called, and L'Eiron disappeared and reappeared before Noel-Len.

"Stay close to me." L'Eiron declared, aware of the numbers surrounding Noel-Len.

It was inevitable that the Excelians grew weary in their form, a form that wasn't indestructible. It was soft and squishy like the skin of a Human.

Noel-Len fired his rifle at the lava monsters. Then watched as a tall overbearing monster approach him, it wore tarnished armour that lined with magma. It dragged an oversized hammer, behind itself and Noel-Len knew there was going to be trouble. The lava monster was ready to strike.

Though something jumped into his vision, and a lava monster attacked the lava monsters that threatened to flatten him. The lava monsters' bit into the lava monsters and not before long the lava monsters screamed a gurgling scream before Noel-Len noted its foaming mouth. Or, he thought it was foaming.

It screeched and leapt from one giant lava monster to another before it clawed at its tongue. Deep magma pooled and squirted everywhere. To Noel-Len's surprise, the beast appeared to have gargled and screamed. Noel-Len watched in horror as an identifiable hole that L'Eiron dug on the lava monster's hardened coat—healed. Both monsters locked onto each other. Then within a heartbeat, they leapt towards each other again, while Noel-Len remained glued to the sidelines.

While the rest of the lava monsters charged at Noel-Len and L'Eiron kept them at bay. "Run," L'Eiron ordered. It had taken a moment or two, but Noel-Len eventually came to and ran past the lava monsters and towards the opening where he sprinted around a corner.

Lava covered the ground before him, and without thinking, he leapt onto an energetic automobile and jumped across the street and towards the wall. Allowing his mind to relax, he clung to the wall and hoisted himself onto the roof, without a second thought.

L'Eiron caught up, "Nice moves." Though, Noel-Len noticed something hidden in L'Eiron's gaze but one that Noel-Len caught.

"Thanks," he said. "It felt natural."

To Noel-Len it appeared that L'Eiron had something to say on the matter but didn't and urged they keep moving as the larva tore down buildings and engulfed streets. L'Eiron gripped Noel-Len and disappeared, they reappeared further down the road and away from the lava. They continued to run before Anaphora beckoned them to their right. Where the lava wouldn't touch them. When the lava passed them, they relaxed a little, and Noel-Len panted. "That's the fastest, I've ever run in my life."

# Epilogue

"REALLY?" ANAPHORA QUESTIONED, surprised.

"It was, why?"

"Nothing . . . It's just you were able to keep up with us." Anaphora said, and L'Eiron nodded in agreement. Noel-Len appeared shocked by her words but never had a chance to comment when Anaphora declared, "Now for the Fragment."

"We have to secure it, somehow." Noel-Len asserted, with a vehemence that caught L'Eiron and Anaphora off guard.

"We will, in time but for now. We have other problems." L'Eiron proclaimed. Anaphora and L'Eiron battled the monsters and not before long, there were distant explosions on the back of the most gigantic monster at the front of the entrance to the Reserve. The beast screeched, and the lava beasts that surrounded them faded away. Then the most colossal monster too faded away. "That can't be good."

Then everyone noticed, the last of the ward began to pull away, leaving their home exposed to the heat and the earth.

"Oh, no." Anaphora declared, then sprinted down the street. L'Eiron and Noel-Len hastily followed, arriving at the house where Michalis lived.

They raced inside, and Noel-Len glanced at the doorway of a room not too far from him. Anaphora and L'Eiron ran upstairs while Noel-Len's curiosity claimed the better of him.

Into the room, he walked, and as he did, shock consumed him. He ran over to Michalis's unmoving body and checked for a pulse, but there was none. By the time, L'Eiron and Anaphora had checked every room, Noel-Len had vacated the office that Michalis's body occupied and pointed them into that room.

Anaphora and L'Eiron kneeled beside his body, and L'Eiron glimpsed the dagger in his back. Pulling it from Michalis's corpse, he scrutinised it. "Who could have done this?" Anaphora questioned, with anger.

"Not entirely sure but I have an idea." L'Eiron declared eyeing the dagger. "Look at the engravings and ironwork. The metal that was used and the design of the hilt." Anaphora's features paled, and Noel-Len couldn't help but question.

Then glanced at the dagger he'd seen for the first time; it was a hunting knife one used by the soldiers of his world. "That knife. It's military-grade."

"Whoever killed Michalis knew what they were doing. They knew who he was. This wasn't a random murder; this was an assassination." L'Eiron clarified and Anaphora's gaze darkened.

"This was a declaration of war by the surface world." Anaphora uttered.

"We don't know that for sure!" Noel-Len attempted. "You can't make such assumptions!"

"Assumptions!" Anaphora bellowed and shot to her feet faster than Noel-Len expected. "How am I making assumptions. There was a dagger in the back of an influential man." Anaphora growled.

"I understand that," Noel-Len began, "I'm just saying, that we need to find out who was responsible rather than assume an entire collection of countries. We don't know what happened, and we especially don't know who could have had access to him while we were gone."

"He's right," L'Eiron proclaimed. "Search the room. There has to be evidence of some kind." L'Eiron scanned the books surrounding Michalis's body and the walls for odd protrusions. Accepting his words, Anaphora searched the room. She noticed a few oddities like the knocked over chair, a puddle of water on the ground from the glass including the undamaged doors and windows. "So, you've come to the same conclusion then?" L'Eiron asked both Anaphora and Noel-Len.

Together they nodded.

"This was an inside job. As for the knife, I'm guessing this was either acquired, or it was owned by the wielder." L'Eiron declared.

"What will the people make of this?" Noel-Len questioned.

"They'll think it's a declaration of war. Just as I had a moment ago, which still does not vacate my mind." Anaphora asserted, lightly. Examining the way Michalis's body laid on the floor. "Regardless, let us give him a proper burial. We need to inform the Peacekeepers." Anaphora stepped away and placed her hand to her ear. Then declared the harsh truth about the Grand Elder.

By the time the Peacekeepers arrived, the magma had solidified, and the monsters were nowhere to be seen. Everyone, including Berith, entered Michalis's mansion to see for himself that the man was dead. "Is that the only reason you came?" Anaphora questioned.

"It is." he had said and L'Eiron rolled his eyes. The way he interacted with both L'Eiron and Anaphora made him think he was a part of their family. However, he didn't say anything on the topic, fearing he could be wrong. They spoke a little more about what had happened then the problem drifted to Gothalia, catching Noel-Len's attention. "Is she . . . is she safe?" Berith questioned.

"I'm not sure how safe she can be, but she's not dead," L'Eiron commented, almost appreciative of his concern.

"*Shh*," Anaphora scolded before continuing. "We mustn't discuss her; she's a traitor remember. And from what I hear she's been executed." This confused L'Eiron then he followed her attention where a Peacekeeper regarded them for a moment with suspicion.

"She's been executed?" L'Eiron played along, genuinely confused. "If so, it clearly wasn't public?"

"No, it wasn't. Grand Elder Michalis had given the order then he wounds up dead." Berith declared, "Very odd timing."

The Peacekeeper that had been eavesdropping on their conversation strolled to them and declared, "You should move now, Lady Anaphora." Though there was a hint of disgust in his gaze, Noel-Len caught it but as quick as it appeared, it vanished.

"Of course," Anaphora declared, "let's go."

The group vacated the manor and Noel-Len was left even more confused. "Okay, what was that all about?" he questioned, once they were out of earshot of the Peacekeepers.

"Gothalia is an enemy of our people," Anaphora declared. "Though, no one knows that she was used as a pawn. The only other person to know was Grand Elder Michalis."

"And that's why he was killed?" Noel-Len questioned, trying to grasp the assassination.

"We suspect." Berith declared. "It's best we get off the streets."

"Agreed. We'll meet at our estate. Later this evening," L'Eiron declared before adding, "We shouldn't be spotted travelling there together."

"I'll see you later this evening, I have a few things to tend to." Berith declared.

"Noel-Len, you and Anaphora head to the estate. I'll join you a little later." Noel-Len nodded. Then both Berith and L'Eiron vacated the area, where they stood beside a building.

"Walk with me," Anaphora beckoned, and Noel-Len did. Through the city, they strode.

Anaphora walked with Noel-Len through the city and towards her estate, one she shared with L'Eiron and Gothalia. Entering the most significant building, she stepped aside to allow Noel-Len to enter and he regarded her for a moment, "I'm not going to bite. Not this time, I promise."

"That makes me feel so much better." Noel-Len sarcastically retorted, and Anaphora smiled at his comment.

Noel-Len entered the manor with interest, observing the architecture and the style of the home. Oddly, it all felt familiar to him. "Is something wrong?" Anaphora questioned, noticing Noel-Len observe the interior a little longer than expected. Though, there was a curl to her lips as she distinguished his curiosity.

"No. No. Nothing's wrong." Noel-Len quickly responded. Though, Anaphora's words come back to him. "Wait, there is something on my mind and has been for a while. You said to Michalis that I was a sibling to Gothalia. How is that possible?"

"How else do you think? Her parents are also; Gaius and Natalia Ignatius."

"But everyone calls her Valdis . . . or something. I'm not sure if I said it right or not."

"You did. It's just . . . where to begin." Anaphora sighed. Then glanced at a photo off to the side, picking it up she handed it to Noel-Len. "This photo," she began, "was taken when you were small. You are in that photo with Gothalia, Gaius and Natalia. L'Eiron and I are also in that photo. It wasn't a celebration that day, it was a day that we all feared. So, we took a photo should you ever come asking for questions."

"That boy in the photo can't possibly be me. Right?" Noel-Len questioned, uncertain.

"It is." Anaphora proclaimed. Noel-Len glanced at the photo a little longer before he recognised his cheekbones, nose and lips that were a lot softer than what they appeared to be now as an adult. Though he couldn't believe his eyes. "So, you see it."

"How come, I don't have any recognition of you? Or Gothalia? Or my mother . . ." he began. Then he thought about it, he could remember a woman but couldn't logically determine if she were his mother, it was just a hunch. It was the way she smiled, the way her voice echoed around in his mind and he couldn't help but remember tender affection.

"That's because she hails from the Valdis clan." Anaphora proclaimed. "And that clan is a clan that everyone hated. They spent years tarnishing their name, damaging their connections and above all, hunting them down until there was none left but you two."

"I don't understand." Noel-Len began, and Anaphora moved over to the kitchen. Turning on the kettle, she prepared two cups. "How come I don't remember?"

"It was because of Lord Michalis, the Grand Elders and the Royal Family. They wiped your memory when you were but a child. Then allow you to live with your father on the surface world while your mother, was imprisoned then executed. As an extra punishment to your father, Michalis had separated both you and Gothalia because you naturally carried the flame of the Ignatius clan, while your sister inherited her mother's power. They especially wiped your memory of that massacre. It is the same with Gothalia. They had to make sure that you two weren't to . . ."

"Weren't to . . . *what*?" Noel-Len questioned.

"Weren't to turn on the Fire Reserve when you became of age." Anaphora declared and Noel-Len stared at her.

"My mother was killed." Noel-Len began, attempting to take it all in.

"That she was."

"My father forced to live elsewhere."

"That he was."

"What about you two?" Noel-Len questioned. "What about you and L'Eiron? Why are you two unpunished?" There was an anger to his voice, but Anaphora had recognised it wasn't entirely filled with rage. There were sadness, confusion and grief that was equally woven into his voice. Enough so, it made Anaphora sad.

*You poor child*, she thought, *all this time you've not known who you really are.*

# Don't miss out!

Visit the website below and you can sign up to receive emails whenever Kalverya Johansson publishes a new book. There's no charge and no obligation.

https://books2read.com/r/B-A-LSEJ-TQBGB

BOOKS 2 READ

Connecting independent readers to independent writers.

# About the Author

Kalverya Johansson spent much of her childhood imagining a world different than one she was living. One with sterling silver knights and super-humans. For eight years, she created numerous novels and is sometimes a chocoholic and coffee fanatic. When she's free, she spends most of her time writing but when she's not writing, she spends her time running K Johansson Studios for other self-published writers. If you like, aliens, demons, monsters and the supernatural; you'll love this new science fiction action-adventure author. Here in this world, she'll create monsters and demons that desire fresh meat while enjoying a treacherous dance.

Read more at https://www.k-johanssonstudios.com.